ABOUT THE AUTHOR

Born in New Orleans, O'Neil De Noux is a former homicide detective and organized crime investigator with the Jefferson Parish Sheriff's Office and the St. Bernard Parish Sheriff's Office in suburban New Orleans. Mr. De Noux has also worked as a U.S. Army combat photographer, a private investigator, a criminal intelligence analyst, a journalist, a magazine editor, and a computer graphics artist. As a police officer, he received seven commendations, primarily for solving difficult murder cases. In 1982 he was named "Homicide Detective of the Year" for the Jefferson Parish Sheriff's Office. In 1989 he was proclaimed an "Expert Witness" on the homicide crime scene by the Criminal District Court in New Orleans.

Mr. De Noux teaches mystery writing at Tulane University College in New Orleans and is the founding editor of two fiction magazines, *Mystery Street* and *New Orleans Stories.* A graduate of Archbishop Rummel High School in Metairie, Louisiana and Alabama's Troy State University, Mr. De Noux is an active member of the Mystery Writers of America and the Private Eye Writers of America, and is the author of four previously published novels and one true crime book.

O'Neil De Noux currently lives in South Louisiana with his wife Debra Gray De Noux and two children, Vincent and Dana.

The BIG SHOW

O'Neil De Noux

This novel is a work of fiction. Any references to historical events, real people (living or dead), and actual locales are used solely to lend the fiction its proper historical setting. All other names, characters, and incidents are fictitious, and any resemblance to actual persons or events is purely coincidental.

 Published by Autumn Books, an imprint of Pontalba Press, 4417 Dryades Street, New Orleans, Louisiana, 70115.

First Edition

Designed by Stephanie Stephens
Cover Photograph by Robert Neil, Jr.

De Noux, O'Neil
The big show / by O'Neil De Noux — 1st ed.
p. cm.
ISBN: 0-9653145-8-8

1. New Orleans (La.)— Fiction. 2. Crime — Fiction I. Title.

PS3554.E66B54 1998 813'.54
QBI98-363

For debb

Acknowledgment: Thanks Uncle Harlan!

In every profession there's a big show

In the army it's the special forces
In the navy it's the seals
In baseball it's the major leagues
In football it's the NFL
In police work it's homicide

Homicide
The big pressure cooker
The big cases
The big show

The Big Show

1	Pleasant Street	11
2	Madison Street	29
3	Neutral Ground	47
4	Vulture Street	63
5	Gentilly Boulevard	81
6	Camelia Street	101
7	Toledano Street	119
8	Burgundy Street	137
9	Louisiana Avenue	155
10	The Colapissa	173
11	Garden District	191
12	Palm Terrace	209
13	Chestnut Street	227
14	Bogue Chitto	245
15	Poeyfarre Street	263
16	Burlwood Road	281
17	Palmetto Street	297
18	Prytania Street	315
19	Leopard Street	329
20	Paris	343

Pleasant Street

LaStanza jammed the brakes of his unmarked LTD, jerking the steering wheel hard to the right in order to miss a burning man running across the street directly in front of him. The man stumbled over the curb and fell face first on the grassy neutral ground along the center of the street.

Flinging open his door, LaStanza grabbed his sport coat and ran around his car to the burning man. Completely engulfed in flames, the man writhed in the grass like a snake in slow motion. LaStanza threw his coat over the man's head and shoulders and rolled him in the grass. The stench of burned flesh stung LaStanza's nostrils along with the strong smell of gasoline.

The man drew his arms and legs up, his muscles contracting. LaStanza had seen it before in burn victims, that death crouch. Only the man wasn't dead. The man's mouth moved, opening and closing as he lay on his back on the grass.

LaStanza leaned over and heard the man hiss. The man's jaw quivered. He gasped and said something that sounded like, "Kee...Kee..." The man's mouth remained open and he stopped moving.

Sitting back on his haunches, LaStanza wiped the man's roasted flesh and burned hair from his shirt sleeves. His own hands burned. His eyes watered from the sting of the flames and the gasoline. He sat back, away from the man, and let his head sink between his knees, his hands at his sides, singed palms up.

Snakebitten. The thought ran through LaStanza's mind. *Jesus, am I snakebitten, or what? Ten minutes before knocking off the evening watch and I run into this.*

Rising slowly, he looked around the quiet residential street, looked back at St. Charles Avenue a half block away, and realized he had turned down Pleasant Street just in time to almost run over the man. Walking back to his car, his hands burning worse now, he realized he was having trouble breathing. LaStanza's lungs felt on fire.

He stumbled to his unit and leaned back against the front passenger door and tried to catch his breath. The unseasonably cool September night air did little to help. The humid New Orleans air felt like ice cubes in his lungs.

Turning slowly, he looked around to see if anyone was on the street. Then he peered over the top of his unit, squinting hard at a well-lit pink Victorian house. He tried to read its address, only his eyes were too teary. He blinked them and felt a sharp burning sensation.

LaStanza reached into the open window of the unit with his right hand and picked up his portable radio, clicked the mike and called headquarters.

"Go ahead 3124," the operator answered.

"I need an ambulance in the 1500 block of Pleasant, just off St. Charles. Possible signal 30. I also need 3122."

"10-4." The operator's voice rose.

"You better send a marked unit too," LaStanza added.

"10-4."

"3123 to 3124," a voice cut in. "I'm enroute." The voice had a slight country accent. The high-plains-drifter himself, Paul Snowood, was enroute.

"10-4, 3123." the operator answered LaStanza's old partner.

"3122 enroute," LaStanza's sergeant told headquarters.

Reaching back into his car, LaStanza dropped his radio back on the front seat. He closed his eyes and waited. He listened as best he could, in case there was someone on the street, but heard nothing except the cars whizzing by along St. Charles.

In the distance, he heard a siren approach. He opened his eyes and looked around one more time, around the neutral ground and across the street, but he was alone. The corpse, lying on its back, its arms and legs curled up, looked like a burned insect.

The oncoming siren turned the corner behind LaStanza, whooping loudly as it closed in. LaStanza looked over his shoulder as a marked unit skidded to a sliding stop in front of his car. Two patrolmen stepped out and moved quickly past LaStanza to the burned man and stood over him, gaping like rookies at their first scene. Their flashlights danced over the corpse. LaStanza recognized one of them. Kurt Owen, with his blond flat top, was no rookie.

Fuck, LaStanza thought, *then again, how many times do you get to see a man burned to death?*

"Hey," LaStanza said, "could you get on the fuckin' horn and hurry that ambulance up?"

"What for?" Owen said. "He's dead."

"For me." LaStanza coughed. "I burned my hands."

Owen turned and walked over to LaStanza. Looking at the detective's outstretched hands, Owen deftly withdrew his portable radio from his gun belt and told headquarters to step up the ambulance.

"You Okay?" Owen asked LaStanza, whose breath was finally returning.

LaStanza nodded. At 5'6", LaStanza was a good six inches smaller than the young patrolman. He felt older than his thirty-four years as he brushed his longish brown hair from his eyes. He patted down his full moustache with the fingers of his right hand, which didn't feel as burned as his left hand.

He noticed Owen's crisp baby-blue shirt, fresh from the cleaners. "Just came on duty, huh?"

Owen nodded and looked around. Putting his hands on his gun belt he said, "You know, you were driving the wrong way down a one-way street."

"What?" LaStanza looked back up at St. Charles then down Pleasant to the next corner, Prytania Street, where a large black-and-white one-way sign stood at the corner.

Mother-Fuck!

"Did you see him and turn down here?"

LaStanza shook his head no. He closed his eyes and leaned his head back against the roof of his car.

"I was just riding around. Killing time before knocking off."

"Well," Owen said as he walked back to the body, "looks like you stumbled on a good one here."

LaStanza pulled his head forward. *The wrong way down a one-way street.* He watched the patrolmen's lights move over the singed body. *The wrong way down a one-way street.* He felt his hair stand up on the back of his neck.

Another siren rounded the corner from St. Charles Avenue as an ambulance turned the wrong way down Pleasant to where LaStanza's unit sat in the center of the narrow street. The ambulance attendants, a pudgy white boy wearing a dress white uniform shirt two sizes took small and blue pants three sizes too small bounced out of the driver's side of the ambulance and hustled to the burned man.

A small black woman, wearing a much better fitting uniform, her long brown hair in a pony tail, climbed out of the passenger side of the ambulance. She carried a first aid kit.

Owen's partner, an Hispanic officer bearing the name tag of *DeLeon,* walked up to LaStanza.

"Hey," LaStanza said. "Can you guys do a quick canvass for me?"

Owen let out an unhappy sigh...unhappy because he was going to have to work now. But that involuntary act was quickly followed by a, "Sure, we can handle that."

"Good," LaStanza said. "Stop anyone on the street and get their ID. Copy it from their driver's license. If they refuse, bring 'em to me. Knock on every door a block in each direction and see if anyone saw anything. Don't miss a house. Both sides of the street. Okay?"

The patrolmen nodded.

"And get the license numbers of all the cars parked in a three block radius. Capish?"

Owen nudged his partner in the ribs and said, "Capish." Backing away, the flat top cop added, "Better let those guys look at your hands."

LaStanza stepped away from his unit and crossed the neutral ground to where the paramedics were stooped over the dead man.

"You can't help him," LaStanza said. "How about looking at my hands?"

The woman paramedic stood up and took LaStanza's hands in hers. Nodding, she leaned over, opened the first aid kit and withdrew a quart sized plastic bottle.

"Over here," she said, leading LaStanza under a street light. "Hold your hands out. Palms up."

LaStanza obeyed. The woman, whose name tag read *Haines*, poured the contents of the bottle over LaStanza's hands. It felt cool.

"How's your breathing?" Haines asked.

"I was having trouble a minute ago."

Another marked unit pulled up on Pleasant Street from Prytania Street. LaStanza watched Sergeant Harry Funder climb out, pull up his gun belt, and stroll over to the neutral ground to take a gander at the corpse. A tall skinny man with hunched shoulders and a long, homely face, Funder was known for his complete lack of humor.

"Don't rub them," Haines said. "Let them drip." Taking the now empty bottle with her, she went to the back of the ambulance. She left LaStanza dripping beneath the street light.

Another car turned on Pleasant from Prytania.

LaStanza recognized it as his sergeant's unmarked black LTD. As soon as it stopped, LaStanza extended his arms outward and shrugged.

Sergeant Mark Land—his *Viva Zapata* moustache curled down in its usual scowl position, his thick black hair disheveled, his white dress shirt as wrinkled as his gray slacks—walked slowly toward LaStanza. Mark was a big boned Napolitano Italian who looked like a larger, burlier, angrier version of LaStanza. Huffing like a Grizzly, Mark stepped up on the neutral ground and growled, "What the fuck is all this?"

Haines tapped LaStanza on the shoulder and said, "Hold your hands out again." She carried a gallon jug this time.

"What is this stuff?" LaStanza asked as he held his hands out again.

"Sterile water," Haines said as she poured the soothing liquid over LaStanza's palms. He felt much better with the water running over his hands.

Looking up at Mark, LaStanza said, "I almost ran over a burning man. He's over there. I managed to put him out."

"You hurt?" Mark leaned closer and looked at LaStanza's hands.

"Only when the water runs out."

"He'll have to go to the hospital," Haines said. "We have to irrigate this."

"Fuck," LaStanza whispered under his breath.

"I heard that," Haines said. She had light brown eyes and a dimple on her left cheek. Just one dimple.

Mark moved around them and went over to look at the burned man. LaStanza watched several other cars arrive and heard an unmistakable voice twang out, "Say Wyatt, what the fuck didja stumble on this time?"

Detective Paul Snowood, decked out in a tan western-cut sport coat, matching pants and dark brown cowboy boots, carried his bone colored Stetson ten-gallon hat in his right hand as he approached, grinning. Behind

Snowood, two newly arrived patrolmen followed.

Harry Funder yelled at the patrolmen to get back on the street. "This ain't no fuckin' circus!," he shouted

"Wait a minute," Mark Land said, stepping in front of the approaching entourage. Pointing to the two new patrolmen, Mark said, "One of you seal off Pleasant up at St. Charles and the other seal it off at Prytania."

Harry Funder's face turned scarlet. He let out an unintelligible curse and stormed off, back to his unit. LaStanza was certain the good sergeant would get right on his radio and scream at anyone who even thought of dropping by. Homicide had already expropriated four of his men. And there wasn't a fuckin' thing Funder could do about it except yell.

Snowood stepped up and looked at LaStanza's hands. "You got dirty or something?"

Jesus, LaStanza thought, *Jesus Fuckin' Christ!*

"They're burned," Haines answered as she continued pouring the wash over LaStanza's hands. She looked up at LaStanza and asked, "How's your breathing?"

"Okay."

"Well," Snowood said, his country-accent in full swing now, "when the coyote goes berserk, it's showdown time." Then he moseyed over to the dead man.

"What'd he say?" Haines asked LaStanza.

"Who the fuck knows?"

The slow-pouring gallon of cool water ran out. "That's gonna start burning again," Haines told LaStanza. "You better come with us." Her chubby partner was already climbing into the driver's seat of the ambulance.

"Not yet," LaStanza said, following Snowood and Mark over to where the burned man lay.

Mark was on his haunches next to the body. He looked up at LaStanza and said, "Ten minutes." Looking back at the body he snarled, "Ten minutes from knocking off and you gotta find this."

"You can say that again," Snowood said.

Mark glared and the detective everyone called

Country-Ass and said, "Where's your fuckin' pen?"

"No," Snowood moaned, knowing what was coming next.

"You're up, my man," Mark said as he rose, his knees cracking loud enough to be heard. "This fucker's yours."

"I fuckin' knew it!"

No way, LaStanza thought. He elbowed Snowood to get his attention.

"Process the scene and take the autopsy in the morning. I'll take it from there."

Mark leaned over LaStanza and growled, "Didn't I hear that girl tell you to go to the hospital?"

"And I got court in the morning, but after that this case is mine."

"No it ain't."

LaStanza looked into Mark's brown eyes. The big Grizzly had broken LaStanza into Homicide, was his first partner in the big show, and was every bit as hard-headed as LaStanza. Maybe more. The two men stared at one another, their faces void of expression for a good half minute before LaStanza said calmly, "I want this one." A second later he added, "It's personal. Okay?"

Mark grimaced, let out a long sigh and shrugged his large shoulder. "All right. Now get over to the hospital."

LaStanza nearly bumped into Haines, who had come up behind him.

"Lead on," he said.

Snowood followed LaStanza and said, "Wyatt." He'd been calling LaStanza "Wyatt" ever since LaStanza gunned down the Twenty-Two Killer three years earlier.

"I'll put a rope on this thing for ya'."

Yeah, LaStanza thought, *so long as you don't have to be saddled with the follow-up.*

Snowood slapped LaStanza on the back and trotted over to his car to get his pen and pad. LaStanza waited for Snowood to come back to tell him to take care of his unit, which was still running.

"Sure," Snowood retreated, the Stetson low on his

brow now, "The trail's a little dusty, but we'll cut 'em off at the pass."

Whatever the fuck that meant!

Before the ambulance pulled off, Haines wrapped LaStanza's fingers in gauze then had him soak his hands in a metal bucket of sterile water. Backing its way up to St. Charles, the ambulance rolled past the a crime lab unit as it arrived. Turning on St. Charles the chubby driver hit the lights and siren.

"Hey!" LaStanza said, "Cut the fuckin' siren!"

The driver turned and mouthed something. LaStanza stood, moved over and flipped off the siren with his right hand, which hurt only half as much as his left.

The driver flinched and said something about regulations.

"The fuck!" LaStanza said and moved back to the bucket. His hands felt much better in the cool liquid.

"Why'd you wrap them?" he asked Haines.

"Keep the fingers separated."

Makes fuckin' sense.

A minute later the driver asked nervously, "So how'd you happen to find that guy?"

LaStanza looked at Haines who snickered under her breath.

"I mean," the driver said, "how did you find him like that?"

"I'm just fuckin' lucky, I guess."

"Oh, wow."

Seated on an emergency room table at Charity Hospital, on a night that was unbelievably quiet for the busiest ER in New Orleans, LaStanza watched an intern with baby blond hair and a peach-fuzz moustache stick one of those nose light things up LaStanza's right nostril. The intern moved the light to his left nostril. The ER smelled of alcohol wipes and old blood. It always smelled that way.

Turning to the freckle-faced nurse behind him, the intern said, "No damage in the nose." The nurse handed him another instrument. It was an eye light.

"Look up," the intern said. Then he had LaStanza look down, then to the right, then to the left. Then the intern switched eyes. The intern told the nurse, "Give him an eye wash and put him on oxygen for an hour."

The intern turned back to LaStanza and flashed his best bedside-manner smile before strolling out into the corridor. LaStanza was a little surprised. Interns at Charity had no bedside manner. They were too shell shocked.

Once, when LaStanza was a Homicide rookie, he watched two interns work over a gunshot victim in the hall because the trauma rooms were all filled. After a sweaty ten minutes, one of the interns turned to the other and said, "Give it up, man."

Pulling off their bloody gloves, the same intern added, "Might as well pull the plug. We're gonna need the machine."

As the second intern pulled the plug from the machine that was measuring the victim's vital signs, the first intern noticed LaStanza leaning against the wall two feet behind them.

"Who the hell are you?" the exhausted intern asked.

"Police," LaStanza said, opening his sport coat to show his star-and-crescent badge clipped to his belt.

The exhausted intern turned quickly back to his partner and said, "Uh, plug that thing back in, Okay?"

Then both interns disappeared down the hall.

LaStanza watched the vital signs indicators of the gunshot victim fade until they registered a long thin line. Actually the dead guy wasn't much of a victim. He was just the loser of a shootout at a drug deal that went awry in the Desire Housing Project. The winner had checked into a Metairie Hospital with a gunshot wound to the leg. He was already in custody. *Typical misdemeanor murder. All paperwork.* One thing LaStanza was sure of, the burned man on Pleasant Street would be no misdemeanor murder. It had whodunit painted all over it.

"Here," the freckle-faced nurse said. She had a thing that looked like an eye cup in her hand. It was full of liquid. "Put your eye here," she said, "then open it and blink a couple times."

After washing out both eyes, LaStanza watched the nurse pour a cup full of ice into the sterile water bath where LaStanza's naked hands soaked.

"What's your name?" he asked her as she started to pull an oxygen mask over his head, adjusting it over his nose and mouth.

"Andrea," she said, picking up a silver instrument that looked like one of those turkey baster things. She stuck the baster into the bucket. She pulled back on the plunger, sucking water into the instrument. "Lift your left hand out," she said. She sprayed the water over his hand again and again. Then she had him switch hands.

"I think we've removed any debris from the burns," Andrea said, pursing her lips as she examined LaStanza's hands. Andrea had short bright red hair. Full figured, she was even shorter than LaStanza. She had round hands, hands that were extremely gentle.

LaStanza readjusted himself and let out a tired sigh. He glanced at his wrist watch lying on the table next to his hands. It was after one in the morning now.

"How much longer?" he asked.

"We have to make sure it's stopped burning and it's well irrigated."

"How much more time?"

"At least an hour on oxygen. How's your breathing?"

LaStanza nodded. Andrea smiled at him and patted his left shoulder with her hand. She had a nice smile.

"I'll be right back. Keep those hands soaking." And she stepped out.

LaStanza closed his eyes and listened to the sound of his own breathing. The oxygen made him light headed. He refused to think about the burned man. There would be plenty of time for that later. He thought of Andrea's smile. It was a familiar smile, a smile very much like Sister

Camille used to give him back in the third grade at Holy Rosary School. It was a friendly, comfortable smile. Somehow the nurse reminded him of the nun.

Okay. If the man ran from my left to my right, he came from the sidewalk along Pleasant Street. Or did he come from the corner of Prytania Street? Jesus!

LaStanza shook his head. If only he'd be paying attention. If he hadn't been daydreaming. *Some fuckin' detective I am!*

He heard the curtain to the trauma room open and opened his eyes.

"Say boy, the doc says you're gonna live," Snowood said, placing his Stetson on the bed next to LaStanza. "Sorry but your friend didn't make it."

Before LaStanza could even think of a retort, the curtain opened again and Jodie Kintyre stepped in. Dressed in a gold short sleeved Saints sweatshirt and jeans, her usually perfect page boy blonde hair messed, her face void of make-up except for a light brush of pink lipstick on her lips, LaStanza's partner stepped over and looked down into the bucket of sterile water and shook her head.

Looking up, she focused her wide-set, hazel eyes on LaStanza and said, "I take one night off..."

"The fuck," LaStanza said. He pulled the oxygen mask off. His hands were stinging too badly for him to spar. *What is this place anyway, Grand Central Fuckin' Station?*

"I brung your partner over so she can drive you home and tuck you in bed," Snowood said, pulling a gray metal chair up in front of LaStanza. Snowood sat backwards in it, draping his long arms across the rear of the high back chair. He spit a glob of brown saliva into the ever-present Styrofoam cup in his left hand and cocked his head toward Jodie and said, "Y'all remember that nice dark blue sport coat with the red specks in it ole Wyatt here used to wear?"

Jodie moved a step back and leaned against the tray table next to the curtain that separated LaStanza's trauma room from the others in the ER.

"We sent it with the crime lab tech to dry out. It's full a burnt gasoline, skin, hair, grass and shit. Got a few holes burned in it too."

LaStanza pulled his hands out of the bath and snatched up one of the fresh towels Andrea had left on the bed, next to the bandage supplies the nurse was supposed to put on him whenever the goddam hour was finished. He dabbed his hands with the towel, keeping his face as expressionless as possible because he knew Jodie's cat eyes were watching him.

"Must be nice," Snowood continued, "having a rich wife to buy you nice sport coats in case you get a hankerin' to put out a fire or two, huh?"

"Shut up Paul," Jodie said as Andrea brushed back into the trauma room. Andrea picked up the oxygen mask and put it back on LaStanza.

"Now I have to put Silvadene on your hands," Andrea said, grabbing a tube from the bandage supplies. Spotting lanky Snowood draped across the chair in his western duds, Andrea did a double take before picking up a white tube. She gently took LaStanza's left hand in hers and carefully spread the cream across the palm of his hand.

"This will keep the fluids in," she said. "Takes the sting away a little too." She spread the cream on each finger. She took his right hand and spread cream on it too. Then she scooped up the bandages and started wrapping his hands. "You follow the directions on these tubes of Silvadene," she said. "And keep them wrapped in sterile bandages and you'll be fine. The doctor told you to go see your family doctor in a couple days, right?"

"Sure."

The wrapping was light, as only the little finger and the ring finger of his left hand needed wrapping. LaStanza noticed Jodie pick up one of the tubes of Silvadene and read the label.

"This here," Andrea said, pointing to a piece of paper, "is a prescription for pain. You can use ice packs if the burning starts again, understand?"

LaStanza nodded.

When she approached him with a syringe, he said, "What's that?"

"Pain killer. You allergic to morphine?"

LaStanza focused his Sicilian eyes on her eyes. He pulled off the oxygen mask. "No morphine," he said in a low determined voice. Andrea opened her mouth to object. He narrowed his eyes. She put the needle down.

"Wrap some ice in a face rag and keep those hands nice and cool at home. Understand?"

"Yes, Ma'am."

Andrea winked at LaStanza. He figured her to be in her mid-thirties, about his age exactly.

"Say Nursey," Snowood said, "ever know anyone to use a brand new Italian sport coat to try to put out a fire on a dead man?"

Andrea shot Snowood a "say what" look, but didn't answer.

"Just ignore him," LaStanza said.

"He looks like he belongs on the third floor," Andrea said as she turned and walked out.

Jodie smiled. Snowood snarled at the place in the curtain where Andrea had departed.

Fuckin' A, LaStanza thought, agreeing with Andrea completely. The third floor of Charity Hospital was the nut ward.

"Hey," LaStanza thought of something and turned to Jodie. "How was your date?"

Jodie crinkled her nose as if she just got a whiff of a Bourbon Street gutter.

"Didja get laid?" Snowood asked.

At least Jodie had learned to ignore Country-Ass. She didn't even blink. She just packed the rest of the bandages and the three tubes of Silvadene in a white paper bag and led the way out.

"Hey, ain't you supposed to check out?" Snowood called out behind them.

It was cooler outside. The night air smelled of rain on the way. LaStanza sucked in a deep, wet mouthful and climbed into the passenger side of his police unit. Snowood was still yakking about something as LaStanza closed the door and waited for his partner to climb in and get them the hell out of there.

Before they pulled away, LaStanza rolled down his window and called back to Country-Ass, "Where's your fuckin' hat?"

Snowood jumped and hurried back into the ER, elbows flying like a human version of Wile E. Coyote. They left him. He'd have to call someone else for a ride.

LaStanza leaned back in the seat and closed his eyes. Jodie and he had partnered long enough for her to take the hint. She never said a word until the unit stopped.

"Need any help?" she asked when LaStanza opened his eyes and recognized that they were at the dead end of Garfield Street at Exposition Boulevard.

He looked over to his right at the mansion he lived in with his rich wife and yawned again. Well lit by the hidden garden lights, the three story white house loomed brightly behind its six foot brick wall that ran alongside Garfield. LaStanza climbed out and opened the back door to get his briefcase.

"I'll get it," Jodie said, climbing out the driver's side.

"I got it," he said, snatching up his case with his right hand.

Jodie stretched as she stood on the other side of the LTD. Reaching her long arms up at the dark sky she said, "Is Lizette in Paris yet?"

LaStanza looked at his watch.

"She'll be landing at Orly in a couple hours." He looked back at his partner, at her messed up hair and face that looked even paler than usual beneath the harsh street light.

"What are you looking at?" she asked.

"So your date was a bummer, huh?"

Jodie's shoulders fell. "Loser City. I'll tell you about it

tomorrow." She climbed back into the LTD and cranked up the motor. Rolling down the front passenger window, she called out, "Pick you up at eight-thirty, right?

"Yeah."

Jodie backed up, made a three point turn in his driveway and pulled away.

LaStanza walked slowly around to the front of his house. He opened the black wrought iron front gate with his left hand, wincing a little as the bandage brushed against the rough iron. The wide expanse of Audubon Park echoed behind him with the sound of the cool breeze rustling through the oaks and the thick-leafed magnolias. It sounded like an ocean, like waves rolling to shore. He turned and looked out at the blackness of the park. He could see the lagoon shining silver under the moonlight.

He had to put his briefcase down to unlock the dead bolt of his cut-glass front door. After disarming the burglar alarm, he relocked the door and re-armed the alarm. He kicked off his penny loafers and left them next to his briefcase in the foyer.

Unfastening his tie and unbuttoning his shirt with his right hand, he walked through the foyer, through the long dining room off to the right and into the kitchen. Immediately he smelled something that made his stomach rumble. He spotted a note on the counter. It was a yellow Post-It that read:

> *Wop,*
> *Gumbo in the fridge. Rice too. Don't eat all the pecan pie.*
>
> *Brulee*

He could hear Aunt Brulee's scratchy voice as he read the note. The old black maid had promised Lizette she'd take care of LaStanza, even if he was an Eye-talian gigolo. Damn scrawny woman kept calling him Wop. He smiled as he stood in the pristine kitchen, next to the built-in porcelain faced ovens—one a regular gas oven—one a deep dish microwave—one a long narrow oven for roasting.

He could smell the oyster okra gumbo. That's what rumbled his stomach. Only there was another smell, a burnt rotten smell, still clinging to the interior walls of his nose. His stomach twisted.

Looking up at the kitchen clock, a large replica of a Barq's root beer bottle cap, he saw that it was closing in on three a.m. And he had to be in court at by nine. *Fuckin' pain-in-the-ass preliminary hearing!*

Opening a cabinet, LaStanza took out a tumbler. He stuck the tumbler into the ice cube slot of their huge side-by-side refrigerator and plopped three cubes into the tumbler. Moving to another cabinet, he pulled out an opened bottle of Chivas Regal and poured himself a stiff belt of Scotch. He poured until all three ice cubes were covered. He took the bottle with him.

Twirling the dark amber liquid around the cubes, LaStanza walked through the kitchen. He turned left through the narrow hall next to the rear stairs and moved back up the main hall to the study. He put the bottle of Chivas on the marble mantle above the fireplace and climbed into the big easy chair that faced the fireplace. He leaned back and kicked up his legs.

He took a sip of Scotch and let the cold liquor burn its way down his throat to his belly. His eyes watered momentarily. He blinked and took another hit of Scotch and then looked up at his favorite picture of his wife that sat in a black lacquer frame atop the fireplace mantle.

Lizette's large golden-brown eyes stared back at him from the eight-by-ten inch close-up. Her long dark hair flowed in an invisible breeze that made the strands of her hair glitter in the sunlight. Her lips looked extra pouty and thick in deep red lipstick.

LaStanza closed his eyes and ran images of Lizette through his mind, like moving snapshots. He saw her creamy white skin, shiny with sun tan oil, as she lay naked on a black pebble beach on the Caribbean isle of their honeymoon. He could feel the sun on his face momentarily. Then he felt the burns on his hands and saw black skin, crinkled and singled. He saw barbecued flesh and smelled it again, that strong stench of burned death.

He opened his eyes and took a long belt of Scotch. He remembered the man's mouth quivering, as the man struggled to say, "Kee...Kee..." LaStanza's stomach twisted from the heat of the Scotch and from the pressure of not eating and of knowing that he had once again crawled into the Homicide Pressure Cooker.

Jesus, a man died in my hands tonight.

He had so much work to do. He had a case to solve, a real heater case.

Snakebitten. Man, am I ever snakebitten.

Madison Street

"Carmen, I'm sick of your fuckin' lying. I don't want to have nothing to do with you anymore, you rotten bitch!"

The thick, deep voice from the tape recorder echoed through the courtroom. LaStanza, perched on the witness stand, readjusted his Smith & Wesson two-and-a-half-inch, stainless steel, .357 magnum revolver in its black leather holster on his right hip, hidden from view by the jacket of his light gray suit. He listened intently as the voice of the accused continued.

"You always fuck with people don't you, Carmen? I tried to help you, tried to be a friend. But you don't give a fuck about *me*, do you?"

The young defense lawyer with a wiry eraser-head hair style had tried his best to block the playing of the recording of the accused, but the judge ruled against him. LaStanza turned his gaze to the accused and did his best to keep a disgusted look from his face.

"I'm coming to see you," the recorded voice echoed. It was followed by the sound of a phone hanging up. The courtroom waited for the next recording to come on. *Thank God criminals are stupid,* LaStanza thought for the thousandth time since he came up to Homicide.

This particular criminal sat next to his eraser-head lawyer and stared straight ahead as if he was staring into some secret inner-space zone. This particular criminal, a muscular white boy of twenty-five, with the incredible name of Lupert Dimetrodon Jones, wore a standard-issue Orleans Parish Prison orange smock and baggy pants and a purple bandanna around his neck. Lupert's mother was into dinosaurs. Her daughter's middle name was Pterodactyl, the poor kid.

Lupert had shaved his head since Jodie and LaStanza arrested him, and had acquired some suspicious bruises along his forehead, of all places, and along his throat. The bluish-purple bruises clashed with his bandanna, which was on the red side of purple.

Stupid Lupert, as LaStanza nicknamed him, was playing his part to the hilt. An occasional resident of the state mental hospital at Mandeville, the wonderful Mr. Jones was on a work-release program when he broke into a New Orleans East duplex and murdered the lone female occupant. That was shortly after he made the first phone call to the answering machine of his former girlfriend Carmen Jacopino. He then made more calls, all of which were recorded. Sitting in his ill fitting orange and purple outfit, Stupid Lupert looked as stone-fuckin-nuts as they came.

The voice came back on the recorder, still deep, but there was an urgency to voice. "Carmen, it's Lupert. I hope you get to the phone before anyone else talks to you. Look, I did something stupid. Something motherfuckin' stupid. I went you see you, but there was no answer. I thought you were passed out or something, so I busted the window and went in the house looking for you."

The voice hesitated a moment before continuing in a deep monotone, now void of any emotion. "I cut the telephone wires too, I think. But this girl inside, she attacked me. And I don't know. I went nuts. I blacked out and when I woke up there was all this blood."

The urgency returned to the voice. "If you hear anything from anybody or see anybody, just tell them you don't know me. No, just don't tell them my name. I think they're gonna question you, the police. Because somebody saw me. Somebody chased me and got my license number." There was another pause.

LaStanza crossed his legs and rested his bandaged hands lightly on his right knee. He continued to watch the killer.

"I don't know, Carmen. I don't know what happened. I blacked out. Maybe I was on some fuckin' dope or something like that. I don't know. Jesus Christ, just don't tell the police who I am." There was the sound of a phone hanging up again.

LaStanza dabbed his moustache with his right index finger and thumb. Stupid Lupert still stared glassy-eyed at the center of the judge's podium.

The voice came on again.

"Carmen, it's me, Lupert again. I really fucked up this time. Jesus Christ, I hope you hear this and don't say nothing. I hope you're not the type of person that offers information. I feel guilty. I know I did wrong, but if you could keep your mouth shut and we can talk about this later or if you can call me as soon as you get home, call me at my mom's. Jesus Christ, Carmen. I fucked up."

The voice suddenly rose in anger. "So where are you? You at your mom's or with your fuckin' husband again? You went back to your fuckin' husband? Jesus Christ! The more I talk to you, the more obsessed I get with you." Stupid Lupert hung up again.

LaStanza waited. There was more.

"Carmen, I hope you don't rat on me. I hope you bail me out of this one, babe. I ask very little of you. This I'm begging for. I hope you answer this phone before you walk down to your neighbor's house or something like that. Oh, Carmen, don't rat me out. I'm gonna get help. I'm going back to the hospital." Again, another hang up.

LaStanza waited. He looked around the courtroom. Besides the Assistant District Attorney, the defense lawyer, Stupid Lupert, LaStanza, and the judge, the only other occupants of the large room were two huge black Orleans Parish Sheriff's Deputies.

The voice came back, this time much lighter, almost cheerful. "Carmen? It's me Lupert, babe. What's going on Sweetie? I been trying to talk to you. I feel ashamed and guilty. But I'm feeling much better now. God, I did fuck up, or what?" There was an audible chuckle. "But I know you're gonna talk to me before you talk to the cops. Call me at my mom's house. Bye babe. Catch ya' later."

She called us first, you asshole.

LaStanza sat up and turned his attention to the short black Assistant District Attorney. Donald Daka rose and turned off the recorder in front of him. Readjusting his vest beneath his blue three-piece suit, Daka said, "Now, Detective LaStanza, armed with the information on this tape and information secured from other witnesses, including the license plate number of Mr. Jones' late model Buick, were you able to secure an arrest warrant?"

"Yes, sir."

Daka picked up several pieces of white legal size paper and brought them to LaStanza.

"Is this the arrest warrant you prepared?"

LaStanza looked it over and said, "Yes, sir."

Daka handed it to the bailiff and asked it marked into evidence. Then he tendered the witness.

Stupid Lupert's attorney stood up quickly, too quickly. He knocked his pen on the floor and had to bend down to get it, his frizzy hair shaking like a loose Brillo pad. "Now," he said loudly, "detective, did you have the voice on this alleged tape scientifically compared to Mr. Jones' voice prior to securing your warrant?"

Alleged tape? He said alleged tape. Jesus, LaStanza thought. *His first name must be Stupid too.*

"No, sir. I did not."

"Then you have no proof that this is Mr. Jones' voice now, do you?"

He's not stupid. He's just dumb.

"I do now. We sent the tape along with comparison

tapes of Mr. Lupert Jones' voice to the F.B.I. lab after the arrest, Sir. The F.B.I. voice print identification experts have positively matched the voice on the tape from Carmen Jacopino's answer machine with the voice on the comparison tapes of Mr. Lupert Jones."

"But you didn't have that information when you prepared the warrant now did you?"

"No, sir."

The lawyer looked smug.

"You just took Carmen Jacopino's word that the voice on her machine was my client's."

LaStanza didn't answer because it wasn't a question.

Suddenly realizing something, the defense lawyer said, "Then you do have some sort of forensic proof after all. Why didn't you say that when I asked you earlier?"

LaStanza looked at the judge for help, but gray haired Judge DeSalvo wouldn't help this time. He had his right hand suspiciously covering his mouth. From the gleam in his eyes, LaStanza knew he was grinning like the proverbial Cheshire fuckin' cat.

LaStanza turned back to the defense lawyer and said, "Sir, I believe you asked if we had the voice on the tape scientifically compared to Mr. Jones' voice prior to securing my warrant. We didn't. We just got the results from the F.B.I. lab yesterday."

"Ah, ha." The lawyer wheeled, went back to his desk and looked at his papers.

LaStanza checked his watch. It was eleven thirty. He sat back and waited. After a couple minutes, Judge DeSalvo told the attorney to step it up. The hand still hid the judge's mouth.

"Now, detective. The only information you had to secure that warrant...the only probable cause you had in order to secure your warrant was the identification of Mr. Jones' voice by this alleged woman Carmen Jacopino, the identification of Mr. Jones' license plate from an alleged witness, and the identification from the photo line-up by the other witnesses, correct?"

"Correct."

Alleged woman? The douche-bag called Carmen Jacopino an alleged woman? Jesus! LaStanza had met Carmen. There was nothing alleged about her.

"What other evidence have you to link Mr. Jones to the crime?"

Daka rose quickly, "Objection!"

LaStanza leaned back and let the lawyers and the judge dicker it out.

Sixty seconds later, LaStanza was out in the hall. He passed Jodie on the way in. Dressed in a prim tan business skirt and jacket, a high collared white shirt beneath, Jodie looked as pristine as usual. Every hair of her light blonde page boy was neatly in place. She looked fresh, as she always managed to do, no matter how little sleep she got.

LaStanza yawned as he sat in the long bench that ran along the wall opposite the courtroom door. Glancing to his right, he spotted Carmen Jacopino. Smoking a cigarette, Carmen stood at the end of the hall looking out the huge glass window of the criminal courts building. When Carmen turned, LaStanza blinked as he realized he could see through her dress.

He looked away, at Carmen's husband who sat across the hall. The husband, sitting in a striped shirt and dress jeans, was playing with one of those game-boy games. LaStanza could hear little beeps as a juvenile smile crossed the husband's face.

He looked back at Carmen as she stood with her right hand on her hip. Her legs, slightly parted, gave LaStanza a clear view of her shape. Carmen Marie Jacopino had a shape all right. Tall and slim, she had nice round hips and breasts about two sizes too large for her frame. LaStanza could make out the cream colored lace of her bra and matching panties beneath her loose fitting white dress.

Carmen reached into her purse, pulled out another cigarette and lit it. LaStanza had to readjust the way he sat and looked back at the husband.

Prissy. The husband looked prissy, looked like the kind of guy who would ask permission before kissing a woman. *Maybe he's rich. Or maybe he has a wide tongue. A very wide tongue.*

LaStanza looked away from both, down the long hall of the criminal courts building, with its high ceiling and marble corridor. Three people moved about down the hall. Two women and a man.

LaStanza let his mind roam back to the case against Lupert Dimetrodon Jones, back to the crime scene, back to the body of a twenty-two year old brunette named Lisa Firenze who looked a little like Carmen Jacopino, who had made the fatal mistake of renting the duplex next to Carmen's, an identical duplex in the apartment-maze area of New Orleans East.

Lisa Firenze was slashed to death with a pair of scissors. Two of her fingers were severed. At her autopsy they counted one hundred and seventy-seven wounds. At the scene they found her side window broken, three neat footprints outside, a pair of cutting pliers next to the severed phone line. They lifted four latent prints from inside the apartment and a partial palm print from the pliers. The palm print and one of the latents were positively identified as coming from the right hand of one Lupert Dimetrodon Jones. The other latents belonged to the victim. Stupid Lupert's lawyer would find out that additional probable cause at the trial.

Just that morning, Jodie, who was the case officer of the "Duplex Murder," received a report from the F.B.I. Criminalistics Lab which positively identified the footprints outside Lisa Firenze's apartment window as having been made by the pair of Thom McCan loafers secured from one Lupert Dimetrodon Jones during the search of Stupid Lupert's room in his mother's house.

Carmen dropped her latest cigarette, stepped on it and walked over to her husband, who was still playing his game-boy. She had a sexy walk, a nice rhythmic flow on high heels. LaStanza quit looking at her when she bent at the waist and whispered something in her husband's left ear.

LaStanza had to get away from this lunacy. He had a murder to work. He had a whodunit on his hands. Hell, he had to find out who the fuck his victim was! He itched to hit the street. He didn't even want to think of the oldest Homicide cliché... "you don't solve murders by sitting on your ass...you solve them out on the street."

Fuck. There he was, cooling it in the hall. He wrung his hands and immediately regretted it. His left hand burned like the dickens. At least his right hand wasn't smarting as much, until he was dumb enough to rub it.

He looked at his watch. It was now ten after twelve. Snowood was probably sitting in the squad room, his cowboy boots kicked up on his desk, his hands behind his head. He had to be finished covering the autopsy of the burned man by now. LaStanza figured Country-Ass was probably arguing with his new partner about where they would eat lunch. Lunch was always Snowood's most important decision of the day.

LaStanza heard her high heels approach before Carmen said, "Excuse me, Detective."

LaStanza stood as she arrived. He could see trouble in her wide brown eyes and along the lines of her well made-up face. Carmen wore dark brown lipstick, the kind Lizette often wore. It was sexy as fuckin' hell. LaStanza felt himself getting excited and fought it.

In a breathless voice, Carmen said, "Is this what they call a lunacy hearing today?"

"Didn't the D.A. explain it all to you?"

"No," she said in almost a gasp.

"This is a preliminary hearing. We have to prove we had probable cause to arrest Lupert. The defense is on a fishing expedition. That's all."

"Then Lupert can't get out today."

"No way." LaStanza tried smiling. It didn't work as well as he thought. "He's got a two million dollar bond."

"Oh." Carmen bit her lower lip and shifted her weight

from her left leg to her right. In her "fuck me" spiked heels she towered a good six inches over LaStanza. He was used to some women towering over him. Hell, he was used to nearly everybody being taller.

Carmen reached out and grabbed LaStanza's left wrist. He flinched and she noticed his bandages, probably for the first time today. She jerked her hand away.

"Oh, I'm sorry," she said, putting her hand over her mouth. "I'm just so shook over this." She had the look of a child who'd been caught with her hand in the cookie jar. She'd been caught all right. The whole damn city knew of her extra-marital dalliance with a stone-fuck-nut-case LaStanza called Stupid Lupert.

"Sit down." LaStanza moved aside. Carmen sat. Thankfully, the door to the courtroom opened and Jodie came hurrying out. Carmen made a squeaky mouse sound.

Jodie walked up and said, "Let's go."

"What happened?" Carmen asked anxiously.

"Lunch," Jodie answered.

Turning back to Carmen, LaStanza asked if she was all right.

She nodded unconvincingly.

LaStanza turned and called out to Carmen's husband, "Hey. Wake up."

The goofy sucker looked up, his jaw falling open.

They left Carmen and headed down the stairs near the South White Street side of the building. LaStanza glanced over his shoulder in time to catch Carmen chasing Donald Daka down the hall. Her husband was still playing his fuckin' game.

"How're your hands?" Jodie asked as they walked around the corner to police headquarters. Whatever coolness was there yesterday was long gone. LaStanza reached under his tie and unbuttoned his top shirt button.

"Want to fill that pain prescription?" Jodie asked.

LaStanza shook his head no. He needed his mind

clear. He had work to do.

"You Okay, or what?"

Turning to Jodie he said, "I was just thinking about a stark naked Carmen standing in front of her sofa asking that dweeb of a husband when he's coming to bed. Know what he'd say?"

"Don't start pulling a Snowood on me," Jodie said.

"He'd say, 'Not now, Carmen. Can't you see...*I'm in the middle of playing my Game-boy!*'"

"You didn't get enough sleep last night, did you?"

Sometimes Jodie sounded just like LaStanza's mother.

Snowood had his feet kicked up on his city-government-issue gray metal desk. He wore his gray lizard boots that day. It went with his black pants and black-and-white shirt with two rows of silver buttons down the front and the string tie with the longhorn steer clasp. His hands were cupped behind his head. He dozed as he leaned back in his gray metal desk chair.

"Think I should?" Jodie asked as she passed, holding a threatening hand over Snowood, as if she would just push him over. LaStanza didn't react so she went over to her desk, across the narrow aisle.

LaStanza found a daily report on his gray metal desk. *Good.* It was better to read a Snowood autopsy report than hear it described by Country-Ass.

New Orleans Police Department
Detective Bureau Daily Report

TO:	Detective Dino LaStanza
FROM:	Detective Paul Snowood
SIGNAL:	14:30 (1st Degree Murder)
VICTIM:	Unknown Black Male
ITEM:	H-080791
LOCATION:	New Orleans Coroner's Office (NOCO)
RE:	Postmortem Exam. At 8:03 a.m., this date, a postmortem exam was conducted

on the cadaver of an unknown black male, approximately 45-55 years of age, who was found burned to death in the 1500 block of Prytania Street.

ATTENDANTS: Dr. B. Matthews, NOCO Pathologist; Det. P. Snowood, NOPD Homicide; and Technician C. Sturtz, NOPD Crime Lab.

EVIDENCE SECURED: One remnant of a green zipper jacket K-Mart brand, Large size; One remnant of a plaid shirt, unknown brand, unknown size; One remnant of a blue tee-shirt; One remnant of a pair of blue dress pants, Questo brand; One pair of black loafers, Stopps brand; Five samples of accelerant chemical (probable gasoline); Powder stipples from the chest area of the victim, Powder residue on the jacket, plaid shirt, and tee-shirt.

NARRATIVE: A detailed report was compiled by the Pathologist. A summary of pertinent information follows:

Unknown subject was burned by use of an accelerant which was ignited by a projectile which struck the victim in the chest. Apparent gunpowder residue was found on the jacket, plaid shirt & tee-shirt. Powder stipples were found embedding in the skin of the victim's chest.

CAUSE OF DEATH: Severe burns over 95% of the victim's body.

MANNER OF DEATH: Homicide

STATUS: Investigation active. Reports to follow.

Snowood might like to clown around sometimes, but when it came to his reports, he was all Homicide.

LaStanza reached over, picked up Snowood's black Stetson and tossed it over his old partner's face. Snowood woke with a jerk, deftly grabbing his hat before it hit the floor.

"Whoa," he said.

"Projectile?" LaStanza asked. "What are you talking about here?" He held up the daily.

"Oh, yeah." Snowood kicked his feet down. "I forgot to tell ya' at the hospital last night, but the crime scene guy found some pieces of a projectile in the grass where you rolled the guy. Looked like some kinda fireworks."

LaStanza picked up his phone and called the Crime Lab. Fat Frank Hammond answered after the second ring. He was eating something, probably an after-lunch snack. LaStanza asked him about the projectile.

"Yeah," Frank said, "I looked at it this morning. It's from a flare gun."

"What?"

"One of those guns you take out on a boat. Common as hell in south Louisiana."

"What else can you tell me about it?"

"Not much. Can't link the projectile to a gun. No markings, no striations, no lands or grooves."

"Thanks." LaStanza said and hung up. He punched out the extension of the communication center and asked for the supervisor in charge.

"I need you to check on something for me," LaStanza began.

"Sure." The supervisor was a patrolman named Cresap. Once a Fourth District patrolman, until an armed robber with a .9 millimeter left him crippled for life by shooting him in the back, Cresap was an infinitely better communication supervisor than the regular civilians hired for the job. He was one of the guys.

"I need to know if anyone called in last night about the burning man on Pleasant Street."

"I heard about that."

"Yeah," LaStanza said. "I called it in on the radio, but I

need to know if any civilians called in. Even if they just called in to ask what was going on. Okay?"

"Okay." Cresap would have to check the tapes. All 911 calls were taped.

LaStanza thanked him and hung up.

Snowood was standing now, his hat on his head, his western jacket in his hand. "Come on," he said impatiently, "my pardner's meeting us at Mr. Gyro's for lunch." Grinning a wide dip-stained grin, he added, "I'm ridin' with y'all."

LaStanza wanted to hit Pleasant Street, but his stomach ached, so he didn't argue. Three cups of coffee and a couple double scotches since lunch the previous day just wasn't enough, even if he wanted to loose the "love handles" that had recently sprouted on his lean runners frame.

Snowood's new partner was holding a table for them at the small Greek Restaurant at the corner of Decatur and Madison Street in the French Quarter. Steve Stevens, new to Homicide, was a five year veteran Robbery Detective. An inch shorter than Snowood's six feet, Stevens was stocky with short choppy light brown hair and a cleft chin. His eyes were his most curious feature, not just because they were extremely light blue, but because his left eye was crooked. It pointed to his nose. Except when Steven flipped out, which he did on occasion, then his left eye would *straighten.*

The place smelled wonderful, which made LaStanza realize just how hungry he was. Their small round table was near the window on the Decatur Street side. LaStanza immediately waved the waitress over.

Dressed in a white shirt and black dress pants, the young waitress smiled as she pulled out her pad and pen.

"Four gyro plates," LaStanza ordered, "and four Barq's." He looked around and there were no complaints. The waitress thanked him, wheeled and walked away. LaStanza noticed she had a nice wide mouth and a deep voice.

"She looks like Katherine Hepburn," Stevens said, resting his chin on his chest as he watched the waitress retreat.

"The fuck," Snowood said. "She's pretty."

"Katherine Hepburn was pretty. When she was young."

Snowood crinkled up his face in a sneer. "Katherine Hepburn was never pretty. She's a battle axe."

LaStanza took his coat off, draped it over the back of his chair and pulled out the note pad and ball point from the interior pocket. He began writing notes to himself about his Pleasant Street Murder. He noticed Jodie watching the passers-by on Decatur, which was a mix of tourists and locals. The tourists were easy to spot. They had glassy looks in their eyes.

"Katherine Hepburn was real pretty in her first couple movies and that girl looks just like she did when she was pretty." Stevens put his elbows on the table to emphasize his point. LaStanza immediately moved his note pad to his knee as the table rocked.

He wrote:

Check patrolmen's reports.

Run all license plates

Pull all police reports from area and time.

Canvass Pleasant from St. Charles to Magazine.

The waitress returned with four icy Barq's root beers in tall bottles and four glasses of ice. LaStanza watched Snowood and Stevens leer at her and watch her retreat.

"What movies?" Snowood challenged. "What movies did Katherine Hepburn every look that good in?"

"I don't remember names," Stevens said.

"Know who she really looks like?" Snowood said. "Audrey Hepburn."

"You're so full-a-shit!"

For the entire month of their partnership, Snowood and Stevens bickered constantly. If something was black to Snowood, it was white to Stevens. If something looked good to Snowood, it was shit to Stevens. If it was Kate

Hepburn to Stevens, it was Audrey to Snowood.

The waitress arrived with a tray with their four plates. She deftly placed each plate in front of the detectives while Snowood and Stevens checked out her boobs and ass.

"What's your name?" LaStanza asked.

"Kathy with a 'K'," the waitress answered with a nice smile. She looked to be about twenty. LaStanza smiled back and thanked her as she put his plate in front of him.

"See," Stevens snapped as soon as she walked away. "Kathy. Katherine Hepburn. I told you!"

"Audrey Hepburn," Snowood said before shoving his gyro into his mouth. At least they remained quiet while stuffing their faces. LaStanza had enough trouble eating a wet gyro sandwich with bandages on his hands...he didn't need to hear any more bickering. The lamb and beef sandwich with the cucumber sauce wrapped in pita bread was wonderful. So were the peppered fries.

Leaving Mr. Gyro's a half hour later, LaStanza noticed that Stevens' striped tie had acquired a glaze of cucumber sauce. Stevens usually wore striped ties. "Especially since they're no longer in fashion," Stevens told LaStanza as he immediately began to pick on LaStanza for wearing the latest fashioned ties, ties decorated with geometric designs or flowered ties. Which pissed LaStanza off because it was Jodie who told Stevens that striped ties were out of fashion. LaStanza had no fuckin' idea. Lizette bought his ties.

Walking up narrow Madison Street, away from Decatur, LaStanza spotted movement to their right. A tall red headed man with two cameras dangling around his neck stood on the sidewalk. One was a box camera, looked like a Mamiya. The other was a 35 mm. Focusing the Mamiya on a tall, slim brunette with long straight hair, a well-made up face, and a body by Playboy, the photographer snapped the shutter. The brunette was sitting on a stoop in front of a narrow wooden building. Directly in front of the brunette sat a black shoe-shine kid of about fifteen. The brunette's right foot was up on the shoe shiner's box, but the shiner wasn't looking at her black high heel. Neither were LaStanza and Snowood and Stevens. They were looking at the sleek curves of the brunette's body that lay very exposed beneath her sheer white teddy.

The cameraman snapped away as the shoe-shiner and LaStanza and Snowood and Stevens stared at the model. Jodie cleared her throat, but no one paid attention.

The model switched legs. The photographer switched positions. Jodie put a hand on LaStanza's shoulder and said, "I don't believe this." At that moment the model stood, her right foot still on the shoe-shiner's box. She put her hands behind her head and turned her body ever-so-slightly to the left. Her breasts bulged at the thin top of the teddy. The dark bush between her legs was about ten inches from the shoe shiner's face.

Noticing the detectives, she smiled, then closed her eyes and lifted her head skyward to let the sun bathed her pretty face. Her nipples nearly poked through the teddy.

"I'm leaving," Jodie said loudly.

"Good," Snowood said.

"Fine," Stevens said.

"Wait a second," LaStanza told his partner, but kept his eyes focused on the model, who finished quickly, waved to the detectives and strolled away with the retreating photographer, leaving the shoe-shiner to pick up his box and catch his breath.

Snowood and Stevens waved back at the model. LaStanza turned to Jodie and said, "Okay, let's go."

"What the hell was that?" Jodie said, pointing to the rear end of the model as the brunette and photographer retreated down Madison toward Decatur.

"You got me," LaStanza said, realizing that he was getting a goddam erection. And Lizette had been gone less that forty-eight hours.

"Can you imagine the traffic jam she's gonna cause on Decatur?" Steven said. Decatur, a thoroughfare, was much busier than tiny Madison Street.

The men followed Jodie to their units parked in the police zone on St. Peter Street, on the other side of St. Louis Cathedral. Jodie walked much faster, as if she was really angry. In front of the cathedral, Stevens turned and started walking backwards. He summed it all up with, "That's what I love about this fuckin' town. Women like that."

"You're sick," Jodie said.

"Know what you need, little lady?" Stevens said.

LaStanza moved aside so Jodie wouldn't hit him by mistake when she slapped the shit outta Stevens. He could see Jodie bracing herself. Her right fist was clenched.

Stevens, grinning now, said, "You need to lighten up. You're too tense."

"Well," Snowood said. "Guess I'll have to go home and poke my old lady tonight. I got a hard on that'd make a buffalo jealous."

Jodie picked up her pace. LaStanza was too busy trying to walk off his own erection to try and catch up.

"Yeah," Snowood continued, "My old lady ain't had it this good since the time we humped outside The Panting Lady Saloon in Whispering Gulch, New Mexico last summer. You ever been to a ghost town?" he asked his partner.

"I been to Shreveport a couple times."

LaStanza picked up his pace immediately. He didn't want to hear any more about Snowood's ghost town adventures. Once Country-Ass got started, there was no stopping him.

Looking back over his shoulder, LaStanza said, "You know who that waitress really looked like?"

"Who?" Snowood and Stevens said in unison.

"Tallulah Bankhead."

"Who?"

Neutral Ground

LaStanza stood over the burned spot on the neutral ground and rubbed the tip of his right penny-loafer through the singed blades of St. Augustine grass. He could still smell the gasoline, along with an acrid burnt smell. He slipped his black portable police radio into the left rear pocket of his suit pants, then fanned his jacket. It had to be near ninety degrees with matching humidity. September in sub-tropical New Orleans was like taking a hot shower under a heat lamp. LaStanza's shirt was damp with perspiration.

He looked at his watch. It was four o'clock now. His shift officially began at four. Never mind that he and Jodie were in court most of the day, never mind that Snowood handled the autopsy that morning, never mind that Stevens was still in the middle of an armed robbery trial. They were the evening watch in the big show. All murders and suicides were theirs until midnight, along with any bad kidnappings and extortions. Thankfully it was Wednesday. Wednesdays were the slowest evenings, if there was ever such a thing in the Crescent City.

LaStanza stepped over to the concrete walkway in the center of the small neutral ground that ran along the 1500 block of Pleasant Street. Pulling his note pad and pen from his coat pocket, he drew a diagram of the neutral ground. He inked in each of the towering oaks, the smaller pecan trees, the tall palm trees and magnolias. He put in the concrete square to his left. He made sure to include each black wrought iron street lights. Electric lights, they looked like old fashioned gas lamps. The one to his right was the one he stood beneath while E.M.T. Haines poured the sterile water over his hands. He drew in the elephant leaf bushes and banana trees and other bushes that dotted the neutral ground. A squirrel scampered to his left and darted up one of the pecan trees.

Jodie, who had been canvassing the 1500 block of Toledano Street, which ran along the other side of the neutral ground, came up behind LaStanza. He looked back at her as she approached. Just as he suspected, there wasn't a hint of perspiration on her fair face. Not a hair of her neat page boy was out of place. In fact, she looked fresh.

"Get anything?" he asked.

"Lady in the yellow Victorian saw 'the commotion on the neutral ground,' but nothing before. She thought you hit him with your car and started the fire."

"Jesus!" LaStanza drew in one final bush. "I got nothing over here," He said, referring to his canvass of the 1500 block of Pleasant. He was disappointed to learn that the pink Victorian house had been unoccupied the previous night. An elderly couple named Fitzgerald had spent the previous evening visiting relatives across the river until returning that afternoon to find a detective on their porch and a burned spot on the neutral ground across from their house.

"Only house I didn't get to is the big one on the corner." Finishing his sketch, he put an "X" over the spot where the body came to rest.

"Didn't the crime lab take measurements?" Jodie asked.

"Sure. I just like to draw."

"Smart Ass."

The crime lab's exacting measurements could provide

a crime scene drawing to scale if needed. LaStanza made certain to draw in the twelve-inch cement curb that surrounded the neutral ground. That's what his victim had stumbled over.

"Let's catch the corner house," he said. He wiped sweat from his brow and put his pad and pen back into his jacket. Stepping over the cement curb, he said, "Know why we call these neutral grounds?"

"Because we're weird."

She had a point. In New Orleans sidewalks were still called "banquettes," a dime was a "silver dime," an "alley" was sometimes the narrow passage between homes, and soft drinks were never "soda pops," but were simply "cokes," unless you wanted a root beer. And everyone drank Barq's root beer and had chicory with their coffee. Well, not everyone. Republicans drank decaf and Tab.

"It's not 'cause we're weird," LaStanza said as they crossed the street to the banquette. Lizette had told him the story, although he had a vague childhood memory of knowing why medians were called neutral grounds.

"Back when Creoles lived on the French Quarter side of Canal Street and the Americans lived on the other side, the middle of the street was neutral ground, sort of a demilitarized zone."

"Oh, yeah. I heard that. I think."

"Bank on it. Lizette the history whiz told me."

"Talk to her yet?"

"She's calling tonight."

LaStanza stopped next to the one-way sign and shook his head. *The wrong way down a one-way street.*

The house at the downtown-lake side corner of Pleasant and Prytania Street was quite a place. A three story white wooden Greek Revival with four thick columns along its front gallery which faced Prytania, the property was surrounded by a wrought iron fence painted white. LaStanza noticed rows of windows on the second and third floor along the Pleasant Street side of the house. Each window had it own small lacework balcony, which overlooked the narrow impeccably trimmed side yard and the street below.

It occurred to LaStanza as he jotted the address and description of the house that he'd used another unique New Orleans description. Directions in New Orleans were never north or south or east or west. Since Lake Pontchartrain was north and the river south, a house on the north side of a street was on the "lake" side and visa versa. Downtown was east and uptown was west. So if a house was on the east side of a street, it was on the downtown side. Simple, unless you were from the rest of America and received a New Orleans police report and wondered what the fuck, "the house was on the uptown-river side" meant.

Leading the way through the front gate, LaStanza climbed the four front concrete steps of the gallery and rang the doorbell. The front door of the house was made of carved hardwood, a real gas lamp on either side. He rang the bell again. A prim black maid answered. Wearing a white dress, white stocking and white shoes, the dark complected woman was about fifty with close cropped salt-and-pepper hair.

"Police," LaStanza said, opening his suit coat to reveal his badge clipped to the front of his belt. "I'm Detective LaStanza. And this is my partner Detective Kintyre." He handed the maid a business card. She took it reluctantly.

"We're investigating the murder that occurred on the neutral ground last night."

"Say what?"

"Last night a man was burned to death in this very neighborhood." LaStanza pulled out his pad and pen again. "He died on the neutral ground. You never heard?"

"No, Sir." The woman had a sharp look to her face, a hawk look. The "Sir" in her voice was automatic.

"We're talking to everyone in the neighborhood in case someone saw something last night."

"I don't stay here at night."

"What's your name, Ma'am?"

"Cleola. Cleola Bracket." The maid looked at LaStanza's card.

"Is there anyone else home?"

"Just the children." She pronounced it "chillren."

"How old?"

"Twelve and two."

"May we speak to the twelve year old?"

Cleola flipped the card around and looked at the blank rear.

"I think you better come back when their parents are here."

"Sure. What's a good time?" LaStanza jotted the maid's name on his pad.

"Come back after supper. 'Round seven."

"Fine. What's their parents' names?"

The fine house on the downtown lake side of the intersection belonged to Doctor and Mrs. B. A. Whippet. LaStanza thanked Cleola and turned to leave.

"We'll be back around seven," Jodie said.

At five-thirty, LaStanza and Jodie stood next to the small park at the corner of Pleasant and Camp Street. LaStanza's shirt was plastered to his chest now. Jodie looked as fresh as she had strolling into court that morning.

The small park smelled anything but fresh. It smelled of cheap wine, vomit, and, faintly, of urine. Besides a set of red monkey-bars, a blue merry-go-round, a metal slide, several futuristic looking square electric lights mounted on pastel green poles, the park featured two men draped across two black iron benches.

On the nearest bench sat a black man with fresh red marks on his dark face. Wearing layers of clothes, the man held a brown paper bag in his left hand, which was wrapped in a soiled ace bandage. LaStanza spotted the green neck of a bottle protruding through the top of the bag in the man's hand.

The man on the other bench fit the same description: homeless, black, fifty to sixty, bruises and red marks on his face, wearing layers of dark clothing, holding a paper bag with a bottle inside.

LaStanza glanced around and realized the park was directly behind the large A&P store on Magazine Street. He stepped through the gate of the wrought iron fence that surrounded the park, a fence painted the same pastel green as the light poles. He heard Jodie following, her low heels clicking on the cement walkway. He maneuvered around an empty bottle of Thunderbird and a broken bottle of Boone's Farm, and stood in front of the first man.

The second man rose and started away. Before LaStanza could raise his hand to indicate that Jodie should cut number two off, Jodie was already moving to intercept the second man.

The man in front of LaStanza didn't look up. LaStanza opened his jacket and said, "Police, man. What's your name?"

"I Raphael Chambliss the fourth. I lives 1595 Camp Street. With Auntie Vanna. I didn't do it. I drinks." The man spoke in a loud, jittery voice.

"What was that?"

"I Raphael Chambliss the fourth. I lives 1595 Camp Street. With Auntie Vanna. I didn't do it. I drinks." The man spoke to LaStanza's penny loafers, rattling off his response in sharp staccato sentences.

LaStanza pulled his radio out of his back pocket and sat on the bench next to Raphael. He crossed his legs and said, "Raphael. We need your help. Somebody you know got killed last night."

Still staring at the spot where LaStanza's penny loafers had been, the man said, "I Raphael Chambliss the fourth. I lives 1595 Camp Street. With Auntie Vanna. I didn't do it. I drinks."

LaStanza looked over at Jodie who had finished with her man and approached shaking her head. Her page boy twisted neatly with the twists of her head.

With an amused snarl, LaStanza said, "This here is Raphael Chambliss the fourth. He lives 1595 Camp Street. With Auntie Vanna. He didn't do it. He drinks."

Turning to Raphael, LaStanza said, "That was Auntie Vanna, right?"

"I Raphael Chambliss the fourth. I lives 1595 Camp Street. With Auntie Vanna. I didn't do it. I drinks."

LaStanza stood and stretched. "Come on," he told his partner. "Let's see if there are any Homo-Sapiens hanging around the front of the A&P."

At six-thirty, LaStanza placed his radio on one of the outside tables of a small cafe at the downtown-river side corner of Toledano and Magazine Street. A heavy-set waiter with oily black hair and a pencil-thin moustache hurried out to hold the chair for Jodie. LaStanza pulled his own chair out and sat across from his partner at the small table with the red and white checkerboard table cloth and the red and blue Cinzano umbrella overhead.

The waiter put plastic-coated menus in front of the detectives and said, "Can I get you anything to drink?"

"Iced tea," LaStanza said.

"Same here," Jodie said, picking up her menu. As the waiter hurried away, she asked LaStanza, "What's the name of this place?"

"Cafe Italiano."

"It smells delicious."

"Tastes even better."

LaStanza ordered green lasagna and a glass of Chianti. Jodie ordered the veal Parmigiana. Across Magazine Street, outside the A&P, LaStanza watched five black men talking as they leaned against the side of the store. The men were sharing two bottles, each wrapped in a brown paper bag. Hopefully, they were talking about what LaStanza and Jodie had asked them a few minutes earlier. Maybe later, no, probably later, much later, one of them would see LaStanza still canvassing the area and say something like, "You know that man who burned. I think his name was..."

The lasagna was outstanding, the wine even better. LaStanza ordered a second glass. His right hand itched like hell. His left hand stung. The wine didn't ease the pain, it just mellowed things out.

Jodie made yummy sounds as she dug into her parmigiana. He had to smile. Jodie was always surprised when he casually said, "Let's eat here." And the place wound up having great food. She shouldn't have been surprised that evening. LaStanza was on his home turf.

It was called the Sixth District, the sixth police district of New Orleans, a thin strip of a precinct that ran from Earhart Boulevard and the Pontchartrain Expressway to Louisiana Avenue down to the river. Crammed in this narrow triangular strip were the elegant homes of the Garden District, the rough and tumble Irish Channel, ten of the city's busiest wharves, and four of its most crowded housing projects: The Melpomene, The Calliope, The St. Thomas, and The Magnolia. Changing some of the project names to Guste Homes, B. W. Cooper and C. J. Peete did nothing to change the sad state of living in abject poverty nor the desperation of the young living next to such affluence mere blocks away.

LaStanza was weaned on the streets of The Bloody Sixth. He worked it as a rookie patrolmen and stayed in The Sixth for over seven years before moving up to Homicide. One of the city's smallest police districts, The Sixth played host to nearly half of the city's murders yearly.

Jodie made small talk, mostly about the food and the curious way the portly waiter fussed over her.

"He can see down your blouse," LaStanza said, which caused Jodie to shoot a hand to her breast until she realized she was wearing one of her high collar blouses.

"Cute, LaStanza. Real cute."

At least she didn't put up a fuss when he paid for dinner. She used to insist they split every bill, even though he'd married one of the wealthiest women in Louisiana. But the longer they were partners and the longer Jodie hung out with Lizette, the more she let LaStanza pay. It wasn't his money.

Just before seven-thirty, LaStanza rang the doorbell of the Whippet house at Pleasant and Prytania. He heard someone running to the door before it opened. He and Jodie both moved to the side automatically. A blonde haired girl threw open the door. Placing a hand on her hip, she said, "Yes? What can I do for you?"

Wearing a Catholic school uniform, a dress white shirt and plaid skirt that reached well below her knees, white socks and black and white Oxford shoes, the girl looked impatient.

"Police," LaStanza said, opening his jacket. "Are your parents home?"

"They might be," the girl said. She had braces and killer baby-blue eyes. "It depends on what you want to talk to them about." She tossed her long hair aside with a flip of her left hand.

"Daphne," a woman's voice called out behind the girl. "Who's at the door, dear?"

"They say they're the police," the girl answered. "But I'm not so sure."

LaStanza smiled. Jodie huffed and stepped through the doorway and called out, "Mrs. Whippet. We *are* the police and we'd like to talk to you and your husband."

Daphne retreated, her hands clasped behind the small of her back, an inquiring look on her face as if she were studying specimens in science class.

A portly woman wearing a long, full flowered dress stepped into the hallway. She had a napkin in her hand. She also had blonde hair, but her eyes were hazel and her mouth far too large for her small head.

Jodie pulled her credentials from her jacket and introduced herself and LaStanza, then began to question Mrs. Whippet, whose first name turned out to be Hazel. Mr. Whippet joined them in the hall, carrying his own napkin. Tall and thin with hunched shoulders and a pair of thick metal-framed glasses on his hawk nose, Mr. Whippet was a mouse of a man who stood behind his wife's abundant skirt, content to let his wife do the talking. LaStanza watched the man look back and forth from Jodie to his wife as the questions were asked and answered. The man's especially round head reminded LaStanza of those plastic football players glued to the dashboard of housing project cars.

No, the Whippets didn't know about the burned man. No, they hadn't seen anything the previous evening. They all go to bed right after the ten o'clock news.

"What about you, Daphne?" LaStanza asked as Jodie put her pad away.

"I'm thinking," Daphne said, twisting her shoulders as she stood leaning against a marble topped table next to the stairs.

"She didn't see anything," Mrs. Whippet said.

Jodie thanked the Whippets and passed one of her cards to Mrs. Whippet. Mr. Whippet, whose first name was Boz, remained behind his wife as the detectives moved back to the door. Daphne stepped over to close the door behind them. As she closed the door, Daphne gave LaStanza a big wink.

"Jesus," Jodie said.

"What? The girl's got taste."

"She's twelve!"

"She won't always be twelve."

Jodie stopped dead. LaStanza continued walking around the corner back over to the neutral ground and waited for his partner. He wanted to keep teasing her, because she was so easy, but he was tired, bone tired. His right hand stung. His left hand burned.

"Come on," he said, when Jodie came up. "I'm kidding."

"You didn't sound like you were kidding."

"Because I'm not. Five years from now I'm asking that little girl out."

LaStanza poured two cups of spring water into the copper espresso machine tucked into a corner of the white kitchen counter of his mansion. Jodie, sitting at the wide counter, her note pad in front of her, yawned as she watched him.

"Brulee leaves you something every night?" she said, nodding to the latest note Aunt Brulee left for LaStanza. The Post-It was stuck to the counter top. It read:

Wop,

Hot sausage sandwich and potato salad in fridge. I took gumbo home. I left pecan pie.

Brulee

"She takes care of me," LaStanza said scooping six measures of espresso grounds into the machine. He flipped on the switch.

"Cappuccino or espresso?" he asked.

"Cappuccino."

He grabbed the matching copper milk carafe and headed for the fridge.

"You're gonna miss the hell out of Lizette," Jodie said.

"Thanks for reminding me."

"Three months is a long time."

"Three and a half months. Nice of you to remind me." He filled the milk carafe half full of low fat milk.

"That's what you get for flirting with a twelve year old."

He wasn't thinking about the twelve year old. He was thinking about Carmen Jacopino's body and that model on Madison Street. He moved back to the espresso maker and held the milk carafe beneath the steam spicket and waited.

Jodie yawned again and then said, "We need to canvass on my case tomorrow night, Okay?"

"Sure."

The steam began to bubble the milk. He moved the

carafe around. *Hell yeah,* he thought. They should canvass on her case. Her case was a real heater case, a hot, high profile, news media case. A University of New Orleans co-ed was raped and strangled in the bedroom of her Gentilly Boulevard apartment. Talk about headlines.

"You get those police reports from last night?" Jodie asked.

LaStanza nodded. She was talking about the patrolmen's reports. Owen and DeLeon had compiled quite a list of license plates from around the crime scene last night, as well as the names and addresses of several passers-by.

"Guess we'll call yours 'Pleasant Street,' right?" Jodie said as she jotted the name of LaStanza's latest case atop her notes.

"Yeah." He watched the milk bubble into a thick foam.

LaStanza's burned man case would be known as Pleasant Street, at least to the detectives. It was an unspoken ritual in Homicide, the naming of cases. In New Orleans, murders were usually named for their location or for something unique about the victim or killer. There was the Unicorn Murder, named such because the victim had been impaled through the forehead with a butcher knife. Then there was the Sock Murder, because the victim was found with a sock stuffed in her mouth. There were so many: the Batture Murders that occurred on the river batture in Algiers; the Gargoyle who had been in the river long enough to have been transformed from a mild mannered accountant into a bloated gargoyle; the Groucho Murder committed by an armed robber wearing a Groucho Marx disguise; the Stupid Lupert Murder; the Four Stooges Murders committed by four escapees from the Tangipahoa Parish Jail. The list was endless.

LaStanza had handled so many...too many. From Dauphine Street to the Gargoyle, Bayou St. John, Coliseum Square, Bywater, Bogue Falaya, Almonaster, Governor Nicholls Street Wharf, Dryades Street, Lee Circle, Cucullu Street, the Desire Streetcar. He remembered them all. He especially remembered the Exposition Boulevard Murder where Lizette's twin sister had been butchered by The Slasher...LaStanza's first case in the big show.

Exposition Boulevard, the double-wide banquette just outside the front gate of Lizette and LaStanza's mansion, was a sidewalk street. Running along the downtown side of Audubon Park, its exclusive addresses faced the park.

Twenty year old Lynette Anne Louvier had been murdered not a hundred yards from her front door as she walked down Exposition Boulevard on a night that changed Lizette's life, as well as LaStanza's.

LaStanza poured the strong espresso liquid into two small cups. He poured two packs of Equal sweetener into each cup, topping them off with the steamed foam milk and a pinch of cinnamon. He brought them to the counter where Jodie sat perched on a stool.

"You're using Equal now?" Jodie asked.

"Love handles," he said, pinching his sides.

Jodie, who stood five-seven and weighed about one hundred and five, had used artificial sweeteners since high school. Maybe that's why she was only five pounds heavier than when she graduated from Dominican High nine years earlier.

"So tell me about your bad date."

Jodie's shoulders sank. She took a sip of cappuccino and let out a heavy sigh. "He lived with his mother until she died a year ago. We're expecting beatification any day now. The woman was a saint."

That was enough said.

"It isn't the date that's got me down. It's my case."

"I know," LaStanza answered softly.

Her hot, high profile, news media case was like a guillotine hanging over the case officer's head. LaStanza knew that Homicide pressure cooker feeling oh so well.

Jodie's case was named for the suspected killer. Because the murder matched the method of operation of a serial rapist striking the lakefront and Gentilly areas for months, it was named for the man known as the pantyhose rapist. The media knew about the similar MO, but didn't know that DNA tests proved the same man who'd committed five rapes, wrapping one leg from a pair of pantyhose around his victim's throat while wearing the other leg of pantyhose over his head and face, had indeed murdered the UNO co-ed on Gentilly Boulevard. To the Homicide dicks the case was simply known as "Pantyhose."

Jodie finished her cappuccino and looked at her watch.

"That's enough to get me home," she said as she rose and stretched her tall, slim frame. "I'll pick you up tomorrow at three forty-five, Right?"

"Yeah."

LaStanza walked her to the kitchen door. The wood and glass door opened to the four brick steps along the Garfield side of the mansion. He left the door open and punched in the lock code on the side gate to let her through to the street. The night was still muggy at midnight.

"You leave your notes for me?" he asked as Jodie stepped through the gate in the tall brick wall.

"They're on the counter."

"Thanks."

Jodie opened the driver's side door.

"You know," LaStanza said, "I'll bet one of those windows along the Pleasant Street side of the Whippet house belongs to Daphne."

"What the fuck is that supposed to mean?"

Jodie was getting the hang of the proper use of the "F" word all right.

"I'll bet that little twelve year old was up last night well past ten-thirty. We gotta talk to her again."

"Yeah. Sure." Jodie climbed in and closed her door.

He waited for her to pull away in their blue unmarked LTD. Looking out at the darkness of the park, he spotted a black cat running breakneck across the front of his house. He smiled as the LTD's headlights disappeared down Calhoun Street. To LaStanza, who wore number thirteen as a baseball player and as a track star at Archbishop Rummel High, a black cat was good luck.

Closing the gate, he made sure it was locked. He also made sure the kitchen door was secure before punching in the burglar alarm code, arming each of the windows and doors for the evening.

LaStanza sat back next to his cappuccino and checked out Jodie's notes. He pulled his notes out of his clipboard and counted the number of houses they'd canvassed that evening. Twenty-seven...they'd checked twenty-seven houses along Pleasant and Toledano and Prytania.

Flipping to a fresh page, he jotted some notes to himself.

Check tomorrow's paper for article.

Check coroner's office for possible IDs.

Expand canvass of Prytania and Magazine areas.

Pull all police reports from entire area.

Finishing off his cappuccino, he poured himself another. The milk was flat, but that was Okay. He jotted himself three more notes:

Run license plates from Owen/DeLeon canvass.

Check out passers-by from Owen/DeLeon canvass.

Computer check of items, complaints, arrests in area.

Jesus, he was fuckin' tired. His hands hurt like hell. He left his notes on the counter and went into the pantry and grabbed a stainless steel bucket. Back in the kitchen, he opened his freezer and scooped a handful of ice cubes from the automatic ice-maker and dumped them in the bucket. He filled the bucket three-quarters full from the kitchen faucet. Waiting for the water, he gingerly pulled off his bandages.

Both hands looked puffy. The skin beneath the bandages looked white and rubbery. He put the bucket on the stool where Jodie had sat and sat back on his stool. Easing his hands into the cold water, he grimaced at the sharp tingles and remembered how the initial twenty-four hours after a murder were the most critical. The first twenty-four hours after the Pleasant Street Murder were long fuckin' gone. And he had nothing. He had an unknown victim and no fuckin' witnesses. Who the fuck ever heard of a dumped body whodunit in the middle of the fuckin' Garden District?

Snakebitten. There's a cottonmouth out there with my name on it!

Snowood hadn't said it yet, but he knew Country-Ass was thinking it. There's goes LaStanza's perfect solution record. Yet maybe Snowood had learned his lesson by now. So many times before he said that exact thing, only to watch LaStanza solve the unsolvable. How did John Paul Jones put it? "I have not yet begun to fight."

The phone rang at twelve-thirty exactly. LaStanza answered it before the second ring.

"Hello Lover," Lizette said in her deep voice. She sounded like she was across the street.

"Hey Babe," he said. "It's good to hear your voice."

"I miss you."

"Yeah? And what are you wearing right now, little girl?"

"Actually, I'm lying here stark naked on the bed of my hotel room." Her voice dropped an octave, sounding even sexier than normal.

"Yeah?"

"Yeah," she said. "I wish I was sucking your dick right now."

Vulture Street

LaStanza dropped his briefcase on his city-government-issue desk on the way to the coffee pot. Scooping up the large blue mug with "Spade & Archer" stenciled on it, a mug Lizette had given him after he dropped and shattered his old mug with "Fuck This Shit" printed on it, he poured himself a thick cup of coffee-and-chicory, adding two packs of Equal sweetener. He took a sip. The brew was stale and smelled burned, probably been on the burner for hours.

Good, nice and fuckin' strong.

He looked up at the clock. It was three p.m., sharp. He reached up and straightened the unofficial emblem of the Homicide Division that hung beneath the clock. The emblem was an art deco painting of a gold NOPD star-and-crescent badge with a vulture perched atop. Someone had taped a dialogue balloon coming out of the vulture's mouth, like in a comic book. It said, "Our Day Begins When Your Day Ends."

On the way back to his desk, LaStanza loosened his Colombian blue tie, a tie dotted with silver geometric designs: triangles and parallelograms and squares. He unbuttoned the top button of his gray Oxford shirt and placed the Spade & Archer mug on his desk. He took off his navy blue suit coat and walked it over to the coat rack outside his lieutenant's office. The door was closed but he could hear a muffled voice talking inside.

He checked the daily reports on his way back to his desk. There was a murder after midnight and one that morning, along with a suicide and an unclassified death. There was nothing about Pleasant Street nor about Jodie's Pantyhose Case in any of the dailies.

Back at his desk, he pulled his *Times-Picayune* from his briefcase, kicked his feet up on the desk and searched for the article about his case. It was buried back in the Metro Section, on page five beneath a D. H. Holmes Department Store ad for microwave ovens.

He read the article.

POLICE SEEK IDENTITY OF MURDER VICTIM

Tight-lipped New Orleans homicide detectives are seeking the identity of a man found burned to death in the 1500 block of Pleasant Street on Tuesday night around 11:30 p.m. The unidentified man was found on the neutral ground that divides Pleasant and Toledano Streets, a block from St. Charles Avenue. Although homicide detectives questioned residents on Pleasant Street Wednesday, no clues were surfaced in this puzzling case.

Described as black, between the ages of 45 and 55, the deceased was wearing a green zipper K-Mart jacket, a plaid shirt, a blue tee-shirt, blue dress Questo brand pants, and black Stopps brand loafers.

Police ask that anyone having information contact Detectives Dino LaStanza and Jodie Kintyre at the homicide division.

LaStanza cut the article out to add to his case file. He noticed the article was written by George Lynn, his old high school buddy who helped him on the Batture Murders.

Good. George Lynn was solid, as solid as any reporter

could be, which meant he could be trusted...almost.

"Tight-lipped," that description had to be Mason. The fine touch of LaStanza's lieutenant was obvious in the press release. There was nothing about the flare gun. Mason believed in keeping at least one important detail from the media, from general knowledge. If the police and the killer were the only ones who knew that detail, it may bring them together.

LaStanza had seen it happen many times before. Killers loved to correct newspaper and television accounts of their escapades, telling their girlfriends or their running padnas that one important detail Mason had omitted from his press release.

"No man, that lady wasn't shot twice, she was shot once, man."

"No man, the dude wasn't stabbed with a ice pick, it was a screw driver."

"No way that fucker drowned. No way."

"He wasn't murdered there. I'm telling ya', he wasn't murdered *there.*"

"Naw, that girl wasn't raped, unless some sick fuck raped her body *after*!"

LaStanza picked up his phone and punched the coroner's office number. He was lucky. A coroner's investigator answered, instead of one of the minimum-wage toe-headed office workers who thought a toe tag was a game played barefoot.

"You get any ID calls on the burned man from Pleasant Street?"

"The crispy critter?"

"Yeah."

"Let me check."

The investigator came back on a minute later with a "no."

LaStanza thanked him. Hanging up, he took another sip of the scorched coffee. He kicked his feet back up on the desk and went back to his newspaper. There was another article about Jodie's Pantyhose Case at the bottom of the front page.

He heard the lieutenant's door open behind him. He heard penny loafers shuffling over. Lieutenant Rob Mason leaned against the side of LaStanza's desk and began drumming his fingers on the desk top.

LaStanza looked up at the lean, triangular face, at the deep set eyes and prominent cheekbones of his fearless leader. Mason blinked twice and nodded, grabbing the edge of the paper. Their lieutenant wore his usual white shirt, dark blue pants and gray tie.

"Damn," Mason said, "the Israelis and Arabs are at it again."

"Huh?"

"Article here says Israeli commandos raided a PLO stronghold in Lebanon, killing nineteen before escaping by boat."

"What's news about that?" LaStanza said. "They run that same article every couple months. Saves time writing up a new one."

"Yeah," Mason smiled. Old chisel face actually smiled. "You'd think they'd all kill each other sooner or later."

LaStanza nodded and went back to his paper. Mason drummed his fingers on the desk top again. LaStanza peeked over the top of the paper and said, "How many days has it been?"

"Five," Mason said. "And I'm fuckin' dying here. *Fuckin' dying!*" Mason wrung his hands tightly, his bony knuckles turning white.

"You try chewing gum?"

Mason started doing knee bends. The son-of-a-gun actually did knee bends there next to LaStanza's desk. Bouncing on his toes, the thin lieutenant with the Marine Corps flat-top went up and down and up and down. LaStanza bit his lower lip to keep from laughing.

"I'm a fuckin' addict," Mason said, punctuating each word with a grunt. "I want a cigarette so fuckin' bad, I'm ready to French kiss a tail pipe!"

LaStanza went back to the Pantyhose article. An industrious reporter found similarities between this case and, of all cases, the Hillside Strangler Case in California.

"My wife keeps cutting out articles about passive smoke from newspapers and magazines." Mason was in full stride now, breathing well as he pumped out knee bend after knee bend.

"She gives me one more article and I'm taking her out."

Wait a minute, LaStanza thought. *There were two Hillside Stranglers, Kenneth Bianchi and his cousin. Named Buono or something. They caught both of them.*

The article went on to explain that, like the Hillside Strangler, all of the victims of the Pantyhose rapist had been sexually molested, and one had been strangled. Trying to play up the fact that the Pantyhose rapist wasn't necessarily one man because descriptions by several of the rape victims varied, the paper pointed out how the Hillside Strangler had an accomplice.

Accomplice? They both were killers. Jesus! And what fuckin' connection was there between the cases?

"I'll make it look like suicide," Mason said as he stopped and stood puffing next to the desk.

"Suicide?"

"Yeah, next person gives me an article about how passive smoke kills, I'm gonna kill 'em and make it look like a suicide." With that Mason turned and went back into his office. He slammed the door so hard it loosened the emblem beneath the clock so the vulture leaned precariously to the left.

LaStanza got up and straightened the emblem. Since he was up, he fixed a fresh pot of coffee-and-chicory. He was careful not to get his bandages wet. He'd reduced the size of the wrapping on his right hand to a single wrap across the palm. He still had to wrap two fingers of his left hand and the entire palm. Both hands still hurt like hell.

By the time he got back to his desk with a fresh cup, Jodie came in. Her hair fluffed and bouncy, she looked as pristine as ever. LaStanza smiled to himself. *She could walk out of a coal mine without a smudge.*

"You early too?" Jodie said as she dropped her briefcase on her desk across the narrow aisle from LaStanza's desk and headed straight for the coffee.

LaStanza reached over and put the paper with the Pantyhose article on her desk.

"Didja read the paper yet?"

"No, it's in my briefcase," she said.

"The paper thinks your killer's two guys, like the Hillside Stranglers?"

"What?"

"Exactly."

Jodie returned to her desk. "Two guys, huh? With the same fuckin' DNA?"

That was another piece of information Mason withheld from the press. DNA fingerprinting was on the cutting edge, something Mason heard about from an old college buddy, now an editor with *Police* magazine in California. The next day Mason called Scotland Yard to get information on the new British forensic breakthrough. Let the media speculate. Let them guess. Sometimes reading the paper was like reading a science-fiction novel.

Jodie snatched up the paper and read it without sitting down. He watched her, watched the visible signs of the pressure cooker working on his partner's face as the inevitable stress of a heater case ate at her. Jodie's jaw tightened as she read. He saw her teeth grinding.

Glancing up at the fluorescents, he saw that several were yellowed behind the beveled plastic light fixtures that dotted the suspended ceiling. Some of the tiles were missing. One, near the sergeant's office, was knocked out when Mark Land threw one of his bear-tantrums and heaved an empty coffee mug up through the tile. There was also a neat hole between the two sergeant's offices, a hole Mark had put his foot through after a screaming match with an A.D.A. who had decided to nolle prosse a first degree murder case because the A.D.A. wasn't sure he could win and the defendant's lawyer categorically refused to accept any plea bargain. Someone hung a sign over the hole that said, "One Small Step For Man."

Jodie sat and cut the article out of the paper. LaStanza stretched and looked over at the wall of windows to his right, windows so dingy he could barely see through them. It looked dark outside. Most of the green tint plastered to the exterior of the windows had peeled away under the unrelenting New Orleans sun. The peeling gave the windows the look of leprosy. LaStanza yawned as rain began to pelt the windows. A sudden semi-tropical rainstorm transformed the leper windows into a kaleidoscope of green tinted wash.

He pulled a stack of papers from his briefcase, and spread them out on his desk. Between sips of coffee, much stronger coffee since he'd made it, he assembled the police reports, the canvass reports, the computer print outs of complaints from the 1400 and 1500 blocks of Pleasant and Toledano Streets and the 3200 and 3300 blocks of Prytania for the last year including arrests, traffic tickets and parking tickets.

He fished out the canvass report from Owen and DeLeon, along with the list of license plate numbers from their canvass the night of the murder. They spoke to nine people that night, three out on the street and six at home, some of the same homes LaStanza and his partner had canvassed later.

"Hey," he called out to Jodie. "Did you notice any boats in the area when we canvassed?"

"Boats?"

"In yards or garages." LaStanza opened his case note book and jotted a big note to himself.

"Look for boats. Ask about boats."

"The flare gun," he explained.

"Oh, yeah." Jodie went back to her paper. "No, I don't remember any boats."

Mason came out of his office. He was jogging in place now. He bounded over to the coffee pot and stopped to pour himself a cup. LaStanza looked back at Jodie and she stared slack-jawed at their lieutenant.

"Nicotine withdrawals," LaStanza said.

Mason hurried back into his office with his coffee and slammed the door again.

"Jesus," Jodie said.

"It'll get worse."

LaStanza couldn't find mention of where the debris from the flare gun was found in the Owen/DeLeon report, so he went fishing through the other reports.

"You talk to Lizette last night?" Jodie asked, putting her paper away.

"Yeah, for a couple hours."

"You tell her about your hands?"

The fuck!

"No."

"Good," Jodie said, which surprised him. "No need to worry her."

"Ah ha!" LaStanza said when he found Harry Funder's report. It was Funder who found the debris from the flare gun projectile in the street at the intersection of Pleasant and Prytania.

"What's with the 'Ah ha'?" Jodie asked.

"Harry Funder found the flare gun debris." Funder had the debris photographed by the crime lab and even took measurements. The debris was only 6'3" from the curb of the downtown-lake side of Prytania and Pleasant, right in front of the Whippet house.

Six feet, three inches. He had to have been on Prytania Street. Good. He came from Prytania Street before crossing Pleasant. Probably. Unless he ran in circles.

"Funder's a pain in the ass sometimes, a Class-A complainer, but he's still a good cop." LaStanza heard himself say aloud.

"Did you eat that hot sausage sandwich?" Jodie asked.

"What? Yeah, for lunch. And what, may I ask, did you have for lunch?" LaStanza said. *If she tells me, then I could die a happy man.*

Jodie described the salad she'd carefully prepared for lunch in detail. LaStanza tuned her out and went back to Owen and DeLeon's canvass report. He re-read a part.

"Officers spoke to Bert Waters of 3203 Chestnut Street who was observed walking his German Shepherd dog in the 3300 block of Prytania at 12:30 a.m. Waters claimed to have seen and heard nothing."

The report listed Waters' vitals: date of birth, driver's license number, and social security number. LaStanza continued to read.

"Officers spoke to Jeanne Bonneau who was standing in her front yard at 1440 Toledano Street at 12:47 a.m. Bonneau said she'd come out after hearing sirens. She also claimed to have seen and heard nothing."

The report listed Bonneau's vitals.

LaStanza read on.

"Officers spoke to William Sherman, 30-year-old white male, of 6711 Yellow Tavern, Enon, Louisiana. Sherman was observed parking his 1984 black Ford pickup at the corner of Prytania and Harmony Streets at 1:08 a.m."

Owen and DeLeon noted Jones' driver's license number, social security number, date of birth, as well as the license number of his 1984 black Ford pickup, and the fact that Sherman had seen nothing. But they didn't say anything about why Sherman was there.

LaStanza jotted himself another note: "Interview Bert Waters, Jeanne Bonneau, and William Sherman from Owen/DeLeon canvass. Locate Enon, Louisiana."

The door opened behind LaStanza and Mason called out, "Kintyre. Come in here. And bring your case file."

LaStanza could feel the heater case sizzling off his partner's back as she went into their lieutenant's office and closed the door. He took another hit of coffee, reached into his upper left desk drawer and pulled out a Daily Report Form.

On the latest beat-up Smith-Corona typewriter LaStanza shared with Snowood, whose desk butted against LaStanza's, he typed out the daily from the previous evening's canvass of Pleasant Street. The typewriter hummed loudly, increasing in pitch the longer it was on.

He managed to finish the daily before the Smith-Corona conked out, which it did when left on too long. It was a race, getting the facts down on paper before the machine sputtered to a halt. Near the end, he was laughing, but not too loudly because his hands burned.

"Beat ya'," he told the Smith-Corona.

Pulling the finished daily from the typewriter, he remembered how Lizette wanted to buy him a portable computer. He'd been practicing on her Macintosh at home and it was so fuckin' easy.

Jodie came out of Mason's office as if she was shot from a cannon. Her face was flushed. Her jaw set and grinding again.

She looked at LaStanza and said, "The fuckin' Chief and the DA are setting up a Task Force on the Pantyhose Rapist!"

"Jesus fuckin' Christ!"

Jodie stopped at her desk and took in a couple deep breaths, as if that would help. Brushing her hair with her right hand she said, "You've worked in a Task Force before haven't you?"

"It was a cluster fuck. Detectives stumbling over each other chasing bogus lead after bogus lead. The more publicity a case gets, the more bogus leads. And there's no publicity like a fuckin' Task Force case."

"Dammit!" Jodie picked up her gray metal trash can and tossed it back across the desk behind her. It careened into another desk and rolled into the aisle, depositing waste paper in its wake. LaStanza preferred drop-kicking his trash can, like a fuckin' field goal kicker.

He took his daily to the copy machine, ran off two copies, dropped the original in the "In" basked on his sergeant's desk. He used the hole-puncher to punch two holes atop one copy and put it on the Daily Report clipboard before returning to his desk with the second copy, for his case file.

"We had a Task Force on my first case," he said.

"The Slasher?" Jodie had her elbows on her desk, her chin resting in her open palms.

"Yeah. It was a disaster. People stumbling over each other like a fuckin' circus of idiots."

Jodie let out a tired sigh.

"Mark and I solved it on our own, away from the Task Force, but we were lucky. Mason let us run with it."

"It's good to be good, but it's better to be lucky," Jodie ran off the homicide cliché without looking at him. She was learning.

"Where the fuck is Enon, Louisiana?" he asked her.

"You got me," Jodie said.

"It's by Bogalusa," Snowood yelled from across the squad room. Country-Ass and his partner were standing in the doorway. LaStanza stood up and stretched before heading for the large Louisiana map on the wall next to the sergeant's office.

"It coulda been a murder too," Stevens said, kicking a desk as he passed.

"What," Snowood said. "Somebody just held him there so the train could cut off his fuckin' head?"

"It could happen."

Snowood dropped his black Stetson on his desk. He pulled off his gray jacket, the one with the tan rawhide strips dangling from the pocket flaps, and hung it on the coat rack. He wore his gray snakeskin boots and another rope tie with a silver longhorn clasp.

LaStanza found Enon on the map. It was fourteen miles southwest of Bogalusa in Washington Parish. Wondering why a country boy like Sherman was parking his pickup at Prytania and Harmony Street at 1:08 a.m., LaStanza went back to his desk.

Could be anything. Sherman could be fuckin' a nice uptown babe or just curious about all the police in the street.

Stevens stopped next to LaStanza's desk, folded his arms and gave LaStanza a mean look.

"Nice fuckin' tie," Stevens said. "Or is that another

bib?"

For a man wearing a maroon sock tie, a lime green shirt and a light yellow sport coat over dark brown pants, Stevens had some nerve. LaStanza glared back at the crooked left eye, grinned, and sat down. Jodie, on the other hand, bounced out of her chair and started in on Stevens.

"You call that piece of knit shit a tie?"

"Don't get in my face, woman." Stevens face remained stony, but it didn't phase Jodie.

She stepped closer and said, "Let me see your socks."

"What?"

"Your socks. Pull up your pants."

Snowood leaning his butt against Jodie's desk and put his two cents in. "Come on. Let's see them socks."

Jodie reached over and yanked Stevens' left trouser leg up.

"Jesus!" she said. "Red socks. You're wearing red and green and yellow and brown and maroon and you criticize *his* tie? What planet are you from anyway?"

A creepy grin crossed Stevens' wide face. "I just said that to see you jump up and protect your boyfriend."

"Yeah, real cute." Jodie wheeled and pushed Snowood out of her way to sit back down.

"I love to see you all hot under the collar," Stevens said. "You're get all bright and perky."

Stevens laughed one of his deep belly laughs, the kind you'd call a guffaw. He sounded ridiculous.

LaStanza looked closely at his partner's outfit. She wore a perfectly coordinated outfit that evening, a light gray blouse, high collared of course, a black fitted skirt well below the knee and black heels. The top two buttons were undone on her blouse as were the lower two on the skirt. That was Lizette's influence, LaStanza was sure.

Opening his note book again, LaStanza had a question for Country-Ass.

"In your daily on the autopsy. Pleasant Street. You forgot to put what was in the guy's stomach."

"Tarnation. I did forget Well all he had was liquid. The doc took it all for analysis. But I can tell you it was probably Thunderbird."

LaStanza nodded and put it in his notes.

"You know," LaStanza said loudly, picking up the list of license plates from the scene, "we had a guy used to work here who used to dress just like you, Stevens."

"Yeah?"

"Yeah. Ever meet Maurice Ferdinand?"

"Yeah, and fuck you too!"

Snowood had to cover his mouth to keep brown shit from spitting all over the squad room. Maurice Ferdinand, better known as M.F., was a limp-dick of a detective that Mason ran out of the Bureau. M.F. was a gutless wonder and the worse dresser in Detective Bureau history, until Stevens.

LaStanza went to the computer and ran the license plates. It was a tedious process. Owen and DeLeon had secured forty-two license numbers. About half way through, Mason walked up, pulling on his blue blazer.

"See you tomorrow. You got the fort."

"Go get some gum."

"Yeah. Yeah." Mason rushed out, his penny loafers clanking loudly on the linoleum floor. He slammed the door on his way out.

Jodie came up behind LaStanza.

"I'd like to canvass tonight, Okay?"

"Sure. I can stop any time." LaStanza pressed the print command and the noisy dot matrix printer printed the information from license plate number twenty-two.

"What are tweedle-dumb and tweedle-dumber doing now?"

"Arguing. They handled a 29S last night while we canvassed. They're also arguing about Mark, about why he's not in yet."

"He took the night off."

"I told them that."

LaStanza wanted to tell her that he didn't like being

put in charge of the squad. But she already knew. Snowood was senior, but both Mason and Mark Land had argued, "You got more department time. And it ain't your choice anyway."

Snowood and Stevens were still arguing when LaStanza and Jodie stepped back into the squad room.

"It's a 29S, Asshole," Snowood said.

"Go ahead. Write it up as a 29S. I'll write my own daily and I'll call it a 30."

Stevens grabbed the beat-up Underwood on his desk and started typing. Snowood reached around and turned the Smith-Corona his way and started his own daily.

LaStanza tucked the print-outs into his case folder. The squad room door opened again. The familiar black face of Detective Sergeant Felicity Jones beamed at LaStanza as Fel strolled into the room, his brown suit coat draped over his shoulder.

"Greetings and salutations," Fel called out. "How are the real police doing today?"

"Shut the fuck up," Snowood answered without looking up.

"You lost or something?" Stevens said.

Grinning broadly, Fel turned sideways as he approached to better show off his new gold sergeant's badge. Tall and muscular, Fel Jones was a dark complected man with an easy smile and enough guts for three cops. Back in LaStanza's time in the Bloody Sixth, Fel had proved again and again just how brave he was. He was the bravest man LaStanza had ever known.

"So, you enjoying the vacation?" Snowood said, still not looking up.

"It is nice," Fel said, referring to his return to the Intelligence Division after a particularly bloody year as Snowood's partner in the big show. "It's quiet. No autopsies. No misdemeanor murders or whodunits or killins'."

"What the fuck you know about whodunits?" Snowood continued while still typing.

Fel turned his attention to LaStanza. "I come to invite

you out Saturday night, white boy."

"You never solved a whodunit in your life," Snowood added. No one paid attention.

LaStanza finished off his coffee and told Fel he'd think about it.

"I figure with Lizette partying in Paris, you might have some free time on your hands. And speaking of your hands, what the fuck happened to them?"

LaStanza looked at the bandage on his left hand and shrugged.

"We don't want that Jacuzzi going to waste on a Saturday night, now do we?" Fel shifted his weight as he leaned on LaStanza's desk. He looked dapper that day in his dark brown suit, beige shirt and light brown and blue flowered tie.

LaStanza reached over and jotted a series of numbers on a scrap of paper. He passed it to Fel.

"That's the combination to the side gate. You know where the towels are in the closet on rear gallery. You know how to work the controls. Help yourself."

LaStanza sat back and then thought to add, "Just don't give the combination to Snowood or Stevens. No redneck peckerwoods allowed."

"Spades and Wops are okay, huh?" Stevens said.

"Fuckin' A." LaStanza was enjoying this.

Snowood stopped typing. He leered at LaStanza, open mouthed.

"You mean you let this porch monkey in your hot tub?" Snowood was doing his best to sound like George Wallace on-a-hot-day-in-front-of-a-schoolhouse-door, but it wasn't working. Fel just grinned at his old partner.

LaStanza figured Snowood was doing this to goad Stevens. Twice the previous winter Snowood and Fel had used the hot tub after particularly long shifts. It was a perfect wind-down from working in the wet cold of icy February nights. Stevens didn't take the bait.

"Seriously man," Fel said. "What happened to your hands?"

"He tried to put out a fire," Snowood said.

"With his hands?" Fel turned to Snowood.

"Yeah. Stupid Wop."

Fel looked at his watch and said, "Gotta go." He pointed his right index finger at LaStanza and pulled the trigger. "See you Saturday night at the hot tub. I'll be the one with the two women."

"Yeah." LaStanza laughed at that, as if Fel's fiancé Wanda wouldn't kick his black ass.

"Thanks," Fel said over his shoulder on his way out.

"Anytime, pisano."

As soon as Fel was out the door, Jodie started in on LaStanza for not taking the sergeants test again. He ignored her. He went back to assembling his case folder. She went on for several minutes before he cut her off with, "Snowood took the test. Look how far it got him."

"You just don't want to be a sergeant, admit it."

"I don't want to be a sergeant."

Jodie shook her head in disbelief. "Why won't you be serious about this one thing?" They'd been over this before, but she just couldn't get it through her thick Scottish skull that he was serious.

"I'm a detective. Not a supervisor."

"You're a supervisor tonight," Snowood said, yanking his daily from the typewriter. Pursing his lips at LaStanza he blew his old partner a kiss and then smiled a brown stained smile at him.

"He just don't wanna stop riding with Sweet Cakes," Stevens said.

"Call me that again and I'll knock you other eye cockeyed!"

Stevens' looked up from his typing, made a face, and looked at his partner. "You finished your daily?"

"Yep," Snowood answered.

"You calling it a suicide?"

"It was a suicide! You stupid fuck!" Leaning toward LaStanza, Snowood said, "We had a guy lie across the railroad tracks under the Claiborne overpass. You know, over in the Fifth. He just laid there until the train came along and clipped his head off neat and clean. You shoulda seen it."

Stevens stepped up next to LaStanza and handed LaStanza the daily he just completed. Under offense, Stevens had typed in RS 14:30 First Degree Murder.

"Is this the same case?" LaStanza asked and immediately wished he hadn't.

"It sure is. I say it's a 30."

"Boy, you are stupider than cowboy on a buffalo mule."

"I say it was murder."

LaStanza scanned the daily, but couldn't find anything that pointed to murder.

"I'm stupid?" Stevens argued back at Country-Ass. "You look like the Cisco Kid on steroids."

Jesus, listen to these guys. Neither makes fuckin' sense. LaStanza felt as if he was in a French movie with bad subtitles. No, a Japanese movie. *Where the fuck is Godzilla when you need him?* He raised his hand and said, "What makes this a 30?"

Stevens leaned a fat paw on LaStanza desk. "There were marks on the man's arms, bruises like he was held down."

Snowood shook his head and let out a long sigh. "The bruises were yellow. They were old. How the fuck do you hold somebody's head over a railroad tie without getting your fuckin' hand chopped off?" Standing now, Country-Ass pulled up his pants.

"The fucker tried to kill himself four times before and left a fuckin' suicide note telling his mother where to find him. It's a 29S. Plain and fuckin' simple!"

"You know what this cowboy son-of-a-bitch wanted to do last night?" Stevens was up on his toes now, both hands on LaStanza's desk as he leaned toward his partner. "He wanted to take the head back to the fucker's mother and ask her, 'Is this your son?' Now, tell me he's not retarded!"

LaStanza looked at Stevens' cock-eye and said, "Where

are your big shoes?"

"What big shoes?"

"The big fuckin' clown shoes that goes with that fuckin' get up you're wearing."

Snowood roared, splattering brown saliva across his desk and the dusty linoleum floor. Stevens' eye straightened, his lips quivered as he snarled at LaStanza. Then he moved around Snowood's side of the desk, picked up Snowood's daily and dropped it in the brown shit.

"Aw, fuck!"

LaStanza closed his briefcase and nodded to Jodie that it was time to fly. Jodie packed up quickly. LaStanza grabbed their coats. They almost made a clean getaway. Not ten feet from the exit door, Snowood yelled, "Hey, what's for supper?"

LaStanza stopped. Jodie continued out, but he could see her stop just outside in the hall. He looked back at S & S and waved them on. Then he went out and waited with Jodie.

Standing just outside the doorway, his briefcase digging into his burned right palm, LaStanza looked back at the neatly stenciled sign tacked to the door. It was a reproduction of a French Quarter street sign, in black and white with a black lacework trim. The sign read: Vulture Street.

Gentilly Boulevard

LaStanza stood between the trunks of two large oaks and watched his partner stare at her victim's house. He knew what Jodie was doing. She was connecting with her victim. Staring at the house, committing even the slightest detail of its description to memory, Jodie was physically connecting herself to the crime scene over and over again with each visit.

He'd been there before. Every homicide dick felt that strong connection, that feeling that you and your victim were bonded. It was the feeling that you were all the victim had left in this world. Sure, there were surviving relatives and friends and even lovers sometimes. But you were the one responsible for bringing in who did it. You were the one to wreck vengeance on the one who committed the greatest sin ever conceived...the murder of human being. It was a great weight to carry, a weight every homicide detective felt again and again when the Grim Reaper snatched someone away.

The Lord might have said, "Vengeance is Mine," but the Lord was nowhere to be found in the Magnolia Housing Project at three a.m. when a young mother is butchered by her boyfriend, or when a man's head is blown off in a drive-by shooting on Carrollton Avenue, or when a monster of a man slips into a woman's bedroom in the middle of a quiet summer night to rape and strangle her.

The Lord must have taken the last train for the coast when that monster of a man climbed through the bedroom window at 3612 Gentilly Boulevard, the bedroom of twenty year old Angie Rinaldi, tied pantyhose around Angie's throat, ripped off her night clothes, and raped her. The Lord wasn't there when the man tightened the ligature around Angie's neck to cut off her breath. The Lord was nowhere to be found when Angie's heart stopped, long before the man was finished with her. The Lord wasn't at her wake nor at her funeral; and He certainly wasn't canvassing the neighborhood again and again, trying to track down Angie's killer. That was Detective Jodie Kintyre.

LaStanza looked up at the towering oaks, at the twisted branches and the leaves that were still mostly green even though some brown ones had crept into the foliage. Yellow light from the street lights cut brightly through the trees, casting black shadows across the lawn in front of the detectives. A warm breeze floated leaves across the ground. The air was musty with the smell of wet leaves and chlorophyll.

Turning, LaStanza looked back at Gentilly Boulevard and noticed that oak trees lined either side of the three-laned boulevard, enclosing the wide boulevard between two rows. So massive in spots, the trees gave the boulevard the look of a tunnel, especially at night.

LaStanza looked back at his partner. Jodie was jotting notes in her note pad now. No telling what details she added to her notes in this, their tenth canvass of the area since Angie Rinaldi's murder nearly four weeks ago. He'd kept count. This canvass made an even ten. Maybe she was just jotting thoughts to herself. Things to do, as he did.

LaStanza looked at the house at 3612 Gentilly Boulevard. An English Tudor, the two-story house was constructed of gray and tan rocks sealed with concrete mortar. The second story was stucco with wide wooden beams criss-crossing its surface, beams painted dark brown, the same as the window sills. The roof rose into three separate points, all narrow and tall.

Along the uptown side of the house was a small stairway of nine steps with a wooden railing, painted the same dark brown. This door led to Angie Rinaldi's apartment. The window which the killer used was around the side of the house. Angie had left the window cracked. The killer used a screw driver to pry off the window screen.

Jodie took three steps to her left and continued writing. LaStanza moved up next to her but did not look at her. Instead, he thought about his first victim. Found lying between two rows of dwarf palms in Audubon Park, near Exposition Boulevard, Lynette Anne Louvier, also twenty years old, had less than a cup of blood left in her body after The Slasher was finished with her. It was a steamy night. The air was thick with the strong coppery smell of blood. LaStanza had certainly connected with Lynette. He married her twin.

Jodie put her note pad away and rubbed her stomach. "God," she said, a sour look on her face. "My po-boy is still in my throat."

"Mine too." LaStanza felt his meatball po-boy stuck in his esophagus.

"That's what we get for eating with S & S," Jodie said. She turned right and started walking away from Angie Rinaldi's house. She was right. Snowood and Stevens had argued through the meal—argued about the Railroad Case, argued about the food, even argued about the Barq's. Snowood's bottle had a blue label and Stevens' was red. The silly fuckers argued over which tasted better, passing each bottle back and forth, spilling globs of root beer on the table.

Back on the sidewalk now, LaStanza followed Jodie through the short blocks of Gentilly from Venus Street to Painters to Iris to Arts Street where they crossed Gentilly to continue their canvass along the lake side of the boulevard.

"I'll take Gentilly," Jodie said, pointing back in the direction of Franklin Avenue. "You take Arts, Okay?"

"Sure."

LaStanza left the boulevard with its tall oaks and wide spaced homes for the closer spaced houses of Arts Street. Walking lake bound up the center of the concrete street, LaStanza noticed how the houses were raised away from the street on steep lawns. It was common in New Orleans, in the largest American city below sea level, for the street to be lower than the houses. Better to accommodate high water in the streets during the unceasing high rains.

He stepped up on the sidewalk that was truly a banquette in front of the first house on the downtown side of the street. He looked around at the mixed bag of houses, mostly brick single story houses. Some of the houses were wooden, old fashioned with green and white striped aluminum awnings and window air conditioning units sticking out of their windows. Some were stucco, some looked like Spanish mission houses. There were only a few trees...a couple pecans, magnolias, and one large palm tree directly in front of the first house.

He took out his note pad and pen and walked up the rising walk to the front door. He rang the door bell and waited. The door was opened by a heavy set man in a white tee-shirt and baggy khaki pants. LaStanza opened his jacket.

"Police," he said. "I'm Detective LaStanza."

The man blinked his red, bleary eyes at LaStanza. He took a step forward and belched.

"Wanna beer?"

One hour and eleven families later LaStanza pulled his portable radio from his rear pocket and called Jodie on the Detective Bureau channel.

"3124 to 3126."

It took a couple seconds for Jodie to respond with a, "Go ahead."

"You better 10-19. I got something over here."

"Be right there."

He waited for her out on the sidewalk in front of 4454 Arts. He jotted a description of the house, a one story red brick with white trim and a garage along the lake side of the house. Its front yard was so high there were six concrete steps between the sidewalk and the walkway up to the front porch. Inside the doorway stood the witness he'd just located, a seventeen year old girl with short straight brown hair and eyes that were even darker brown. The girl wore a thick red pullover shirt, jeans and white tennis shoes.

Jodie rounded the corner and he waved at her. She picked up her pace as he tucked his note pad back into his coat pocket. Jodie's low heeled pumps clapped on the sidewalk. LaStanza looked at his watch. It was almost 8:00 now. Jodie stepped up and looked over at the girl in the doorway.

"Her name's Maria Garcia. She just might have seen something."

Jodie's wide-set cat eyes narrowed a millimeter. She pulled her note pad and pen from her purse and led the way back to the doorway.

"This is Detective Kintyre. She's in charge of the case," LaStanza said as they followed Maria into the comfortable living room of the house. Standing uncomfortably in her own home, Maria wrung her hands and said, in a slight Hispanic accent, "My parents will be home any minute."

"Good," Jodie said, a slight smile crossing her face. "Mind if we sit?"

Maria nodded.

"Good," Jodie said, sitting on the dark green sofa to the right of the front door, which remained open. LaStanza pulled his radio out of his back pocket and sat in the tan recliner against the opposite wall. Jodie nodded for Maria to sit and the girl sat at the other end of the sofa.

"Maria saw a man get out of a light blue car on the night the woman was murdered on Gentilly Boulevard,"

LaStanza said.

Maria bit her lower lip. She stared at Jodie.

"You sure it was the same night?"

Maria nodded. "It was a Friday night. I saw it on TV the next day and in the paper."

"What time are we talking about?"

Maria looked at LaStanza who smiled at the girl and said, "Go ahead."

Maria crossed her legs and took in a deep breath. When she told LaStanza the story a few minutes earlier she was excited and willing. Now she chose her words carefully as Jodie took notes.

"I was parked outside my house with my boyfriend, Jimmy Dore. We were...talking. And kissing." Maria covered her mouth with her left hand for a moment, then continued. "I saw a man park a light blue car up at the corner. No," she stopped suddenly, "first I saw him drive by us slow like. I thought he was a police car because he was moving so slow. But he didn't stop. He went up to the corner and parked on the other side of the street."

Jodie raised her left hand, continuing to write with her right.

"What time are we talking about?"

Maria uncrossed her legs. "It wasn't long before midnight. 11:30 maybe."

"Okay, then what happened?"

Maria re-crossed her legs. LaStanza noticed a faint sweet smell in the room, a faint perfume smell.

"Jimmy was telling me about practice. Jimmy's on the Holy Cross football team. I wasn't looking at Jimmy though, I was looking at the man get out of the blue car. I was curious because he was under a streetlight, but I couldn't see if he was white or black." Maria was excited again.

LaStanza could see Jodie writing furiously. He pulled out his pad and checked his notes against this second telling of Maria's story, adding what she added as she went on.

"I couldn't see his face because he was wearing a sweatshirt with a hood. It was black. And his hands were in his pockets. He walked around to the front of the car and leaned against the front of his car. He never looked our way. He kept looking at Gentilly.

"He looked scary. I don't know why, but I was scared. I told Jimmy and he looked over. We watched the man stand there for a good five minutes or ten minutes. Then the man walked off fast toward Gentilly and turned the corner."

It took Jodie a couple seconds to catch up.

"Which way did he turn?"

"Toward Franklin."

That was the right way.

"Did you see him come back?"

"No, ma'am. My papa came out and told us to come in and we did. We watched TV and Jimmy didn't leave until two or three in the morning. I looked over then and the blue car was gone."

"Was it a big car?"

"Yes. An American car. Full size. And it was light blue, sky blue."

"Did you see the license plate?" Jodie had to ask that one.

"No, ma'am."

"Now you're sure this was the night, the Friday night the woman was murdered on Gentilly Boulevard."

"That girl Angie. I'm positive. I talk to Jimmy about it and we're both positive."

"Did you know Angie?" LaStanza asked.

"Oh, no. Her name's been in the paper. On TV."

Maria looked at Jodie who continuing writing. After a minute Maria went on. "I was scared, but Jimmy told me it wasn't nothing to worry about. He told me the killer was a short man. The man we saw was big, over six feet, and stocky."

Maria looked from Jodie to LaStanza and back again. She folded her arms and drew her legs up under her.

Moving her gaze back to LaStanza he could see her searching, reaching out, asking with her eyes, "The killer was short wasn't he?"

LaStanza let Jodie answer the obvious.

"Maria," Jodie said, "we don't know what the killer looks like at all. Do you know how Jimmy knows he was short?"

"Jimmy said he heard it."

Both LaStanza and Jodie made note.

"What's Jimmy's address?" Jodie asked.

Maria rattled off an address on Feliciana Drive.

"Where's that?"

"Gentilly Woods."

LaStanza had already explained to Jodie that this part of town was Gentilly Terrace. Gentilly Woods was the next section of the old town.

"And his phone number?"

Maria gave the phone number in a voice that was much more quiet.

Jodie looked up at the girl and said, "Now, Maria, um, why didn't you tell the police about this man?"

"I did...we did. Jimmy's father is a police. He works at the Fifth District Station. We told him."

Jesus Fuckin' Christ! LaStanza felt a knot forming in his stomach. Jodie's face was getting red.

"Maria," LaStanza said, "have you ever seen that car around here before or after?"

"No."

Under his note that said, *Interview Jimmy Dore and father*, LaStanza wrote, *Check houses on and around corner of Gentilly and Arts about light blue car.*

A car pulled into Maria's driveway, just as headquarters called LaStanza on the radio. He picked up his radio and said, "Go ahead, headquarters."

"The Seventh District's requesting a homicide team at the Mianteen Bar on Chef Highway. Signal 30."

LaStanza closed his eyes and said, "10-4."

"And the First District just received a 30-29S at Smith's

Hotel on Camp Street. They're calling for Homicide too."

Jodie's head sank forward until her chin was against her chest. Maria was up and standing in her doorway. A short, stocky man with a receding hairline stepped in, followed by a older version of Maria, wearing a dark blue dress with small white flowers.

Jodie handled the introductions and explanation as LaStanza slipped outside. Fanning his jacket in the nonexistent breeze, he called Snowood and Stevens on the radio, asking them to handle Smith's Hotel while he and Jodie handled the Mianteen Bar. No sense in calling the other squad. LaStanza heard them earlier, rolling over to Algiers to the wonderful and picturesque Fischer Housing Project to handle a dumped body.

Snakebitten. Put me in charge and the whole fuckin' unit gets nailed by cottonmouths!

What did they call it in hospitals? Triage work. Patch up a stabbing victim because behind the next curtain a man's been shot in the head and behind the third curtain a pregnant woman's hemorrhaging and the EMTs are on their way with two head injuries from the same car wreck. Patch them up and go on to the next case.

Homicide work in the big city had become triage work long before LaStanza moved up from the Sixth. Like puppets on deadly strings, detectives dart from crime scene to crime scene, hurriedly putting whatever time they could on a case until another pulls them away.

LaStanza felt the strings tugging at his elbows as he stood outside the Mianteen Bar at the corner of Chef Menteur Highway and Coronado Street, interviewing a barmaid with stringy blond hair and linebacker thighs.

"Wait a second," he said, "the guy in the yellow shirt had a gun too?"

Her name was Kat, but everybody called her Cat with a "C." LaStanza greeted that witticism with a cold Sicilian stare. Kat brushed her badly-split hair with a spidery hand

and said, "Yeah. The first guy that came in. The guy in the red shirt pulled a pistol out and shot the dude in the blue shirt twice. *Then* the guy in the yellow shirt pulled out his gun and shot the dude twice too."

LaStanza reviewed his notes while Kat leaned her abundant butt against the side of Mianteen's. She popped her bubble-gum in nice even rhythms.

Two perpetrators, both Vietnamese between 5'4" and 5'6", both thin with black hair, clean shaven. *Thank God they were wearing different shirts.*

"If you saw these men again, could you identify them?"

"If you catch 'em tonight before they change their shirts."

Kat called 'em *Vietmanese.* LaStanza heard that particular variation on the Viets before, particularly from white trash. He hadn't bothered putting his jacket on, preferring to work in his shirt sleeves, his Colombian tie now loosened even more. He wiped perspiration from his brow.

"Can we go back inside? We got air-conditioning."

LaStanza shook his head no. Jodie was inside with two Seventh District patrolmen and the crime lab technician processing the scene.

"Hey!" LaStanza pointed his pen at a Vietnamese man who had opened the door to the bar and was peeking in. "Get back up against that fuckin' wall!"

He waved to one of the bored patrolmen leaning against the crime lab van. "Keep these witnesses up against the wall. And don't let them talk to each other, OK?"

"Sure," a patrolman with long curly brown hair said, pointing an eighteen inch black Kel-lite flashlight as big as a Louisville slugger at the man who had just peeked into the bar. "Say boy. What's the matter wit' you. You stupid?"

LaStanza shifted his weight to his left leg as he stood out in the shell parking lot. Kat was smiling at him. "Goddam gooks," she said softly enough for only him to hear.

"They're not gooks," he said.

"Huh?"

"What type of pistol did the first man have? The man in the red shirt?"

"What do ya' mean, 'What type'?"

LaStanza turned to his left to show his magnum in its black holster on his right hip. "Was it silver colored or black?"

"Silver. I think."

"Was it a revolver like this, or was it small and square like an automatic."

"It was little and square. So was the one the other guy had too."

LaStanza figured as much. He's spotted three brass casings on the dirty floor of Mianteen's when he and Jodie arrived. The casings were between the door and the body as it lay next to the first pool table.

"Course, the other man's gun was like yours. It was a revolver, only black."

"What other man?"

"The one that was shot. He showed it to everyone before the men came in and shot him. It's in his right front pocket."

Jesus. Our victim's got a gun too!

"Say, Baby," Kat said.

God, he hated it when barmaids called him "Baby." He didn't look up from his notes.

"Baby, what happened to your hand?" Kat reached over and touched the bandage on LaStanza's left hand.

"It's a fungus I got in 'Nam." LaStanza looked into Kat's bleary eyes and added, "Won't go away. It's very contagious."

Kat tried to secretly wipe her hand on her pants.

LaStanza spotted the patrolman with the Louisville Slugger Kel-lite waving at him.

"This one says he knows the perpetrators' names. The dead guy's his cousin." The big cop twisted his head at

LaStanza the way a dog does when you whistle at it. LaStanza couldn't help but let a slight smile cross his lips.

Before the coroner's office assistant arrived with their black body bag and stainless steel gurney, LaStanza had the perpetrators' first names and had isolated three excellent eye-witnesses from the crowd of black haired men assembled against the filthy gray wall of The Mianteen Bar.

"Don't let anybody leave," he told the patrolmen. "Especially these three." LaStanza pointed to his witnesses. He had their driver's licenses in his pocket anyway, in case they got a case of the rabbits.

He went back into the bar. Jodie was putting the finishing touches on her notes. The crime lab tech was calling out the final measurements, triangulating the distance between the victim's body and the walls of the lovely establishment. The place reeked of beer and the sweet coppery smell of dried blood. The faint odor of cordite remained in the air from the gunpowder.

LaStanza tugged on Jodie's left elbow.

"You're going to have to NA the victim," he said. "He's got a gun in his pocket."

"Shit." Jodie let out a long sigh then told the crime lab tech to run a neutron activation test on the victim's hands. LaStanza had gone over this with Jodie before. If a victim's armed, especially with an open breech weapon like a revolver, you better run a test for gunpowder residue. Otherwise, a sharp defense lawyer will make it look like you did something wrong. LaStanza had seen it before.

"But officer. Why didn't you run a gunpowder residue test to *prove* the victim hadn't fired a weapon? Why didn't you process the entire scene? What were you covering up?"

The slumped shoulder technician was not thrilled, but he complied, running swabs over both of the victim's hands.

"How many casings you got?" LaStanza asked Jodie.

"Four. Two .22 calibers. Two .25 calibers."

"Good. And wounds?"

"Four entry wounds. Three in the back. One in the neck."

That's what accounted to the massive amount of blood around the victim. Sucker bled to death. His compact, thin body was curled in a fetal position in the center of a wide pool of blackish red blood.

When the technician finished, he tip-toed out of the blood pool. Jodie waved the coroner's assistants over. Both were black and middle aged.

"Let's make sure we have no exit wounds," Jodie said.

The assistants rolled the body over, pulled up the shirt and wiped away the blood with their rubber gloves. There were no exit wounds on the torso or neck or jawline.

"Good," Jodie said. "Is an investigator coming?"

The taller of the two assistants said no. Then he gave Jodie the name of the doctor declaring death.

"He's all yours," she said, turning away.

LaStanza noticed a wallet sitting up on the pool table. A driver's license had been removed. He looked at the picture. It was the victim. He looked better dead than in his Bureau of Motor Vehicles picture. Most people usually do. *Except Lizette,* he thought. *She looked like she modeled for hers.*

As the body was being loaded on the gurney, LaStanza tapped on his partner's shoulder again.

"We forgot the gun in his pocket."

"Shit!"

She made the taller assistant open the body bag and fish out the gun. The crime lab tech processed it. Taking photographs before opening the cylinder. The gun was a Targa .22 caliber with a three inch barrel, blue steel with a black plastic grip. It held nine rounds, none of which had been fired.

"Casing's in good shape?" He asked Jodie. "No body step on them?"

She nodded.

"Good." Casings were as good as projectiles at times, especially with small caliber weapons. Firing pins leave markings on bullet casings that are just as easy to link to a weapon as the projectile is to link to the striations and grooves left from its path through a particular gun barrel. Particularly on drive-by shootings when a good projectile is hard to find, casings left lying in the street can link weapons from crime scene to crime scene to an eventual perpetrator. *If we ever catch them,* LaStanza thought.

There was an old Homicide cliché that applied here. "You can't have enough evidence." Another cliché came to mind also. "A victim dies once. A crime scene is murdered a thousand times."

Then again, LaStanza remembered. *The crime scene's post mortem in court is the coup de grace. Fuckin' lawyers!*

LaStanza finished the last statement, yanking the sheet out of the Smith-Corona as the typewriter sputtered and coughed and then expired.

"Beat ya'."

"What?" said the thin Vietnamese sitting next to LaStanza's desk. Tran Vinh Son, at 5'3", was a good three inches shorter than LaStanza and, at 110 pounds, was a good 30 pounds lighter than the detective. Then again, LaStanza had a moustache. Tran was a second cousin of the man shot to death while playing pool at the Mianteen Bar earlier than evening.

"Can I see the pictures again?" Tran asked.

"Sure." LaStanza pulled out the two photographic line-ups. Each line-up consisted of six color police identification photos of Oriental males. He spread each line-up on the desk in front of Tran, who had already identified the perpetrators, one from each line-up. So had one of Tran's cousins and the victim's brother. The brilliant perpetrators had made the mistake of shooting someone with too many relatives in the fuckin' bar.

LaStanza and Jodie solved the murder fifteen minutes after arriving at the Bureau. They put together seven line-ups of Viets arrested in New Orleans the last three years, including all with the first name of Nguyen and Phan. Sometimes you just get lucky. Both perpetrators had been arrested before on minor charges.

Tran nodded his approval and repeated with conviction. "This is the man with the red shirt." He pointed to the mug of Nguyen Can Tho, Vietnamese male, age 22. "This one was wearing the blue shirt." He pointed to Phan Rang Minh, Vietnamese male, age 23.

LaStanza passed Tran the three page statement they'd just completed.

"You need to read it carefully and sign at the bottom of each page," LaStanza said.

"OK."

LaStanza pointed to four typos. "Put your initials next to each one, OK?"

"OK."

No need to explain any more. Tran was an honor's student at the University of New Orleans. He was probably mentally correcting LaStanza's grammar as the detective went back to the coffee pot for a fresh cup.

"You're so full a shit!" Snowood's voice boomed from across the squad room. He and his partner entered, slamming into desks as they argued.

"She wasn't bad looking. 'Cept for the fuckin' hole in her head." Stevens said, swinging his briefcase in a tight circle, his shirt half pulled out of his pants.

Snowood didn't look much better. His shirt was rumpled and dotted with dirt spots. Turning back to his partner he said, "She was a rail, a porch rail. She looked like a Nazi Concentration Camp victim."

"No fuckin' way, man. She was a fox."

"A fox hound!"

Spotting LaStanza next to the coffee pot, Snowood tossed his briefcase on his desk and said, "Thanks for nothin', you buzzard!"

LaStanza turned and looked up at the Vulture, then looked back at Snowood and grinned. Snowood collided with his partner as Stevens tried to pass. Turning to Tran Vinh Son, Stevens said,

"What the hell you looking at?"

Tran looked at LaStanza with frightened eyes.

LaStanza said, "He's probably wondering what you did with your big clown shoes."

"Very fuckin' funny!" Stevens collapsed in his desk chair and covered his face with his arms.

Snowood moved up next to LaStanza and grabbed the coffee pot. There was a smudge of dirt on Country-Ass' left cheek, but LaStanza didn't mention it.

"Real cute, sending us to fuckin' Smith's Hotel. Ever been there?" Snowood's eyes bulged. He was on his toes, leaning against the table. "Smelled like a fuckin' pig sty, and I ain't talking no cliché here." When Snowood was real mad, his country accent faded. "It smelled like pig shit. And the bodies weren't what smelled. They were fresh!"

Snowood poured himself a cup, took a sip of it black and said, "Hot tamale. That's good."

Turning toward Stevens, he said, "It was a typical 29-30." Which meant a suicide-murder.

"Only Bozo over there," Snowood said as he pointed at Stevens with his chin, "he thought the dead girl, the murder victim, was *pretty*. She looked like Olive Oil with a bullet in her head."

"He called her a fox." LaStanza said, trying not to laugh.

"Yeah. He's stone fuckin' nuts."

LaStanza took a hit of coffee. Tran stood up, so he went over and showed the man exactly where to sign his name.

"You can go now," LaStanza said.

Tran shook his hand and walked out of the Squad Room.

Snowood plopped into his desk chair and kicked his boots up on his desk. The bottoms were dotted with gobs of black tar-looking shit.

LaStanza took another hit of coffee, then said, "We were on Gentilly. Right down the street from the Mianteen Bar."

"Huh?" Snowood said, suddenly groggy.

"That's why we took the Mianteen and you got Smith's."

"Oh."

Gentilly Boulevard became Chef Menteur Highway on the other side of the Industrial Canal. They were only a few miles away. He just wanted Snowood to know why he was sent to the lovely Smith's Hotel.

"Hey," Stevens called out, "where's Meat?"

"Call her that to her face," LaStanza said. "I wanna see her slap the shit out of you."

Stevens shook his head. His hands were behind his head now. Turning his cock-eye toward LaStanza he said, "What's with all the gooks in the hall?"

"They're not gooks," LaStanza said.

"Oh, excuse me. You with the A.C.L.U. now?"

"They're zipper-heads," LaStanza said in an even voice. "Koreans are gooks."

"He should know," Snowood said. His hands were also behind his head. "He was over there."

"He was in Nam?" Stevens said. "No way. He's too young."

A snap shot of the jungle hell-hole came into LaStanza's mind. He blinked the image away immediately. In a tired voice, he said, "I got in at the end of the war, when everyone was hauling ass to get the fuck out."

"Why did you call them zipper-heads?" Snowood asked.

"Fuck if I know." LaStanza yawned. "We also called them dinks and slopes and Charlie. Sometimes, when the tough little bastards hit us hard, we called them Charles."

The squad room door opened again and Jodie walked in briskly. Legal sized papers protruded from the folder under her left arm. She walked straight to her desk and fell into her chair. A strand of her page boy fell out of place across her nose. She blew it out of the way.

"You look beat, little miss," Stevens said. He didn't call her Meat.

Jodie's back stiffened. She looked at LaStanza and said, "I have the warrants. I dropped off a copy at NCIC. You think you can leave a note for the day watch to catch our autopsies in the morning?"

"What about ours?" Snowood said.

"I said *our* autopsies. That's collective." Jodie said in a voice meant for a first grader.

"Yeah," Snowood said, turning his chin to LaStanza, "how about writing a note, fearless leader? Or are you afraid to make a decision?"

LaStanza yawned. He already had a note sitting in the day shift sergeant's 'In' tray. He was enjoying this too much to say anything yet.

"They're both misdemeanor murders," Jodie added.

"No, yours is a killin'," Snowood corrected.

"Yeah."

There were three types of murders in New Orleans. The whodunit, which involved some investigative technique, was the only murder worth working. The misdemeanor murder, which was any murder involving a husband and wife, boyfriend and girlfriend, or other instances in which the victim and perpetrator were closely related, was a paperwork case. The third was not a murder at all, it was a killin', which usually occurred in a bar, requiring either the victim or the perpetrator to have consumed intoxicants. Killins' resulted in a manslaughter conviction at best and required about as much paperwork as a routine suicide. Murders in housing projects were classified as killins' for years, until the fuckers started killing children in cross-fires. Mason and LaStanza changed the rules then. Any killing of a child was a whodunit, even if the killer was waiting at the scene to hand over his gun. The only murder that was worse than the murder of a child was the murder of a police officer.

Only, when a child was murdered, people actually cared enough to help.

"I seen them. It was Johnny Johnson and Keith Simmons. They done shot little Jeffrey."

LaStanza sat in his chair and looked at the clock. It was closing in on two a.m. now. He'd missed his call from Lizette. Autopsies started at eight a.m., sharp.

"I don't know," he said. "I think you're muling me because Mark's not here."

"Fuck you!" Snowood said.

"Double fuck you!" Stevens said.

LaStanza looked at his partner. She stuck her tongue out at him. "Don't be an asshole," she said.

"I wrote a memo an hour ago," he said. "It's in the day sergeant's 'In' tray."

Snowood went and checked anyway.

LaStanza told Jodie she could finish her daily on Gentilly tomorrow. "I already wrote a daily on the Mianteen Murder. It's in Mason's 'In' tray."

"Thanks."

"You know," Snowood said as he tucked a glob of brown shit between his lip and gum, "the Cheyenne have a phrase for nights like this."

LaStanza stood and started packing his briefcase. Jodie followed suit. Even Stevens stood up, probably because everyone else was standing.

"This is the kind of night the Cheyenne called 'Touch the Sky'." Snowood paused a second before adding, "Wait a minute. It might be called 'The Night of Wolf Who Hunts Smiling'."

Whatever the fuck that meant.

Camelia Street

LaStanza watched Aunt Brulee's gnarled black hands as she picked up a butcher knife and deftly sliced two shrimp po-boys in half. The old woman's knuckles looked like chestnuts, her fingers like twigs from a twisted magnolia tree. Brulee mumbled under her breath as she put the sandwiches on plates. She shoved one of the po-boys along the kitchen counter to LaStanza.

"Get up all hours of the day..."

LaStanza took a hit of iced tea and waited until Brulee sat in one of the stools across from him. The fried shrimp smelled delicious. His stomach rumbled.

Still mumbling, Brulee sat, picked up half of her po-boy and turned her gaze out of the kitchen window. LaStanza glanced out at the light blue sky. He could see a thick white cloud in the distance.

"Got all the money he needs and he work like a slave..."

"Tea's great," LaStanza said.

Brulee took a bite of po-boy and nodded, still looking out the window. Today she wore the same type of white maid's uniform worn by Cleola Bracket, the Whippet's maid. *That's right, it's Friday.* On Monday, Wednesday, and Friday, Brulee worked at Lizette's parents estate on St. Charles Avenue. Although she did the cooking, cleaning and washing for Lizette and LaStanza, she only cooked at the estate. Still, Lizette's mother bought Brulee new ultra-while uniforms after the move to St. Charles.

LaStanza bit into his po-boy, savoring the taste of fresh French bread, the sweet mayonnaise, the tangy shrimp and sharp touch of Tabasco. His hair was still wet from his shower and his face still stung from the pull of his electric razor. Time for new blades. Reaching over with his left hand, he gingerly opened the morning paper. His hand still smarted. There was a Pantyhose Case article along the right side of page one.

"Victim's Classmates Live in Fear" was the title of the article. LaStanza glanced at the byline. He'd never heard of the reporter. Between bites of po-boy and gulps of iced tea, he read the latest news of his partner's heater case.

It seems that Angie Rinaldi's classmates were terrified of being raped and murdered in their bedrooms. One nineteen year old girl relayed how her father had put burglar bars on her window. Another never goes out at night alone. A third, this one a male classmate, said he carries a gun now everywhere he goes. "I'd rather stand trial than be carried by pallbearers."

Sounded like the old police cliché that went, "I'd rather be tried by twelve than carried by six."

LaStanza flipped to page four where the story continued. Brulee was still looking out the kitchen window. She chewed her po-boy carefully, her taught jaw muscles moving slowly, her dark brown eyes fixed on the window. LaStanza figured he'd never get used to having a maid. Every so often, he would hold a chair for Aunt Brulee, or pick up something for her when she dropped it, only to be swatted on the hand by a spatula or batted with an oven mitt.

"Boy, you got no sense," Brulee would scold him. "You don't hold a chair out for no maid! I *work* here." Brulee took pride in her work, well deserved pride. She damn near raised Lizette, her twin sister Lynette, and their little brother.

LaStanza flipped through the rest of the front section of the paper. There was nothing about his case. There was an article about the Mianteen Bar Killin' on page three of the Metro Section. Not only was the name of the bar misspelled, but every name in the article, including Jodie's, was misspelled. According to the article the victim had been shot four times by three men. LaStanza wondered if science-fiction writers started out as reporters before moving over to more realistic writing endeavors.

"You got shrimp gumbo and rice in the ice box," Brulee said, picking up the second half of her po-boy. She was looking at him now. "You can get pizza or go to McDonald's over the weekend."

He smiled and nodded and then bit his lower lip to prevent himself from pointing out to Brulee that he had been a bachelor until thirty-two.

"The po-boy's great," he said. "Thanks."

She huffed at him and looked out the kitchen window again. She'd told him that he wasn't supposed to thank a maid, but that was one instruction he ignored.

"You look terrible, boy," she said. "You keep runnin' yourself down at night and you'll look like an old man by the time Lizette come back."

"Just working," he said, picked up the sports section.

"You are dumber than you look," she said. He waited, but she didn't call him a gigolo as she usually did.

From the other side of the paper he told her, "You know. You're taking some good care of me." He paused a second before adding, "Deep down, I know you love me."

Brulee snorted loudly and said, "Zif!"

LaStanza cranked up the new charcoal gray Maserati Biturbo 425I, the car Lizette bought him after his midnight blue Maserati was stolen from Jackson Avenue while he worked the Batture Murders. He let it warm up in the garage for a minute. He put on a pair of dark, mirrored sunglasses, gangster glasses. The engine was so quiet it felt as if it killed. He touched the gas pedal and the engine roared.

Slipping a cassette into the enhanced stereo, he waited as black voices started talking, followed by aching music and the smooth voice of Marvin Gaye. He turned the stereo up, allowing "What's Goin' On" to reverberate through the Maserati. He backed slowly out of the garage, bobbing his head to the music.

The garage door descended behind him as he pulled away down Garfield across Calhoun to take a quick left on Henry Clay Avenue up to St. Charles Avenue. He turned up the air-conditioner and caught sight of the Swiss clock on the rosewood dash. It was a quarter until two o'clock. The leather seat felt cool on his bare legs. Clad in red running shorts and a thin blue New York Yankees tee-shirt and white tennis shoes, LaStanza laid his .357 magnum on the passenger bucket seat, next to his pad and pen.

Turning right on St. Charles, he proceeded downtown in the heavy afternoon traffic past the finest homes of the Crescent City. Passing beneath huge branches of ancient oaks and towering magnolias, green streetcars clanking along their rails to his left, LaStanza glanced around at the fine lawns and palatial homes. Crossing State Street, he looked to his left across the neutral ground at a private street called Rose Park which ran off the lake side of St. Charles Avenue. Nestled on the downtown corner of St. Charles and Rosa Park was a three story immaculately white Greek Revival estate with twenty wide marble front steps that led from the manicured front lawn up to the wide front gallery with its twelve Ionic columns and second story veranda with its six smaller columns and the sheltered driveway along the Rosa Park side with more Greek columns holding up a gingerbread overhang. Parked in the sheltered driveway was Lizette's mother's white Mercedes four door.

The traffic lightened up past Jefferson Avenue. The Maserati crossed Napoleon Avenue and turned right on Toledano Street. LaStanza cut the air-conditioner and powered the front windows down. Someone was cutting their grass. A strong scent of chlorophyll filled the car.

Slowly, LaStanza cruised down Toledano all the way to Magazine Street. Turning right he drove over to Louisiana Avenue and made a quick right back on Camp Street to Pleasant Street and then up Pleasant to Prytania. He cruised up and down Prytania and every street within a six block radius of Pleasant and Prytania before returning home on Magazine with the addresses of three houses with boats parked in their driveways.

Before changing for work, he picked up the kitchen phone and called the coroner's office.

"It is I, Detective LaStanza from Homicide. Anybody called to identify the burned man from Pleasant Street?"

"Say what?"

"Let me speak to your boss, OK?"

"OK."

LaStanza waited for an investigator, or if he was lucky, one of the pathologists. He wanted to ask about his victim's fingerprints.

"Turn here. By the Frostop." he told Jodie as they approached the 7300 block of Chef Menteur Highway.

"You coulda warned me," Jodie hit the brakes and stopped the LTD in the middle of the intersection of Chef and Plum Orchard and waited for traffic to clear. LaStanza looked back at the Frostop, at the huge mug of frosty root beer perched above the brown and white cafe.

"Ever have a Lot-o-burger?" he said.

"What?" Jodie shot him an annoyed look. He could see her squinting at him from behind her green framed sunglasses.

"A Lot-o-burger. Ever have one?"

Jodie gunned the LTD when there was an opening, crossing the Chef, turning up blacktop Plum Orchard.

"What are you talking about?" Jodie said.

"A Lot-o-burger. At Frostop. You had Frostops uptown when you were a kid didn't you?"

"Yeah, but I never ate at one." She was tightening up. He could see it by the way she gripped the steering wheel. Nervous. He'd seen it before with her. She was afraid. Not of getting hurt, afraid of messing up. If there was one thing he knew quite well about Detective Jodie Kintyre, she was hard on herself. Too hard.

"You're dress is climbing up," he told her, gleeking her legs over the top of his gangster glasses.

"Go ahead and look." Jodie's tan skirt had ridden about three inches above her knees. LaStanza had mentioned, when she picked him up, that her skirt was a little on the tight side and was actually *above her knees.* Of course, she also wore a high collar white blouse. Her matching tan jacket hung from a hanger in the back seat, across from LaStanza's navy blue suit coat.

"Which way?" Jodie asked as they closed in on a fork in the road.

The houses along Plum Orchard were one story wood frames with wider than usual yards with few trees. The yards were well kept and there were no abandoned cars littering the street. The street was crowded with children. It looked like a normal middle class neighborhood. LaStanza noticed the mix of black and Vietnamese children.

"Left," he said. "You see that fuckin' get-up Stevens had on this afternoon?"

"That's why I put on my sunglasses." She shot him a nervous grin.

Stevens iridescent green tie was muted compared to his green and yellow plaid pants.

A hint of a smile stayed on Jodie's lips, which were shaded with red lipstick. More of Lizette's influence. Jodie used to wear pink and other pale lipsticks before hanging around with LaStanza's wife.

"Turn right here," he told her as they almost overshot Camelia Street.

"What's the address again?"

He looked at the computer print out in his lap.

Beneath the name of Nguyen Can Tho was the address 4642 Camelia Street. He gave her the number and looked around. There were more kids on the street now.

"It's on your side," he told her as two black kids around ten darted across the street in front of them. Jodie hit the brakes then continued on more slowly.

He could see her jaw tightened again.

"That's it," he said as pointing to a white wood frame house with green trim. Jodie eased the LTD to the curb. LaStanza pulled out his magnum, opened the cylinder and checked his rounds. Snapping the cylinder shut he looked at his partner and said, as seriously as he could, "Let me shoot him, OK. I haven't shot anyone in a while."

Jodie smiled this time.

LaStanza slipped his magnum back into the holster on his right hip but didn't fasten the holster before climbing out. He spotted Jodie tapping the butt of her revolver as she climbed out.

"Say white girl," he said in a lower voice, holding up his portable radio in his still bandaged left hand "Where's your LFR?"

Jodie reached in and grabbed her portable radio, her LFR...little fuckin' radio. Which was compared, obviously, to the BFR carried on the shoulder of occupants of the cities picturesque housing projects.

"Remember," he said. "We're on Charlie's turf now."

"I know," she said. "Pongee sticks and tunnel rats, right?"

LaStanza grinned. He watched the house as they approached in single file. There were three windows facing the street. The front porch was a concrete block with four black lattice railings holding up an aluminum overhang. The front door was off to the right, facing back toward Chef Menteur. Jodie led the way up four concrete steps painted green up to the porch. She opened the screen and tapped the front door with her LFR.

LaStanza kept watching the windows for movement. The door opened and a Vietnamese woman with steel gray hair peeked out at them.

"Police," Jodie said. "You speak English?"

The woman nodded. Wearing a cotton flower dress with a round white collar, the woman wrung her hands in a towel and peered out at them.

"May we come in?" Jodie asked.

The woman nodded and backed away. The living room was dark and cool and smelled of rich Asian food, spicy, like a good Chinese Restaurant. The woman stood in the center of a room with a dark blue sofa, a matching recliner and thick wooden end tables and a coffee table atop a purplish oriental rug.

"We're looking for Nguyen Can Tho," Jodie said as LaStanza pulled Tho's mug shot from his dress shirt pocket and showed it to the woman.

The woman nodded at the picture and finally spoke, "Nguyen not here. I his mother." The woman focused her wide brown eyes at LaStanza.

LaStanza pointed to Jodie and said, "Talk to her. She's in charge." He stepped aside and looked down a small hall an open bathroom and a kitchen on the left.

"Mind if we have a look around?" Jodie said.

The woman nodded again and LaStanza searched the three small bedrooms on either side of the living room, the hall and kitchen. He looked out the back window at a yard featuring a tall willow tree and a ditch along its back side. He peeked into a large stainless steel pot atop a gas stove—soup bubbled, slices of roast pork rising around a thick mix of Chinese vegetables.

Jodie was still questioning Nguyen's mother, jotting something on her note pad. LaStanza shook his head no to Jodie when she looked up. Pointing to the woman with her ball point, Jodie said, "Nguyen hasn't lived here for a year. She doesn't know where he stays but thinks it's across the river."

"Algiers," the woman said.

Jodie gave the woman a business card and told her it would be better for Nguyen to call and surrender than be stopped on the street by an overeager patrolman. "He's wanted for a serious crime. Understand?"

The woman nodded and bowed her head as the detectives left.

Two Vietnamese girls and a black boy were playing on the rear bumper of the LTD. The older Vietnamese girl appeared to be about seven, the small one about four, the same age as the boy.

"You know," Jodie said as they walked back to the car. "She didn't ask any details. What her son is accused of."

"They never do." Walking up to the children, LaStanza stopped and went down on his haunches. He smiled at them and asked if they knew the man in the picture. He held out Nguyen's mug shot. The older Vietnamese girl nodded. The smaller one pulled her dress up to her mouth and stood squirming and smiling back at LaStanza.

"When was the last time you saw him?"

"I don't remember," the older girl said.

"What kind of car does he drive?" LaStanza tapped the rear quarter panel of the LTD.

"A red car."

"Is it big like this one?"

"No. It's small. It's a Toyota," the older girl added proudly.

"He come around here much?"

"No. He used to."

LaStanza rose and shrugged at Jodie. The smaller girl twisted sideways as she stared up at the detectives, the hem of her dress still in her mouth.

"Women should do that until they're at least fifty," LaStanza said.

"Cute, LaStanza. Real cute." Jodie climbed into the LTD.

Pulling away, they made a three point turn at the next intersection. Jodie took it slow with all the kids running the streets.

"Stop," LaStanza said just as Jodie was pulling back

down Camelia Street. "Look at that street sign."

Typically, the street names were stenciled in black on white placards attached to the sides of telephone poles at the corner. LaStanza pointed to the sign and said, "It's spelled with one 'L'."

"So?"

"So, the Camellia Grill is spelled with two 'L's."

"So," Jodie said as she pulled away.

"I just wish they'd be consistent."

LaStanza watched Alfred's sinewy black hands as the waiter pulled the ends off the paper covering three straws and held them out to LaStanza, Jodie, and Mark Land as they sat at the large "W" shaped counter of the Camellia Grill. Each grabbed their straw and put them in their Cokes.

Alfred pulled out a small note pad and leaned his hip on the counter and said, "What's it gonna be tonight?"

Tall and lean with a touch of gray in his short hair, Alfred was one of the most famous waiters in the city. The Camellia Grill, that white ante-bellum short order grill just up Carrollton from St. Charles Avenue, sold posters of a large hot-pink camellia with a green stem in the shape of a fork. They went for $10. If signed by Alfred, they sold for $20.

Jodie ordered a cheese omelet. Mark ordered a triple decker grilled ham and cheese. LaStanza ordered his usual, a cheeseburger and fries.

"So, how's Miss Lizette tonight?" Alfred asked, flashing a wide smile at LaStanza.

"She's in Paris."

"My, Lord. What you doin' here, then?"

"You got me."

Alfred laughed and moved to the grill, wiping his hands on his white apron. LaStanza watched him. Alfred never wasted a movement. Cracking two eggs to drip on the grill with one hand, Alfred flopped a fresh hamburger patty next to the eggs with the other hand, tapping open the lower portion of the stainless steel refrigerator with his left foot before stepping over to pull out a bag of frozen French fries to plop in the hot grease pit next to the grill. Strong cooking aromas added steam to the atmosphere, mixing in with the rich smells of the food others ate as they sat on stools up and down the counter.

Mostly college students from Loyola and Tulane, there was a also a healthy mix of uptowners, men with manicured fingernails, women with gems on most of their fingers.

LaStanza thought of his victim's hands, how the man's fingers curled as the muscles contracted from the heat, how the pathologist had to cut off the man's fingers and soak them in saline to get them to straighten, how the burned skin was peeled away later to get to the second layer of skin in order to roll the fingers to get their fingerprints.

"Hey," Mark said, poking LaStanza with his elbow, nearly knocking him off the stool. "What you day dreaming about?"

"Nothing."

Mark was so large he spilled over his stool. That's why they sat him at one of the corners of the "W" shaped counter. Leaning his elbows on the counter, he nearly blotted out Jodie on the other side him.

Turning to Jodie, Mark said, "How'd your post go this morning?" "Post" sounded better than "autopsy" at dinner time. He was asking about the Mianteen Murder.

"Four penetrating wounds," Jodie said. Placing her hand near the center of her back she said, "Three entries on the right side of the spinal column." She moved her hand to the back of her neck. "One here."

Arching her back like a cat, she stretched and added, "Got four good projectiles. All small caliber. Just like the .22 and .25 casings at the scene. Two were fatal wounds. Clipped the aorta."

Mark was nodding. "That'll do it." Turning to LaStanza, he said, "What's new on Pleasant Street?"

"The crime lab's got his prints now. But what the fuck do I do with them?" It wasn't a question as much as a statement. Without a name, the prints just sat and waited.

"No ID calls?"

"Not a one."

"Well," Mark rubbed his chin with his bear-paw of a left hand, "we should make bums wear dog tags."

LaStanza took a sip of Coke.

"You sure ain't got much going on that one, do ya?"

"Nope," LaStanza agreed. All he could do for now was canvass...canvass...canvass. And hope to get lucky.

Mark suddenly slapped LaStanza on the back and said, "You'll solve it. You always do." He laughed.

"That's a load off my mind."

Alfred brought all three dishes at the same time, sliding them into the right places on the counter smoothly and easily. Pointing a long index finger at the bandage on LaStanza's left hand, he said, "What happened?"

"Dog bite."

"Oh."

Mark snapped up his sandwich, took a bite and said, "Alfred. One more, OK?"

"Sure."

"Glad you suggested eating here," Mark told LaStanza. "I used to eat here a lot when I worked the Second."

In his shirt sleeves, wearing a tie alarmingly similar to LaStanza's aqua blue flowered tie, he looked like an oversized, unmade version of LaStanza. When they were partners they were often mistook for brothers.

Jodie spoke from the other side of the big sergeant, "Thank God you didn't invite S & S."

Mark leaned back, allowing LaStanza to see his partner, who was sipping the straw in her Coke.

"Yeah," Mark agreed. "They're tough to eat with. Like eating with Belushi in *Animal House*."

"Naw," LaStanza said, "more like eating with Crazy Horse and Custer."

"Fuckin' A!" Jodie said.

Even Alfred looked at her.

LaStanza and Jodie just turned off Stephen Girard on to Feliciana Drive, slowing down to spot Jimmy Dore's address when Mark called them on the radio.

"Go ahead," LaStanza said.

"10-19," Mark said. "The subjects from Feliciana Drive are at the Bureau."

Fifteen minutes later, Jodie led the way into the office. A curly haired man in a Hawaiian shirt and jeans was sitting at Snowood's desk. A skinny boy of about twenty, wearing an oversized tee shirt and jeans stood next to Mark Land by the coffee table. He looked like a fresher version of the man at Snowood's desk.

"Meet Henry Dore," Mark said, waving to the man in the Hawaiian shirt. "And this here's Jimmy. Henry works the Fifth District."

Jodie dropped her purse on her desk and introduced herself. Jimmy Dore stepped forward and she waved him to LaStanza's desk chair. LaStanza sat on the edge of his desk as Jodie broke out her note pad.

A few preliminary questions confirmed that yes, Jimmy Dore was Maria Garcia's boyfriend, and yes he remembered seeing the man in the light blue car on the night of the murder on Gentilly Boulevard.

"I told my Dad all about it."

Jodie turned to the man in the Hawaiian shirt, who shrugged and said, "I sent you a memo."

"What memo?" Jodie looked over at Mark who was still leaning against the coffee table, a mug in his right hand. He shrugged.

Henry Dore reached into the top pocket of his Hawaiian shirt and pulled out a piece of paper. He unfolded it and passed it to LaStanza. It was Xerox of an NOPD Memo Form. Subject: 10-18 in reference to the murder of Angie Rinaldi. It was all there, the blue car, the big man in the hooded sweatshirt. LaStanza passed it to his partner.

"I keep copies of all my memos," Henry explained without anyone asking. "Our 10-5 system's pretty fucked up."

It sure was. The memo never made it to the Detective Bureau.

LaStanza headed for the coffee. Calling back to Henry, he said, "Can I get you a cup?

"Naw. What happened to your hand?"

"Dog bite."

LaStanza grabbed the Spade & Archer mug and poured himself a strong cup, adding two packs of Equal. Standing next to Mark, he watched his partner go over the facts again with Jimmy Dore. When she finished, she slumped back in her chair, brushed a renegade strand of hair from her eyes and asked LaStanza if he had any questions.

"Yeah. Jimmy, did you tell Maria you heard the killer was short."

"Yes sir. I knew she'd be afraid, so I told her that to calm her down."

"You made it up?"

Jimmy looked at his father and made a "sorry" face. "I've been careful bringing her home and making sure she keeps everything locked up."

Just as the Dores left, Snowood and Stevens came into the squad room. Slamming the door so hard it rattled, Stevens boomed, "I don't give a fuck! I'm tired a that shit."

"You didn't have to break it, you fuckin' gorilla."

"You lucky I didn't break your skinny ass!"

Kicking chairs out of their way, the two stormed across the squad room. Stevens led the way, still dressed in his iridescent green tie and loud green and yellow plaid pants. Snowood followed, grinning a brown stained grin, a black Stetson atop his pointed head. Dressed in a dark blue shirt, a bright yellow cavalry bandanna tied as a tie around his neck, dark blue pants and black cowboy boots, Snowood waved at Mark and said, "Sarge. I want a new partner."

"No, *I* want a new partner!" Stevens bellowed. Dropping his briefcase on the floor next to LaStanza's desk, Stevens moved up right in Mark's face and said, "I can't take no more *country-fuckin-music!*"

Mark dropped his right paw on Stevens chest and backed the multicolored dick back two steps.

Snowood stepped past Mark for the coffee pot and leaned around the big sergeant to tell his partner, "Why don't you tell him what you did to my radio?"

"Your LFR?" Mark asked.

"No, our car radio." Snowood turned back to his partner.

Stevens folded his arms and said, "I broke it! I can't take no more hillbillies crying about broken hearts and train wrecks and cheatin' wives!"

LaStanza looked over at his partner. Jodie had her head buried between her hands, her elbows propped up on her desk. Between her elbows was a stack of papers. LaStanza stood and stretched and leaned over. Sure enough, she was going over her Pantyhose Case notes. He saw her jaw twitching. She was so deep in the pressure cooker, she didn't even hear S & S.

He grabbed his briefcase and tapped her on the shoulder.

"Let's go," he said.

She rose lethargically, scooping her notes into her briefcase. LaStanza grabbed their jackets and led the way out. Mark was now standing between S & S, his arms folded, his head down. Stevens snarled at Snowood who laughed back at him like a lunatic hyena.

LaStanza hoped they would escape before Mark exploded. No such luck. Just as he grabbed the door handle, a volcanic voice erupted behind them.

"*Shut the Fuck Up!*"

LaStanza drove. It must have rained while they were talking to the Dores. LaStanza rolled down his window and let the damp, rain swelled air flow over him. Jodie sat silently looking out the front passenger window.

LaStanza took Broad Avenue all the way to Gentilly Boulevard, the wet tires hissing beneath the LTD. Slowing in the 3600 block of Gentilly, LaStanza pulled up and parked in front of Angie Rinaldi's house at 3612. Well lit by the new spotlights the landlord put in recently, the two story English Tudor rock house loomed like a cold castle rising from the wet earth.

A half hour later, LaStanza cranked up the LTD and drove slowly around the corner, turning again at the next right to come up behind the house along Wisteria Street. The LTD crept along Wisteria to Iris, back up to Gentilly and then in and out of the streets that ran up and down the Boulevard. Twisting like a snake, they passed blue street signs...Music Street and Arts Street, Painters, Venus, Franklin, Eads, LaFaye, Baccich, Eastern...back to St. Roch, Spain, Mandeville, Marigny to Elysian Fields Avenue and back again. Driving to Franklin, the LTD crept down past Wisteria again, to Jasmine, Verbena, Gladiolus, Jonquil, Lavender, Clover, Acacia, Myrtle, Elder, Sage and Bay, then back up Franklin to Lombard and Carnot and Mirabeau to Elysian Fields again. Returning to Gentilly, the LTD eased up and down Clematis, Montpelier, Fairmont, Claremont, Piedmont, and St. Vincent.

Jodie remained silent. They weren't looking for anything in particular. Maybe a light blue car, a full sized American car. LaStanza just knew they had to be there.

His mind wandered as the LTD moved over the damp street. His mind flashed a inner vision of silky thighs, of a brunette in a tight miniskirt crossing her legs next to him in the Maserati she bought for him after he was stupid enough to get his first car stolen. He day dreamed of Lizette's oversized breasts and hard nipples when she rode him, her back arched, her ass cupped in his hands, his dick buried deep in her wet pussy. He dreamed of her soft, silken pubic hair and his tongue licking her, making her buck against him. He thought of her lips, of those thick, pouty lips, those extra kissable lips. He thought of the way she walked naked around their house, upstairs and downstairs and even out on the rear deck by the Jacuzzi in broad daylight, the ease at the way she moved, the beauty of her naked body.

He remembered how she looked when he took her to the airport for her flight to Paris. Decked out in a red light-weight double-breasted, body hugging coat-dress that was cut just above her knees and opened up nicely when she sat, showing a healthy slice of thigh, she looked so sexy. He envied whoever sat next to her on the plane.

She had curled her long brown hair that morning, parting it on the side, pinning it back in a gold barrette. Her lips were painted in crimson lipstick, a deeper hue than even her dress. She wore her tortoise shell glasses, wide glasses that seemed to highlight her gold-brown eyes.

She kissed him good-byc, smearing her lipstick across his lips, running her tongue over his. On her toes she hugged him tightly and whispered in his ear, "I'm gonna miss you, Babe. So much."

Looking back at her he could see tears in her eyes. Choking back a laugh, she said it was silly. It was only one semester. Yet her hand squeezed his hard, very hard, until she had to let go. She called him from New York, before crossing the Atlantic. She said she missed him. He could feel it in his heart, the ache.

"Hey, we're going the wrong way on a one-way street," Jodie said.

A car blew its horn at them, a defiant fist reaching out a driver's side window of a black Chevrolet that swerved to miss the slow moving LTD.

LaStanza grinned at Jodie and said, "Sometimes I just love pissing off the public."

Toledano Street

LaStanza rang the doorbell, then wiped perspiration from his brow with the bandage on his left hand. Stepping back, he looked at the enormous black front door of 1440 Toledano. He noticed the matching black shutters on the four windows along the front of the house. He saw a movement behind the curtain in the window nearest the door. He reached forward and rang the bell again. He looked around the wide front gallery with its black wood railing. Several dead magnolia leaves dotted the otherwise pristine gallery.

His LFR tucked in the back pocket of his Gitano blue jeans, his off duty Smith & Wesson .38 caliber Model 60 comfortable in its holster along the small of his back, LaStanza fanned his sky blue short-sleeved dress shirt. The dress shirt, worn unbuttoned and out over a pale yellow tee-shirt, concealed the Model 60. Open in front, it allowed easy view of his badge clipped to his belt just above his left front pocket.

He heard the enormous front door creak open and looked back as a green eye peeked out at him. LaStanza opened his shirt and said, "Police. I'm looking for Jeanne Bonneau."

The door opened enough for a round nose to poke out and half a pair of lips which said, "I'm Jeanne

Bonneau. What do you want?"

"I'm Detective LaStanza, Homicide. Last Wednesday morning at twelve forty-seven a.m. you spoke to two patrolmen out by your front gate. I need to talk to you a little more about it."

Jeanne Bonneau's moon face emerged from behind the door. She wore a unicorn earring in her right ear and a gold rope necklace around her neck. LaStanza could see the top of a light green blouse. A faint, sickly whiff of strong perfume slithered out from behind the door. Jeanne's brown hair was plastered straight back. It looked oily.

"You're the detective that's been snooping around here with that tall blonde haired police woman, aren't you?"

"Guilty. May I come in?"

"No." Bonneau's eyes widened, as if LaStanza had asked something improper.

It's just a hundred degrees out here, Lady!

He felt a cool breath of air-conditioned air eek out of the door and brush across his face. Bonneau closed the door a little and said, "What do you want to talk to me about? I already told the officers..."

"What I'd like to know, Miss Bonneau, was what were you doing before you were standing out in your front yard at twelve forty-seven a.m.?"

"What?"

Snowood would have described the ensuing conversation as, "It was like pulling teeth from a prairie chicken."

Before closing the door on LaStanza's face, the moon faced woman concluded her statement with, "I should have done the same thing to you I did when that blonde haired detective knocked on my door."

"What was that?"

"I didn't answer my door."

Twelve minutes after ringing Jeanne Bonneau's doorbell, LaStanza moved down the eight brick steps from the wide gallery, past the elephant-ear plants and the rubber plants to the small black wrought iron gate, which he left open on purpose.

He walked down Toledano to the next house and rang the doorbell. A man in a wheelchair answered. Not only had he not seen anything, the man had no idea anyone had died a block away, nor did he care, or so he said before shoving his door closed.

LaStanza rang the bell again. The door opened quickly.

"Do you own a boat?" LaStanza asked.

"Hell no!" The door closed again.

Back on the sidewalk, LaStanza looked at his notes. The owners of all three boats he'd spotted yesterday had no flare guns. Neighborhood busybody Jeanne Bonneau did not have a boat, nor had she seen anything before all the police lights and sirens attracted her attention out across Prytania along the neutral ground on Pleasant Street. By not seeing anything, she had given LaStanza something. With her window curtains open and sitting in her front room reading, she could not have missed a flaming man run past her house. The victim did not come from Toledano Street.

LaStanza moved back up to the corner of Toledano and Prytania and looked up and then down Prytania. Since the pieces of the flare projectile were found near the corner of Pleasant and Prytania, it appeared the victim came from either Prytania or up Pleasant before crossing in front of LaStanza's car to the neutral ground.

Checking his notes, he confirmed that either he or Jodie had canvassed every house in the 1400 and 1500 blocks of Toledano and Pleasant, as well as some in the 1300 blocks and most of the houses along the 3200 block of Prytania. He found Jodie's note next to Jeanne Bonneau's address of 1440 Toledano. Jodie'd had written, "No answer."

LaStanza checked his watch. It was three-thirty p.m. He could put in another hour and a half easily and have time to grab a quick bite and still catch Lizette's call at six. He looked back down narrow Toledano, at the closely spaced houses on either side of the street. He noticed how the houses along the odd side of the street were even more closely spaced. The neutral ground that ran between Pleasant and Toledano ended at Prytania. Houses were crammed back to back along the area once occupied by the neutral ground. The large trees in the small front yards gave the 1400 and 1300 blocks of Toledano a tunnel feeling.

Walking over to Pleasant, he dodged an over-eager Catahoula hound as the big brown dog ran headlong toward Louisiana Avenue, not even pausing when it crossed Toledano. He looked over at the Whippet house at the corner of Pleasant and Prytania. He didn't see Daphne.

He needed to talk to Daphne. But he didn't want to knock on her door. He wanted to run into her, sort of casually, and ask which window was the window of her bedroom, ask her what she was doing after the news that particular Tuesday night when all the commotion happened out on the neutral ground. He had a gut feeling about that girl. But he knew, with some witnesses, especially young witnesses, you couldn't push.

LaStanza canvassed his way down Pleasant Street all the way to Bert Water's house at 3203 Chestnut Street. Checking his notes carefully, he knocked on the door of every house along Pleasant that he and Jodie had received no answer on their previous canvass. He found another boat owner in the 1400 block of Pleasant, a Bing Crosby look-alike with a pipe in his mouth. No, the man had seen nothing. No, the man had no flare gun. Yes, the man had seen *The Bells of St. Mary's.*

"Why do you ask?"

"Just curious," LaStanza said before walking off, fanning his shirt.

Back at the second house from Prytania on Pleasant, a narrow shotgun half-hidden behind two large pecan trees, LaStanza found a heavy-set woman knitting in a rocker on her small front gallery.

"Oh, I remember that evening well," she said rocking back and forth. "That was that cool night, wasn't it?" Cool evenings in New Orleans were as rare as an iceberg in the gulf.

"Did you happen to see anything or hear anything before all the commotion on the neutral ground?" LaStanza pointed back up Pleasant. Standing on the bottom step of the wooden gallery, he watched the woman's mouth twitch as she knitted, as if the movement of her mouth guided her chubby hands. She said her name was Mrs. Roger Whittaker, no relation to the singer. She wore a light blue seer-sucker dress, high collared and ankle length. She looked to be about sixty, with standard-issue old-lady-blue hair.

"I never saw anything. I heard sirens. But that happens a lot around here."

"What time did you turn in that night?" LaStanza wiped more sweat from his brow.

"Oh, I never go to bed before midnight - one in the morning. I watch cable until all hours." She nodded her head back at the open front door. LaStanza could see it was her living room.

He put his right foot up on the next step and leaned closer before asking. "Did you have your windows open that night?"

"Of course." Shotguns were built long before air conditioning, built to allow whatever breeze there was to flow through the house.

"If a burning man ran past here, let's say just before midnight, would you have noticed?"

"Mercy yes. I keep my screen latched, but my front door was open. I sit right in there." She nodded her head toward her living room. "Sometimes the people out here on the street are better than the TV."

"Do you remember seeing anyone out on the street that night, around eleven-thirty to midnight? Anyone at all."

Mrs. Whittaker looked up at him, squinted her eyes

and said, "No. It was very quiet out here until the police started arriving."

LaStanza thanked her and left a business card on the railing at the top of the steps.

Since there was no answer at Bert Waters' house, LaStanza wedged a business card between the door frame and the man's front door. On the back he wrote, "Please call Monday after four p.m."

At a quarter to five, LaStanza scrambled back to Lizette's burgundy Maserati just as a rainstorm struck. Huge drops peppered him, soaking his hair before he tossed his LFR in and jumped into the car, which he'd parked at the corner of Pleasant and St. Charles. He let the engine warm and the AC cool off his body. He pulled out his Model 60 and laid it on the front passenger seat next to his portable radio.

He jotted a note on his pad, *Canvass 3100 and 3300 blocks of Prytania. Carefully.* He needed the exact path of his victim. He had to make sure to ask about that. He had to be sure.

Looking at the rain blurring the Maserati's windows, he knew it was out there. The solution to the mystery was out there. He just had to find it. He had to tap that right someone on the shoulder and ask the right question. That someone could be sitting in their living room right now, waiting for him to ask. They would say, "Sure. I saw someone dowsing black man with gasoline" or "I saw someone with a flare pistol chasing a black man. I just don't want to get involved."

Damn, I shoulda talked to Daphne. He made a quick note to follow up on that gut feeling.

Slipping the Maserati into first gear, he eased across St. Charles and took a quick left. His mind wandered back to when he was about twelve or thirteen. There was a story out of New York, about a woman hideously stabbed to death while thirty-eight people watched and did nothing. The papers made a big deal about the growing apathy in America. He never forgot the victim's name. Kitty

Genovese. The police eventually found the thirty-eight eyewitnesses. Nearly all of them said, "I didn't want to get involved." One man, a neighbor of Kitty Genovese, turned up his stereo to drown out the woman's screams.

LaStanza remembered how it had bothered him. Now, as a grown-up in Homicide, it was an every day occurrence. A modern urban horror was now commonplace; not just the horror of a woman hideously knifed to death over a city block in an attack that took an hour to complete, but the apathy.

"Do I have to testify? Do I have to go to court? Do I have to be...*bothered?*" Sometimes he wanted to grab people like that by the throat and shake the fuck out of them, rattle their brains.

The Maserati knew the way home automatically, even if it was a standard. He'd asked Lizette why anyone who drove in New Orleans would buy a car with a standard transmission.

"This is a high performance sports sedan," she said. "Nothing like a sexy brunette in an Italian sports car, huh?"

He'd promised to keep both Maseratis running, so he'd taken hers out that Saturday. By the time he pulled into the garage, about a hundred-and-fifty shift changes since Pleasant Street, he was happy to turn off the engine.

Mason reached across LaStanza's kitchen counter for a piece of pizza and said, "You sure you don't mind?"

"Would you just shut up and eat." LaStanza looked at the kitchen wall clock. It was five-thirty.

Mason scooped up a slice of bacon cheddar cheese pizza, pulling it away slowly, dripping strings of mozzarella, and held it up to let it cool a minute. In an orange USMC tee-shirt and green army-surplus pants, his flat-top freshly cut, Mason looked like an off duty drill instructor. All he needed was a Yogi Bear hat.

"I just didn't want you to eat all alone," Mason said, a smirk on his chiseled face. "I'll pay for my half of pizza."

"The fuck. We got a charge account at Domino's." LaStanza bit into his first piece. It was crisp and hot, just the way he liked it, and delivered to his door within thirty minutes.

"What do you mean, 'The fuck'?" Mason said between chews.

"Your wife ran your skinny ass out, didn't she?"

Mason choked momentarily, put the pizza down and grabbed the chilly Abita beer LaStanza just opened for him.

LaStanza was grinning now as he ate.

"What were you doing? Thumping your fingers on the kitchen table to the tune of 'Zorba The Greek'? Push ups in front of the TV while she was trying to watch Tom Cruise on HBO?" LaStanza raised his hand, "Don't tell me. You were running in place and slipped into gear and knocked all kinds of shit over in your living room."

"Very funny."

LaStanza took a hit of his beer.

"I knew you'd be here all alone in this big fuckin' mansion and thought you'd like a little company on a Saturday night. That's all."

LaStanza looked at the clock again and said, "Lizette's calling from Paris at six."

Mason looked at the clock and chewed faster.

The sun was settling outside, falling behind the oaks of Audubon Park. A bright stream of orange-red light streamed through LaStanza's kitchen window, giving the room a golden glow.

"So," Mason said, grabbing a second piece, "what's happening with Pleasant Street?"

The job was never far from Mason's mind. LaStanza expected as much as soon as he answered his doorbell and found his lieutenant on his front gallery with a six pack of St. Pauli Girl in his hand.

"Well, I got nothing. Zip. I got a whodunit and a whoisit, a dead black guy and a shitload of uppity white folk who saw nothing."

Mason had obviously read LaStanza's dailies because he didn't ask any superfluous questions. He just made small talk until he got around to the real subject he wanted to talk about.

"This Pantyhose Case is getting to be a big time heater."

LaStanza nodded and took another bite.

"Kintyre met with the Sex Crimes Unit today."

LaStanza knew that.

"They went over the list of sex offenders the unit has under surveillance.

"Too bad we can't just compare the DNA."

"Yeah."

The technology was too new. No data base yet, at least not in New Orleans.

Mason took a sip of beer, put it down and said, "I've been checking Kintyre's dailies. She's doing a good job. A thorough job. Only..."

"Only what?"

"Only I can't stop the fuckin' chief from starting up a goddam Task Force."

"Fuck!"

The detectives became silent as the kitchen changed from gold to red, then to an eerie red-gray. LaStanza eventually went over and flipped on the overhead fluorescents. He had to squint for a second as he went to the freezer to get each of them an icy St. Pauli Girl.

Just as Mason said it was getting dark too early, a thunderstorm struck. It came in sheets, slamming against the kitchen windows. Thunder bellowing like some angry god.

They finished the pizza in silence.

Mason insisted on leaving five minutes before six.

"Come on, wait out the rain."

"Hell no, the street'll probably flood."

"Then have another beer," LaStanza said.

"Naw. I gotta go. Catch ya' Monday." Exiting through the side gate on Garfield, Mason called back. "Thanks for the pizza."

"Thanks for the St. Pauli Girls."

The gutters on Garfield were already flooded.

LaStanza went up the rear stairs to their second floor bedroom. He lay on the bed on his back and closed his eyes and waited. He was just feeling that drowsy nap-feeling when Lizette's sky blue Princess telephone rang on the night stand.

He picked it up before the second ring. He noticed the clock. It was six-twenty.

"Hello, Darlin'," Lizette said, her voice deep and sexy.

"Hey, Babe."

"So how was your day?" She sounded wide awake, even though it was one-twenty a.m., Paris time.

"I got rained on and Mason had pizza with me for supper. He said he didn't want me eating alone, but I think his wife had enough of his I'm-going-stone-fuckin'-nuts-giving-up cigarettes and kicked his skinny ass out for a while."

Lizette laughed.

"So what are you wearing?"

She laughed again and said, "I'm taking off my heels right now. They're black. And I'm wearing black stockings and that dark gray minidress, the one I got at Macy's, remember?"

He remembered. The dress was a body hugger with a scoop neckline.

"What else?"

"Hold on while I slip out of my dress."

She picked up the phone three seconds later and said, "No bra, of course." He closed his eyes and saw her large breasts floating free, her nipples round and hard.

"Any panties?"

"White and very very sheer."

He could hear her switching the phone around to her other ear.

"Now," she said, "I'm naked."

"Good."

"And I forgot to close the French doors on my balcony. I'm lying here on my bed and there's a nice breeze flowing over my naked ass."

LaStanza readjusted his dick in his jeans and said, "Balcony? What balcony?"

"Oh, yes. I've got a permanent room now. I'm at the Hotel Colbert, room 24. You'd love this place. It's an eighteenth century building just across the Seine from Notre Dame."

"What happened to the other hotel?" LaStanza dug a pad and pen from his wife's night stand. He wrote down "Hotel Colbert. Room 24."

"Oh, it was closer to The Sorbonne, but it had too many students. This is the left bank you know, the Latin Quarter. Cafes, bookstores, art studios. They have naked models out on the street standing around modeling for Eurotrash and Asiantrash artists, not to mention all night parties. This place is like the French Quarter on steroids."

"You don't like it?"

"No, I love Paris. It's truly the most exciting city on earth. I just don't want to live like a bohemian. The Hotel Colbert is perfect. I can walk to class but I don't have to *live* with the students."

He closed his eyes again and pictured her lying on her belly on a small bed in a cozy room.

"Is the Colbert one of those quaint little place above a bakery?"

"Oh no. It's a full service hotel. The most expensive in the Latin Quarter. That's what I mean about getting away from the students. A girl needs her privacy."

"That's why you left your balcony doors open?"

"All anyone could see are my feet. The bed's against the wall."

He pictured her now on a large bed in a plush room, the skyline of The City of Light illuminated outside her balcony, the curtains flowing in with the breeze.

"What's the number to your hotel?"

Lizette gave him the phone number to the Colbert.

He put the pad back on the night stand.

"I wish you were here," she said. "I had a wonderful dinner tonight at Le Pactole on the Boulevard St.-Germain. Crowded, but the veal was perfect."

She went on to describe the restaurant and the people and the food and wine. Then she told him about Professor LeGris again, the sixty-five year old instructor who was sponsoring her at the University of Paris, the man who held the Chair on the French Revolution at The Sorbonne. Tomorrow the prof and his wife were taking Lizette to the Place de la Concorde, which used to be the Place de la Revolution, where the heroes of her dissertation, Robespierre and St. Just, were guillotined. They were also going to the tomb of Napoleon at L'Invalides.

"It's going to be great seeing it all first hand. All the primary sources I need for my doctorate are right here."

He smiled to himself. His wife would soon be Dr. Lizette Louvier, Ph.D. He was glad she kept her maiden name. He never thought of her as anyone but Lizette Marie Louvier. Everything at the mansion, the power, the phone, the gas, even the house was in Lizette's name. Then again, it was hers.

No use advertising to criminals that she was a LaStanza. It wouldn't fool everyone, but most criminals were too stupid to find out who he married or where he lived. Anyway, his mother was Mrs. LaStanza.

"Remember *An American in Paris*?" Remember when Gene Kelly and Leslie Caron danced next to the river?"

"Uh huh." He remembered.

"Well, my room looks out on the Seine. I can see where they danced. God I wish you were here with me. Paris is *so* romantic."

He told her how much he missed her too, how he had dreamed about her every night.

"Last night I dreamed you were exercising, like aerobics, only you were naked."

"And," she prodded.

"Nothing. It was like I was looking at you through the

lens of a camera. I'd zoom in on your face and then your boobs then your pussy. It was nice."

"I can see Notre Dame from here too," Lizette said, her voice changing, getting softer. "If you were here right now, I'd climb all over you."

LaStanza had a full fledged diamond cutter erection now.

Fuckin' great. All I need.

Lizette let out a frustrated sigh, then changed her voice, perking it up. "So how's your case coming along?"

"The case is going nowhere."

"No leads?" Her voice sounded higher. "I'm sitting up now, cross-legged."

He fidgeted with his jeans again and said, "It's as if he dropped from a spaceship right on Pleasant Street."

"What about Jodie? How's her case coming along?"

"They're passing out the Vaseline Monday. They're starting a Task Force on her case."

"No!"

Lizette let out a long sigh and then said, "Guess you haven't had time to start reading *A Moveable Feast* yet?" Before he could answer she quickly added, "You don't have to, you know. I just thought you might like it."

"I read the first chapter last night. I liked the girl in the cafe."

"The one with the black hair cut diagonally across her cheek?"

"Yeah." He also liked the way the book opened, with bad weather. It reminded him of New Orleans.

"You should see Valerie LeGris. She's stunning. She's from Martinique. You'd like her. Thirty years old, she has long straight dark brown hair and olive skin."

So the prof's got a young wife.

"Lay down on your back," he said.

"All right." He heard her move. "Better now?"

"Much. Now open your legs a little."

"All right." Her voice sounded low and sexy. "Is that better?"

"Much."

He could see her lying there, her long brown hair draped over her pillow, her back curled, her knees bent slightly, the dark bush of her silky pubic hair waiting for him.

"What was that about naked models?"

"Deeno!" Lizette let out a sharp sigh, followed by a giggle. "I saw two naked girls today standing out on the street modeling for painters. Tourists were passing and taking pictures of them."

"Out on the street?"

"I know what you're getting at. You think I'm an exhibitionist. Compared to these girls, I'm an amateur."

"Out on the street? In broad daylight?"

"Sometimes you sound like an eight year old."

He'd told her before, but he said it again. "All men are eight year olds at heart."

Some nights LaStanza dreamed of brains dripping down walls, like mozzarella cheese. Some nights he dreamed of autopsies, of entrails squirming like snakes. Some nights he dreamed of processing crime scenes while standing in a pool of blood that nearly covered his shoes completely.

That night LaStanza dreamed of a Vietnamese whore he'd known for one steamy Saigon night. He had paid her to model for him when he was a combat photographer in a war that was better off forgotten than recorded on Plus-X Pan Kodak film.

Her name was Luanne. At twenty, her body still tight, her face still smooth and pretty, she was truly beautiful, so long as you didn't look in her eyes. LaStanza picked her up at an out-door cafe near Tan Son Nut and brought her to a hotel with a French name. They fucked on a bed with squeaky springs then fucked against the shuttered balcony doors as the monsoon rain swept in on them through the door's louvers, cooling their slick hot bodies. Then they fucked on the floor, doggy style, like animals.

He hadn't been with a woman for six months, hadn't

seen many women except frightened mama-sans and little girls with frog eyes staring at him as if he was a Tyrannosaur stomping through their home. He was a dinosaur all right, the last of the Americans still in country, taking pictures of a place where Americans should have never been.

Luanne slept curled in his arm that night after they exhausted themselves, her short straight black hair against his cheek. She flinched in her sleep, twitching at times. He remembered how, when he moved, she pulled him closer. They slept in their combined sweat, the thick humid air a damp blanket over them.

In the morning, LaStanza went down to a bakery up the street. He bought croissants and coffee-and-chicory from a tiny mama-san who used to be a maid at a French plantation. After eating, he and Luanne showered together in an open-air shower in the courtyard of the hotel with the French name. Children peeked out at them from the rooms.

It was after the shower that LaStanza picked up his Nikon and had Luanne pose for him. Still wet from the shower, she posed in the courtyard, among bent-up wicker chairs and broken bamboo head-boards.

The strong Southeast Asian sun beat down on her wet body, glistening the sleek curves of Luanne's body as she put her hands behind her head and twisted her torso, bending her right knee forward. LaStanza took full length pictures of Luanne and then close-ups of her face, her eyes closed as she faced the sun, then close-ups of small round, perfectly formed breasts, then close-ups of her thick mat of black pubic hair between her slender legs.

He had her sit in one of the bent-up chairs, straddling the chair, her legs open. He took two thirty-six shot rolls of Luanne and became very excited again. Back up in their room they fucked again on the bed, longer and slower this time, Luanne hanging on to his neck as he came in her.

Most whores wouldn't kiss their johns. Luanne French kissed LaStanza so much his tongue ached. He remember her lips were so delicate. Her tongue was anything but delicate.

LaStanza developed the film himself and printed each frame carefully. Laying them out on his cot on a steamy afternoon the following week, he felt a tightness in his throat as he looked at Luanne's face, at her charcoal eyes.

He always wanted to take pictures of women like the pictures in *Playboy* and *Penthouse*. He wanted to capture the complete naked beauty of a woman on film. Nothing on earth was more beautiful.

The photos he'd taken of Luanne were some of the best he'd ever taken. Her body was gorgeous in the bright sunlight. She was a natural model. Only, the more he looked at the pictures, the more his eyes were drawn to hers, to her flat, lifeless eyes. The more he looked at the pictures, the more Luanne looked like a mannequin to him.

He went to see Luanne again but she wasn't at the cafe near the air base. She wasn't at the hotel with the French name. He looked for her up and down the ratty streets, even talked to the local police, showing them one of the close-ups of Luanne's face. But he never found her. Not a trace. He even went to the morgue. But he never saw her again.

At first, the only pictures he kept of Luanne were the ones with her eyes closed as she stood facing the sun. But later, as the weeks crept along, he pulled out the others. He wanted the vacant eyes, the more vacant the better. He wanted to see Luanne's dark eyes staring though the camera lens. As if he wasn't there.

That night, after hanging up with his wife in Paris, LaStanza dreamed of Luanne standing naked on a Parisian street, posing for a bearded Romanian artist with an angry face and peasant hands. Tourists stopped on they way by and took photos of Luanne, who stood facing a bright European sun.

In the dream, LaStanza stood across the street and watched as people moved past Luanne and leered at her, at women pulling their husbands away, at youngsters staring at the naked lady, at sailors rubbing their crotches as they passed. He dreamed of Luanne's sleek body, of the way she kissed him, of her dark hollow eyes.

LaStanza woke shortly before three in the morning to in-coming rounds, mortar rounds, falling like dominos, one after the other, blowing holes in the soggy earth, exploding hollow eyes from a pretty face that did not scream. He sat up in bed and ran his hand over his soft cotton sheets. Catching his breath, he got up and went to the bathroom. After relieving his bladder, he climbed back into bed.

He pressed his mind to dream of the Caribbean, of turquoise water streaked in midnight blue and powder blue and purple. Like a video tape, he played back a vision of Lizette lying next to him on a black pebble beach. On her belly, her bikini top unfastened, he applied suntan oil to her soft skin. Rubbing the thick oil that smelled of sweet coconut along the small of her back, Lizette raised her hips and he untied the bottom of her bikini and pulled it away. He rubbed the oil on her ass and down her legs.

Kneeling next to his wife, he patted her on the ass and she rolled over on her back. He rubbed oil on her throat and across her breasts and down to her navel and through her pubic hair and down her legs as she lay naked on the beach.

She bit her lip as his hands returned to her breasts and kneaded them, rubbing across her pointy nipples. His fingers slipped down to her soft pubic hair and into her pussy as she raised her hips slightly and began to move her hips to his touch.

He fingered her gently, along the top of her pussy. Moving over her, he kissed her and felt her hot tongue against his as she worked her pelvis in rhythm to his fingering.

She reached over and started working his trunks down, pulling out his swollen dick, guiding him over her and then into her. Lizette wrapped her oily legs around him as he sank into her and fucked her there on the beach.

Lizette was so hot, she came immediately, grabbing his ass, pulling him against her as she gasped and bucked violently. He continued humping her after she released, shoving his dick deeply in her, working his dick along the sweet walls of her velvet pussy until she started up again.

When she came again, crying and bucking against him, he exploded in her and felt his semen shoot in her in long, hot streams.

Son-of-a bitch. This ain't working!

LaStanza sat up and flipped on the lamp. To his surprise it was after six a.m. *I must have fallen asleep.*

Reaching over to his night stand, he scooped up the paperback of *A Moveable Feast* and flipped to the second chapter and read about Paris in the winter, about clear sharp winds and bare trees without leaves that looked like sculpture.

Burgundy Street

The sixth victim of the Pantyhose Rapist sat uncomfortably on her tan sofa and ran her fingers through her short blond hair. Her name was Jane Berry. She was twenty.

LaStanza, standing in the open front door of the victim's apartment, watched her without staring at her. His right hand tucked into the front pocket of his beige suit pants, he ran the fingers of his left hand down over his moustache.

"Uh...I was unlocking my door when he came up behind me," the victim told the two Sex Crimes detectives standing at the end of the sofa.

LaStanza looked over at his partner. Jodie sat in an easy chair on the other side of the room. She jotted furiously in her note pad. In dress black slacks and a high-collared white blouse, Jodie wore her shoulder rig, her new stainless steel .9 mm Smith and Wesson Parabellum suspended in a canvass holster under her left arm pit.

"He shoved me down on the floor and jumped on top me."

Jane Berry pointed to the carpet a few feet in front of LaStanza's feet. The tan carpet looked new and clean. Looking up, LaStanza caught Jane staring at him with wide blue eyes.

He looked away quickly, looked around the apartment,

at the neat wooden end table on the far side of the sofa, at the matching coffee table, at the marble mantle above the fireplace on the wall that divided the Creole cottage into a duplex.

"He shoved my face into the carpet and wrapped pantyhose around my neck." Jane ran her left hand across her throat. There was a red mark on the right side of her neck, half hidden behind the collar of her white blouse.

Rotten bastard! LaStanza felt the leopard inside stretching its claws. He felt his hot Sicilian anger rising, felt that leopard feeling, that feeling of wanting to rip someone's head clean off.

LaStanza caught a whiff of automobile exhaust, turned and looked back out the front door at the dark street outside the Creole cottage that sat along the river side of Burgundy Street in the residential part of the French Quarter, 1214 Burgundy to be exact. An empty green French Quarter mini-bus chugged past along Burgundy. Decorated to look like a streetcar, the mini-bus coughed loudly, its tires hissing over wet blacktop.

Two uniformed patrolmen stood out in the rain beneath a yellow street light across the street. Shielding their note pads with the top of their aluminum clipboards, they copied the license plate number of every car that passed down Burgundy. LaStanza spotted more uniforms. Accompanied by other Sex Crimes detectives, three other patrolmen carefully canvassed the entire 1200 block of Burgundy, from Governor Nicholls to Barracks Street and beyond. He knew others were stopping everyone in a three block radius as well as copying the license plate number of every car parked in the area.

"He shoved my skirt up."

Jane took in a deep breath. She was wearing jeans now. She directed her voice to the floor.

"He tore my panties off and then rolled me over. There's a scratch on my leg. Do you need to see it?" She looked up at the commander of the Sex Crimes Unit as he stood with his arms folded at the end of the sofa.

"No," Sergeant Frank Savage said, raising his right hand. "The doctor will examine you." Savage folded his arms again, his eyes narrowed, his lips thin and flat. LaStanza watched the man's lean hawk-like face, a tired, angry face. He had the look of a man with the weight of the planet on his round shoulders. Savage wore rumpled gray pants and a dress white shirt and an equally rumpled black tie. His straight black hair was wet from the rain. Pushing forty, he looked older.

LaStanza glanced over at the other Sex Crimes detective. Darlene Wilson was the first black woman to ride the Sixth District, back when LaStanza was still on the road. Darlene stood in her maroon pants-suit, her head bent over her note pad as she took notes.

"He had a stocking over his face," Jane said, running a shaky hand through her hair. "He yanked me up by the stocking around my neck and pulled me into the bedroom and raped me."

Darlene looked up and went into the bedroom. Passing LaStanza, she gave him a half-hearted wink. Heavy set and a good three inches shorter than LaStanza, she was only a shade darker than the olive-skinned Homicide dick.

Frank Savage unfolded his arms and cleared his throat. "You told the patrolman this happened at around seven o'clock, is that correct?"

Jane nodded. "As soon as he left I looked at the clock next to my bed and it was exactly seven p.m. I got up and locked my door then called 911."

Darlene stepped back into the front room just as a Crime Scene Technician named Sturtz arrived behind LaStanza. Adjusting his horn-rimmed glasses with his free hand, Sturtz held up his large black crime scene kit in his right hand. Savage waved the technician in.

"Miss Berry," Savage said. "Detective Wilson will take you to the hospital now. Don't worry, we'll lock up your house."

Jane covered her face with her hands for a moment, then stood up and said, "I'll need my purse."

Darlene moved out of the way and touched LaStanza on the shoulder.

"Goddam Monday," she said in a low voice.

LaStanza nodded. Leaning his back against the door frame, he closed his eyes and rubbed them with his knuckles and remembered a bedroom on Gentilly Boulevard.

Also twenty years old, Angie Rinaldi lay spread eagle across her bed, her lemon yellow blouse pushed up to her neck, her right hand resting on an end table at the far end of the bed. Her lifeless eyes were pointed straight up at the ceiling, her mouth open, and saliva swathed her chin. Half of a pair of pantyhose was wrapped around her throat so tightly it had drawn blood.

What LaStanza remembered most clearly about the scene was Angie's right hand lying atop the end table. Curled slightly, her hand was so white and childlike. Angie Rinaldi had tiny perfect hands.

The fuck!

LaStanza's eyes snapped open. He took in a deep breath as Jane Berry came out of the bedroom, a brown purse hanging from her right shoulder. LaStanza stepped out on the front stoop to let them pass. As the victim passed, she turned and looked into LaStanza's eyes and he said, "We're gonna get him, you know." His voice was firm and low and even he believed it.

Jane Berry's lips quivered for a moment before she looked away and took the three brick steps down to the banquette.

Darlene elbowed LaStanza as she passed and said, "You know something we don't?"

He narrowed his eyes and then shrugged.

He watched the two women move to a dark blue unmarked LTD parked near the corner. The rain had slackened. LaStanza sank his hands into his pockets and looked up the wet street, at the side-by-side buildings pressed up against the banquette. Back up at the corner of Burgundy and Governor Nicholls Street stood a red brick two story building with a black lacework balcony along its second floor. The balcony wrapped around the corner of the building. An identical building stood directly across Burgundy. There were businesses on the first floors of the buildings, businesses that were already closed. LaStanza saw patrolmen knocking on the worn wooden doors.

An old woman in a faded red housecoat stood on the balcony of the building on the river side of the street and yelled down at the patrolmen. "They're closed!"

The blue LTD pulled away slowly. LaStanza felt the leopard again, pacing inside, back and forth. He'd seen the look Jane Berry had given him before when she first flashed her blue eyes at him. It was a look of degradation, of violation of a woman who had been violated so deeply no man could ever understand. He knew it wasn't sex. It was violence. It was pure and simple violence, brutal and evil. Only the bastard used sex to brutalize her.

LaStanza took in a deep breath of rain-swelled air and wished, with all his might, that he could step outside and know which way to turn to stalk down the bastard, to chase him down, to catch him, to go directly for the jugular and then carry the bastard's carcass up into a tree for everyone to see.

Moving back into the apartment, LaStanza saw a flash go off in the bedroom. He stepped into the bedroom doorway and watched Sturtz put his camera down and pull a large brown paper bag from his kit. Carefully, the technician removed the top sheet from the bed, folding it to make sure evidence, like pubic hair, did not fall away. Frank Savage watched, his tired eyes narrow and sunken. Sturtz followed the same procedure with the bottom sheet. Even more carefully, Sturtz bagged the victim's torn panties, her dark blue skirt, bra, and yellow blouse, each in its own brown paper bag.

When Sturtz started with the fingerprint powder,

LaStanza turned back to the living room. Jodie wasn't there. He found her outside, across the street, staring down Burgundy. LaStanza stepped down the three brick steps to the banquette and crossed the narrow street. He stood next to Jodie, directly across from the victim's house and looked back at the Creole cottage, at the single story building nestled between two multi-story buildings with more lace balconies. The cottage was built of brick between cypress support beams covered with masonry. LaStanza remembered his Louisiana history. First the French, then the Spanish, built cottages with brick-between-cypress timber construction along swampy south Louisiana, especially along the wide crescent in the Mississippi in the little town the French named Nouvelle Orleans. Painted pastel yellow, the masonry had wore away from parts of the front of 1214 Burgundy, revealing upright and diagonal timbers cut from swamp cypress two hundred years ago.

Jodie switched her LFR to her left hand and pointed her chin toward the victim's cottage. "Savage says the other side of the double's unoccupied."

LaStanza nodded. A fine mist of rain, swept in by a sudden breeze, rolled over them momentarily. Jodie turned her back to the breeze. LaStanza faced it, feeling the cool water on his face.

"Can you believe this shit?" someone said loudly from across the street. LaStanza turned in time to spot Ben Gately crossing Burgundy. Gately, plump and pale, shook his head and said, "Son-of-a-bitch hits five times in Gentilly. Now this."

"The miracle of automotive travel," LaStanza said, stepping back to allow Gately to get out of the street as another faux-streetcar bus lumbered past. Gately, in his mid-forties, sported a flat top haircut and wore a dark green polyester suit and two tone brown shoes. LaStanza knew him when he was twenty pounds thinner and fifteen years younger. When LaStanza's big brother graduated from the academy, Gately was his first partner. That was in the Second District, the uptown police.

Gately stood next to LaStanza, his hands in his pants pockets, note pad tucking under his left armpit. Like LaStanza, Gately's LFR was in his left rear pocket.

"You know," Gately said. "I keep thinking I'm too old for this shit, then a cock-sucker like this comes along and all I wanna do is...stop him."

"I want to make him suck my pistol," LaStanza said.

"That's your M.O., ain't it?"

LaStanza could see Jodie shooting dagger-eyes at Gately, who didn't even notice her looking at him. And they stayed that way for a few minutes, on a rainy Monday night, as the sergeant and crime lab technician processed the crime scene, as other Sex Crimes detectives and patrolmen canvassed the area, as Darlene Wilson drove Jane Berry to Charity Hospital to an emergency room intern who would examine her to check for bruising or other marking before swabbing her vagina for seminal fluid and combing her pubic hair to secure any dissimilar pubic hairs and then asking Jane to pull several pubic hairs for comparison. The intern would secure whatever physical evidence was available for Technician Sturtz to pick up and bring to the crime lab for analysis. Of course, a nurse would be present during the examination. Modern rape investigation was anything but private.

"I'm hungry," Ben Gately said, rubbing his left hand over his belly. "Y'all wanna get something to eat?"

"Better ask your sergeant," Jodie said, pointing to Frank Savage now standing on the stoop of Jane Berry's cottage. Savage waved Gately over.

"You know," Jodie said when Gately was out of ear shot. "He's such a dork."

LaStanza arched his left eyebrow.

"Back when he was in the Second, no one would ride with him until they put my brother with him."

He could see Jodie tense up. LaStanza was used to just about everyone tensing up whenever he mentioned his brother. It came with the territory. Joseph LaStanza, killed in the line of duty, was even more popular than their father, Captain Anthony LaStanza, who retired not long after his oldest son was gunned down by a pair of burglars at the intersection of St. Claude and Elysian Fields on the worst night of Dino LaStanza's life.

As the rest of the detectives and patrolmen assembled across the street, Jodie and LaStanza joined them. Savage looked worn. The other Sex Crimes detectives moved in slow motion, as if their bones ached.

"I want every house canvassed," Frank Savage said, "from Rampart to Dauphine, from St. Philip to Esplanade. That's both sides of Rampart and both sides of Esplanade. And I want the license plate number of every fuckin' car parked in a six block radius, especially along Rampart."

Looking over at LaStanza, Savage said, "Can you guys stay?"

"Unless somebody dies."

Savage almost smiled.

Turning to Gately, Savage added, "Ben, make sure you check all the bars on Rampart for witnesses, anything. And everyone, remember that powder blue car." Savage pointed his pen at Jodie. "Anyone find one parked around here, call me immediately."

LaStanza volunteered to take Esplanade Avenue. He tapped the two youngest looking patrolmen to come along. They looked eager. With Jodie's heels clicking on the uneven banquette, they moved past the small park at Burgundy and Barracks Street, crossed Barracks to the narrow avenue that ran along the end of the Quarter.

LaStanza felt his stomach tightening from hunger as they began their canvass of the dark avenue with its small neutral ground covered by ancient oaks and magnolias. He could smell the rain in the trees and the sweet, sickly scent of the water-logged magnolias.

At one o'clock in the morning, LaStanza parked their LTD in a no parking zone next to the fire station on

Esplanade across from the old U.S. Mint. Slapping the blue light up on the dash board, LaStanza climbed out and stretched. The Mint, which had been renovated and turned into another tourist attraction, was illuminated by spotlights behinds its black wrought iron fence. It's dark red facade absorbed the lights reflecting none of the light back into that dark corner of the Quarter.

"There's someplace to eat around here?" Jodie said as climbed out of the car.

LaStanza turned and said, "There are three great burgers in New Orleans. The Camellia Grill. The Clover Grill on Bourbon. And Ruby Red's." LaStanza pointed at the sign to Jodie's left.

She looked and said, "That's a restaurant?"

LaStanza closed his door and walked around the back of the car.

"Look at the good side. No S & S tonight."

"Thank God for little miracles."

Snowood and Stevens avoided the Pantyhose Case as if it was the plague.

Passing the front window of Ruby Red's, Jodie reached for the door knob. LaStanza continued past the ornate black wrought iron pillars that supported a balcony along the front of the restaurant and pointed to the alley along the river side of the place. He waited until Jodie quit shaking the door knob and looked.

"This way."

Jodie followed him down the narrow alley to the open courtyard at the rear of the restaurant, a courtyard littered with trash cans, empty wooden Coca-Cola cases, and other assorted trash, along with the restrooms which occupied the first floor of what once was a slave quarters.

"Jesus," Jodie said, "should I take out my gun?"

"Naw. It'll only piss off the roaches."

LaStanza made a sharp left and led the way into a restaurant that was darker than the alley outside. He stopped and took in a deep breath of sizzling beef and grilled onions. It smelled wonderful.

A black man in a white chef's hat stood over a grill to the right, beneath a yellowed Tiffany light. A tall waiter with a beard waved them to the second table from the back door. At the only other occupied table sat another tall man reading a large blue book.

"You really want to eat here?" Jodie said as soon as the waiter walked away after depositing menus on their rickety round table.

LaStanza was bone weary. His stomach felt sour from not eating. He waved the waiter back over and said, "Two burgers all the way. And two Dixies."

Jodie let out a long sigh and said, "This better be good."

LaStanza watched the waiter go behind the 1890's bar and pop the tops off two Dixie longnecks. He brought frosted mugs with the beers and placed them on the table.

The first belt was cold and sharp and tasted sweet. LaStanza took another long gulp. Jodie put her mug down and exhaled and nodded.

"You know," LaStanza said, when his mouth recovered. "I miss working the street. Back in patrol."

"Why? So you can pass shit like this off to detectives?"

"No, I miss the action. I miss catching bad guys. I mean *physically* catching them."

"You're strange tonight."

He wanted to tell her about the leopard. He wanted to tell her about how it paced back and forth inside. Ever since the day his father leaned over his hospital bed and called him, "Mio leopardo piccolo"...*my little leopard*...he felt it inside. It was always there of course, but after he had stalked and killed an out-of-control La Cosa Nostra hit man, felt the recoil of his .357 magnum as he blew the fucker's brains all over Audubon Park, ever since he smelled the man's blood he felt the leopard within.

There is an old saying along the sandy hills of Sicily. A Siciliano kills quickly and silently like a leopard, pound-for-pound nature's most efficient killing machine.

"3120 to 3126."

Jodie picked up her LFR and answered Mason.

"Go ahead."

"Call me at home."

"10-4."

Jodie narrowed her cat eyes at LaStanza. A call from Mason after midnight was never good news.

"Pay phone's outside the bathrooms," LaStanza said, reaching into his pocket for a quarter.

"Thanks."

The waiter arrived with their burgers and thick fries. He dressed his and poured ketchup next to his fries and picked at them until Jodie returned.

Sitting heavily, she closed her burger and took a bite.

He took a bite of his and waited. The charbroiled beef was delicious and felt so damn good in his stomach. He wiped juice from the sides of his mouth with the pristine white napkin next to his utensils.

Jodie picked up a French fry and said, "I have to meet with the Gentilly Task Force tomorrow at nine o'clock."

LaStanza thought about it a minute then said aloud, "I guess they can't call it the Pantyhose Task Force, could they?"

Jodie shook her head as she took another bite of burger.

"You'll be okay," LaStanza said. "Just bring lots of Vaseline."

"Bring yours too."

LaStanza felt his stomach bottom out. He closed his eyes.

"No," he said.

"Oh, yes. We're both assigned to the wonderful world of the Task Force."

"I don't fuckin' believe it."

"Mason sends his apologies. He said he was going to tell you yesterday, but he couldn't find you."

"Yesterday?" LaStanza's stomach felt sour again.

"Yeah, Sunday. You weren't home yesterday?"

LaStanza took another hit of beer.

"I spent the day with my folks."

"Oh." Jodie went back to her burger.

LaStanza took a bite of his and followed it with another fry.

"You know," Jodie said. "I know it's par for the course, but it's hard to believe no one saw anything tonight. No lead whatsoever. It's like he comes and goes like a ghost."

"He's no fuckin' ghost. He just knows how to blend in. The Slasher was like that. He was just an ordinary fat fuck that no one paid attention to until he started slicing up women."

LaStanza turned and waved to the waiter for two more Dixies. He went back to his burger and finished it off, along with his fries. Jodie ate more slowly. Leaning back, he took his time with the second beer.

The rain started up again just as they stepped out the back door of Ruby Red's. LaStanza picked up his pace but slacked off when he looked back and saw Jodie had given up and was walking slowly, her page boy drenched. She looked nice, all wet and revived. He wanted to tell her, but figured she'd just slap him, especially if he mentioned how he could almost make out her nipples.

He unlocked her side of the car, cracked the door and then went around and climbed in the driver's side. Jodie climbed in, wiped the rain from her face and fell back on the seat and closed her eyes.

LaStanza took his time in the rain. No special hurry. He drove back up Esplanade, turned left on Dauphine and went back into the Quarter all the way to Dumaine where he turned right up to Burgundy for another right. Cutting in front of a French Quarter mini-bus, he slowed down to a crawl all the way back to Esplanade.

Around St. Philip, Jodie opened her eyes and said, "Where are you going?"

"I'm lookin' for a powder blue car."

Jodie sank her head back and said, "I pulled two over yesterday. One was driven by a priest, the other by an

ADA."

At Esplanade, LaStanza turned right again and went all the way down to Decatur to pass back through the Quarter toward home. Somewhere along Magazine Street, he told Jodie, "My brother didn't want to ride with Gately at first."

"What?" Jodie opened her eyes.

"Joe thought Gately was too laid back, too slow moving. Joe wanted action. You know what its like when you're rookie-brave. He wanted blood and guts, sex and violence. You know. The America dream."

They caught the light at Magazine and Jackson Avenue, where the rain promptly stopped.

"But you know Gately was the perfect partner. He slowed Joe down. It took a while for Joe to realize, but he always told me Gately was the best partner he ever had."

The light changed and LaStanza waited for two cars to run the red light before proceeding. In New Orleans, if you gunned it as soon as your light turned green, you'd be in Charity or taking up permanent residence in one of the Canal Cemeteries.

"Gately sounds like *your* first partner."

"What?"

"Yeah," Jodie said, trying her best to hold back a grin, "Didn't Stan Smith teach you everything you know?"

"The fuck! You know what he taught me? He taught me how to hang out the window of police cars and swing a nightstick at people with their elbows sticking out of car windows."

"What? Wait, slow down."

LaStanza touched the brake.

"Not the car. Your story."

LaStanza shrugged, eased back on the gas pedal and went on. "The stone-fuckin'-lunatic used to hang out of our police car and try to hit people's arms if they stuck their arm out of the car window."

"Why?"

"He'd tell them that they could lose that arm if they

didn't keep it in the car. Once, we almost got run off Claiborne by a tractor-trailer rig. Stan went ballistic, especially when he saw a fat black elbow sticking out of the drive's side window. He screamed at me to pull it over and hit the siren. When we finally got the truck over, Stan yelled over the P.A. system, 'Get your black ass out of that truck.'

LaStanza slowed down to allow two black kids on bikes to cut across Magazine.

"So what happened?"

"You know how high those rigs are?"

Jodie nodded.

"When the guy got out his head didn't go down. He was the biggest man I've ever seen. Fuckin' huge. I told Stan that he wanted him, go get him. Stan turned on the P.A. again and said, 'You. Get the fuck out of the Sixth District. Now!'

"The guy climbed back in and left. Stan started telling everyone about this truck driver we saw once by the name of Tyrone Bunyan."

Jodie sat up suddenly and said, "Wait a minute. Didn't Gately jump in the river once to save somebody?"

"A goat."

"A *what?*"

LaStanza raised his right hand, palm toward his partner and said, "It was a goat. Joe was there. They were on the Nashville Avenue wharf with the Harbor police pulling a floater out of the river. Joe heard something out in the river. He thought it was a kid, but it turned out to be a white nanny goat baying and crying and trying to get to shore. Apparently it sounded pretty pathetic. Joe said he felt bad for it and thought of throwing it a rope, as if that would do any good. He didn't see Gately take off his gun belt and shoes. Next thing he knew Gately jumped in the fuckin' river and pulled the fuckin' goat out."

Jodie laughed. "So the dork saved a goat's life."

"Only for a minute."

"Huh?"

"Well, as soon as the goat recovered, it tore through the empty wharf and ran in front of an eighteen wheeler on Tchoupitoulas Street."

"No!"

"They found its head and one hoof."

"Jesus." Jodie's nose crinkled as if the dead goat was on her lap.

Ten minutes after dropping Jodie off at her shotgun double on Milan Street, LaStanza parked the LTD next to the Whippet house on Pleasant Street. Climbing out of the car, he stretched and inhaled a deep draft of damp air, musty with the smell of wet pecans and oaks. Looking up at the Whippet house, he noted only a faint light inside the first floor area. The windows along the second floor were dark.

Crossing the narrow street to the neutral ground, he walked around the burned spot to the concrete walkway that ran down the center of the neutral ground. Standing with his hands in his pants pockets, occasional heavy drops of rain falling on him from the over drenched trees, he looked around at the fine homes, at the Victorians and the Greek Revivals, at the Antebellums and two story doubles, at the refurbished wooden houses with their French Quarter black wrought iron balconies. He noticed there were no cars parked on Pleasant or Toledano along either side of the neutral ground, except his LTD. All were safe in their garages.

Like the mansion he lived in now, each home had a little red light by its front door, the tell-tale burglar alarm. Many had barred windows. He listened and heard only the rustle of the leaves in the trees and the sound of the cars going by along St. Charles Avenue.

He closed his eyes and saw the man's face again, the charred black face as the man's mouth opened and closed, as the man hissed and gasped what sounded like, "Kee...Kee..."

LaStanza felt an itch beneath the bandage on his left

hand. He pulled it off and scratched the new pink skin and thought, *What a horrible fuckin' way to die.* He remembered how much his hands hurt and his lungs.

In movies, dying looked easy. People who get shot always get blown off their feet and die instantly. In real life, it'd take a mortar or artillery shell to knock someone off his feet. A double blast from a 12 gauge shotgun at close range might do the trick, but certainly not a pistol, not even Clint Eastwood's vaunted .44 magnum. Hell, if it could knock a man down, then Eastwood would be on his ass too. LaStanza heard a firearms examiner explain it once. Something about equal and opposite force.

In real life dying usually took a long time. People sliced up with a butcher knife had to bleed to death. People shot usually died of internal hemorrhaging. That takes time. Unless it's a head shot or one through the pumper, people cried and screamed and kicked and howled like fuckin' werewolves, or lay on the grass trying their best to say, "Kee. Kee." Even with their body singed like burnt barbecue.

Stepping back across the grass to the one foot cement wall at the edge of the neutral ground, LaStanza spotted a car turning from St. Charles the wrong way down Pleasant Street, as he had nearly a week earlier. He stepped back away from it's bright lights and saw that it was a marked police car.

The car stopped next to him and the interior light came on. It was Kurt Owen, alone, in another crisp shirt. He widened his eyes in a mock surprise, opening his mouth as if he'd just caught LaStanza doing something strange.

LaStanza walked around the front of the unit to the driver's window, which was open. Owen's beefy left arm was resting, elbow out, on the door. Owen was bobbing his head like one of those plastic dogs from the dashboard of beat up Cadillacs in the Melpomene Housing Project.

"So, what it is?" Owen said in fluent project-Negro.

"You been cruisin' around here much?"

"Every fuckin' night. Two. Three times a shift." Pointing to Prytania Street, he said, "I park over there and write my reports."

It was LaStanza's turn to nod.

"Seen anything?"

"Not a fuckin' thing. I been asking too. Can't find a soul who saw anything. You come up with anything?"

LaStanza shook his head no.

"No ID?"

LaStanza kept shaking his head, then shrugged and stretched again.

"Where's your partner?"

"She's home. Where's your partner?"

"He took his kid to Disneyworld. Ever been there?"

LaStanza fought off a yawn and managed to say, "No."

"It's the most perfect place in America. I ain't shiting you. Streets are clean. No crime. No violence. No poverty. It's perfect. Only it don't last. You run out of money."

For some reason that struck LaStanza as funny and he laughed. Owen laughed too then said, "Say, confidentially. Is your partner a good lay or what?"

It's called the Sicilian stare. LaStanza had it down pat. Without showing a scintilla of emotion on his face, his eyes bore through Owen's blue eyes all the way to the back of the man's skull.

"Shit," Owen said. "God dammit, I'm sorry. It was a joke. He told me you'd get a kick out of it. Man, I'm really sorry."

LaStanza leaned back on his heels.

He felt the fine touch of Stan-The-Man Smith along the hair at the back of his neck. No doubt, the lunatic had struck again. No fuckin' doubt.

Louisiana Avenue

LaStanza made his way through the crowd in the squad room and looked up at the clock above the vulture. It was ten until nine. He dropped his briefcase on his desk and scooped up the phone receiver and punched out the number to Communications.

"Let me speak to Cresap," he said when an operator answered. Removing the off-white linen jacket Lizette had bought him, he folded the jacket over his left arm and waited on the line. Lizette had told him it was off-white. He thought it was light tan.

A half minute later Cresap came on the line with a cheerful, "Hello, who's calling."

"LaStanza. Have you been able to check those logs for me?"

"Yeah. I sent you a memo."

Fuck!

LaStanza lowered his voice. "I didn't get it."

"Yeah, well I checked all logs, all calls, all the tapes. I even checked the Second and Sixth District stations. No calls at all."

"Thanks."

"You want me to send another copy of the memo. I kept a copy."

"Naw, that's OK. Thanks. Really."

"Anytime."

Hanging up, LaStanza kicked his chair and shouted. "I'd like to know who the fuck's stealing all our fuckin' memos!"

A Sex Crimes detective resting his butt on Snowood's desk jumped as if he was goosed.

"Call the police!" someone said behind LaStanza. "We got a thief in headquarters."

LaStanza wheeled and saw it was Ken Davenport, the other Sex Crimes sergeant, a smallish man with a thick mop of black hair and a perpetually happy face. LaStanza hated perpetually happy faces, but liked Davenport. So he shut up and went and picked up his chair, which was lying on its side behind Jodie's desk.

Then he went and hung his jacket on the coat rack before moving over to the coffee pot. Davenport joined him. LaStanza dropped two teaspoons of sugar and a thick slurp of Pet Milk into his coffee and stirred. He held his gold and navy blue tie up against his short-sleeve dress white shirt as he stirred. He'd dunked too many ties in his coffee.

"Nice tie," Davenport said. He wore a typical policeman's K-Mart outfit: tan cotton pants, white shirt, and a red and blue striped tie with his dark blue blazer. He reached over and turned LaStanza's tie around and said, "Italian silk."

LaStanza spotted the top of Jodie's blonde head moving through the crowded room. Looking back at Davenport's smiling face, he said, "My wife bought it for me."

"Tell me," Davenport said, resting a friendly arm on LaStanza's shoulder. "Is she as good a lay as she looks?"

"Better than *your* wife, as I recall."

Davenport laughed and shook his lead as he left. "Okay. Okay," he said. "Touché. Touché."

Jodie slipped through the crowd and dropped her briefcase on her desk. She dug her mug out of her desk drawer and headed toward LaStanza, drawing looks from the men as she passed. LaStanza smiled for the first time that morning as his partner approached. How did Lizette put it? "A woman doesn't have to say anything. She makes a statement with her clothes."

Jodie wore a pale yellow suit, its long jacket fastened by one buttoned at the waist, its skirt nice and tight and just above her knees. She was thin enough to wear her shoulder rig under her light jacket, which LaStanza saw as a slight bulge to the left of her left breast. He blinked as she approached to be sure. Beneath her jacket, she wore a flesh colored blouse, which made it appear she wore nothing beneath the jacket.

He snickered as she stopped and poured herself a cup.

"Quit it," she said in a low voice.

That only made it worse. He put his hand over his mouth.

"Wait until Savage sees you."

"I passed him in the hall. He didn't notice."

Looking back at the room, LaStanza saw they were the focus of attention. He started laughing again and his partner gave him a quick shot in the ribs. He leaned his mug away, to keep from spilling any on his navy blue pants.

A black hand reached out and steadied LaStanza's arm.

"Watch out boy," Felicity Jones said, grinning at LaStanza.

LaStanza narrowed his eyes and said, "Don't tell me."

"Yep. Looks like I'm gonna be working with y'all again."

LaStanza wasn't buying. People in Intelligence never worked.

"You volunteered, didn't you?"

Fel just smiled.

"I don't believe it," Jodie said.

Fel loosened his red tie and tucked his thumbs in the top of his black Sans-a-belt pants. He also wore a dress white shirt, but no gun.

"You're going to need a gun," Jodie said, moving aside to let Fel to the coffee. "We arrest people in the Bureau."

"It's on my ankle," Fel said, then turned and told LaStanza, "Thanks for the hot tub Saturday night."

"You used it?"

"Yeah. We didn't leave no mess did we?"

Must have brought their own towels, LaStanza figured.

Frank Savage stepped into the squad room and made his way to the front of the room. LaStanza and his partner, with Fel in tow, moved to their desks. Before sitting, LaStanza leaned over and told Jodie, "I knew Fel used my hot tub."

"Huh?"

"He left enough African-American pubic hair to make a Brillo pad."

Jodie slugged him on the shoulder, spilling coffee all over the top of his desk.

"All right," Savage said in a tired, raspy voice. "May I have your attention."

LaStanza blotted up the coffee with Kleenex as Savage held up the morning's *Times-Picayune.* "Gentilly Rapist strikes in Quarter," ran the thick black headline. LaStanza had already read the article over his early morning coffee at home.

His friend George Lynn wrote the article, which cited sources in the coroner's office who said that elements of the attack in the Quarter were identical to the four previous attacks in Gentilly, including the attack that killed Angie Rinaldi.

"As you can see," Savage said, "this fuckin' heater case has gone ballistic. Right now the chief's upstairs with the three television stations trying to explain why we haven't caught the fuck yet. He's also announcing this Task Force."

Savage continued in a tired voice.

"We have twenty-three police officers assigned to this Task Force, two secretaries from our unit, and one A.D.A. who isn't here today because she's in court."

That brought a couple snickers from the back of the room, including a couple veiled coughs of, "Blow job. Blow job."

Savage ignored them and went on to introduce everyone. LaStanza sat in his chair and took sketchy notes. Besides half of the Sex Crimes Unit, which totaled ten detectives, they had two dicks from Robbery, two from Burglary, six Follow-Up plainclothesmen, one Intelligence officer, and two from Homicide. LaStanza noted the Follow-Up officers were from the Fifth, the Third, and the Vieux Carré Districts. He looked up at Fel who was leaning on his desk. Fel had a toothpick in his mouth now. In a shark-skin Kelly green jacket, he kinda stood out in the crowd.

Jodie, with her note pad in her lap and her long legs crossed, still garnered most of the stares. He wasn't sure, but she looked like she'd put on heavier make-up than usual. She was pushing, all right.

Savage let out a long, tired sigh and said, "We had eleven suspects under surveillance Monday evening, which means we've eliminated eleven more men. So far we've eliminated thirty-five suspects by having them under direct surveillance when an attack occurred."

"What about the DNA?" one of the Follow-Up officers asked.

Savage explained, patiently, about the lack of a data base, about the cutting-edge technology, about how it would be useful, goddam fuckin' useful *after* they caught the fuck!

"We just have to catch him the old fashioned way," Savage lifted his left foot to show the worn sole of his black oxford shoe. "We work the streets."

Then he went over the rapes, one by one, in chronological order, finishing with the known description of the perpetrator. "Although none of the victims can identify him because of the stocking over his face, we know he's white, around six feet tall, husky, with dark brown hair."

"That narrows it down," a fresh faced Follow-up officer

said sarcastically.

"Sounds like half this room," Davenport added.

"Except LaStanza," Fel said, which brought automatic snickers. Son-of-a-bitch used to call LaStanza "Short People" when they rode together until LaStanza started calling him "Chicken Dick. That's right, the only black man with the dick of a chicken."

Savage gave out the assignments. The Task Force would meet every morning in the squad room at nine a.m., where assignments would be confirmed. The two Sex Crimes secretaries would man the new Task Force phone lines, which the chief was giving to the media at that moment. The Sex Crimes detectives and Robbery and Burglary dicks would concentrate on known and suspected sex offenders. The Follow-Up officers, along with Fel Jones, would follow-up the call-in leads.

"The Homicide team will concentrate on the Rinaldi Murder Case and that powder blue car."

"What car," someone in the back said.

Savage explained about the car.

Jodie turned to LaStanza, a surprised look in her hazel eyes. LaStanza shrugged and slapped his forehead in a mock dumb-Italian expression. Jodie rolled her eyes and looked back at Savage who finished up his speech with, "Any questions?"

Davenport stepped forward and said, "Yeah, who's going to handle the missing memos?"

"What?" Savage said.

LaStanza picked up his mug and stuffed it back in his desk.

"Someone's stealing LaStanza's memos."

"What are you talking about?" Clearly Savage was in no joking mood.

"All right," Davenport announced loudly. "No body leaves this room until we discover who's been stealing LaStanza's memos. Gately, bar the door."

LaStanza picked up his briefcase and LFR, stepped over and grabbed his jacket and headed for the door,

Jodie right behind. Davenport was dividing the squad room into search patterns for a buncha chuckling detectives, including Fel Jones, who said, "Sounds like a conspiracy to me. Someone call Jim Garrison."

Gately opened the door for LaStanza and said, "Sometimes I hate this job." Only Gately was grinning. "This isn't one of those times."

When they were in the elevator, Jodie said, "You ask for it sometimes, you know."

"No. I don't know." Still hot under the collar, he tried not to snap at her.

"Come on. You're smart enough to know you're a prima donna."

"A prima donna?"

"Yeah." Jodie turned her cat eyes to him. In her heels she was a couple inches taller than LaStanza. "Think about it. You stand out a lot."

LaStanza looked at her chest and said, "And this outfit isn't for standing out."

The elevator finally opened on the first floor and Jodie stepped out quickly. Over her shoulder she said, "I have you know I planned on dressing like this until they moved me back to the squad."

"Now you don't have to."

"I know," she said, turning back. "We can work full time on my case. I don't believe it."

"Yeah," LaStanza said. He thought of Pleasant Street immediately. He might be working full time on the Pantyhose Case during the day, but he knew where he'd be in the evening.

It was still in the nineties when LaStanza parked his Maserati at six p.m., behind Bultman's Funeral Home at the corner of Prytania and Louisiana Avenue. He left his jacket in the car, slipped his LFR into his right rear pocket, loosened his tie and headed down Prytania. He noted two apartment houses across the street along the 3300 block of Prytania, a beat-up shotgun double sandwiched between the apartment houses.

Along the lake side of the street, he passed a pale purple two story Victorian with white columns along its front gallery. Two Greek Revivals were next. He crossed Toledano to the neutral ground and crossed Pleasant to the Whippet house and rang the doorbell.

Cleola answered before he had to ring again. She stood in the doorway, in her white maid's outfit, and gave LaStanza a stern, inquisitive look, the kind nuns used to give him at Holy Rosary when he cut up in class.

"Miss Bracket," he said. "Sorry to be a bother, but I'd like to talk to Daphne."

"Well she ain't here. Nobody here. They all in Disneyworld."

LaStanza looked at his watch for a second and said, "What about school?"

"It ain't crowded in Disneyworld now." Cleola put a fist on her hip. "Missing school ain't gonna hurt that child. She can't get nothing but straight As."

"Uh. When will they get back?"

"What you want to talk to that little girl about?"

LaStanza almost smiled at that.

"Murder," he said.

It was Cleola's turn to be puzzled. She leaned back on her heels and said, "They'll be gone a week."

"I'll be back," LaStanza said and turned away.

"Suit yourself," Cleola said.

He heard the door shut behind him.

As he walked back to the 3300 block of Prytania to continue his canvass, he thought about Disneyworld. He couldn't imagine, when he and his brother were growing up, that his mother would take them out of school...to go on vacation.

Four houses and two apartment buildings later, his shirt plastered to his back, LaStanza stood beneath a street light at the corner of Prytania and Louisiana Avenue and looked across the street at his Maserati. It was still there, sandwiched between a black Lincoln and a gold Cadillac. A bored security guard leaned against the trunk of the Caddy.

LaStanza felt a pang of hunger and thought about calling it a night, but there was one apartment house to go and he'd be finished with the 3300 block of Prytania. Turning back to the house, he noticed that the two story pink stucco building was nearly identical to the other two apartment houses along that block of Prytania, only this one faced Louisiana Avenue.

LaStanza looked across Louisiana at a Popeyes Fried Chicken outlet all lit up on the uptown riverside corner of the street, across from a Tastee Donuts with its yellow roof. He felt hunger again and rubbed his stomach.

God, I'm so out of shape. He missed running. He'd started running in Audubon Park, but lately he couldn't find the time with the case load. He looked back at the Popeyes and there was a time, a night he ran past that chicken place, in hot foot pursuit of an armed robber who insisted on taking a family box full of extra spicy with all the money.

The stupid fuck was still inside, waving his chrome Saturday night special around when LaStanza and Fel Jones rounded the corner from Prytania Street in their blue and white marked unit. Spotting them, the fuck dropped the box of extra spicy and the chrome revolver, which slid across the floor all the way back to the counter. He beat feet out the door down Louisiana Avenue, ducking behind the huge oaks along the sidewalk.

They lost sight of the fuck who was dressed in black tee-shirt and jeans. Fel stopped and got out just as the fuck started up again and it was off to the races. Fel Jones, a former quarterback at St. Augustine, gained on the fuck, who turned out to have played wide receiver for St. Augustine four years after Fel. LaStanza, the miler from Rummel, pulled up the rear. At Chestnut, the robber crossed the wide neutral ground and was lost momentarily in the darkness behind the large oaks along the downtown side of the avenue.

By that time, LaStanza had overtaken Fel, who was so shocked he stumbled. Later he claimed he stumbled on the broken sidewalk. The robber re-crossed Louisiana again near Constance Street, dodging a public service bus before running headlong into the Second District.

LaStanza caught the fuck at Constance and Antonine, running him down, giving the wheezing fuck a nice shove from behind. The robber tumbled, scraping his face on the blacktop and breaking his left collarbone.

In the subsequent lawsuit, LaStanza had to explain to a federal jury that he did not beat up the fuck, that the man broke his collarbone when he fell. The robber was convicted in state court and sentenced to ninety-nine years at hard labor. It was his second armed robbery conviction. In federal court, however, he won a settlement of $125,000 against the NOPD for physical abuse during arrest. His industrious lawyer produced three doctors who testified that there was no way the robber could have broken his collar bone in a fall. No way.

Fel Jones suffered a sprained ankle and a bad case of how-the-fuck-did-a-white-boy-outrun-me-blues. They both got their asses chewed by their captain who said, "You two stupid fucks. Left a perfectly good running automobile in the middle of the street to run down a robber. You coulda drove there!"

A sudden breeze down Prytania felt cool against LaStanza's shirt. Readjusting his LFR in his back pocket, he turned the corner and heard footsteps behind. He wheeled as the Catahoula hound raced toward him. The dog deftly sidestepped him and glided across Louisiana without slowing and continued down Prytania. LaStanza looked back in the direction where the dog had come, but there was no one.

Weird fuckin' dog.

An old green Chevy with a gray primer fender slowed as it passed up Louisiana. The two black male occupants checked LaStanza out as it proceeded on. No doubt they couldn't miss the magnum on his hip or the badge clipped to his belt.

LaStanza looked around the avenue, at the wide neutral ground, at the Popeyes once again and the dark looming oaks, their trunks so black they stood out like gnarled black holes in the darkness.

LaStanza stepped up to the front door of the pink stucco apartment house, which bore the address of 1489 Louisiana Avenue. Chiseled in the worn concrete arch above the front door was the name, "The Colapissa." A black sign next to the doorbell box read, "Private Property." The building's windows were trimmed in dark green. Its narrow front garden featured several decaying elephant ear plants and plenty of black mud. A naked yellow bulb dangled from a rusty fixture to the left of the front door, which was multicolored, but mostly a dull brown.

LaStanza checked the door. Locked. So he pushed the lowest doorbell and continued up the line until a tinny old lady's voice came on over the P.A.

"Police," LaStanza said.

The lady said something like, "Gort Klatu Barata Nikto."

"It's the police, lady. You wanna push the buzzer?"

He barely heard the buzzer, which sounded more like a clicking. He pulled the door open and walked into a well lit and surprisingly clean foyer.

A man stood at the bottom of a stairwell and glared at LaStanza. The man, who had to be pushing sixty, held a broom stick in his plump right hand. He wore an tight undershirt that was once white over his round chest and a pair of green plaid shorts below his abundant belly. The man was about LaStanza's size, albeit twice as wide.

"Who the hell are you?" the man said, taking a step forward, raising the stick up to shoulder level. The man wore no shoes. Nearly bald, the man's face had lost a serious fight with gravity. He had a basset hound face, droopy cheeks, wide slobbery lips.

LaStanza pointed to his gold badge, then to his .357 magnum and grinned at the geezer.

"Police," he said.

"I know that! What's your name?"

"Detective LaStanza. Homicide. You can put the stick down."

Pine Sol. The place smelled of pine oil. God, LaStanza hated that smell. His mother used to mop everything, even the steps outside their house, even the sidewalk, with Pine Sol.

"What you doing here?" The man lowered the stick slightly.

"I'm investigating a murder," LaStanza said, opening his note pad. "What's your name, mister?"

"What'd you say your name was again?" The man had tiny eyes and squinted in the bright hall light.

LaStanza told him again.

"That's a dago name."

LaStanza clenched his teeth.

"You one of Badalamente's boys?"

Stupid fuck thinks I'm La Cosa Nostra.

Bristling, his neck turning slowly red, LaStanza said, "Ever hear of Harold Lemoni?"

"Who?"

"He was Badalamente's nephew."

"Friend of yours?" The man put his left hand on the stair railing.

"No," LaStanza said, "I blew his brains out in Audubon Park with this magnum on my hip. Maybe you read about it in the paper?"

"Don't read *The Picayune.* It's a *communist* paper!"

Jesus help me.

"Okay, so what's your name?"

"Why do I have to tell you my name?"

"Because I asked you. You got a problem with that?"

"Yeah. According to the Constitution, I only have to identify myself to a cop if I committed a crime." The man's southern accent was more apparent now as his voice rose.

Now, LaStanza. This is a potential witness. You don't want to shove that stick up his ass. Not yet, anyway.

LaStanza closed his note pad and moved to the first door to his right and knocked on it. A tall, dark complected woman of about forty answered the door. Smiling slightly, she wiped her hands on the small white apron on the front of her green dress and let LaStanza in.

The man with the broom stick was gone when LaStanza stepped back into the foyer ten minutes later. He looked for the man each time he exited an apartment but the man was nowhere to be found.

He found the landlady in the last apartment, along the rear second floor of the building. Frail looking, with cotton-candy white hair, Mrs. Wagner was a little jittery talking to a homicide detective, but welcomed LaStanza into her tidy apartment.

Smelling of roses, the cozy flat was furnished with a thick cushioned sofa and chairs. Mrs. Wagner, tucking her ankle length print dress around her calves as she sat in one of the thick chairs, told LaStanza she was unaware of any murder at all in the neighborhood. It was the same story he'd received from every occupant of The Colapissa.

A man died horribly a block away and no one even knew.

"Who's the heavy-set man downstairs? Bald with a droopy face. About sixty."

"Was he carrying a broom handle?"

"Yes, ma'am."

"That would be Billy Day." Mrs. Wagner smiled. "He's cranky, but his bark's worse than his bite."

"He live here?"

"In 5A."

LaStanza glanced at his note. No one answered his knock at 5A.

Probably on purpose.

"Where's Mr. Day from? He has an accent."

"Mississippi, I believe. Or Alabama." Mrs. Wagner climbed out of her chair and went over to a large folding table with two letter-sized cardboard filing boxes on top. She started thumbing through the first box.

"He's been a tenant for a quite a while. From before I became landlady."

Mrs. Wagner fished out a manila folder and turned to hand it to LaStanza. He got up and thanked her.

"Mr. Day takes care of things around here," the landlady said on her way back to her chair.

"You mean maintenance?"

"Goodness no. We have a maintenance man comes in Mondays and Fridays from eight a.m. to noon."

LaStanza jotted notes from Billy Day's rental agreement, which was dated ten years ago in 1975.

"No," Mrs. Wagner went on. "Mr. Day looks after the place. Keeps the bad kids away. Vandals and stuff like that."

Billy Day, now fifty-five, was from Tupelo, Mississippi. He listed his occupation as retired. LaStanza gave the file back to Mrs. Wagner and thanked her.

"If you hear anything at all, from anyone, about the man who burned to death last Tuesday night, call me." He gave her a card and left.

Billy Day was sitting on the bottom step in the foyer. LaStanza moved past him without speaking. He almost made a clean getaway.

"Tell your bosses if they got business in The Colapissa," Billy Day said. "Tell 'em to send a white man next time." He mispronounced Colapissa, dragging the end of word into a urine derivation of *piss-a.*

LaStanza turned and looked without expression at the basset face. The man leered back at him.

Fuck. It's been a long day. LaStanza turned to leave again.

Behind his back, Billy Day said, "Little shit."

LaStanza turned slowly and walked back to the man. Billy Day sat up defiantly. LaStanza leaned right up in the man's face and said, in a low voice, "I'm coming back here tomorrow night. You talk shit to me tomorrow night, I'm gonna put you in Charity Hospital, you ignorant asshole."

The man opened his mouth. LaStanza raised his right index finger and pointed it between the man's eyes.

"Just shut the fuck up!"

The skinny eyes glared at him

Billy Day waited until LaStanza opened the door before mumbling, "Mother-fucker."

LaStanza stopped, door knob still in hand. Over his shoulder, he said, "I don't usually beat the fuck out of fat old men. But I'll make an exception in your case." He waited for a response. When he received none, LaStanza stepped out of the door back into the wet-as-a-rag humidity. He rubbed his stomach as he moved away from The Colapissa.

It's pronounced like the leaning tower of Pisa, you dumb fuck. Cola - piza. Piza. Not 'piss - a'.

He spotted the Catahoula sitting under the streetlight at the corner of Prytania. Panting, the hound looked his way, then darted off down Prytania. By the time LaStanza reached the lamp, the dog was gone.

Weird fuckin' dog.

LaStanza had a gut feeling about Mr. Billy Day, the Mississippi broom handler with the personality of a wart hog. There was something about him. Something bad. LaStanza felt it in his gut when he woke up, felt it as he drank his morning coffee, felt it as he sat in front of the office computer at eight forty-five a.m., punching up the man's social security number on the screen.

Just as Frank Savage called the Task Force meeting together at five after nine, LaStanza pushed the computer print out button and waited for the noisy dot matrix printer to spit out the information he'd discovered on old basset face. He brought it back to his desk and studied it as Savage spoke.

"We received forty-two calls yesterday," Savage said. His voice was hoarse. LaStanza looked up at him and noticed his hair was wet, as if he just stepped out of the shower. The armpits of his dress green shirt were also damp.

Savage went on to explain about how they weeded through most of the leads.

LaStanza looked back at the print out. According to the computer, basset face's real name was Kaiser Billyday, alias William Day, alias Billy Davis. Born in Bissell, Mississippi, in 1930, he'd been arrested three times for arson. Convicted once, Billyday spent eleven years in Mississippi's lovely Parchman State Penitentiary, before being paroled in 1975.

Arson. Fuckin' arson. He set things on fuckin fire!

LaStanza bounced in his chair. He turned to Jodie. She was dutifully taking notes. He tried to get her attention. Giving up, he looked over at Savage who was explaining about their canvass for the light blue car.

"...and talked to most of the residents around Arts and Gentilly with negative results. No one knew anyone with a light blue car."

"Is this light blue car a definite thing," a red headed follow-up officer from the 2nd asked. "I mean, is he definitely driving a light blue car."

"Ain't nothin' definite about this case," Savage said as politely as he could.

"Except," Davenport cut in, "except that he'll hit again."

The room was silent for a moment before Savage started up again, doling out assignments.

LaStanza turned to his partner and threw a pencil at her. It careened off her note pad and struck her right breast. She looked up and glared at him. He smiled at her and held up the print out.

She squinted her eyes and shook her head no and went back to her notes. He leaned back in his chair and tried to keep still until the meeting ended.

Ten long minutes later, when the meeting did end, he bolted from his chair and reached Jodie before she could close her note pad.

"Look," he said, shoving the print out under her round nose.

She brushed it away and said, "What's your problem?"

"Problem?" LaStanza rocked back on his heels. "I just found a fuckin' arsonist living a block away from my murder scene."

"What?" Jodie snatched the paper from his hand.

LaStanza bounced on the balls of his feet. He ran his left had down over his moustache. He stepped aside to let some of the dicks pass when a hand shoved another piece of paper under his nose.

It was Savage.

"Here," Savage said. "It's a lead on your light blue car."

"A what?" LaStanza took the paper.

"A lady on Arts Street says she knows who drives your blue car."

Jodie snatched the paper from LaStanza's hand.

"It was on Arts Street your witness saw the man park the car on the night of the Rinaldi murder, wasn't it?" Savage grabbed the front of his shirt and fanned it.

"Yeah," Jodie said, passing both papers back to LaStanza.

"Well, let me know," Savage said and moved away.

Jodie stood up and started packing her briefcase. LaStanza moved back to his desk and did the same.

"Kintyre," someone called from the back of the room. "Line two."

Jodie scooped up her phone. LaStanza saw her shoulders sag as she picked up a pen and jotted something in her note pad.

"Goddamit!" Jodie slammed the receiver down so hard it bounced off, and she had to reposition it again. She fell back in her chair and kicked her desk. She closed her eyes and let her head fall back to face the ceiling.

LaStanza stepped back over and leaned against the side of her desk. He folded his arms and said in a low voice, "The middle button on your blouse is unbuttoned." She wore a dark green silky blouse and black slacks.

"Who gives a shit?"

"I can see your bra."

Jodie looked down and brought her hands to her chest and discovered her blouse was not unbuttoned.

"Real cute!" she said and picked up her note pad and added, "Remember Nguyen Can Tho?"

"Mianteen Murder?" LaStanza pointed at her note pad. "Camelia Street?"

"He was picked up an hour ago by a Seventh District unit. He's in Central Lockup."

LaStanza looked back at his desk, at the print-out and the paper with the lead on the light blue car.

"Jesus Christ!"

Jodie stood up slowly and said, "Soon as I'm finished with the gook, I'll call you on the LFR."

She was right. She had to interview Nguyen before he was arraigned and got a goddam lawyer who would tell him, as every lawyer told their criminal defendant clients, "Don't say anything to the police. Not one word."

Dammit! There would be no sneaking over to Pleasant Street until the p.m.

Jodie's teeth were grinding. He could see the muscles moving beneath her jaw.

"Okay," he said. "I'll handle Arts Street, but soon as I can, I'm heading to Pleasant Street. I got a hot lead."

Jodie shook her head and said the obvious, "Everything at once."

"Welcome to Homicide."

Jodie picked up her phone again and called downstairs. She told them to get Nguyen ready to be picked up. LaStanza shoved the Billyday print out into his briefcase and the Arts Street paper into the front right pocket of his blue suit pants.

"Hey," he told his partner when she got off the phone. "He's not a gook. He's a zipper-head."

"Shut the fuck up."

"I love it when you talk dirty, white girl."

With her hands on her hips and her jaw jutting toward him, she tried her best to look angry. She looked so cute.

The Colapissa

"Yes," the woman behind the screen door said. "I'm the one called. Are you with the police?" The woman looked around LaStanza as if Son of Sam was out on the sidewalk, or the Boston Strangler at least.

"Detective LaStanza. Homicide." He pointed to his badge and revolver. He'd left his blue suit coat in the car.

The woman looked around him again so he moved a little to his right to give her a better view.

"Are you alone?"

"Yes." LaStanza adjusted his mirrored sunglasses—gangster glasses.

"The sergeant said he was sending a team."

"My partner's interviewing a murderer." LaStanza took the note from Savage out of his pocket and said, "Are you Myrtle Bezou?"

The woman nodded and put both her hands up to her throat.

"May I come in?"

"The sergeant said he was sending a team."

LaStanza turned and went back to the LTD, unlocked the door, reached in and pulled his credentials out of his coat pocket. His jaw set tightly, he returned to the woman who was still standing behind the screen door and pressed his open creds against the screen. He pushed his gangster glasses up on his head, like Pacino did in *Serpico.*

"I'm the only policeman you're gonna get lady. You got something to report about someone who owns a powder blue car, now's the time to talk." He pulled the creds away and slipped them into his right rear pocket.

"Well," the woman said, unlatching the door with a shaky left hand. "I'm just so nervous." She backed away from the door.

The house, two doors from Gentilly on Arts Street, was a one story white wood frame with a green shingle roof. LaStanza couldn't recognize the smell inside, but the AC felt cool on his damp shirt.

Myrtle Bezou backed herself into an easy chair that faced the screen door. She sat stiffly, her knees pressed together, her hands in fists at her sides. LaStanza's mind registered a quick police description: white female, mid-forties, 5'4", 145, brown hair and eyes. Myrtle wore a purple blouse over bright blue slacks and white sandals, which LaStanza noticed when she suddenly crossed her legs.

"Who do you know who owns a light blue car?" LaStanza got right to the point as he put his LFR on the coffee table to his right. He hoped she wouldn't correct with by telling him he should have said, "Whom."

"Um. The man who cuts my grass has a light blue car."

LaStanza said nothing. He just looked at her, knowing she would automatically continue.

"His name is Randy Pain. He does my lawn once every two weeks."

LaStanza kept staring.

"He drives a Chevrolet or Oldsmobile. It's light blue. You know, powder blue. Baby blue."

LaStanza nodded slightly. The room smelled like air freshener.

"Do you want his address?"

"What does he look like?"

"He's big."

Myrtle here's the kind of witness you want at a bank robbery.

LaStanza jotted the word "big" in his notes. "What's his address?"

Myrtle popped out of her chair. "He lives on South White Street." Moving over to the coffee table, she picked up a brown address book. "I had to bring him home once, when his car wouldn't start. He lives right next to Parish Prison. Oh, and he has a receding hairline."

"He's black?"

"Oh my, yes." She showed LaStanza the address book, and he wrote down the vitals on Pain.

LaStanza scooped up his LFR and slipped it into his left rear pocket and thanked Myrtle. He spotted a can of air-freshener on an end table next to the front door. It was honeysuckle scent. He knew if he touched it, it would still be warm.

"Um," Myrtle said behind LaStanza as he started out the door. "Randy's not going to get in any trouble is he?"

"No ma'am." LaStanza turned back and tapped his gangster glasses back down over his eyes. "He's not in any trouble at all."

Myrtle's face was scrunched up with the kind of look a four year old would give you if you tried to explain how Ronald Reagan became president.

"He's black," LaStanza said and left.

LaStanza led Randy Pain through the squad room and into one of the tiny interview rooms and sat him in the uncomfortable straight-back wooden chair and left him there. He went back out and put his briefcase on his desk and dug out the Spade & Archer mug. He arrived at the coffee pot just as his partner came out of one of the other interview rooms with a black haired zipper-head wearing an Hawaiian shirt and baggy black pants. Nguyen was handcuffed behind his back.

"Yo, Nguyen," LaStanza said grinning. "You're Nguyen Can Tho, aren't you?

The zipper-head stopped and shot LaStanza a hard look. LaStanza stepped around Jodie and moved up close to Nguyen who gave the detective his meanest look.

LaStanza smiled and said, "Say, Nguyen. You lose a brother during the war?"

Nguyen narrowed his eyes and tried to look even meaner.

"You know," LaStanza told Jodie, "I killed a zipper-head looked just like this guy at the Chosin Reservoir." Addressing Nguyen again, he asked the Vietnamese if he was sure he hadn't lost a brother in the war.

Jodie reached around, grabbed Nguyen's arm and led him to the chair next to her desk. She came back with her mug.

"So," LaStanza said in a low voice, stirring his coffee, "what it is?"

"I got an inculpatory. Says he shot at the victim, but missed. His padna, Phan Rang Minh, did the actual killing." Jodie poured herself a mug full. "I didn't tell him about the bullets from two different guns in the victim's body. I'll let it surprise him and his goddam lawyer in court."

"Good. He tell you where his gun is?"

"Sold it to a black named Leroy in the Fischer Housing Project."

Yeah. Right! The Fischer had more Leroys than Vietnam had Nguyens.

LaStanza nodded to the interview room where Randy Pain waited and told Jodie what he had.

"He ain't the killer. He's black. But he could be..."

"The man who parked the light blue car," Jodie finished the sentence.

"He lives around the corner on South White. He was so nervous he was attracting too much attention, I scooped him. He was all confused when I asked about the blue car. People were coming outta everywhere like roaches."

"Well, I gotta book my asshole," Jodie said.

"Did he say where his padna is?"

"Long Beach."

"Mississippi?"

"No, California."

"Then you gotta send a teletype too," he said.

"I know. Long Beach P.D."

"I'll be inside," LaStanza said, pointing to the interview room.

"Right."

Just as Jodie left with her killer in tow, Mason came bounding out of his office. Squinting his beady eyes at LaStanza, he carried a brown envelope in his left hand and one of those metal hand exercisers in his right hand. Mason's right hand worked the exerciser with ferocity.

"Here," he said, passing the envelope to LaStanza. "It's your autopsy report from Pleasant Street."

"Already?"

"I asked them to step it up."

"Thanks."

Mason had worked up a sweat, which painted the armpits of his khaki colored dress shirt. His green tie was loosened and dangled like a dead lizard all the way to the brown belt holding up his dark brown pants.

"Not much in the report," Mason said as he reached for the New Mexico mug Snowood had brought him from one the Country-Ass vacations to the badlands. Still working the hand exerciser Mason poured the last of the coffee into his mug. He took a hit of coffee, nodded and darted back into his office.

LaStanza tossed the autopsy report on his desk, picked up his note pad and headed for the room that held the nervous Randy Pain.

By the time Jodie returned from booking the Mianteen murderer, LaStanza was back at his desk with a fresh cup of coffee-and-chicory, the autopsy report on his UNSUB in front of him.

"So what happened?" Jodie asked.

He smiled at her and said, "Randy Pain sold his baby blue car to a fella named Leroy in the St. Thomas Project three weeks ago."

"Come on."

"Dead fuckin' serious. Anyway, he says he's never been along Arts Street at night, with our without the blue car."

Jodie looked around. "Where is he?"

"He walked home. How about lunch?"

"Yeah, I'm famished," she said. "But I got a couple teletypes to send."

LaStanza took the time to read the autopsy report. Mason was right. The report wasn't much. The pathologist estimated the man to be at least sixty-five. He'd had some dental work, probably military, which included a gold front tooth. He'd had his appendix removed, along with his right kidney, some time ago. His liver was yellowed with advance cirrhosis. Toxicology was forthcoming. The cause of death was listed as asphyxia from extensive burns. The manner of death: homicide.

When Jodie came back, LaStanza was packed and ready. She waited until they were in the elevator to ask, "You really shoot someone at that reservoir."

"The Chosin Reservoir is in Korea."

She gave him the same look Myrtle gave him, that are-you-retarded look.

"You're so weird sometimes."

"I'm just a prima donna."

She slugged him in the shoulder. Again.

"Do you know where Billy Day is?" LaStanza asked Mrs. Wagner when the landlady of The Colapissa answered her door. Mrs. Wagner wore a yellow jogging suit on an afternoon that was pushing ninety.

She smiled from her doorway and said, "No. I don't know where he is. Have you checked his apartment?"

Do I look stupid today or what?

"Yes, Ma'am. He's not there and his neighbors haven't seen him."

"Sometimes," Mrs. Wagner put a finger over her lips as if she was about to divulge a state secret, "Mr. Day leaves before dawn and doesn't come back until after dark."

LaStanza smelled something wonderful coming out of the woman's apartment, something from her kitchen. Red beans maybe.

"Um, who are Mr. Day's closest friends around here?"

"Oh my, he and Reverend Dothan are very good friends."

LaStanza jotted it down in his notes. "And where does Reverend Dothan live?"

"Two doors down Prytania at The Elton Apartments." Mrs. Wagner pointed over her shoulder. "That's the other pink stucco building. Just like The Colapissa. Only it faces Prytania."

LaStanza nodded and handed Mrs. Wagner another business card. "As soon as you see Mr. Day, please call me. It's important I talk to him."

The woman smiled, took the card and smiled again.

The Elton was more flesh colored than pink and looked older than The Colapissa. LaStanza had to lean on several buttons until someone buzzed him in. He'd been inside The Elton the evening before on his canvass of the 3300 block of Prytania, had spoken to several residents, but had received no answer at most of the doors.

Ten minutes after entering the tired building, he found the good Reverend Opp C. Dothan in a second story apartment whose window overlooked the tiny rear back yard, a yard overgrown with camellia bushes and rubber plants and enough weeds to re-populate a desert.

"Y'all come on in," Reverend Dothan said, opening his bright green door. "Anything I can do to help our boys in blue."

Obviously, from Dothan's accent, he and Billy Day were soul brothers. He sounded like Big Daddy from a hillbilly production of "Cat On A Hot Tin Roof."

Tall and stooped, with spider-web gray hair, Reverend Dothan wore a red and white striped polo shirt with blue and yellow plaid Bermuda shorts, dark blue socks and his brown sandals. His apartment smelled faintly of mildew.

"Course I know Billy Day. Been knowing him for goin'

on five years. We bowl together every Friday night and play poker every Tuesday night."

No. Don't fuckin' tell me!

LaStanza put his LFR on a rickety end table next to an orange couch and pulled out his note pad.

"Every Tuesday night?" He started in on his notes.

"Nine o'clock until midnight, one, two in the morning. We bowl every..."

"Last night?"

"What?"

"You play poker last night?"

"Sure did. Me and Billy and Sam Grover and Sam Perkins and Sam Elliot played until one thirty a.m. Sam's a retired policeman from your department."

LaStanza looked up into the man's mud brown eyes. He was getting a headache.

"Which Sam?"

"Sam Elliot."

After writing the names and addresses of the three Sams, LaStanza eased up on the important question. "Last Tuesday night. You guys played poker?"

"Every Tuesday night. We play here in my apartment. It'll be five years this Halloween."

"Billy Day played?"

Reverend Dothan was sure. They played late that night, to nearly three a.m.

Sam Grover, who lived on the first floor of The Elton, thought they stopped around two-thirty. Sam Perkins, who lived back at The Colapissa, thought it was more like ten until three. Sam Elliot, who had indeed retired from the NOPD a year before LaStanza's rookie year, and who lived along the backside of The Colapissa in a roomy three bedroom flat, was positive he got home just before three last Wednesday morning.

"You see any police out on Prytania Street?"

"We go the back way, through the back yards."

"And Billy Day was with you guys?"

"Yeah. And how's your father doing now days?"

Sam Elliot was sixty-five with a round beer belly, a purple drinker's nose, a face as wrinkled as a dry chamois, and a pair of piercing green eyes that still seemed sharp. He noticed the LFR right away, the new channels along top. He noticed how LaStanza favored his mother. He even noticed the thin scar along the left side of LaStanza's neck where Harold Lemoni's 9 mm nicked him that night in Audubon Park, the night LaStanza blew the fucker's brains all over the base of a magnolia tree. No doubt Elliot would have noticed Billy Day slip away from a poker game to torch someone.

"Do you know anyone around here who has a flare pistol?" LaStanza tried pulling straws.

"Nope."

Old basset hound face was waiting for LaStanza at the bottom of the stairs of The Colapissa. Wearing a gray Ole Miss Rebel tee-shirt and blue shorts, he was barefoot again, the ever-present broom handle in his left hand.

"I here you been askin' about me, dago?"

LaStanza continued down the stairs and shook his head as he approached the man and said, "You sure are an asshole, Kaiser Billyday."

The man's jowls quivered as if he'd been slapped. He retreated a step and moved aside as LaStanza passed.

"Tell me, Kaiser. How was Parchman?"

Billy Day retreated another step. Gaining control of his basset jowls, he frowned angrily and slowly raised the stick.

LaStanza stopped.

"Try it. I'll kick your ball up through your throat."

The man took two steps back and lowered the stick slowly until it was covering his crotch.

"What kind of shit hole is Bissell, Mississippi anyway?"

The jowls shook violently as the man growled, "I'm from Tupelo."

"Elvis was from Tupelo. You hound-dog-face looking mother-fucker are from Bissell."

Billy Day stuck his chest out, as if that would do any good. His lips slobbered as he said, "Elvis was a punk. All he ever wanted to be was a nigger."

Jesus! A southern boy talking down the King. I don't fuckin' believe this.

"Goddam niggers and wops and spicks." Billy Day was talking himself into bravery. "I remember when we used to put y'all at the back of the bus." Puffing now, he raised his voice, "Wop! Didn't I tell you to send a white man next time..."

LaStanza took three quick steps over to the man and snatched the stick out of the fat hand. He broke the stick over his right leg and dropped it on the foyer.

"You say one more word before I leave and I swear I'll rip out your fucking throat, you low life fuck!"

LaStanza turned slowly and left. Stepping out into the late afternoon humidity, he was glad to leave the Pine Sol stink and the smell of Kaiser Billyday behind. He looked around for the Catahoula, but the dog was no where to be seen. He walked back to his car. For a second he thought about the 3200 block of Prytania toward Harmony Street. That was next, but not today. Today it was straight home and a call to Lizette's hotel room. Five o'clock in New Orleans was midnight in Paris.

On his way home, he thought about the black and white "colored only" signs at the back of the streetcars, back when he was growing up in the segregated Fifties and Sixties. He remembered Archbishop Joseph Francis Rummel standing up to the segregationists, integrating the Catholic Schools and all the churches, excommunicating some die-hard Confederates who were still fighting the civil war nearly a hundred years after Appomattox. He remembered John Kennedy pissing off the old time southerners and Martin Luther King scaring the hell out of insecure whites.

"Get to the back of the car, boy." LaStanza heard streetcar drivers again and again telling that to the blacks.

He also remembered a lame joke—Luigi was told to

get to the back of a bus and said, "Wait. I'm Italian."

"Italian? Get off the bus."

The balconies of the Orpheum Theater and the Joy and the Saenger were for Negroes. Supermarkets had two drinking fountains, one marked "colored" and one marked "white." There were four bathrooms, two for each sex. No way a black could pee next to a white man. No fuckin' way.

LaStanza's big brother warned him not to drink out of the colored fountains. "They put stuff in their water," Joe said. "The manager at Schwegmann's told me."

The bad old days. Kaiser Billyday was still there—along with the George Wallace standing in the door of the university—those guys murdered and buried in Philadelphia, Mississippi—Viola Liuzza gunned down—burning crosses—and enraged chants of "Segregation today. Segregation tomorrow. Segregation forever."

LaStanza found a fresh Post-it from Aunt Brulee on the kitchen counter:

Wop,
Chicken salad in the fridge. Banana pudding too and fresh ice tea. I'll get potato chips at grocery tomorrow. You got Fritos in cupboard.
Brulee

Chicken Salad—Brulee's chicken salad— was the best. Ever.

LaStanza left his LFR on the counter and went upstairs to call. Lizette answered after the first ring.

"Hello, Babe," she said in a deep, sleepy voice.

"You asleep?"

"No, just drifting. I was thinking about you, Babe."

He heard her rustling for a second. Probably her sheets. He lay back on their bed and kicked his penny loafers off on the floor.

"I miss you, Babe," she said in a velvety voice.

"Boy, do I miss you."

The sound of her voice was so sexy.

"I saw a movie tonight," she said. "With an actor who looked so much like you, it was scary."

"Pacino?"

"No, his name is Vincent Spano."

"Who?"

"He looks so much like you, I got all choked up in the show."

"What?"

She told him about an American theater on the Place Contrescarpe. She'd gone with a couple of students from The Sorbonne and Valerie LeGris. "I was sitting between these two boys and got all choked up watching the movie. God, put a moustache on Vincent Spano and he's *you.*"

"What two boys?" He remembered the Place Contrescarpe from *A Moveable Feast.*

Her voice rose in amusement. "Oh, just Louis and Rene. They're in my class. They're both nineteen. Rene's a little on the chubby side, but Louis thinks he's a lady's man."

"Been putting the move on you?"

"Every time he tries, I start talking about my husband the homicide dick. That's a real turn off to someone who thinks he's a lady's man."

He heard her rustling again.

"So, what's happening on your case?"

He closed his eyes and said, "It's been a long fuckin' day. I found an arsonist living a block away. A real muggle-head and a racist to boot. Only he's got a better alibi than Capone had for the St. Valentine's Day Massacre." He told her all about Billy Day, alias Kaiser Billyday, and the broom handle and Myrtle Bezou and hitting Jodie on the boob with his pencil and about the powder blue car and even the Catahoula.

"They have blue eyes," she said. Her voice was soft again.

"Really?"

"Most of them do."

If he ever got a close look at the hound, he'd check it out.

"So, what did you wear tonight?"

Lizette made a sexy sound deep in her throat, a soft sound and said, "Casual. White blouse and denim miniskirt." Her voice dropped an octave. "The real short one you like."

"With the pin-strips?"

"Yeah. I'm sure Rene got a couple good shots of my panties when I climbed out of Valerie's car."

"What about Louis? He get a shot?"

"Maybe. The skirt's awfully short."

LaStanza felt his dick stirring, felt it growing as he thought of how tight and short Lizette's pin-striped skirt was. So short, that when she sat, even like a lady, he could still see her panties. Climbing out of a car provided a wide open view of her crotch.

Lizette wore that same miniskirt one day last summer while trying on shoes. On a lazy summer Saturday, they had gone to the French Quarter to look around. Lizette spotted a pair of navy blue shoes in the window of a shoe boutique on Royal Street, right across from the Vieux Carre Police Station. Without a hint of hesitation, she plopped down in a chair facing the window and the street and let a fat bald man help her into three pair of shoes. LaStanza moved around in front of his wife and watched as she sat there lifting each leg, raising each knee very high, revealing the entire front of her white panties, along with a nice slice of dark pubic hair peeking out the sides of her thin panties.

The fat man got more than a good look. So did some of the passersby along Royal, including a couple patrolman LaStanza did not know, thankfully.

Squirming once, Lizette tugged at the sides of her skirt and said to the fat man, "Miniskirts aren't made for trying on shoes." The man had noticed. He'd been staring at her crotch since he'd started with the first pair, his face only a couple feet away.

Later, in their Jacuzzi, Lizette said she'd done it on purpose. "I saw you watching," she said. "That's why I threw each leg over the side of the man's stool, so my legs would be wide open for a second."

She'd left her legs open for more than a second. Trying on the last pair, Lizette leaned back in the chair. As soon as the second shoe was on her foot, she dropped her foot around the other side of the fat man's stool, and sat there, her legs draped around either side of the stool. Looking down at the shoes, she twisted her feet and dug the soles of the shoes into the carpet of the narrow store before standing up to walk around in the shoes.

"So, what's the name of this movie?"

"*Alphabet City*. You'd like it. Sex and violence."

"And what's this Vincent Spano like?"

"Dark. Good looking. Taut cheeks. Intense eyes. He even has your pointy chin. A great smile, just like you. And a Roman nose too."

"Thanks."

"What alibi did Capone have for the St. Valentine's Day Massacre?"

"He was in Miami."

He heard her rustling again.

"Now," she said. "I'm lying on my back. Close your eyes and you can see me in the moonlight coming through the French doors."

He could see her in his mind, her long dark hair draped over her pillow, her back curled again, her legs opening slowly, the pink slit between her soft silky pubic hair. LaStanza's dick could cut a diamond now. By the time he hung up, a half hour later, his dick was as hard as Stone Mountain.

A long cold shower did little good. LaStanza hurried to pull on a pair of red running shorts as soon as he stepped out because someone was leaning on his doorbell. Rubbing a towel through his hair, he went down to the cut glass front door and looked out and saw the last person he wanted to see. He opened the door and looked at a tall uniformed police sergeant with blond hair and an evil grin on his clean-shaven face.

"Say hay, Candy Ass. What took you so long?" Stan Smith brushed by LaStanza and went through the foyer an into the dining room. Rubbing the towel over his hair, LaStanza followed the man who'd been his first partner during those first extra-dark days and nights in the Bloody Sixth.

Stan moved straight into the kitchen and said, "You got anything to eat?"

LaStanza wouldn't answer.

"Fel Jones tells me you gave him the combination to your house so he could use your hot tub. That true?"

LaStanza continued rubbing his hair with the towel as he went through the kitchen and up the back stairs to get his hairbrush.

Stan shouted behind him, "He fucked his girlfriend in your hot tub."

When LaStanza returned to the kitchen, Stan was helping himself to Brulee's chicken salad, a cold Dixie beer in front of him.

"Hey, this shit's good," Stan said taking another bite of a thick sandwich he'd made himself.

LaStanza snatched the bowl of chicken salad from Stan and made himself a sandwich before it was gone.

"Aren't you gonna congratulate me?" Stan said.

LaStanza ignored him, but that never discouraged Stan the Man.

"I just got chosen to be a pubic hair measurer for the Miss Nude America Contest."

LaStanza went to the refrigerator to dig out the poppy seed dressing and his own Dixie longneck. He settled at the counter across from Stan and spread the dressing over the chicken salad of his open sandwich.

"Does your partner have one of those big hairy bushes or does she keep her pubs close cropped?"

LaStanza closed his sandwich, sliced it in half and took a bite. Brulee had out done herself this time.

"You got any chips?"

LaStanza looked over at the cupboard.

"I know your wife's got a hairy pussy," Stan said as he went to the cupboard. "When she wears those miniskirts I can see her drawers and I saw some pubic hair peeking out the side of her panties once." Stan brought the Fritos back to the counter, pausing for emphasis. "I like pubic hair peeking out at me."

LaStanza took a hit of Dixie.

Stan ripped open the bag of Fritos and shoved a handful of the gold chips into his mouth. Chewing didn't slow his talking down.

"You must be getting pretty horny with Hot Lips gone."

LaStanza went back to his sandwich.

"We caught those smash-and-grab punks on Claiborne. Three young boot lips from the Melpomene. We bushwhacked them. It was sweet."

Stan paused for a drink of beer.

"I cold cocked one when he tried to rabbit. They'd just terrorized an old woman. Almost pulled her out of her car when she wouldn't let go of her purse. The fucks."

LaStanza grabbed some Fritos and put them in his plate.

"We caught the albino robbers last night. Caught 'em in the act down on Magazine. They tried to hold up a warehouse. Foreman hit the silent alarm. Only they weren't albinos. They were just pink skinned white boys."

LaStanza started the second half of his sandwich.

"Saw your in-laws last weekend. I had a detail at one of those garden parties. For charity. At the Latter Library."

LaStanza took another bite and followed it with two salty Fritos.

"Lizette's old lady's not a bad looking woman. Does she always have that sour look on her face?"

LaStanza washed it down with beer.

"I like her old man. He came over and talked to us. Had food and Coke sent out to the cops. He's a decent guy. Looks awfully young."

Fucker can't take a hint.

"He's always cool. Ever notice that? That's what old money will do to you. Take everything in stride."

LaStanza went back to his sandwich.

Stan took a bite too, finished off his beer and went for a second.

"Saw your old man yesterday."

Oh No.

"He was driving along Magazine. He looked pretty tanked up. Swerving that old Lincoln all over the fuckin' place." Stan returned, twisted the top off another Dixie longneck and took a quick hit.

"I followed him home. He didn't hit anything."

LaStanza finished his sandwich, ate a couple more Fritos and went for a second beer.

"You're not talking to me." Stan said.

LaStanza turned back and shot him the cold, emotionless Sicilian stare. *Took you long enough to notice.*

"Be that way," Stan said. "I can talk all night. I like the sound of my voice."

No fuckin' kidding.

Garden District

Jodie came up behind LaStanza and leaned over his shoulder to read an article in the morning *Picayune* about a rape victim in Arkansas who'd tracked down her attacker and castrated him with a Bowie knife. LaStanza caught a whiff of her perfume as the ends of her page boy brushed his right cheek. He reached for Spade & Archer, which he'd just filled to the brim.

"Good girl," Jodie said.

As LaStanza raised the mug to his lips, their sergeant's door slammed open, careening off the wall. They both jumped, LaStanza spilling coffee all over the paper.

"Jesus Christ!" Jodie said. "Y'all look like shit."

Mark Land led the way out of his tiny office, followed slowly by Stevens and Snowood. Tie dangling like a dead brown tongue from his thick neck, Mark's shirt tail was completely out, and he was *barefoot.* His baggy brown pants looked as if he'd played a couple quarters of rugby—no forward passes, no substitution, no time-outs. His hair had a windblown, I-don't-give-a-rat's-ass look to it. Mark stood outside his door and glared at LaStanza and Jodie with reddish eyes.

Stevens moved around the big sergeant, shuffling slowly to his desk. His hair matted and greasy looking, his orange tie sticking out of the left breast pocket of his yellow shirt, Stevens sat slowly in his chair, as if his ass ached.

Snowood also stepped around Mark. He moved like a zombie in a bad Spaghetti-Western straight to the coffee pot. The left row of buttons of his John Wayne blue shirt were unbuttoned. His brown western pants had pleats along their sides, where they weren't supposed to be. Snowood poured LaStanza's strong brew into a Styrofoam cup and started sipping it—black.

LaStanza waited for Mark to say something, but the big bear just stood there, breathing heavily until Jodie said it again, "You guys look terrible."

LaStanza cringed as Mark growled. He actually growled.

"Enjoying your vacation?" Mark said.

"Huh?" *Jodie actually said, "Huh"?*

LaStanza covered his eyes.

"Well, the fuckin' vacation's over!" Mark's voice echoed off the walls of the squad room. "LaStanza's back on the squad. We switch to days tomorrow. Capito?"

"Capito," LaStanza said from behind his hands.

The door slammed again. LaStanza looked in time to see Mark storm off, shoes in one hand, briefcase in the other. Mark's voice boomed again. "Up to our asses in fuckin' bodies and we gotta work short!"

He slammed the squad room door so hard, the vulture across the room tilted to one side again. LaStanza went and straightened it, watching Snowood take a long, slow, purposeful walk to his desk and sink into his chair across from LaStanza's.

Jodie held up the paper to let it air dry, careful not to get any coffee on her gray blouse or her black slacks. She wore that shoulder rig again, the one that gave her back problems. LaStanza had warned her.

He took another sip from Spade & Archer and watched Snowood's head fall back, mouth wide open. If he only had a balled up piece of paper, they could play basketball. Snowood's big nose would be a perfect back-board. LaStanza would love to dunk one.

"I like him better like this," Jodie said.

Two Juvenile dicks and a Follow-up Officer from the Task Force came into the room through the door Mark almost ripped from its hinges.

"What's the matter with you?" Jodie said, pointing to Stevens who face grimaced as he readjusted himself in his chair.

"I got prostrate problems."

LaStanza felt his stomach twitch. *Jesus.* He didn't even want to hear about it. He closed his briefcase and took another hurried drink of coffee.

"You mean pros*tate*," Jodie said.

Steven's left eye straightened again. LaStanza hated when he did that.

"I didn't say prostate. I said pros*trate.* I can't lie down. I got problems straightening out my back."

LaStanza opened the gate of yet another black wrought iron fence, this one in front of an immaculately white, three story ante-bellum home a block down from the Whippet house. Firmly in the Garden District, the property featured a flower bed of roses along its fence, a bed of azalea and camellia bushes along its front and side, and a manicured lawn that smelled freshly cut, although there wasn't a blade lying around as evidence.

The house stood at the downtown-riverside corner of Prytania and Harmony Streets. LaStanza wiped sweat from his brow—again—as he took the twenty concrete front steps up to the front gallery. He rang the doorbell next to the large white wooden door with its two cut glass ovals. The brass doorbell had silver crossed-sabers above and below.

He stepped back and copied the address in his notes, 3138 Prytania. He rang the doorbell again and noticed the chimes rang the opening bars of "Dixie." A large mockingbird alighted on the white wooden railing of the gallery, which was painted gray with six thick square front pillars supporting the ornate gingerbread overhang. The mockingbird bounced twice, let out a litany of chirps, and flew away, its gray and white wings in contrast against the dark green leaves of the magnolia trees out in front of the house next to the street.

The door opened and a teenaged boy in a light green school uniform stood in the doorway blinking a pair of blue eyes at LaStanza.

"Police," LaStanza said, pointing to his badge on his belt. "What's your name, son?"

The boy blinked at him and said, "My mother's inside. You want to come in?"

"Sure." LaStanza said, following the boy into a foyer with a slate floor. He couldn't help notice the wide staircase off to his right. The end post of the staircase had a huge brass eagle perched on it.

The boy led the way to the left, through a sitting room into a large living room that smelled of lemon cleaner. The afternoon sun filled the room, streaming in through a row of windows facing Prytania Street. In the center of the room were three couches, one occupied by a woman wearing an off-white blouse and matching pants. The woman had her bare feet up on the couch as she sipped a clear drink from a champagne glass.

"Um, Mom. There's someone here," the boy said, moving off to the left. The woman turned, blinked at LaStanza and then flashed a very warm, very friendly smile at the detective.

Her gaze moved down to his badge. She blinked and said, "You must want my husband?"

LaStanza looked around to be sure no one else was in the large room and said, "Why do you think I want your husband?"

The woman smiled broadly. "Come in," she said in a lush uptown voice that made sure it pronounced every syllable perfectly, even if she'd had too much to drink. "Have a seat."

The woman waved the boy off, but LaStanza stepped in the boy's way.

"What's your name, son?"

"Me?"

No, the fuckin' monkey standing behind you. LaStanza was willing to bet the green uniform wasn't from a Catholic school.

"My name's Biff."

LaStanza jotted it in his notes, then looked back at the boy.

"What school do you go to?"

"Me?"

Jesus, I'm speaking English! I recognize the fuckin' language. LaStanza stared at the boy again.

"I go to the Vandeer Academy on Perrier Street."

LaStanza nodded and decided he'd talk to the boy later, much later. He turned back to the woman as the boy left the room. She was sitting up now and filling two glasses from a crystal shaker. The glasses had an olive in each. The woman raised one for LaStanza.

"No thanks. I'm allergic to martinis."

"Gin or Vodka?" the woman said, crossing her legs as she leaned way back on the couch.

LaStanza pulled a card out of his top pocket and put it on the coffee table next to the martini pitcher.

"I'm Detective LaStanza. Homicide." He watched to see if it registered. The blue eyes seemed alert enough.

"I'm working the murder that occurred down the street Tuesday before last."

"What murder?" The woman put her right arm up on the back of the couch. With her brown hair up in a bun, she looked like a dipsy Sally Field.

"A man was torched about a block away from here the other night."

"Mercy. Who was it?" The woman finished off her drink and reached for the one she'd prepared for LaStanza.

"We have no idea. Do you recall what you were doing Tuesday before last, around eleven o'clock to midnight?"

She threw back her head and laughed a gurgling

laugh. Managing to swallow and not get any on her blouse, the woman said, "I'm asleep by ten every night."

LaStanza put pen to paper again and asked the woman her name. When she told him, he felt that twitch in his stomach again.

"Would you mind repeating that?"

"My name is Buffy Stone."

"And is Mr. Stone in?"

"Mr. Stone is my father and he's dead. My husband's name is Norwood."

It was like a veil lifting from in front of his eyes. The manicured lawn, the crossed-sabers, the doorbell that played "Dixie," the bronze eagle, the ultimate whiteness of the place, especially Buffy and Biff, including the blue eyes.

"Norwood?" LaStanza said. "As in Byron Norwood?"

"My husband. The father of my adoring fourteen year old son Biff. Yes." She leveled her blue eyes at him and said, "You had no idea, did you?" She didn't have to add—"and what kind of detective are you anyhow?" The look in her eyes said it.

"Is your husband home?" LaStanza's voice was even and smooth.

"He's in Atlanta. Be back tomorrow afternoon."

"Does anyone else live here?"

"My oh my. Aren't we the inquisitive type." Her voice had a hint of slur in it. She popped the olive from LaStanza's drink into her mouth and bit it before saying, "Let me make it easy for you. No. No one else lives here. Last Tuesday night I went to bed early. Biff was in his room doing his homework. Byron was in Nashville or Memphis. I forget." She shook out her hair.

"How do I know that? When Byron's out of town, like tonight, I'll be lucky to make the five o'clock news. When he's home, I sometimes make the ten o'clock news."

"Mind if I talk to your son?"

Buffy smiled and said, "Go ahead. But see me before you leave."

LaStanza nodded and went back out through the sitting room and foyer to another sitting room where Biff stood staring out one of the front windows. The boy rocked back and forth on his heels and toes, back and forth. The boy had his mother's brown hair, but definitely his father's straight-back posture.

"Biff?"

The boy wheeled and lost the stiff back. Smiling nervously, he stepped behind a high back chair.

"Do you remember what you were doing the Tuesday night before last?"

"What?" The boy had inherited none of his father's shrewdness.

"Sit down," LaStanza said, pulling his LFR out of his back pocket and putting it on an end table. He sat in the matching high back chair and pointed to the one Biff stood behind.

LaStanza had to work at it, had to get Biff to re-live each evening back to the Tuesday before last. No, he didn't know about the murder. He didn't see anyone out on the street, because he couldn't. His bedroom faced the back yard. He had gone to bed after the ten o'clock news every night last week. He remembered because he was reading *Moby Dick*, the poor kid.

Constantly looking away, Biff answered LaStanza's questions carefully. The boy was so nervous LaStanza couldn't tell which of his questions bothered him the most, couldn't get a good read on the boy at all, except a feeling in his gut, a bad feeling.

He made a mental note to talk to Biff again. He filed it next to the note to talk to Daphne Whippet. "Biff, do you know Daphne Whippet?"

The boy shook his head no.

Rising to leave, LaStanza reached out to shake the boy's hand. It was sweaty. With a dipso mother and a stone lunatic father like Byron Norwood, it was a miracle the boy could communicate at all.

Buffy Stone Norwood was out on the front gallery

when LaStanza finished with the boy. Sitting in the wooden swing at the far end of the gallery, she had her hair down now. It looked freshly brushed out. Her thin lips were covered in a fresh coat of pink lipstick. She a pretty woman actually, even with the bleary eyes and the age lines showing on her face now that she was out in the sunlight.

"Would you like some iced tea?" she asked.

He shook his head no.

She had also changed into a pink blouse and long skirt. Like most uptown women, she wore clothes that were way too large, clothes that hid her figure.

"Could you tell me about the murder?"

He told her, instinctively rubbing the new pink skin in his left palm when he told her about his burns. He told her as much as he thought she should know. He didn't hold much back because there wasn't much to hold back. He watched her face, but there was nothing but curiosity there.

"You better take this down," she said when he finished. Shielding her eyes from the sunlight, she turned and looked out at her yard.

"You might want to check my husband's bodyguards. Willie Sherman works every Tuesday and Thursday night from dusk to dawn."

William Sherman! Of course, Owen and DeLeon spoke to him around one a.m. LaStanza remembered something about parking a pickup.

"My husband has them park on Harmony Street." Buffy pointed to the corner. "Willie Sherman, George Meade, and Benny Butler."

Buffy turned and put her legs up on the swing. Then she raised her knees and pulled her feet up against her, making sure to tuck her long skirt around her ankles lest someone zipping by along Prytania might see up her skirt.

"Willie will be here tonight," she said, "between six and seven."

Good. LaStanza would have time to re-read Owen and DeLeon's report and re-read his own notes and gather his thoughts. This was getting interesting. Very interesting.

"Do you or your husband own a boat?" LaStanza asked.

Buffy turned her blue eyes to him.

"We have a Four Winns express cruiser out at the marina. Berth 1117. I haven't been on it in years."

He was about to ask about a flare gun, but thought better of it.

"I'll be back to talk to Mr. Sherman later. And your husband tomorrow evening."

"How do you pronounce your name again?" Buffy had his card in her hand now.

LaStanza repeated his name.

"Well, Detective Dino LaStanza of Homicide. Willie Sherman's no mister. He's just a redneck asshole."

LaStanza was just about to wave the waiter over, when Jodie called him on the radio. Instead he reached for his LFR and answered, "Go ahead 3126."

"10-20?" she asked.

"Magazine and Toledano."

"Can I meet you?"

"10-4. I'm outside."

"10-4."

LaStanza put his menu next to his iced tea and dug the Owen-DeLeon report out of his briefcase. He started a new note page with the information about William Sherman—white male, thirty years old, of 6711 Yellow Tavern Road, Enon, Louisiana, who parked his black 1984 Ford pickup at the corner of Prytania and Harmony Streets at 1:08 a.m. He checked the computer print outs and found where he'd run Sherman. No criminal record.

Then he checked the print out of the 3200 block of Prytania to see if the name Norwood was there. He knew Byron Norwood had a record when he was younger, but Norwood lived in Lakeview back then. He found one listing for the address 3138 Prytania. Buffy had reported her son's bicycle stolen from their front yard two years ago. He felt better because the listing was under the name Buffy Stone. He looked through every print out, from lists of arrested subjects, to lists of incidents reported to police, to victims, to license plate numbers of cars parked in the neighborhood. The name Norwood was no where to be found. He felt better because he hadn't missed it.

Jodie pulled up in the LTD and parked across the street from Cafe Italiano. As she crossed Magazine, a sudden river breeze flipped her short hair. She'd already removed her shoulder rig. The same heavy-set waiter who'd waited them the last time, the one with the oily black hair and pencil-thin moustache, approached and asked if he was ready to order.

"In a minute," LaStanza pointed to Jodie. The waiter pulled a chair out for her and handed her a menu.

"Nice disappearing act, mister." She sat stiffly across from LaStanza.

"You heard. I'm off the Task Force. I got a murder to solve."

Jodie huffed and studied her menu. The breeze began to flap the papers in front of LaStanza. He quickly scooped them up and shoved everything back into his briefcase.

He waved the waiter back over and ordered ravioli and iced tea.

"What?" Jodie said, "no wine?"

"I got an important interview a little later."

She ordered veal parmigiana and said, "And what kind of wine was that last time?"

"Chianti," the waiter said with a broad smile.

"What's your name?" LaStanza said, passing his menu to the waiter.

"Hymie. Hymie Rosenberg."

Nice Italian name.

The waiter leaned over and said, "We tried a Kosher deli once. Lost our shirts."

"Well, you hit it right this time," LaStanza said. "Your

chef's great."

As soon as Hymie was gone, Jodie put her LFR next to LaStanza's, turned hers way down and said, "You realize this is the first time we're not gonna be working together."

Her wide-set cat eyes were giving him that cold feline stare.

"You don't need the tit anymore," he said.

"I know." She flashed him a hard glint then looked out at Magazine Street and said, "Just don't be a stranger."

"OK."

"You come up with something," she said, "let me know. Don't be a lone wolf."

He wanted to tell her a leopard hunts alone, but he knew that wasn't true.

A smile crept across his face as Hymie arrived with their drinks and a plate of warm bread wrapped in a red-and-white checked napkin. Jodie waited until they were alone again to say, "What are you grinning about?"

"Guess who lives in the 3200 block of Prytania, a block from my murder scene?"

Jodie shrugged.

"Byron fuckin' Norwood."

He wish he had a video camera. Jodie's eyes widened. Her mouth made a nice round "O." She let out her breath and said, "Jesus, Dino."

He didn't have to say anything else. He could see her mind working behind furrowed brows. Hymie arrived with their main courses. And over steamy parmigiana and zesty ravioli, a train of thoughts ran through LaStanza's mind.

Would a man who burned crosses burn a black street bum? Fuckin' A! Would a man who paraded around high school in khakis with a swastika on his arm—a man who joined the Nazi Party while at the University of New Orleans and regularly delivered hate speeches against mongrel races—a man raved who against those no-good jigaboo-nigger-coon-bone headed-boot lipped neegroes—a man who rose to Grand Wizard of the

Knights of the White Magnolia—a man who slithered away from the Klan when he lost an election to form the National Movement for the Advancement of White People—Would he slither out one night, douse a street bum with gasoline and torch him? Fuckin' A, he would. Now did he? That was the real question.

"You know, he's probably going to run for governor," Jodie said as she reached for her Chianti.

LaStanza nodded.

OK, so a man who lost last year's U.S. Senate election by a dozen percentage points, a new Republican who's a shoe-in for a run off position in next year's governor's race overcrowded with Democrats—so he isn't likely to go out at night near his own house and torch a man. Logically, he wouldn't. But Norwood's not logical. Hate isn't logical. Hate is too powerful.

"It was a crime of opportunity," LaStanza said. "My victim was in the wrong place at the wrong time."

He didn't have to tell her a good homicide dick didn't believe in coincidences. She already knew it.

"So you're interviewing Norwood later."

"No. One of his bodyguards. That guy Sherman who was stopped by Owen and DeLeon on Prytania Street at one a.m."

"Oh, yeah. Mind if I come along?"

"Actually, I was thinking of using you later on this. I have a feeling I'm going to need a tall, blonde, ass-kicking partner as a secret weapon on this one. Capish?"

"I guess so." She seemed more puzzled than miffed. Good.

LaStanza watched Willie Sherman park his black pickup along the Harmony Street side of the Norwood House at 6:15 p.m. Sherman, wearing a dark blue baseball cap with a red brim, a black tee-shirt, and blue jeans, along with white tennis shoes, walked through a side gate and up to a side entrance of the house. There was a cupola that protruded from that part of the house with its own concrete steps, wrought iron railing and gray porch.

Sherman came out ten minutes later, locked the door behind him with a key and climbed into his truck. He didn't see LaStanza approach and jumped when the detective tapped on the driver's side door with his LFR.

"Police," LaStanza said from behind the driver's side post. Sherman had to crane his neck back to see him. "Step outside Sherman. I want to talk to you."

LaStanza retreated a step and slipped his LFR back into his left rear pocket. Sherman opened the door and climbed out. A little under six feet, Sherman was thin and wiry with sunburned arms and neck, and a day's growth on his unshaven face.

Sherman removed his Atlanta Braves cap to run his hand through his balding hair. "What is it?" he said. His voice had a slight north Looisiana country twang. He looked down at LaStanza's magnum.

"Detective LaStanza. Homicide." LaStanza opened his note pad and said, "You remember talking to two policemen a few nights ago, around one a.m.?"

"Sure." Pronounced "shore."

Sherman looked around, as street lights struggled to peek through the thick magnolias and oak trees.

"Did you see anything that night, before the police arrived?"

"Naw." Sherman looked down at his feet and rubbed the toe of his tennis shoe on the concrete. "I just came back from getting a beer when the officers came up and talked to me. I'd been gone for about an hour."

"Where'd you go?"

Sherman looked up and smiled a dip stained smile a-la-Paul Snowood. He spat off to his right and said, "Copeland's up on St. Charles. I had a bite to eat too. But I don't remember 'zackly what."

"What were you doing back here at one a.m.?"

"Workin'." Sherman slipped his hands into the back pockets of his jeans. "I work for the movement."

"The white people's movement?"

"The National Movement for the Advancement of White People." Sherman stuck his chest out a little.

"What work were you doing at one o'clock in the morning?"

"Guard duty."

LaStanza looked into the man's blue eyes and said, "You parked your truck here that night, right?"

Sherman nodded. "Every Tuesday and Thursday."

"You see anyone out on the street that night?"

Sherman shook his head.

"You see any street bums around here that night?"

Sherman continued to shake his head.

"You ever see any street bums around here?"

"Nope." The eyes didn't even blink but the boy was getting impatient. He pulled his hands out of his back pockets, folded his arms, and began to tap his left foot.

"Did you see Byron Norwood that night?"

LaStanza waited for an answer, keeping his Sicilian eyes from revealing anything as he stared back at Sherman.

"I don't rightly recall." The smile was back. Sherman recalled very little, the more he thought about it. LaStanza kept the questions coming, watching the foot tap, the brown spit fly across the narrow street. He asked about the other bodyguards and about the white people's movement. Sherman tried to be cagey, but LaStanza wasn't after any movement secrets. LaStanza wanted to know how a man on guard duty never saw any street people.

Finally, as Sherman was getting real itchy, a man in an overcoat stopped by one of the oaks across Prytania. The man reached into a large brown paper bag he carried in his left hand and pulled out something and started to eat it as he walked off.

LaStanza nodded over Sherman's shoulder, which caused Sherman to turn and look.

"That's the second one since we been talking," LaStanza said.

Sherman turned his blue eyes back and said, "So?"

"So, I think you're a fuckin' liar."

Sherman's head snapped back. LaStanza took a step forward, narrowing his light green eyes.

"You never saw anything that night. You never see any street people around here." LaStanza's face was expressionless, his voice deep and even. "This ain't no fuckin' game, Willie. This is the big show. The major leagues. This is homicide, cocksucker."

Sherman took a step back and looked over LaStanza's shoulder.

"What you looking for, Willie. I'm alone. It's just you and me."

Sherman looked away and spat again. His chest rose as he breathed heavier. LaStanza knew he own pulse was smooth and even. *Ice in the veins*, he told himself. He'd hit that plane, that icy Sicilian plane when it was all even and cool.

"Man," Sherman said in a high pitched voice, "you're crazy or somethin'." He put his hands up, palms out. "Man, I don't want no trouble with the police. Even if you're crazy as shit." Sherman folded his arms again. Typical defensive position.

LaStanza slowly reached into his front pocket, pulled out a business card and stuck it between Sherman's arms.

"I'll be around Willie."

LaStanza backed away slowly. Raising his right hand, his index finger extended, his thumb up like the hammer of a pistol, he pointed his finger at Sherman and mouthed the word, "Bang."

Sherman looked at the business card, then looked up and said, "How do you say your name?"

"That's right, I'm one of those Papists. One of those Catholic Sicilian mother-fuckers. You know what Sicilians are, don't you?"

Sherman refolded his arms.

LaStanza let him think about it.

Off to LaStanza's left, a mass of roaches wallowed in Sherman's brown spit, wading in to drink, doing the breast-stroke, having a good ole fuckin' time. LaStanza turned and walked back to his Maserati parked beneath a huge magnolia at the corner of Harmony and Coliseum Streets.

Sherman was leaning against the door of his truck when he pulled away.

There were two messages on the phone machine at the mansion. The first was from Lizette.

"Hey, Babe," she said in a deep, sleepy voice. "I just wanted to tell you how much I miss you tonight. It's raining, lightning and thunder here. I can see the silhouette of Notre Dame with lightning all around. It looks so...medieval. It woke me, so I thought I'd call and tell you how much I miss you." She purred and then said, "I'm going back to sleep now. I love you, Babe." Then she hung up.

The second message was from Jodie.

"Hey, it's almost seven. Call me when you get in. OK?"

Dropping his handcuffs and speed loaders on the bed, he punched out his partner's number.

"Hello." She sounded up.

"Yeah. It's me."

"How'd it go?"

"You missed it. He copped out. It's all over."

"What?" Her voice rose.

He counted to himself. *One. Two.*

"You dumb shit."

He told her about the Braves baseball cap and the stained teeth and how Willie boy never saw any street people and how he'd called Willie a fuckin' liar. LaStanza sat on his bed and kicked off his penny loafers.

"So," Jodie said. "When do you get to talk to Norwood?

"Tomorrow evening. First I gotta canvass around that immaculately white house."

His leg tossed over the side of the big easy chair in the study of his mansion, LaStanza leaned the chair all the way back and took a sip of scotch rocks. Bob Marley & The Wailers finished "Jamming" and started up LaStanza's favorite "Waiting in Vain," the easy driving reggae music echoing from the giant stereo system half hidden on one of the many bookshelves of the room.

Ever since the honeymoon, where he and Lizette were serenaded nightly by a steel drum band in the tiny restaurant of the Hotel St. Just, he'd added reggae to his list of favorites, along with Motown, The Beatles, and most rock and roll from the scary Sixties—The Doors, Cream, Iron Butterfly, The Stones, The Animals, Crosby-Stills-Nash & Young, and so many more.

Closing his eyes, he could see the shiny, smiling black faces of the steel drum band, feel Lizette's body moving against his, the smell of perfume in her hair, the warmth of the rum in his belly, the banana trees and palms swaying in the sea breeze just outside the restaurant. In the distance he could see the shimmering Caribbean rolling on to a black pebble beach.

Opening his eyes, he took another belt of scotch and thought about where all the fuckin' confederates had come from, all of a sudden. Uptown? No, they just lived there. Billy Day was from Mississippi and Sherman was from Enon and Norwood was from Lakeview. Like roaches, they just seemed to swarm along Prytania Street.

He tried to remember the first time he'd heard of Byron Norwood. Was it when he was trying to work his way through Loyola and Norwood was prancing around U.N.O. waving a Nazi flag? Was it the TV coverage when Norwood and the boys-n-the-sheets turned that meeting in City Park into a full fuckin' riot when he grabbed the microphone and pointed out two police intelligence officers in the background?

No.

But it was in City Park. He remembered now. It was at a track meet at Tad Gormley Stadium. George Lynn pointed out a group of assholes in khakis wearing swastikas in the bleachers. They were from a very exclusive, lily white private school in Lakeview.

"Come on," Lynn said as he grabbed a couple ace bandages and a black Marks-A-Lot. He and Lynn drew a Star of David on the ace bandages and put them on their arms before the 440 race. They were the only members of an all boys Catholic high school track team to win a 440 wearing Stars of David on their arms.

Brother Alain wasn't amused at first, until LaStanza pointed to the Nazis in the stands. He remembered what the red headed brother said.

"Jesus! You could have worn a cross, too!"

Palm Terrace

Fel Jones frowned as he passed another eight-by-ten black-and-white to LaStanza. The picture featured Byron Norwood standing next to a burning cross. Norwood, dressed in a white robe, held his KKK hood in his left hand, his right hand pressed over his heart, a peaceful far-away look on his face.

"That's when he was the Grand Wizard of the Knights of the White Magnolia," Fel said as he dug through the Intelligence Division's thick file on Norwood. LaStanza noticed the file was labeled "Volume 1."

"He bleaches his hair now," Fel said, passing another photo, this one had Norwood standing with six other knights, all in robes. Norwood was the only one with his hood off.

"He's had a chin job to fix his weak chin," Fel said, going back to the file. "And a cheekbone job to *enhance* his cheekbones. And an ass job."

"You fuckin' me?"

"No. He wants an Afro-ass. Only he's still gonna have a needle dick." Fel loosened his tan tie, which matched his pants exactly.

LaStanza had never seen Fel like this before, with his ears turned back like a lion watching a herd of Zebra. Even on the street, Fel was always a hair's breath away from a big grin. Even on Dryades Street, with shards of glass in his hair, his sweaty black face spotted with flour after a fusillade of police bullets destroyed the convenience store where Fel and LaStanza were staked-out, almost killing both, even with his eyes bulging and his lips quivering, Fel smiled.

But this morning, sitting behind his own gray metal desk up in the Intelligence Division Office, Fel didn't smile as he rooted through Byron Norwood's file and passed pictures to LaStanza.

"Fucker dresses nice now that he thinks he's legit," Fel said, handing LaStanza a color eight-by-ten of Norwood in a gray silk suit. LaStanza had on a gray linen suit that morning, charcoal gray with a turquoise tie dotted with silver triangles and squares.

"He's written three books," Fel said, pulling out Volume 2.

LaStanza could imagine the titles—*White Like Me,* or maybe *I Was A Teen-age Nazi,* or maybe even *Attack of the Fifty Foot Negro.*

The real titles were worse.

Fel passed LaStanza an orange paperback with a title in bright green print, *The Myth of the Six Million.*

"The fuck."

"Yeah," Fel agreed. "Fucker wrote an entire book about how the Holocaust was a propaganda stunt concocted by the Soviets."

"Jesus."

Fel handed LaStanza a thin leather hardback with its title in gold leaf, *The Mongrel Races.* No need to explain that one. Anyone from that sandy island off the Italian boot knew what it was like to be a mongrel. Sicily had been conquered by the Phoenicians, the Greeks, Carthaginians, Romans, Saracens, French, and then the Napolitanos before the Americans and British in WWII. Talk about a mongrel race.

"My favorite," Fel said, "is this one." He held up a red hardback with a black lettered title, *The Pure Wife.*

LaStanza gave Fel that look, the look a six year old would give if someone tried to explain that the guy in the movie with Bonzo, the chimp, that guy was the most important man in the country.

Fel leaned back in his chair and put his hands behind his head.

"I Read that one all the way through," he said. "Bet you didn't know that men are ruled by reason and logic. And women, they're ruled by emotions. That's why we gotta take care of them."

Reason? Logic? The fuck.

"Fucker should write Science Fiction," LaStanza said. "You know, *Today the World—Tomorrow the Stars!* or *What Entropy Doesn't Mean To Me.*"

"Entropy?"

"Yeah. I went to Catholic School. I learned big words."

Fel passed LaStanza a computer print out of Norwood's arrest record. He was surprised to see more than one arrest. Everyone knew of the well publicized enciting a riot charge. LaStanza read the disposition listed next to that charge. Convicted. Sentenced to 6 months. Sentence suspended. Active Probation for 12 months.

The next entry was an arrest for ROMV—Reckless Operation of a Moving Vehicle (2 counts). The charge was dismissed. No surprise there. Fuckin D.A.'s Office dropped so many charges it was a miracle they didn't cause earthquakes. Norwood must have been on a joy ride, or ran one too many red lights and pissed off the police.

The next entry was the most interesting. Three years ago, long after Norwood was past those self-proclaimed "misjudgments of youth," he was arrested in Athens, Georgia, by the ATF for possession of an explosive device.

LaStanza showed the entry to Fel, who leaned forward and said, "Oh, yeah."

The disposition of the charge was a nolle prosse.

"No prosecution?"

Fel leaned back again and looked up at the ratty ceiling. "Ever hear of Providencia?"

LaStanza was getting a headache now. He shook his head no.

"It's an island about a hundred miles off the coast of Nicaragua. It was all over the news. About two years ago. A buncha skin heads tried to take the island and set up some sort of Aryan nation."

"Yeah," LaStanza remembered something in the paper. Bald headed assholes in handcuffs being led off by Feds. "What happened? I forgot."

"Stupid fucks never made it out of Louisiana."

LaStanza waited for the punchline. He knew Fel Jones well enough to know there had to be a weenie. He could see the hint of a glint in his old partner's dark eyes.

"Guess who was an unindicted co-conspirator?"

"No shit?"

"I think that's why that explosive device charge was nolle prossed."

It took a second for that one to sink in. LaStanza stood up.

"He copped out on the others?"

Fel shrugged. "The Feds don't tell us shit like that."

LaStanza sat back down. "What else have you got?" It wasn't a real headache because it was already gone.

LaStanza stepped out from under the canopy of thick oak branches across the street from the Norwood house. Raindrops left from the day's shower fell from the leaves, peppering him as he crossed Prytania. At least it was cooler in the late afternoon after all the rain. He had to jump a puddle next to the curb and step over a muddy spot beneath the wet magnolias across the sidewalk from the immaculately white house.

Norwood answered the doorbell. Dressed in an off-white safari shirt and baggy light gray pants and tan boat shoes, Norwood pulled a pipe from his mouth, smiled and extended a friendly right hand to shake.

"Detective LaStanza, I presume."

LaStanza shook the hand firmly and then reached into his coat pocket and withdrew his credentials. Norwood examined the photo ID and said, "How does a gimlet sound to you?"

"I didn't catch that," LaStanza said.

"Gimlet," Norwood said, flashing an ultra white smile.

Gimlet? That's a tool. LaStanza's father used one to bore holes in wood when he made the wooden wagon for his boys.

"Gin and lime juice, Old Sport." Norwood said as he pat LaStanza on the shoulder as if they were college chums.

Old Sport?

"They're quite refreshing," Norwood said, as he slipped the pipe back between his teeth and led the way through the house to the living room with the three sofas. Darker with the shades drawn, the room smelled of pipe smoke and air conditioning.

"I saw you talking earlier to the Smiths across the street," Norwood said. "That's called canvassing, isn't it?"

LaStanza nodded and looked around the room, at the vases and tables, at the pictures of Byron, Buffy, and Biff at varies ages, at the two framed Audubon prints on easels at the back of the room.

So he watched me canvass his neighbors. Good. LaStanza wanted his attention.

Norwood stepped over to a table next to a large bookcase and poured two drinks into tumblers, dropped a slice of lime in each and turned back to LaStanza.

"No thanks."

"Don't give me that old 'I'm on duty' cliché."

LaStanza pulled his note pad out and said, "I'm not here to drink."

Norwood put his pipe on the table and brought both glasses to the coffee table and sat in the same sofa his wife had used the previous evening.

"OK. Shoot," he said with a smile, crossing his legs like

a woman. Norwood took a sip of his drink and waved to the sofa on the other side of the coffee table. "Sit down, Old Sport."

LaStanza put his Little Fuckin' Radio on the coffee table and sat, readjusting his magnum on his hip.

"What do you know about the murder down the street, Tuesday before last?"

"That's what I like. A direct question." Norwood put his drink down. "Actually I wasn't aware of it until this morning, when Willie Sherman called and told me about your conversation last night." Norwood shook his head. His styled blond hair didn't move one millimeter when she shook it. "A terrible thing." Norwood reached for his drink. "I feel awful that something like that happened so close to my home and I wasn't even aware."

He said it like it was LaStanza's fault for not running over and saying, "Massa Norwood. One of the darkies got hisself all burned up."

"Where were you that night?"

The politician smile was back. "Out of town," Norwood said smoothly. "In Nashville. I was with Senator Dickson of Metairie. I came back around six the following evening."

Dickson was a big wig Republican. LaStanza had seen his thin face all over the tube, bragging about Reagan's new Republicanism.

Norwood took another sip.

"You should try this. It's awfully refreshing, Old Sport. It's a British drink. You can make it with vodka, but I prefer gin."

"I'd also like the names and addresses of your bodyguards. The ones that guard this house at night."

"Certainly. Anything I can do for our boys in blue."

Yeah? What about the time you stood up with that microphone and pointed out the cops in the crowd? You fuckin' low life.

LaStanza looked back at Norwood's blue politician eyes. It wasn't a contest to see who'd blink first, but it was a stare. LaStanza let his light green Sicilian eyes return an emotionless stare for a couple seconds before he said, "I'll take that list now."

"Fine," Norwood said, scooping up his drink and rising. LaStanza grabbed his LFR and followed Norwood back through the house to his office, which was behind the room where Biff had been looking out the window yesterday. With wall-to-wall bookshelves along three walls and double windows that faced Harmony Street, the office was dominated by a large mahogany desk.

Norwood walked around the desk and placed his gimlet on its green blotter. "One second," he said, stepping into an office behind his. LaStanza could see there was a larger office back there with at least two desks, several phones and a copy machine. Norwood made a copy of the sheet he'd fished out of a file cabinet and and gave it to LaStanza.

"These are the men who guard my house," he said. "If you like I could ask them about..."

"No thanks. That's what the city pays me to do." LaStanza folded the sheet and slipped them into his jacket pocket.

"If there's anything else I can do to help..."

"I'll be in touch."

Norwood led LaStanza back through the house. They stepped into the foyer as someone bounded up the stairs. LaStanza spotted Biff just as the boy darted into a room.

"Don't run up the stairs, son," Norwood said loudly, then added to LaStanza in a hushed voice, "Kids."

"You know," he said as he grabbed the front door knob. "Your reputation preceded you, Detective LaStanza."

LaStanza waited.

"You've got quite a reputation."

LaStanza still waited.

Norwood smiled and said, "A prefect solution record in Homicide. Tell me, seriously. What does it feel like to shoot someone?"

LaStanza narrowed his left eye and said, "You writing another book?"

"No. No offense. I've just always wanted to ask that question of someone who knew the answer." The blue eyes were at it again, trying to see something in LaStanza's eyes. If Norwood could look deep enough, he just might see the leopard pacing back and forth.

Norwood opened the door and stepped back, allowing a fresh breath of rain-filled air to swirl in. The rain had started up again.

"Would you like an umbrella?"

"No thanks. I like the rain." LaStanza slipped his LFR into his back pocket and his note pad into his coat pocket, turned up the lapels of his linen jacket and walked off the gallery into a nice autumn rain.

At the corner of Prytania and Eighth, he stopped beneath another magnolia and watched the rain stop. He moved from the shelter of the tree and crossed Eighth. Just as he reached the first house, Mark Land called him on the radio.

LaStanza pulled his LFR out and clicked the mike and said, "Go ahead, 3122."

"I need you over on Palm Terrace. 29S. Second District needs some help."

LaStanza stopped and leaned on the front gate of the fence.

"3122 to 3124. I know you hear me. Are you 10-4?"

"10-4."

LaStanza looked at his watch—3:15 p.m.

Fuck me! He felt like shouting it, but instead he sucked it in, slipped his LFR into his back pocket once again and headed for the Maserati, which he'd parked again in the parking lot behind Bultman's Funeral Home.

Fuckin' interruptions!

He turned just in time to spot the Catahoula racing his way. LaStanza folded his arms as the hound glided past, tongue hanging out. For the first time LaStanza noticed that it was actually multicolored with different shades of brown splotches. The dog loped across Louisiana and continued down Prytania.

Turning off St. Charles Avenue onto the narrow one-way street called Palm Terrace, LaStanza remembered what he told Jodie the first time she handled a suicide. She looked nervous.

"You know that they say about suicide?" he said.

"No, what?"

"Suicide'll kill ya'."

She gave him that sour look for the first time, the one with her nose crinkled and her cat eyes squinted all up.

LaStanza pulled up behind a marked unit parked along the left side of the street. He spotted a uniform standing outside what looked like a garage along the right side of a small white bungalow with a red tile roof and green trim.

Climbing out of the Maserati, LaStanza looked around at a street in a time warp. A series of nearly identical stucco doubles lined either side of Palm Terrace. The doubles were connected at their garages, recessed from the street by driveways. The front doors faced the driveways, suspended in alcoves beneath archways supported by white spiral columns.

The doubles across the street bore even numbers—2, 4, 6. The odd numbers were on his side. The bungalows were old fashioned like from the nineteen-twenties or thirties, a lot like the bungalow he lived in near City Park, the one the crazy fuckin' Colombians blew up during the Electric Daughter case. The architecture reminded LaStanza of an old time black-and-white movie. He expected Cagney or Bogie to step up and say, "What do you want, Copper?"

One thing LaStanza noticed, on his way up the small steep driveway to where the uniformed officer waited, was that there were no palm trees on Palm Terrace. In fact there were no trees, except for the oaks back along St. Charles.

A balding sergeant with salt-and-pepper hair and a thick moustache met LaStanza at the top of the driveway. At least this face was familiar. LaStanza wrote the sergeant's name in his notes—Daniel Dravot.

"Pretty sure it's a suicide," Dravot said in a gravel voice, "but it's a doozie. Go take a look." Dravot pointed to the open garage.

Moving closer, LaStanza passed a woman in a gray dress sitting on a low brick wall between the alcove and the garage. The woman had her head forward, resting in her hands. Three steps later, LaStanza took in the bizarre sight in the garage.

A patrolman with a silver clipboard stood just inside the doors. In front of him was a gallows—a genuine American wooden gallows straight out of the old west with six steps leading up to a platform with a hanging rope suspended from a crossbeam supported by two upright beams. A turned-over stool lay on the platform. Its trap door was open. Beneath the trap door lay the body of an obese white male in a green tee-shirt and blue pants.

LaStanza stepped into the garage and took a few steps to the right. He could see the body was barefoot and decapitated. Its head lay about ten feet on the far side of the body, facing the driveway and the street. LaStanza looked up at the rope again and saw blood on the noose.

"There's a suicide note up next to the stool," the patrolman said.

"Who's the woman?"

"Wife. She found him."

LaStanza stepped back to the door of the garage. "What's your name?"

"Carnehan. David Carnehan. You're LaStanza right?"

LaStanza nodded. Looking at the severed head from a different angle, he said, "Have you called the crime lab?"

"I certainly did," Carnehan dragged out the word so it sounded like, "cer...tain...ly."

"And don't touch anything."

"No pro...blem...o. I'm not a rookie." The patrolman smiled at LaStanza. Solidly built with curly brown hair, the man looked a lot like Michael Caine, the actor.

LaStanza went out to talk with the wife. He asked if it was OK to sit next to her. She nodded without lifting her head from her hands.

"I'm Detective LaStanza," he said. "I'm gonna need your husband's name."

"Manny Peldecular."

He had her spell it, as well as her first name, which was Wilhomena.

No wonder he killed himself!

"When did you find him?"

Wilhomena lifted her head up and pulled her hair away from a plain face. She turned her deep set, green eyes to him and told him how she'd found Manny about an hour ago when she returned home from shopping.

"He'd been depressed for some time now," she said. "Got laid off from Shell Oil two years ago. He was an engineer. He had medical problems. Back problems, vision problems, prostatitis." That sent a shiver up LaStanza's spine.

He made quick work of the interview, finishing just as the crime lab technician finally arrived at the same time two of Wilhomena's sisters drove up in a brown stationwagon.

LaStanza had one more question of the widow Peldecular. "Did you know he was building a gallows in your garage?"

"The garage was his. I was just happy that he was working on something."

LaStanza pulled away from Wilhomena's shiny eyes, leaving her to share her private pain with her now weeping sisters.

LaStanza followed the bespectacled tech into the garage and watched him take photos and measurements. He went up on the scaffold before the tech recovered the suicide note. The scaffold smelled of fresh cut lumber and faintly of blood.

Leaning over he read the note printed in neat block letters.

> *Willy—insurance papers in the top drawer of my desk.*
> *Police—I killed myself. I committed suicide.*
> *Press—Shell Oil drove me to this, the bastards.*
> *Not bad, huh? I built it myself.*
>
> *Sincerely,*
> *Manuel Josephus Peldecular*

LaStanza watched the tech photograph the body—the limp hands lying palms up, the bare feet pointing outward in either direction, the bloody stump of the man's neck, the severed vertebrae, the ripped blood vessels and torn muscles.

Manny Peldecular's head was photographed before the tech measured its distance from fixed points in the garage. Then the tech triangulated measurements from the body to fixed points. LaStanza looked closely at Manny's head, at the flaccid cheeks, the half-opened dull eyes, the jagged tear where the rope ripped his head off. A foot beyond the head lay a pair of thick-lensed glasses.

"Hey," LaStanza told the tech. "Get shots of the glasses. And measure it too." He meant triangulate measurements to and from the glasses.

The tech, whose name was Simmons, said, "Yeah. Yeah."

"And I want exact measurements of the gallows too."

"Why?"

"Because I plan to build one to personally fuckin' hang the next crime lab tech that asks me why. Capish?"

Simmons readjusted his glasses and said, "Jesus, what's got into you?"

"Just do it, OK?"

All LaStanza needed was to be dragged in front of a

fuckin' grand jury and asked for exact measurements because some wise-ass wanted to know if the gallows could really hang someone.

Dravot and Carnehan were watching from the open garage door. LaStanza moved next to them and said, "Who opened the garage door?"

"We couldn't find his head," Dravot said, "so I opened it."

"It was too dark inside," Carnehan said.

Made sense.

Folding his arms Carnehan added, "I saw a flick on cable the other night. A man built himself a giant mouse-trap, laid his head on the release pin and killed himself. When his wife found his body she told the detective she thought she'd married a man but wound up marrying a mouse. She had a real bitchy voice."

"That's a real case," Dravot said. "Happened in Wisconsin."

"No shit?"

"Fuckin' A."

Dravot turned to LaStanza and said, "What did this guy do for a living?"

"Engineer. Got laid off from Shell a couple years ago."

"Well," Carnehan said, "he did a helluva job building this thing."

"I'd say he needed to work on his physics," Dravot said, "or he'd still have his head."

"Too fat," Carnehan said, like the second on a good comedy tag team.

"Fuckin' right," LaStanza said moving out of the way of the two coroner's assistant who stepped in with a black body bag atop a stainless steel gurney.

"You got a small bag to go along with that big one?" Dravot asked.

The assistants didn't answer. You had as much luck getting a rise out of a cadaver as you would one of them.

LaStanza spotted a white flash to his right and saw a poodle dart into the garage and make a bee-line for the head. Turning, LaStanza spotted a tall woman in a low cut red blouse tight gold pedal-pushers, spiked high heels and a gold bandanna around her head out on the sidewalk. She cupped her hands around her mouth and called out, "Bootsie, Bootsie! Come out of there."

One of the coroner's assistants said, "Hey, y'all better come get this dog. He's latched on to the head."

"Hey," Dravot called back to the woman on the sidewalk. "You know Manny Peldecular?"

The woman smiled and said yes.

"Well, you better come get your dog before he eats Manny's head."

LaStanza had to hand it to Dravot, the man said it cool as shit.

LaStanza called Lizette at five-thirty and then again at six. No answer. At six-thirty he left a message with the concierge, then went down to the refrigerator and pulled out the white beans and rice and breaded pork chops Brulee had left for him.

He ate in the large dining room at a table that sat sixteen, beneath a crystal chandelier the size of a basketball goal, backboard included. The table was cherrywood. The setting was china, not the fine china, just the everyday china. The silverware was silver, not stainless steel. Food tasted better on silver. Even beans.

LaStanza thought about all that, thought about a mid-city boy living in an uptown mansion. What was that drink again? A gimlet? LaStanza remembered watching his father build that big old wagon for his boys, boring out the axle holes with a spiral shank tool he called a gimlet. The muscles of his father's large arms twisted as he worked. They were round and sweaty. He remembered his father's strong hands hammering the boards together.

He remembered how his brother pulled him in the wagon that first glorious day, away from their house, down bumpy North Bernadotte Street, across City Park Avenue, and between the huge oaks of City Park. His brother pulled him through the long beards of Spanish Moss that felt itchy on his face. He remembered them both pulling that wagon around the neighborhood searching for bottles to turn in for their deposits so they could buy the latest issues of *Spider-Man, Daredevil,* and *The Fantastic Four.*

LaStanza closed his eyes and saw his brother's face again, as if he were watching a video tape. He saw Joe turn and look at him and laugh. Joe always laughed at Dino, cruelly sometimes, as big brothers often did. For a second Joe was ten, his hair cut in a crew-cut; then Joe was a teen-angel again in a leather jacket, hair slicked back; then Joe was a police sergeant laughing at his little brother the rookie.

If he concentrated hard enough he could hear Joe's voice, that soft familiar voice of his big brother telling him it was OK to hold his hand when they passed the Canal Cemeteries on their way back from seeing *Thirteen Ghosts* and *House on Haunted Hill* at the Carrollton Theater.

He could feel Joe's strong hand around his.

LaStanza got up, picked up his plate and glass, and put them in the dishwasher. He fixed himself a stiff scotch rocks and went into the study, turning off every light on the way. Sitting in the big easy chair in front of a fireplace they never used, he sipped the cold burning scotch and let his mind roll back to a time when comic books cost twelve cents, a Milky Way was a nickel; to summer nights listening to the Yankees beat everyone, and watermelon fights, and playing cavalry in the backyard, and climbing the ancient oaks of City Park to fight dragons and rescue princesses—to a world where his brother was still alive, still running and playing along the trails of City Park, his blue jeans torn and dusty.

He could hear the LaStanza boys racing home for supper, washing up with their old man in the kitchen sink, squirming into straight back chairs under a bright kitchen light for their mother's spaghetti and meat balls.

Sometimes, if he concentrated hard enough he could feel Joe lying in bed next to him, could feel the weight of his big brother who had spent the day slaying dragons and fighting those *Marvel* villains—*Doctor Doom,* and *Magneto,* and *Kraven The Hunter.* Joe could vanquish any monster that had the audacity to try to live under their bed. Joe could out-run, out-hit, out-think any kid they ever knew.

Then, one night it all went away. Joe went away. Killed in the line of duty. Killed in the line of duty.

Fuck duty! His brother was gone.

LaStanza sat up. He saw Joe lying in his coffin, all decked out in New Orleans blue. He said it before and he'd say it until the day he died. He should have died when he was eight—when the world was full of wonder and Joe was still alive.

God, he missed his brother.

The phone rang.

He stumbled over to Lizette's desk and picked up the receiver and croaked out an hello.

"Babe, are you all right?" Lizette said.

"What time is it?"

"It's two-thirty in the morning here."

"Where were you?"

"Dinner and then we went to the Folies-Bergere."

"The what?" LaStanza pulled the secretary chair out from Lizette's desk and sat heavily in it.

"The Folies. It's a show. Huge sets and half naked dancers. It's wild." Lizette cleared her throat and said, "Are you OK, you sound strange."

"Just one of those days."

"Tell me about it while I strip."

"Let me see. A dog tried to steal the head of my latest suicide victim and guess who lives a block away from my Pleasant Street murder scene?"

"What dog?"

"Byron Norwood."

"Wait, you're going too fast. Something happened to

Byron Norwood's dog?"

LaStanza took in a breath and said, "No. I said a dog tried to steal a dead guy's head—and I found out that Byron Norwood lives a block away from my murder scene. Do I make sense now?"

"No. Yeah, I think so."

He could hear her moving the receiver around as she took off her clothes.

"What are you wearing?"

"Now all I have on are panties. But I was wearing a red sequin minidress, black pantyhose, red heels, a white bra and panties."

LaStanza rubbed his eyes. "What sequin minidress?"

"I bought it here. You're gonna love it. It's very tight."

"You were out awfully late," he said.

"I'm sorry I missed your call," she said, her voice dropping an octave.

LaStanza reached for his drink and realized he had none. He could use another.

"I interviewed Norwood today."

"What's he like?"

"He kept calling me Old Sport."

Lizette let out a breath and said, "Oh, yeah. You remember *The Great Gatsby*, don't you?"

He'd read it his second year at Loyola in a Twentieth Century American Lit Class.

"Yeah, I remember."

"Gatsby kept calling Nick 'Old Sport'."

"Oh yeah."

LaStanza thought of something else. How did Manny put it? "Not bad, huh? I built it myself."

"What did you say?"

LaStanza found he was laughing.

"What's so funny."

"I just remembered how Gatsby ended up."

Chestnut Street

With the stink of Manny Peldecular's autopsy still in his nostrils, LaStanza walked up to the rear of the dark green pickup parked next to the Norwood house. The man in the driver's seat saw him coming and looked back as LaStanza tapped on the side of the truck with is LFR.

"Hi ya'‘," the man said nodding to LaStanza.

"You mind stepping out?"

"Sure."

LaStanza took a step back as a large man with a round chest and linebacker arms climbed out of the cab and stretched. With shaggy light brown hair and a thick moustache two shades darker, the man had a craggy face with a deep cleft in his chin. Smiling at LaStanza, he looked like a bloated Kirk Douglas.

The man stuck his hand out to shake and said, "George Meade. You must be LaStanza."

The handshake was firm and quick. LaStanza slipped the LFR into the back pocket of his faded jeans. He pulled the ball point pen and small note pad out of the front pocket of his dress white shirt, which he'd worn out, over a maroon Loyola tee-shirt.

"You know why I'm here," LaStanza said, jotting the date atop a fresh page.

"Yeah, but you're gonna have to say pretty please." The

man crossed his arms and grinned.

LaStanza gleeked him, tapping down his gangster sunglasses to peek over the top at Meade. "Say what?"

"I'm just fuckin' with ya'," Meade said, smiling wider. "I'm ex-police. What can I do for you?"

Jesus. Ex-cops could be the best witness or a policeman's worst nightmare because they knew it all.

"What do you know about the murder down the street?"

"Let me see. I have this memorized. I wasn't here that night. I saw it in the paper. Yes, I've seen plenty street people around here. No, they're never any trouble. So let me see, I don't know much that can help you, except that you really pulled Willie's chain the other day."

LaStanza tucked that away, about Willie. Good to get a reaction like that.

"Anything else I can help you with?"

Before LaStanza could ask his next question a cool breeze passed over the men, a *cool* breeze—as if someone opened a refrigerator door.

Meade turned completely around. LaStanza fanned his shirt as the breeze increased momentarily before fading. Meade looked back with a what-the-hell-was-that expression on his face.

LaStanza cleared his throat and said, "How long have you worked for Norwood?"

Meade nodded, as if he saw it coming. "A year. And I'm not ashamed of what I do. I'm just an ex-cop. Shit, I don't know anything else." Shrugging as he scraped the heel of his left boot on the street, he said, "I don't give a shit what Norwood preaches. This is the best paying job I had since I left JP."

LaStanza put "JP" in his notes. Meade was an ex-Jefferson Parish deputy.

"How long were you a cop?"

"Twelve years."

"You hang around much with Willie Sherman and the other bodyguard?"

"Benny Butler. No. You know how there's always a shucker on every platoon, someone who won't handle his calls, who does he best to avoid work?"

LaStanza nodded.

"Willie and Benny are shucker deluxes. Couple of real muggle-heads."

"Know what they do when they're not bodyguarding?"

"Tormenting dogs. Sniffing bicycles seats. Comparing dick sizes with a magnifying glass."

LaStanza heard enough. He pulled a business card out of his ID folder and handed it to Meade.

"Yeah," Meade said as LaStanza turned to walk away. "If I hear anything, I'll call ya'."

It could have been a con job. Meade could be as rabid a nigger hater as any of them. Maybe it was the way described street people—"No, they're never any trouble." Sometimes you have to follow a gut instinct.

Anyway, LaStanza figured most of what Meade fed him was true. True enough for him to move away, back down Harmony, to knock on yet more doors.

The house directly behind Norwood's was occupied by an insurance salesman with a plain face and Harpo Marx hair. He knew where Prytania Street was all right, but wasn't sure that Pleasant Street was a block from his house. "Isn't it on the other side of Louisiana Avenue?"

Stepping back on Harmony Street, LaStanza felt that breeze again. He turned and faced it. No doubt it was coming off the lake, filtering over the city on its way down to the gulf. It wasn't a rain-swelled breeze or even a damp breeze. It was uncharacteristically dry. Yes, Autumn was arriving all right. Finally.

That's how it went in New Orleans. One minute it was steamy, the next moment the humidity vanished and a ten degree drop in temperature meant Autumn had arrived.

Moving on to the next house, LaStanza remembered what Tennessee Williams said on that PBS show Lizette had found on cable one night. It was dated, and ole

Tennessee was sitting next to the pool in the patio of his French Quarter home. Laughing, Tennessee said the only time to live in New Orleans was the spring and the autumn—the summer was a steam bath and winter—too damn wet, cold and windy.

LaStanza worked his way down Harmony Street all the way to Chestnut Street where that other witness lived, the one stopped by Owen and DeLeon walking his dog the night of the murder.

Chestnut was more narrow than Harmony because of the trees lining each side of the street, and because the houses were closer to the sidewalks. Shaded by oaks and several huge weeping willows, the street was so dark LaStanza pulled off his gangster glasses and hooked an arm of the glasses down the front of his tee-shirt.

It wasn't as cool on Chestnut, away from the breeze. LaStanza rang the doorbell of 3203 Chestnut. The ring was answered by loud barking. He took a step back from the white wooden door and leaned against the green railing of the porch and waited. He looked around the narrow front yard then back at the green shutters of the white wooden house. He heard a male voice and locks being unlatched. The door opened and a tall man with white hair leaned against the screen door and said, "Yes?"

LaStanza opened his shirt to show his badge and introduced himself.

"Bert Waters," the man said, reaching down to grab the collar of a large German shepherd that nuzzled its snout against the screen door. The dog yapped twice, then started panting.

"What can I do you for?"

LaStanza hated it when people talked like that.

"A couple weeks ago, you were questioned by uniformed officers on Prytania Street, about 12:30 in the morning,"

"Yes, are you the detective who left his card on my door?"

"Yeah."

"I left two messages for you but you never called back."

Fuck!

"We got a message-eating monster at headquarters," LaStanza said in disgust.

"Well, come on in," Bert Waters said, pulling the dog back in. "Have a seat while I put Otto in the back yard."

LaStanza put his LFR on an end table next to a plush dark green sofa and looked around a room out of an interior design magazine—wall etchings in gold leaf frames, Chinese vases, oriental rugs, a bookcase filled with leather-bound books, and two brass-and-porcelain Casablanca ceiling fans.

"I walk Otto every night," Waters said as he came back in with two bottles of Coca-Cola. He put one on a coaster in front of LaStanza. Slivers of ice slowly worked their way down the sides of the Coke bottle.

"Thanks," LaStanza said reaching for the drink.

Waters sat in a matching straight back chair off to LaStanza's right. Wearing a white polo shirt over faded baggy jeans, Waters also wore brown sandals *and* white socks.

"In summer I walk after the Channel Four news and *M*A*S*H*. Too hot to walk during daylight. During the winter, we walk after the six o'clock news. I don't worry about getting jumped. Not with Otto. He's an Alsatian you know. Pedigree. We take the same route, which you need to know."

Waters pointed to the note pad LaStanza just pulled out. He wiggled his finger like the nuns used to when it was time to takes notes because they were about to say something very fuckin' important.

"We always walk over to Harmony and down across Camp, across Magazine, across Constance to Laurel, where I grew up as child. I lived in that little yellow shotgun at Harmony and Laurel."

Oh yeah. Sure. I know the house. Everybody knows that little fuckin' yellow house.

"Then we go uptown across Pleasant, across Toledano,

Louisiana, Delachaise to Aline, where I used to teach. You know, that big gray building that's now gone condo?"

Doesn't everyone?

"Then we walk up Aline across Constance, Magazine, Camp, Chestnut, Coliseum..."

The goofy fuck's gonna give me every street name. Watch.

"...up to Prytania, Pitt, across St. Charles, Carondelet, Baronne, up to Dryades and over to Foucher. I used to teach at Cohen High. You know Cohen?"

"Handled a suicide there last year," LaStanza said.

"Suicide?"

They didn't tell you? The nerve.

"Yeah, a janitor hanged himself in the girl's locker room."

"What was his name?"

"I don't remember."

"Was it Charlie?"

I don't fuckin' remember.

LaStanza shrugged.

"Was it Jerome?"

"I think his name was Izoslavich or Jonoslavich," LaStanza lied.

"I didn't know him," Waters said in obvious relief. He took a sip of Coke, wiped his mouth with the back of his left hand, and said, "Did you discover why he killed himself?"

"Not really." LaStanza wasn't about to tell him that *why* wasn't one tenth as important as *who, what, when, where* and especially *how*—to a homicide dick.

"OK. Where was I?"

"Foucher Street."

And so it went until finally, Waters rounded Louisiana on to Prytania Street and ran into two uniformed officers.

"I didn't see anyone on the street until I saw those officers and that was at 12:30 a.m., exactly. After they questioned me, I went back home via Louisiana Avenue down to Chestnut. Usually I take Harmony home."

LaStanza took another sip of the icy Coke. There were

slivers of ice floating in the drink. He loved Coke that cold.

Bert Waters picked up his phone, punched out a number and said, "It's Bert. Why don't you come over? And bring Bertha."

LaStanza almost made a clean getaway, quickly downing the rest of the Coke and finishing off his notes. He even managed to stand before there was a knock at the door. Waters jumped up, opened the door, and let in two creatures who introduced themselves as Bertha Dale and Judd Cole. Bertha looked so much like Aunt Bee from the old Andy Griffith Show that LaStanza did a double take. Judd Cole was the spitting image of Johnny Jacolucci, the ugliest boy in the history of Rummel High.

Judd had the same mis-matched eyes, the left one a half inch higher than the right, the same hook nose, the same lipless mouth that slobbered when he talked. He even had the same frizzy carrot-red hair.

"Oh my," Bertha, the Aunt-Bee-clone said, "A detective."

"Yep," Judd slobbered, a thin string of saliva slinging down to his skinny neck.

"We have something to tell you," Bertha said, running her hands down the side of her abundant hips. She wore an Aunt Bee high-collared dress to her ankles.

I got to get the fuck out of here, LaStanza thought just as Bertha said, "Have you been to that white house at the corner of Harmony and Prytania?"

LaStanza cleared his throat and said, "Yes."

"Men have been carrying shotguns in and out of that place."

"Gasoline cans too," Judd added. His physique was showcased by his gray undershirt that hung like a wet rag from his bony shoulders and went half-way down his baggy yellow shorts.

"Gasoline cans?" LaStanza said as he sat back down.

"And the parties," Bertha said, raising her hands and shaking them like a revival preacher. "Wild parties like you wouldn't believe."

LaStanza pulled his note pad and pen out again and settled back on the thick sofa and said, "Gasoline cans?"

An hour and an excruciating headache later LaStanza escaped Waters' house and made his way back up Harmony Street. Meade's pickup wasn't there. LaStanza glanced at his watch—four o'clock. He felt a sour rumbling in his belly so he turned up Prytania to walk back to Bultman's for his car.

The breeze picked up as he crossed Pleasant Street. It stirred the cicadas in the trees, and they began their listless singsong buzzing. The buzzing echoed down the streets. At his car, he stopped and closed his eyes a minute and remembered late summer days sitting out on the front porch with Joe back on Bernadotte Street, listening to the call of the cicadas echo from the oaks of City Park, the sky orange with the setting sun.

On the way home, he thought about another Saturday night alone in the mansion. Then he thought about Sunday, about his mother's spaghetti dinner and watching another useless Saints game with his old man. His mother would have her hair up in a bun and sit quietly across the white porcelain-top table in their kitchen and pick at her spaghetti. Stoic, she would retreat into her private world where Joe still lived. She would mouth words in silence, as if she was talking to her sons and her husband back when his hair was still dark and he never drank. If she caught LaStanza watching her, she would smile and ask how the spaghetti was, then go back to hers and slowly drift away again.

The old man would be half looped before dinner and completely looped by the third quarter, sitting in the old easy chair in front of the Zenith, watching the Saints drop another. His mother would be at the far end of the couch, away from the TV, doing needlepoint.

Then again, maybe the Saints would win one, or maybe the old man would be out by the fourth quarter and LaStanza could sink back on the couch and take a nice long nap in a house where he grew up, among the familiar smells, and all the memories.

Watching the Whippets unpack, LaStanza rolled down the front windows of Lizette's Maserati to let in the nice Sunday afternoon breeze. Mr. Whippet did most of the carrying, while his wife shoo-shooed their black-and-tan terrier into the house. Besides a bright yellow tee-shirt, Mr. Whippet's get-up included plaid shorts, white sandals and black knee-hi socks held up by those sock garters—garters and shorts!

Daphne wore an oversized Disney tee-shirt over extra baggy shorts that reached below her knees and carried her own loot into the house. Cleola stood at the front door and greeted each. She wasn't about to do any toting. *Smart woman.*

LaStanza leaned back in the seat and ran through the information busy-body Bertha and her compadre Judd had given him about the Norwood house. Bertha had personally seen men carrying shotguns in and out of the house on two occasions. Judd had seen "wild parties" with women and men at the same party and once witnessed a mini cross-burning in the backyard.

Although both were sure men had toted gasoline cans in and out of the house, they were fuzzy about the details. "You told me that," Bertha said, pointing to Judd. "No," he argued. "You told *me.*"

Stretching behind the steering wheel, LaStanza watched Daphne Whippet leave the front door and hurry two doors down to a cream colored house along the same side of Prytania. She carried a large white plastic bag with her. LaStanza remembered canvassing that house. They had kids.

He looked at his watch. It was five-thirty. Climbing out of the car, he slipped his off-duty .38 into the holster at the small of his back and pulled his dress blue shirt on to cover the gun and badge clipped to his belt. He grabbed his LFR and stretched. The cicadas started up again, buzzing and echoing.

He walked down to Harmony Street and approached the red and black pickup from the front. The man behind the wheel still didn't see him until he tapped on the door with his LFR. The man jumped and let out a nervous laugh.

"Police," LaStanza said, "you wanna step out."

The man had a problem climbing out. Balding, he stood near six feet and weighed close to three hundred pounds. Wearing a tight fitting gray tee-shirt and jeans held up by a wide cowboy belt that he had to keep pulling up, the man nodded and said, "Willie told me you'd be around."

"You have a driver's license?"

The man pulled out a long black wallet with a chrome chain attached to his belt, as if he carried state secrets. He produced a bent up license. LaStanza ran his fingers over the plastic coated license and felt a half dozen staple holes. It was an old cop trick. In Louisiana, when you get a ticket you have to surrender your driver's license. The license is stapled to the traffic ticket. The more staples, the more times the driver had pissed off the police enough to get a ticket. Real assholes had their licenses stapled three or four times to one ticket.

His name was Benjamin Butler and he lived in Bogalusa. LaStanza jotted the pertinent information in his notes before passing the license back to Butler.

"You know why I'm here," he said.

"I sure do. But I don't know anything 'bout no murder."

LaStanza went through the routine, asking all the questions, getting the predictable answers. He watched Butler. The man wasn't nervous, like ole Willie, didn't appear too bright or observant, nor seemed to care.

LaStanza thanked him and saw a wave of relief cross the wide face as Butler prepared to climb back into his truck. Backing away, LaStanza added, "They still hold those big barbecue rallies up by Bogalusa?"

"Sure do," Butler said, opening the door.

"I used to go out with a girl from Franklinton," LaStanza lied. "We went to a couple barbecues that went well into the night. They had fireworks on the river."

"Yeah," Butler said, rubbing his belly. "I done ate more than my share. Drank more, too."

LaStanza pretended to yawn before he said, "I can't remember exactly, but was that on the Bogue Chitto or the Pearl?"

"Bogue Chitto River," Butler said, "about a mile from Willie's place." As soon as he said that, his face took on a puzzled look and he looked away.

LaStanza smiled and walked back to the Maserati. He barely had to break stride to squash a cockroach lumbering down the sidewalk in front of him. It popped nicely beneath his tennis shoe. He wiped the shoe in the grass before climbing back into Lizette's car.

He rolled down the front windows again, to allow the early evening air to flow through and thought back to when he first heard about the Klan barbecue rallies outside Bogalusa. He couldn't remember. He figured the bodyguards were regular customers. He just wasn't sure they still held those rallies, until now.

The drone of the cicadas rose. A patrol car turned off Eighth Street and head his way. It slowed as it crossed Pleasant Street and crossed over the wrong way to his side of the street. He recognized Owen behind the wheel, his elbow leaning out the driver's side window, and DeLeon with his elbow out the window on the other side.

"Nice short," Owen said, stopping the unit.

"My wife's," LaStanza said, forcing back a genuine yawn. Looking at DeLeon he said, "How was the House of the Mouse?"

"Tiring. My son wore me out."

Owen signaled to an on-coming car they'd better go around in case they hadn't noticed he was in a police car...and wasn't going to fuckin' move.

LaStanza waited until Owen looked back before he

said, "Remember Willie Sherman, the guy in the pickup y'all stopped that night?"

"Yeah. The redneck."

"He's one of Byron Norwood's bodyguards. Norwood owns that white house at Prytania and Harmony."

DeLeon looked back toward the house.

"There's always a bodyguard out there in a pickup," LaStanza said. "Y'all ever run into them?"

Owen shook his head and smiled, "We will now."

A beep tone came over Owen's radio, followed up by a 103F in progress at Sidney's Newsstand on South Carrollton.

Owen shook his head and hit the blue lights. Looking back at LaStanza he said, "Fighting over fuckin' *Playboys* again, no doubt."

LaStanza watched them zoom off up Prytania to Louisiana and then right. When he looked back down Prytania, he spotted Daphne Whippet, without the white bag, walking back to her house. He climbed out and crossed the street to intercept her before she reached her front gate.

"Hello," he said, "remember me?"

Daphne stopped and smiled and said, "Yes. You're that detective." Her blue eyes lit up as she put her hands behind the small of her back and rolled her shoulders slightly.

"So how was Disneyworld?"

She stopped rolling her shoulders. "How did you know?"

"I'm a detective, aren't I?"

The smile came back, larger this time, showing off her braces.

"Actually," he said in a conspiratory voice, "Cleola told me when I came and asked to see you."

Daphne's jaw dropped. "You came to see *me*?"

"Yeah." LaStanza leaned his left hand against the white wrought iron fence of the Whippet house. "Tell me. Your bedroom faces Pleasant Street, doesn't it?"

Daphne nodded.

He dropped his voice into a deep, serious tone. "You remember the night the man died on that neutral ground, don't you?"

Daphne looked away, turning her gaze across Prytania.

"Did you see something that night?"

Daphne shrugged and said, "I saw all the police on the neutral ground."

LaStanza slipped his right hand into a rear pocket of his faded jeans. "Did you see anything before all the police cars came?"

"I...saw you put the man on fire out." Her voice dropped. "It was kinda awful."

LaStanza nodded and asked the million dollar question.

"Did you see which way he came from?"

"Huh?"

"Did he come up Pleasant or from Prytania Street."

"Oh." She let out a sigh, put her left hand on her hip and said, "He didn't come up Pleasant Street. I woulda seen him, I think. I was reading by the moonlight."

"Moonlight?"

"I have to put out the light in my room after the ten o'clock news. Sometimes I open my blinds and read by the street lights and the moonlight. My bed is next to the windows. I can see the street all the way to Prytania."

LaStanza turned around and said, "He must have come this way, from Prytania. He crossed in front of my car."

"He had to."

He heard the door open behind him, but ignored it. He asked Daphne, "Do you know Biff Norwood? He lives in the white house back there on the corner."

Daphne looked back and shook her head no, her long hair bouncing.

"Little girl," a voice called out behind LaStanza. He didn't have to turn to know it was Cleola.

"Y'all come on in now," Cleola said.

Daphne let out a bored sigh, as if to say, "Really!"

LaStanza pulled a business card from his front pocket and gave it to Daphne. "You think of anything else. Or you hear anything, call me, Okay?"

"Sure." The braces-smile was back. Daphne winked and moved around him, walking slowly and purposefully as if he was just another boy in the hall that she'd just talked to and wanted everyone to know she'd just talked to him.

LaStanza kept his face from grinning as the little girl walked through her front gate. Cleola held the gate open for Daphne and watched her climb the steps of the three story Greek Revival and go in before she looked over at LaStanza and said, "'Bout time you showed up. I left you two messages for you Friday."

Don't fuckin' tell me.

"Messages?"

"Well, I forgot your name so I told them I wanted to talk to that Al Pacino looking detective with the moustache."

Cleola had cut her salt-and-pepper hair even shorter and wore her usual white maid's dress, white shoes and stockings. Her eyebrows were furrowed as she stepped up to LaStanza and crossed her arms.

"I been givin' food to some of the people out on the street. Leftovers. You know."

Leaning around LaStanza, she looked down Prytania toward Harmony Street.

"Sometimes I walk the Whippet's dog." She took in a deep breath and said, "Well, them men over at the house on the corner, they been talking 'bout frying porch monkeys loud enough so I can hear."

"Men in pickups?"

"Yeah. One real fat and the other real skinny."

Sounded like Sherman and Butler.

"They say anything else?"

"No, they just laugh."

LaStanza nodded.

Cleola cleared her throat before asking, "Why you talk to that little girl?"

"I thought she might have seen something. From her room the night the man was burned, but she didn't."

"Don't go puttin' no fool notions in that little girl's head. She too old for her age now."

LaStanza narrowed his eyes and let a sly smile come across his face.

"Miz Bracket," he said, "that's the last thing I wanna do."

"Good," she said with a firm nod of her head.

"You ever feed a man with a gold tooth, about sixty-five?"

Cleola scrunched up her face and said, "I never look at their *teeth*!"

LaStanza picked up three ham and cheese po-boys and a six pack of Budweiser and walked around the back of the A&P to the small park at the corner of Pleasant and Camp Street. Three black men sat on three wrought iron benches.

They pretended they weren't watching him as he moved to the empty bench, pulled the six pack out and the three po-boys and said, "Anyone want a po-boy and a beer?"

A tall man with a scar on the left side of his jaw stood up and walked over. Wearing a navy pea-coat and brown corduroy pants and mis-matched tennis shoes, the man stood a few feet from LaStanza and said, "What you talkin' about?" The man's two front teeth were missing.

LaStanza opened his shirt to show his badge and said, "I'm with the police union. We give food away all the time, man. You want a sandwich or what?

The man turned to his compadres and waved them forward. LaStanza stepped back and let them at it. They each grabbed a sandwich and two beers and went back to their benches. He waited until they finished half their po-boys before he said, "Y'all heard about the man burned to death up the street?"

The shortest of the three looked over at him with crossed eyes and shrugged. The man wore a long red sweater over a dark tee-shirt and army fatigue pants.

"You a vet?" LaStanza asked him.

The man nodded as he took another bite.

"I was regular army," LaStanza said.

With his mouth full, the short one managed to say he was in the Corps.

"Were you in country?"

The man nodded and said, "Sixty-eight."

LaStanza was still in high school then but told the man how he'd been with the Big Red One at Bien Hua. The short man was at Da Nang.

LaStanza looked at the third man who wore a beat up orange polyester dress coat, a gray sweatshirt and jeans so worn they looked transparent. Turning back to the short one, he said, "Y'all missing anyone? Is there anyone you used to hang out with gone now?"

The short man opened his second beer and said, "We ain't missing nobody."

"And nothin'," the tall one added as they all moved away from the detective.

LaStanza picked up a shrimp po-boy on his way home, laid it out on his kitchen counter and popped open an icy Barq's. Two bites into his po-boy the phone rang. It was Jodie. She sounded down in the mouth.

"Sometimes Sunday-with-the-folks is a pain in the ass," she said.

"You too?" He always thought Jodie grew up in a Norman Rockwell painting. Her Dad looked like a Kansas corner druggist, her mother like Mother Goose.

"Yeah. They just didn't figure their little girl would end up a dick."

LaStanza wasn't about to touch that one, so he took another bite.

"You eating?"

"Shrimp po-boy."

"Want me to call back?"

"No, I can eat and talk at the same time. I'm Italian."

He heard her moving the phone around, but no laugh for his lame joke.

"This goddam Task Force is fuckin' killing me."

"Yeah?"

"All I've been doing is following a fuckin' known sex offender." She moved the phone around again.

"What are you doing?" he asked.

"There," she said. "I took off my clothes."

"Quick. Go open your the blinds."

"They're open."

He dropped two globs of ketchup on the counter. They left a nice red stain when he wiped them up with a napkin. She was being cute again.

"You ever try following someone in this fuckin' city? Asshole drivers. We've been shadowing known sex offenders around the clock. We only lost our guy three times today." She was getting angrier by the second.

"Wanna use one of the Maseratis?"

"No."

"I'm not kidding. They're insured."

"No, but I could use a new partner."

He took another bite.

"Mine smokes."

"Anybody I know?" He took a quick sip of root beer.

"Hadley. Third District Follow-Up. More muscles than brains. Thinks he's a stud."

LaStanza couldn't resist. "You fuckin' him?"

Jodie's silence told him she was in no mood.

"You missed a good one Friday," he said. "Fucker tried to hang himself and ripped his head clean off."

"No way."

"He weighed over three hundred."

"Oh."

She got quiet, so he took another bite. When she hadn't said something by the time he finished chewing and taking another sip of drink, he said, "You shoulda seen my old man today. He threw the remote control through the front window when the Colts ran back that kickoff."

"Come on."

"Serious. Then he tried to blame me when my mother came in to see what happened."

"My old man fell asleep after dinner."

"Mine too, after his second six pack."

"You wanna link up for lunch tomorrow?"

"Actually, I was gonna try and talk Mark into giving me a half day off."

"Oh?"

"Yeah. It's time for a road trip. I've never been to Bogalusa."

"Dammit. Take me!"

Bogue Chitto

A north breeze whipped the brown water of Lake Pontchartrain into small white caps as LaStanza crossed the Causeway, the windows of his Maserati down, the dry air cool on his face and arms. Keeping the car under fifty-five—because a Causeway cop would give his mother a ticket to make his quota—LaStanza watched two brown pelicans off to his right, gliding nearly motionless in the face of the sweet north breeze. When he was a kid he thought pelicans were too goofy-looking to be the state bird, until he saw them in flight.

He turned up the stereo on Crosby Stills & Nash as Stephen Stills started up *Suite: Judy Blue Eyes.* With the strings and sweet harmonies echoing in the car, the purr of the Maserati's turbocharged engine barely discernible, the autumn air tosseling his hair and his gangster glasses firmly set on his Roman nose, with his dark green tie loosened and his light gray suit coat on a hanger behind his head, with his magnum on his hip and his LFR turned off in the trunk, with the extra-bright sun resting at high noon, LaStanza headed for the piney woods of the Florida parishes, those hilly parishes north of the lake that were once part of New Spain, a long, long time ago.

Past the small towns of St. Tammany—Mandeville, Abita Springs, Waldheim, and Bush, LaStanza crossed the swift moving Bogue Chitto River just south of Sun. He took a left on LA 16 and eased into Washington Parish, riding parallel along the river toward a little place called Enon, where Willie Sherman lived.

He stopped at a corrugated tin store near the intersection of 16 and LA 60. Two pickups were parked in the oyster shell parking lot. A hand painted sign above the open front door of the store read: Ruby's Fresh Goods. Stretching, LaStanza slipped on his jacket and pushed his badge clip to the left so it wouldn't be seen so easily. He noticed how the air was clean and dry, thick with the scent of pine needles.

He climbed the six wooden steps to the porch, patted a sleepy bloodhound on the head and stepped into the store as a heavy set woman with dyed crimson hair was telling a skinny man in a gray jumpsuit how that wasn't no werewolf, it was a bobcat.

"Ain't you never heard a bobcat cry at night?" The woman had a slight accent, a hybrid Northshore-Mississippi drawl. Not as slow as an Alabama accent, a Mississippi accent was the classic southern belle accent.

LaStanza dug a bottle of Pepsi out of a chest half filled with ice and moved back to the counter.

The skinny man said in the same accent, "That was no bobcat."

The woman smiled and told LaStanza, "Fifty cents. American."

Cute. He was gonna try and slip them pesos.

LaStanza smiled back, handed her a dollar said, "Y'all know where Yellow Tavern Road is?"

The skinny man said, "It's in Enon." He stared at LaStanza with thin muddy brown eyes.

The woman nodded her head and said, "Take a left at the light at LA 437. It's a half mile on the right, just before you cross the river." She ran a rag over the yellow Formica counter and added, "Who you looking for, Officer?"

Narrowing his left eye, LaStanza said, "Willie

Sherman."

The woman rang up fifty cents on the old-fashioned black cash register. "He lives in the second trailer on the left down Yellow Tavern." She put two quarters on the counter.

The skinny man leaned on the counter and said, "You police?"

"New Orleans," LaStanza said and turned back to the woman, "Are you Ruby?"

The woman leaned against the cash register and said, "All my life."

LaStanza took out a business card and passed it to her. She read it.

"What did Willie do now?" the man asked.

"What did he do before?"

The man folded his arms and said, "I dunno."

"Come on," Ruby said, raising her voice, "besides being banned from here, Willie's too ignorant to do anything real bad."

LaStanza opened the Pepsi and took a sip. "Why'd you ban him?"

"Shoplifting."

LaStanza looked around the tiny store.

"I told you he's ignorant," Ruby said. "If he ain't home, he'll be at the Coral Club or in N'Awlins. He works in the city."

The skinny moved over to the door and said, "What kinda car is that?"

"Maserati."

"Say what?"

"Ever hear of a Ferrari?"

"Yeah."

"That ain't one."

LaStanza thanked Ruby, left the change on the counter and paused as he stepped around the skinny man. Turning back to Ruby, he said, "Where's the Coral Club?"

"It's on 437 about a mile past Yellow Tavern. It's just

the other side of the bridge. On the right."

LaStanza petted the bloodhound on his way out, hung his coat back up on the hanger, climbed into the Maserati and eased out of the parking lot, making sure he didn't skid his tires. Didn't want to careen shells off the pickups. One was probably Ruby's.

He almost missed Yellow Tavern Road. There was a street sign all right, nailed to a pine tree. The road was blacktop once, but was mostly dirt now. The first trailer on the left was an old silver Air Streamer rusted badly and leaning against two pine trees bent from its weight.

The second trailer was a blue and white house trailer, half hidden from view in the piney woods. LaStanza turned into the dirt driveway and parked.

Leaving his coat, he walked through the woods to the concrete steps up to the trailer. He knocked on the louvered glass window next to the front door and waited. He knocked again, then took a walk around the trailer. There was a small electrical pole out back with a working meter. He jotted the meter number in his notes, in case he had to call his LP&L source.

Besides two rusted bicycle frames, a couple dozen beer cans littered the brush around the trailer. He knocked on the door again before walking back up to the road to check the silver mailbox perched precariously on a pine tree stump. He found five pieces of junk mail addressed to resident or occupant before finding Willie Sherman's electric bill.

The sound of a woodpecker echoed through the woods behind LaStanza. He turned and shaded his eyes with the mail and looked for it, but there was no way he could spot it. So he put the mail back and climbed intc the Maserati.

The next house down Yellow Tavern Road was a good quarter mile away. LaStanza knocked on the screen door of the clapboard house and soon discovered its occupant, an elderly man who needed a walker to get around, did not know Sherman. Neither did the occupant of the only other house on Yellow Tavern a quarter mile further down the road.

Driving back to LA 437, LaStanza took a right and crossed the Bogue Chitto again before turning into another oyster shell parking lot in front of a long, low wooden building with a green shingle roof and a red neon sign in its lone front window that announced it was indeed "The Coral Club."

He parked the Maserati next to a black Camaro, away from the three pickups, left the gangster glasses on the padded tan leather dash and slipped into his coat. Before he opened the beat up wooden door of The Coral Club, he heard the twang of some shit-kicker moaning about two-timing women.

The smoke-filled room smelled of beer and sweat. Two men with cowboy hats leaned against the long bar to the right, two more shot pool off to the left. The bartender, an Ernest Borgnine look-alike without the smile, grunted when LaStanza asked for a Bud.

A half hour and an ear-ache later, with no new information whatsoever, LaStanza left in the middle of a song about a dead dog and a no good woman with crystal hooters—whatever the fuck that meant. He put his coat back on its hanger and heard a woodpecker again. He looked over at the tall pines to his left and smiled to himself, as if he'd be able to spot it. He cranked up the Maserati, slipped on his gangster glasses, popped in a B. B. King tape and cranked up the volume, letting the bluesy strains of "The Thrill is Gone" cleanse his mind for a minute before slipping the car into gear.

Recrossing the Bogue Chitto, LaStanza spotted a marked Washington Parish Sheriff's Office car parked down at a camping area next to the river. The picnic tables were empty. He could see the deputy inside was writing a report, his windows down.

The Maserati wormed its way down the dirt road to the picnic area. LaStanza checked out the black and white unit with the word "Sheriff" emblazoned in block letters on its front door. He couldn't help notice the green and yellow lightning bolts on the side of the car.

Pulling around the unit, LaStanza remembered how he used to park along the wharves to get a peaceful moment away from the public to write his reports. Climbing out, he stretched and caught the deputy checking out his badge and weapon on his belt.

Cooler next to the churning brown water, LaStanza noticed how narrow the river was, how the woods ran right up against the bank, except where man had cleared away the trees. He watched a tree limb float by, spin in a small whirlpool, and continue on. The woods smelled wetter and mustier here.

"It's pretty deep," the deputy said, resting his elbow out the window. "We pull a body or two out ever so often. Kids mostly. City people come up here and like to dive off our bridges. Good way to die." His accent was barely discernible.

"I never knew we had white water in Louisiana," LaStanza said, referring to the white-capped rapids.

He walked over to the unit and noticed the deputy ogling the Maserati. Blond, with a light moustache, the deputy looked to be in his mid-twenties. His uniform was khaki with brown epaulets and a gold six point star badge. His name tag read *Courane.*

"Nice car," the deputy said.

LaStanza pulled a business card from his shirt pocket and handed it to the deputy. "We all get sports cars in Homicide," he said.

"You shittin' me. That's a police car? I thought the city was broke."

"It is now."

Courane eyeballed him, looking to see if his leg was being pulled.

"Those lightning bolts make your car faster?"

Courane's face remained serious.

"I'm kiddin'," LaStanza said. "It's my wife's car."

"Yeah," Courane said, finally looking at the business

card.

The woodpecker started up again, but LaStanza didn't look for it.

"You know a fella named Willie Sherman? Lives in a trailer on Yellow Tavern Road about a half mile back."

Courane shook his head no.

"He's got no record on the state computer," LaStanza said, "but I hear he gets into local trouble."

"If he does, it's gotta be small time."

LaStanza looked up at the bridge and said, "He hangs out at The Coral Club."

"Then he's a loser all right. Country music and all that shit."

"You from around here?"

"Naw. Covington. I married a girl from Bogalusa."

LaStanza turned and leaned his rear against the front quarter panel of the unit. "Isn't there a big campground around here?"

Courane pointed his chin down river and said, "Lincoln Park's about a mile down. Almost in St. Tammany Parish."

"They still have those barbecue's there?"

Courane didn't answer, so LaStanza looked back at the deputy, who was smiling now. "You pumping me?" Courane said.

LaStanza nodded and shrugged.

"Let's see. The Coral Club. Lincoln Park. Some of our whiter boys in trouble down in the Crescent City, or what?"

"Somebody torched an African-American right in the Garden District."

Courane laughed. "Sounds like you got your hands full." He looked back at the card and said, "Detective LaStanza. *La*Stanza." He ran his hand through his hair and added, "The big show's in April. Around Adolph Hitler's birthday. Fireworks. Cross burnings. Watermelon fights. You see, Lincoln's a private park."

Courane stuck LaStanza's card into his silver clipboard

on the front seat, slipped on a pair of dark sunglasses and started up the engine.

"Hitler's birthday?" LaStanza asked.

"Yep." Courane slipped the car into gear and said, "Better watch who you question up here, Mr. Eye-talian detective. This place is full a white boys."

LaStanza made it home just before five, so he called Lizette, but she wasn't home. Flipping on the portable TV at the far end of the kitchen counter, he slipped the plate of red beans and rice and two pork chops Brulee left him into the microwave. He changed to Channel 4 to catch the news, opened a cold Barq's and watched Anchorman Bill Elder start in on a story about arrests at the Liberty Monument. Before he could take his first sip, LaStanza saw Willie Sherman and Byron Norwood at the head of a crowd in front of a white obelisk. His mouth fell open as the story unfolded.

The bespectacled Elder explained how two groups clashed at the monument at the foot of Canal Street, a monument honoring the White League's victory over a biracial police force in the Reconstruction-era Battle of Liberty Place in 1874. LaStanza spotted the defiant face of state Representative Boyd Richards as the old black civil rights leader led his crowd forward, singing and chanting, toward the monument where Norwood and his white boys stood waving confederate battle flags, surrounded by about twenty NOPD uniformed officers. LaStanza didn't recognize any. He did notice, however, that all were white, all wearing dark sunglasses, their short hair neatly styled with mousse or hairspray.

Richards and some of his followers started pushing the police.

Oh, no!

The officers pushed back, using their PR 24 nightsticks. It escalated quickly. A young officer grabbed Richards around the neck and wrestled the geriatric case to the ground. Helped by a second officer, they put

Richards down gently, sort of, before slapping on the cuffs.

Elder explained how eighty-two year old Richards, along with three fellow protesters, were charged with simple battery on police and resisting arrest. Police spokesman Major Sam Quarters explained, "When someone tries to physically break through a line of police officers, they're gonna be arrested." He sounded smooth, all right. Even if he had a weasel face. LaStanza never liked him. It was personal. Quarters was an asshole, plain and simple.

With the camera panning the obelisk, Elder explained how it was erected in the 1890's to honor the twenty-seven members of the White League killed in the conflict. As the camera returned to the front of the monument, it focused on Byron Norwood who explained that if blacks removed this monument, they'd be after the statue Robert E. Lee at Lee Circle next, then Jefferson Davis and General Beauregard would have to go.

"The man who founded New Orleans, Bienville, owned slaves," Norwood said. "Should we tear down his statue from in front of Union Passenger Terminal? Will seculars demand we tear down the statue of Joan of Arc? Why not rip Andrew Jackson off his horse in Jackson Square because his troops killed Creek and Cherokees?"

Norwood was now flanked by Benny Butler and Sherman. Norwood dropped his voice to emphasize his next point. "We may be a minority in this city. But we still have civil rights. This monument was dedicated to those who died to protect these rights."

The story cut away back to Elder at the anchor desk. "Representative Richards has responded with a statement calling the monument a symbol of humiliation for black people, representing racism and slavery."

The microwave pinged behind LaStanza. Turning away, as another story filled the screen, he remembered how his old man called Richards an uppity nigger back in the Sixties, when Richards was young and spouted revolution. Now the old man was being choked by a young white cop ' n the Five O'clock News. He felt acid in his surly stomach as he thought of what Norwood said. Son-of-a-bitch was shrewd as hell.

With one stroke Norwood had managed to label whites as the new minority. Elect him governor and he'd be pushing for affirmative actions for white males.

The rest of the news rolled by in a blur as LaStanza ate his beans and rice and chops. In the middle of Dan Rather, he loaded the dishwasher and reached for the soap powder. The phone rang.

It took a second for LaStanza to recognize Mason's voice. It sounded hoarse.

"What you doing?" Mason asked.

"Eating."

"Soon as you're finished, can you 10-19 the 7500 block of Maple Street? Jodie and I could use a little help."

LaStanza felt a pang in his stomach.

"Pantyhose?"

"Yeah," Mason said. "He raped a sixteen-year-old around two o'clock over here and..." Mason coughed and cleared his throat.

LaStanza waited. The "and" sounded ominous.

"And while we were all over here, he raped a woman on West End Boulevard."

"Son-of-a-bitch!"

"Might as well come over here. It's closer and Jodie's beat." He gave LaStanza the address.

LaStanza jotted the address on the Post-it Brulee had left him about the red beans.

"I'll be right there."

He climbed into a pair of jeans, and pulled on a dark blue tee-shirt with "POLICE" stenciled in red across the chest—where the hell Lizette found the shirt was beyond him.

He picked out a wide brown belt, slipped a pouch with two speed loaders inside next to the holster. He took his service revolver this time. Like the speed loaders, his weapon carried semi-jacketed .357 magnum hollow points. *Fuck regulations.*

Gripping the steering wheel of his Maserati, LaStanza felt the leopard growling lowly inside as he gunned the engine and drove the wrong way up Calhoun to St. Charles to take a hard left. Blowing the red light at Broadway, he pulled up behind Mason's white LTD parked under a row of trees across the street from the Maple Street Children's Book Shop.

His pulse was even now, his light eyes wide in the encroaching rainy darkness as he crossed the street. Pulling a dress gray short-sleeved shirt over his tee-shirt, he shoved his LFR into his right rear pocket and jumped the three steps up to the gallery where Mason stood smoking a cigarette.

"Come on," Mason said, dropping the butt on the wooden porch and stomping it out. "Let's canvass."

LaStanza led the way down the stairs, but let Mason lead the way across the street to start their canvass.

"Jodie inside?"

"Hospital with the victim. He nearly crushed her larynx. They're trying to take a written statement from her."

Mason's burgundy tie was loosened, his white shirt soiled across the back, his tan pants dotted with patches of dirt.

"He forced his way in when she opened the front door. She was coming home from school."

Stepping through the open gate of a shotgun double, Mason stopped and said, "The fuck caught a woman coming home with groceries on West End. He left her tied up, nearly choking to death. Her teen aged son found her."

Two hours of useless canvassing later, LaStanza and Mason watched Jodie pull up and park behind the Maserati. Leaning against his car next to Mason, LaStanza watched his partner climb out and walk over.

He actually spotted a strand of her page boy out of place. Her white blouse wasn't crisp. Her navy blue slacks were actually wrinkled. She looked at him with tired eyes and said, "Y'all come up with anything?"

"Just a fuckin' headache," Mason said from the other side of LaStanza.

Jodie leaned against the Maserati. She ran her hands through her hair and said, "We had fifteen sex offenders under surveillance today."

"So we've eliminated fifteen more," Mason said. "How's the little girl?"

"Her voice box is damaged, but they don't think they'll have to operate." Her voice dropped as she said, "She was a virgin. She's pretty ripped up."

LaStanza heard cicadas again, in the distance.

"So how did it go up by Bogalusa today?" Jodie asked.

LaStanza shrugged. Folding his arms, he felt perspiration in his arm pits. There wasn't a breath of air on the street.

"They're still canvassing up at West End," Mason said, holding up his little fuckin' radio. He reached into his front pants pocket, pulled out a pack of Juicy Fruit and unwrapped two sticks. He offered some around, but found no takers. He stuffed both pieces into his mouth.

"I guess we can call it a night," he said.

"Fine by me," Jodie said.

LaStanza yawned. When he finished, he said, "Anyone for a Jacuzzi?"

Mason shook his head no.

Jodie yawned and said, "It so happens I've been carrying around a bathing suit in my trunk." She poked him in the side with a fist.

All three pushed away from the car at the same time. Mason grabbed LaStanza's arm and said, "Oh yeah. I forgot to tell you. You're back on the Task Force."

LaStanza opened the French doors at the back of his kitchen, stepped out on the deck and dropped two large towels on one of the padded wrought-iron lawn chairs next to the hot tub. He pulled the vinyl insulated top off the Jacuzzi and checked the temperature. 100 degrees.

Nice and toasty. He turned on the jets and climbed in.

He moved to the center, sank all the way to his neck, bobbed his head underwater for a second and then sat up, the water bubbling at chest level. Jodie was in the doorway now, her hands on her hips. She wore a one piece black suit. She looked nice.

"You have a suit on, don't you?"

"Yeah," he said in a tired voice.

"You better." She stepped gingerly out on the deck and crossed over to the other side of the hot tub. It took a couple seconds to get her long limbs in.

"It's awfully dark out here."

"The light from the kitchen's enough," he said. "Quit complaining."

LaStanza put his arms up on the Fiberglass edge of the Jacuzzi, rested his head back against the side and just let the water gurgle over him.

"It's hot," she said.

"It feels good," he said. "Give it a minute."

He blinked his watery eyes and saw her sinking lower. "If it gets too hot," he said, "sit up on the edge."

She closed her eyes and nodded.

He let his feet rise, careful not to brush against her, closed his eyes again and floated in the churning water. Under the teakwood and glass overhang, behind the seven foot brick wall, with the banana trees and magnolias the small backyard, he got that feeling again—that he was in some tropical place.

He thought back to his honeymoon, back to the black pebble beaches of Guadeloupe, of a naked Lizette glistening under the sun as he rubbed coconut scented suntan oil over every inch of his bride.

His eyes snapped open.

Gotta stop that. Don't need a hard on.

"What's tomorrow?" Jodie asked.

"Tuesday?"

"I'll pick you up in the morning, right?"

"I guess so."

He let his legs sink back and sat up on a higher level along the side of the tub away from the kitchen. The evening air felt cool on his chest now. He ran his hands through his hair.

"So, what's Bogalusa like?" She had one eye open, her arms up along the back of the tub now.

"Did you know we have white water like rapids in Louisiana?"

"Huh?" She sat up, moving to the higher level across the wide tub.

"The Bogue Chitto near Enon, where Willie Sherman lives, they're rapids there. It's kinda pretty, except for the rednecks."

"So what did you find out?"

"Not much. Only that Sherman and the Hitler youth meet at this private park. Burn a cross or two."

He climbed up on the edge, but left his legs still in the tub.

"So you think this Sherman might be..."

"Don't fuckin' know." LaStanza shook his head, cool drops of water falling on his shoulders. "He's just the best game in town."

"Talk to Lizette today?"

"She's not home much," he said and had to smile.

Jodie sank up to her throat and moaned, "Paris!"

"I know. I know."

God he missed her. Although he was getting more than a little anxious, it wasn't just the sex his missed. He missed not seeing her—not being with her. He missed her smile, the way her long hair draped over her shoulders. He missed her face so much, it hurt. He missed the sound of her voice, the way she snuggled next to him in bed, her breath falling on his shoulder at night. Most of all he missed her gold-brown eyes, topaz eyes—the color of crisp autumn leaves. No, most of all he missed being with her, being *with* her.

"I thought you were gonna explode when Mason said you were back on the Task Force. Saving it for tomorrow?"

He shook his head no, shook the image of his wife away for the moment.

"We'll be partners again," Jodie said.

He nodded.

"What's the matter. You too tired to talk?"

"No. I'm mad."

Jodie climbed up and sat on the edge and stared at him.

He looked back at her eyes and said, "I'm gonna get that mother-fuckin' rapist. *We're* gonna get him."

"That's what we've been trying to do."

"No," he said evenly. "We've been going through the motions. You and I are going to get him like we got the Batture Murderer. You and me, partner. We're gonna nail his ass."

"Fine by me."

LaStanza climbed out of the tub and walked over to the lawn chairs, pulled onc away from the overhang and sat in it. He looked up at the full moon and the bright starry sky.

"So, how we gonna catch him?" Jodie said as she climbed out.

"The streets. He's out there on the streets...riding around."

Jodie grabbed a towel and sat in the other chair. "They're gonna assign us to a new sex offender to follow around."

"No. I'm gonna talk to Savage in the morning. We're Homicide dicks. We've got a murder to solve. We're gonna use every snitch, every trick, every smoke and mirror we got. Savage'll see the light because I'm gonna tell him to leave you and me alone and we'll reel-in the fucker."

When he looked at his partner, her nose was crinkled.

"I know," he said. "I'm such a prima donna."

Jodie smiled and ran the towel over her long legs.

LaStanza looked back at the sky. He heard a knocking

and for a second thought it was a woodpecker, but only for a second. Turning, he spotted a smiling black face as Fel Jones entered through the side gate.

"Am I interrupting anything?" Fel said as he pulled off his brown suit coat and climbed up on the deck.

"Nope," Jodie said rising. "I was just leaving."

Fel dropped his coat on her chair and started in on his tie. Grinning at her, he said, "At least wait 'til I'm naked."

The nose crinkled again.

"I mean it," LaStanza said, looking at his partner.

Jodie turned to him.

"He's gonna fuck up and we're gonna be right there to slam dunk the fuck. We're gonna get him, then we're gonna nail my murderer." He almost added, "You know me. I always get 'em." But she knew that.

Fel pulled off his shirt and started in on his belt.

"I'm getting an itchy trigger finger," LaStanza said, looking back up at the sky. "I ain't shot anybody in a while."

"Fine by me," Jodie said, turning toward the kitchen.

Fel dropped his pants and drawers, pulled off his shoes and socks and climbed into the tub. He let out a yummy sound and then said, "Since when you wear a bathing suit in your own tub?"

LaStanza spotted a falling star for a second, then it was gone. He closed his eyes. He felt his heart racing and took a minute to calm it down. He felt the leopard again, crouched and ready to pounce.

He heard the sliding door open behind him.

"You stand up and I'll shoot your dick off," Jodie said.

He looked back and saw his partner was dressed now, her wide-set eyes flashing a hard glint at Fel in the tub. She stepped up and told LaStanza, "I'll pick you up in the morning."

LaStanza stood up and stretched and yawned. When he finished he put a hand up on his partner's shoulder and said, "I'm gonna kill somebody this time. I can feel it."

Jodie's eyes turned into ovals. She pursed her lips tightly. She let out a breath and poked him in the belly.

"I got goose bumps," she said and turned away and left.

Looking around at Fel, LaStanza raised an index finger and said, "Shut the fuck up."

Poeyfarre Street

LaStanza spotted the white LTD turn off Louisiana Avenue and head his way down wet Prytania Street. Sitting up behind the steering wheel of Lizette's burgundy Maserati, he looked at his watch with a sinking feeling in his belly. Mason at two o'clock in the morning was never good news.

LaStanza twisted his back around to work the kinks out and told himself he should have stayed home and gone to bed when he had the chance.

Mason pulled up next to the Maserati, rolled down his window and tossed a butt out on the wet pavement. "Jodie figured you'd be here."

The egg rolls LaStanza wolfed down at midnight kicked him in the stomach. LaStanza closed his eyes and said, "I don't fuckin' wanna hear this."

"He struck again."

LaStanza's chin sank to his chest. He and Jodie had put in sixteen hour days the last two days...or was it three days? Cruising the dark streets, talking to every snitch they knew, they talked to so many fuckin' people it was numbing. So now on Thursday night, when he couldn't sleep, he fired up the Maserati, picked up some egg rolls and thought he'd watch Sherman a while. The black pick-up was still parked a block away at the corner of Harmony and Prytania. Sherman had probably spotted the Maserati now and was watching them.

"It's bad," Mason said.

LaStanza looked over at his lieutenant's drawn face.

"Another 30," Mason said.

Another fuckin' murder.

"Jesus! Where?"

"Warehouse District. Off Tchoupitoulas."

LaStanza started up the Maserati.

"You know," Mason said. "It'd help if you kept your radio on." Rolling up his window he added, "Follow me."

It was a good thing he said that. LaStanza would have wrapped the Maserati around a telephone pole on the wet streets if he didn't have to follow Mason's slow moving LTD. He turned on his LFR and left it face up on the front passenger seat, next to his off-duty .38.

LaStanza's right foot itched to gun the accelerator of the turbocharged engine. His hands felt sweaty on the padded steering wheel as he followed the LTD down Prytania all the way to Melpomene down to Constance where Mason took a left and headed toward the CBD.

Passing under the concrete pillars of the Pontchartrain Expressway, Mason slowed and turn the wrong way down one-way Poeyfarre Street and parked immediately to the right. LaStanza had to drive past, slowing so he wouldn't run over the three patrolmen standing in the narrow street. He found a spot to park near the end of the block by Annunciation Street.

Climbing out, LaStanza slipped his LFR into the left rear pocket of his jeans and his .38 into the holster at the small of his back. He reached in and scooped up his pad and pen and walked back up Poeyfarre.

He glanced to his right at a dark, two story red brick warehouse. To his left, where Mason stood with two patrolmen, stood a hulking three story brown brick warehouse that had obviously been converted into Condos in this new yuppie residential Warehouse District. LaStanza looked at the rows of well-lit windows facing Poeyfarre.

The building was still ugly—with worn bricks and cement window sills dotted with pigeon droppings.

Grabbing the end post of a cast iron fence coated with thick silver paint, LaStanza swung around and bounced up the brick porch to where his lieutenant stood.

"I remember this place," Mason said. "Used to be a clothing warehouse."

LaStanza looked up at the silver numerals 944 above the door. The air smelled wet and musty next to the building. There were six large search lights above the front door but it was still dark as hell. The old bricks absorbed the light.

"Nice fuckin' shirt," Mason said as he turned and motioned to the patrolmen to open one of the glass double doors of the ancient building.

LaStanza looked down at the purple tee-shirt he'd put on with his jeans before heading for the egg rolls. He'd bought the tee-shirt outside Tiger Stadium at last year's LSU-Tulane game. Across the chest, in gold was printed: TUCK FULANE!

He followed Mason through a well-lit, immaculate foyer that smelled of lilac, down a pristine hall to an elevator with a stainless-steel door. The elevator smelled of lilac too.

They got out on the second floor, turned right and walked down to the last door on the right, where yet another patrolman stood next to Frank Savage. The door had black numbers 201 on it. Savage's hair was wet again, his dress white shirt and black tie rumpled again. He looked at LaStanza wearily and stepped back out of the way.

Mason stopped just inside the door. LaStanza peeked in as a flash went off. Sturtz, the bespectacled crime lab tech, leaned around a wooden coffee table and stood over a pair of naked legs and snapped another picture.

Jodie, who stood behind Sturtz, looked at LaStanza with a tired look, until she spotted his shirt. She almost smiled. Closing her eyes momentarily, she switched her weight from her right leg to her left. In a white tee-shirt and black jeans, her page boy and make-up perfect, she looked as crisp as ever—except for the weary eyes.

Mason waved Jodie over. She took a roundabout route to them, hugging the walls. LaStanza led the way back into the hall. Mason leaned against the far wall and lit up another cigarette.

"Talk to me," he said.

Jodie opened her clipboard and said, in a scratchy voice, "Her name was Daisy Armstrong. Twenty-five. Lived here a year and a half. Worked at D. H. Holmes on Canal. Woman across the hall in 204 found her." Looking up at LaStanza she added, "The fuck left the door wide open. The body was spotted from the hall. It's a fresh kill. She's still warm."

"Same M.O.?" Mason said.

"Pantyhose around the neck," Jodie said. Her cheeks looked suddenly drawn.

Mason pulled the cigarette from his mouth and said, "Tell Sturtz I want the works. Vacuum. Everything." He tapped LaStanza on the arm and started down the hall.

"Nice shirt," Jodie told LaStanza as he backed away, following Mason. Waiting for the elevator, he spotted Gately and Wilson come out of an apartment down the hall and move to the next door.

As soon as they stepped outside, Mason waved two patrolmen over and told them to write every license plate on every car within a three block radius. "Stop anyone on the street and bring them to him." He pointed to LaStanza.

"You handle the canvass," he told LaStanza, turned and went back into the building.

Ten minutes into the canvass a fine mist moved in like a wet fog. LaStanza found a car with a warm engine parked behind the victim's building along John Churchill Chase Street. He found it's owner, a sixty-five year old retired fireman sitting alone in the Down Under Bar at the corner of Chase and Constance. So drunk, the fireman could barely talk. LaStanza made him pull out his driver's license and noted the man stood a good inch smaller than himself. The bartender, a barrel-chested Aussie with a full blond beard gave LaStanza a description of his customers that morning, both of them.

Two hours after starting their canvass, LaStanza and the three patrolmen hurried back into the victim's building. Standing in the foyer, they turned and watched the rain move in like sheets in the wind, hammering the sidewalk in waves. It lasted ten minutes exactly, then vanished, leaving a moon-filled sky littered with stars so bright they looked as if they'd been freshly washed.

"This shit's getting old." Savage said as they all settled at tables at Cafe DuMonde. A breeze filtered over them from the north, over the spires of St. Louis Cathedral, down across Jackson Square, as a gray dawn crept through the French Quarter. LaStanza pulled up a chair next to Jodie. Savage and Mason sat at the same table, while Gately, Wilson, Davenport and Fel Jones, who had arrived with the second wave of troops in time to help finish off the canvass of the Poeyfarre neighborhood, sat at the next table.

LaStanza felt sore, the muscles on his arms ached, his legs twitched as he sat. He rubbed his eyes for a good minute while Mason ordered cafe-au-lait and beignets for everyone. The only other customers in the open air cafe nestled between the sea wall and Decatur Street were two black cabbies and a brunette woman in a white evening gown. She looked familiar to LaStanza as she sat staring out at the street, her legs crossed, three empty cups in front of her.

The strong coffee did little to revive LaStanza. He passed on the powdered-sugar coated beignets, which left a white ring around Fel's mouth.

"You look like a negative of Al Jolson," Mason told Fel, who grinned back at the lieutenant.

Jodie sat very still across from her partner. She stared

at the gray sea wall. The breeze blew a strand of her blonde hair across her lips. It clung to her lipstick momentarily, before she brushed it away.

LaStanza wanted to say something to her, wanted to say something funny, something that would make her laugh, but couldn't think of a fuckin' thing to say. So he watched her sit there with her perfect posture, her mouth pursed, her elbow now on the table top, her chin resting in the palm of her hand as she stared at the sea wall.

He suddenly felt like leaning over and kissing Jodie. For the hell of it. He wanted to reach over, cup her face in his hands, turn her head and French kiss his partner right there in front of everyone.

"You okay?" Jodie said.

"Huh?"

"You look sick."

LaStanza almost laughed.

"Take a look at Fel," she said. "He looks like it's his last meal."

She'd been watching.

"Can't help myself," Fel said. "These babies are good."

The brunette in the white evening gown stepped up behind them and asked Mason for a light. She had a thin cigar in her right hand. Mason handed her his Bic lighter and told her to keep it. She brushed her long straight hair out of her eyes and lit the cigar then put the lighter down in front of Mason. Stepping over to the other table, she picked up a napkin, dabbed it in Fel's water glass and wiped his face for him. Then she turned and pointed to LaStanza and said, "Nice shirt."

She turned to leave.

LaStanza said, "How's the modeling going?"

She stopped and looked back at him over her shoulder.

"Madison Street. You in a teddy with a shoe shine boy."

The woman's face remained expressionless. She nodded and left, her hips moving back and forth between the close-spaced tables, all the way to Decatur.

Fel turned to LaStanza with a "What the fuck is going on?" look.

So LaStanza told him about the model in the teddy posing with the shoe shiner and the red-headed cameraman.

"I love this town," Fel said.

Jodie crossed her arms and asked LaStanza, "How'd you recognize her?"

He was going to remind her he was good with faces, even when a woman wore a teddy, but this called for a Snowood quote. So he said, "When the coyote howls, the owl listens." Whatever the fuck that meant.

Later, crowded into the Chamber of Horrors they witnessed the autopsy of another young woman snatched from the world by a fuckin' monster. LaStanza watched two large black coroner's assistants remove the victim's clothes and pass each piece to Sturtz who put each in a separate brown paper bag.

The victim lay naked on the stainless-steel table on her back, her short black hair disheveled, her body unmarked except for the stocking knotted around her neck. Her face was blue, her swollen purple tongue protruded from her small mouth. Her eyes were closed, as if to shut out the evil that took her life.

What was she like? What were her dreams? What had she done on the last day of her life? LaStanza shook those thought away. What was the use?

He felt the coffee sour in his stomach now. A silent belch caused it to bubble half-way up his esophagus momentarily. He took a step back just as the pathologist strolled in and said, "There too many of you in here."

No one moved.

"Anyone gets in my way, I'm booting all of you out," Dr. Horace Holmes said.

Who's he gonna call? The police?

Tall and prissy, Holmes wore thick glasses on his hook nose. Looking at the group, he inched forward, tapped down his glasses and gleeked LaStanza's tee-shirt.

The hook nose rose and Holmes said, "I went to Tulane." He put his hands on his hips as if he expected a response.

LaStanza met his eyes and said, "So you're used to losing."

He heard Jodie let out a little cry behind him.

"What did you say?" Holmes was on his toes now.

"What word didn't you understand?"

"All right," Mason said. "That's enough."

Holmes shook his head and turned away and said, "Goddam cops."

"No shit, Sherlock," Fel said.

Holmes shot him an angry look.

Mason stepped in Fel's face and growled, "Cool it."

And so the autopsy was performed in silence. Jodie was the only one to break the silence, getting the minimum details she needed from Holmes who worked as quickly as he could to be rid of them.

Which suited LaStanza fine. He never liked the prissy bastard.

Mason told LaStanza to go home right after the post-mortem. Pointing to Jodie he said, "Soon as you knock out a quick daily, you go get some sleep." Turning to Savage he said, "They'll be back tomorrow morning, OK?"

Savage nodded wearily.

"I'll call you tonight," Jodie said.

LaStanza watched her and Mason turn the corner before he crossed South White Street to the D.A.'s parking lot where he'd parked the Maserati.

He left a message for Lizette with the concierge before climbing into bed. For a second he thought about taking a shower. He rolled over on his belly and the next thing he heard was a ringing. Faintly, as if in a fog, the ringing continued until he realized it was the phone.

Fumbling with the receiver, he dropped it, pulled it up by the cord and croaked, "Hello."

"You sleeping, Babe?"

"No. Uh, yeah." He looked at the clock. It was four p.m. already.

"You all right?"

"Yeah." He rolled over on his back and said, "Talk to me. I wanna hear your voice."

"God, I miss you so much, Babe."

He closed his eyes and listened to an animated Lizette describe her classes that day, something new she learned about Robespierre, and the dinner she just had with a classmate named Michelle, who was from a place in France called Arles.

"That's where Van Gogh painted his sunflowers."

They ate at a little bistro near the Luxembourg Gardens called the Polidor, where Hemingway and James Joyce used to eat. It was funky old and reminded Lizette of the Napoleon House on Chartres Street.

The mention of food stirred his stomach. He thought he smelled something. Sitting up, he did smell something wonderful wafting from downstairs. Brulee was cooking something that smelled so fuckin' good his belly rumbled.

LaStanza sank back in his bed and listened to Lizette's voice, envisioning what she looked like as she spoke on the phone. He missed her face so badly. Her face was as close to perfection as he'd ever known. Her face was stunning at times, so much that heads turned. He loved waking with that face—most of all when she wore no makeup and was still sleepy-eyed and smiled at him like a little girl. God, he missed her. Hell, they were still newly weds, even if they'd been married two years.

"Babe," she said when she sounded like she was getting tired. "Did you check to see how many vacation days you have?"

"Actually I did. I've got a hundred and two."

"My, God. I'll buy you a ticket tomorrow. You'll love Paris. You can sit around the Colbert all day and we can play around all night."

"Not yet," he said when she quieted down. "I've got a

couple murderers to catch."

"I know," she said softly. "But we're spending Christmas in Paris. Remember."

"I'll be there long before that."

"Good."

After a quick shower, LaStanza climbed into a Colombian blue Rummel tee-shirt with John Churchill Chase's moustachioed Raider stenciled in white across his chest, and a pair of red jogging shorts and went downstairs with his hair still wet.

He caught Brulee leaning over the kitchen stove, a ladle in her right hand. She turned her gaunt face to him and said, "Big night last night?" Her face was the color of dark mahogany.

"Bad night," he said, moving over to the stove.

He spotted grits in a large bowl atop one burner and candid yams cooling in a baking pan next to it.

"What's in the oven?"

"Grillades. What else you gonna eat wit' grits?"

Brulee put the ladle on one of those spoon holders on the top of the stove and moved over and washed her hands in the sink.

"Bout time you got up," she said, drying her gnarled hands. "Give the grillades another half hour. The grits'll be done in ten minutes."

She pointed to a round aluminum thing on the counter.

"Put that garlic bread in the oven ten minutes before you take out the grillades. I know you Wops gotta have your daily intake of garlic."

Brulee pulled a thin white sweater over her white maid's dress and scooped her large brown purse from the counter. "You talk to your wife lately?"

"Just got off the phone with her."

"She called me last night," Brulee said, jutting her jaw out. "She's sure having a good time in Paris." With that, she went out the kitchen door.

LaStanza peeked in at the wide pan of grillades and

sucked in a deep breath of the simmering veal roasting in its spicy roux. As he closed the door the phone rang. He snatched the phone off the wall.

"You up?" It was Jodie.

"Yeah. Have you eaten?"

"No. I just got up."

"How about grillades and grits?"

"You kidding?" Her voice rose.

"Brulee says to give them another half hour."

"I'll be right there."

She arrived just as LaStanza was pulling the aluminum wrapped bread from the oven. She asked if he needed any help and he sent her into the dining room where the grillades and grits and candid yams were already laid out, with two settings.

"Nice, huh?" he said as he opened the bread.

"You telling me?"

He still wasn't used to all this rich people shit.

Jodie had pulled on a white tee-shirt and cut-offs. Her hair looked freshly blow dried. His was everywhere. He had to keep brushing it from his eyes as he dug into the veal medallions and the thick brown gravy that he poured over the grits.

Brulee had outdone herself. The grillades were rich and delicious, the grits fluffy, the candid yams sweet and tangy. Even the iced tea was perfect.

"Kelly finally asked me out," Jodie said with a sly smile.

"About time." LaStanza nodded. "You're gonna have to educate that boy."

Jodie smiled.

Kelly was a tall rookie from the Fourth District who'd helped them with the Batture Murders last year. It had taken him that long to get around to asking Jodie out.

"When are you going out?"

"Next Saturday."

"*Next* Saturday?"

"He's cautious. And shy," she said.

"He's not Italian."

"Yeah, but he's a hunk."

"You had a wet-on for him from the start."

She tossed a piece of garlic bread that careered off LaStanza's elbow. He picked it up and ate it.

"I brought my notes," Jodie said.

"No. No shop talk. We're taking the night off."

"Yeah?"

"Yeah."

Jodie helped pick up. As soon as the dishes were in the dishwasher, LaStanza grabbed two cold Dixie longnecks and headed for the living room.

"Sit," he told her, handing her one of the beers and motioning to the wide sofa.

He slipped a tape in the VCR and sat at the other end of the sofa.

"What are we watching?"

"True genius," he said, twisting the cap off the beer and leaning way back.

They watched Peter Ustinov as Hercule Poirot in *Death On The Nile* without commercials, without interruptions, as if the rest of the world had slipped away.

Just before the murder, LaStanza hurried out to the kitchen and popped popcorn and grabbed two more beers.

Ustinov's Poirot was a kick in the ass. LaStanza loved those movies, loved watching the overweight Belgian use his little gray cells to outwit those clever killers.

"Hey," he said as Poirot was telling everyone that Simon Doyle had indeed murdered his wife, "how about a good Marlowe next?" He was thinking about Bogey's "The Big Sleep."

Only Jodie didn't answer. She was cutting "Zs" now. So he let her sleep and watched Poirot explain, in meticulous detail, how Simon Doyle only faked getting shot by his ex-lover so he could pull off his shoes, rambled down the other side of the steamboat to slip into his wife's room and put a bullet in her head, then ramble back, shoot himself in the leg for real this time, replace one of the spent casings in the pistol, wrap the murder weapon, a red stained handkerchief, and an ash tray in the stool he'd pinched from the Bette Davis character and throw them all overboard through the open window, into the Nile.

He woke Jodie when the movie ended.

"The husband and the girlfriend did it," he said.

"Who?"

He walked her out the side door and out to Garfield Street.

"Hey, do you have the combination to the gate?" he asked.

"What?"

"For the hot tub. *Next* Saturday night. You and Kelly. It's a great ice breaker. Get naked. There's nothing like fuckin' in a Jacuzzi."

She made that sour face again.

"I'll disappear."

"I'll pick you up in the morning, mister. We're gonna canvass the fuck out of Poeyfarre tomorrow and all weekend. Capish?"

"Capish."

Another long fuckin' weekend. Fat lot of good it'll do. But they had to do something. The Pantyhose Rapist wasn't perfect. He had to make a mistake. All they had to do was find it, like Son of Sam getting a parking ticket near his last murder scene. They all make mistakes.

Jodie climbed in the LTD and pulled away.

Yawning, LaStanza felt this evening was a respite, a calm before the storm. He felt something else, felt a creepy feeling along the back of his neck. He turned his pale eyes around to the haunted oaks of Audubon Park with their Spanish moss beards. He felt a tingling and smiled to himself. He couldn't fuckin' wait.

Mason came out of his office as LaStanza put his briefcase on his desk on bright, cool Monday morning.

"Good," he said. "you wore something good."

LaStanza looked down at his tan and gold tie and light blue shirt that seemed to go well with his off-white linen suit and brown penny loafers.

"The last time we went up to the Chief you wore a tee-shirt and jeans."

It was a Yankees jersey. LaStanza was off-duty.

"Don't fuckin' tell me," LaStanza said.

"Come on. The fat fuck's expecting us."

LaStanza looked at Jodie and shrugged.

"Close your mouth," he said as he followed Mason out.

"This shit's getting old," Mason said when they were in the elevator. "If this is what I think it is, we're going straight to the civil service commission after."

LaStanza didn't give a rat's ass. He was just angry he'd left his gangster glasses down in the LTD.

His rotudness, Chief of Police Ron Miles, sat behind his wide desk, his short arms crossed over his round belly. He looked like a statue of Buddha. His wispy white hair was curled atop his cantaloupe head. He turned his Porky Pig nose up as Mason and LaStanza walked into his office.

To his left sat Lieutenant Bob Kay of the Training Academy. Kay, with his usual crew cut and glasses, was actually in a suit, instead of the usual sweat suit. He had a pained look on his face.

LaStanzas winked at his old friend as he sat in one of the two chairs in front of the Chief's desk. Mason took the other, just as the door to their right opened and the fat Chinaman waddled in and sat in a chair next to the Chief.

Political advisor extraordinaire, as the Chief described his constant companion, the Chinese was referred to derisively by every police officer as the fat Chinaman. The man looked so much like Jabba-The-Hutt from that *Star Wars* movie, it was uncanny.

Miles cleared his throat and said, "You are not to speak until I tell you to speak. Now, Detective LaStanz, I called you in because you were AWOL from your post at the Task Force yesterday evening and had to be searched out and found." The fat fuck loved calling him "LaStanz."

Am I in another dimension, or what?

LaStanza noticed Mason taking notes.

"I believe you were located near the house of political candidate Byron Norwood. You have been spending a great deal of time near that house." Miles raised his hand as if LaStanza was going to say something, which was as far away from reality as this entire meeting.

"I'm aware that there was a murder near there. But I'm also aware that since you've been assigned to the Task Force, you have spent more time working that particular murder, instead of your assigned duties at the Task Force."

Glancing at the fat Chinaman momentarily, Miles continued, "I called this meeting to advise you and your lieutenant of two things. First, you are ordered to discontinue your work on Prytania Street. That particular case will be assigned to another detective. You will devote your time to the Task Force."

Miles picked up a piece of paper from his desk and said, "And second, I want to remind you that at a previous hearing, your conduct was found to be unstable due to your penchant for violence," He was reading now, "In that you have been involved either directly or indirectly in five shooting incidents which resulted in loss of life. You are reminded that if you become involved in any further act of extreme violence, be it justified or not, you will be immediately transferred to the Records Section. Permanently."

Miles dropped the paper on his desk and said, "That's all."

LaStanza looked at Kay whose mouth was open.

"That's all, I said."

Mason rose and tapped LaStanza on the shoulder. LaStanza stood slowly, raised his right index finger, closed his left eye, pointed the finger at the abundant belly of his rotundity, cocked his thumb back and mouthed the word "bang" as his thumb fell forward like the hammer of his .357 magnum, his hand recoiling from the shot. He winked at Kay on his way out.

The word "gelding" came to mind as he followed Mason into the elevator. That fat fuck planned to de-nut LaStanza and ice him away in the Record Section. The fuck! Before the ink on the transfer order could dry, LaStanza would be long gone lonesome blues. He'd fly straight to Lizette and watch her face explode into the biggest smile this side of Buddha.

Mason stormed into the Bureau, lighting a cigarette as he crossed the room. LaStanza picked up Spade & Archer and headed for the coffee pot where Jodie stood with Fel Jones. He held his hand up before they could even ask and pointed to Mason, who stopped just outside his door and boomed, "I'm taking that fat mother-fucker straight to the civil service commission!"

Jabbing his finger toward LaStanza, he shouted, "He thinks he's taken your gun out of your hands. I'm gonna blow his balls off. He can't do that to an officer in the field. No fuckin' way!"

Stepping forward, he added, "I want accurate time sheets on all the overtime you ain't been claiming. I'm filing a formal complaint on that fuck. Capish?"

"Capish." LaStanza smiled. He loved it when Mason bounced on his toes. Mason only did that when taking care of his men. Both knew LaStanza wouldn't hesitate to shoot anyone. Hell, he was itching to shoot someone.

Mason slammed his door so hard, he knocked two mugs off the coffee table.

"So what happened?" Jodie asked.

"I think Monsieur Norwood's been pulling political strings." LaStanza reached for the coffee.

"Norwood? He called you up because of Norwood?" Jodie had her hand on her hips. She's forgone the shoulder rig and wore her .9 millimeter in a holster on the belt of her dress gray pants.

"He thinks he just took me off the Pleasant Street Case."

"He sure don't know you." Fel said. He wore his maroon suit again.

"Maybe he does know you," Jodie said. "He gunning for you."

"The man has no dick," LaStanza said as he put the pot down and reached for the cream and sugar.

"You're thinking with your dick," Jodie said, her voice rising. She turned and walked off.

LaStanza looked at Fel and shrugged.

"Hey," he called out to his partner. "What've we got on tap with the Task Force today?"

Jodie sat in her chair, folded her arms, and turned her back to them.

Turning to Fel, he said, "Boy, am I gonna have fun fuckin' with that Nazi. He ain't seen nothing yet."

Fel grabbed his elbow, causing him to spill coffee all over the table.

"Jesus!"

Fel's face lit up. "Can I come?"

Burlwood Road

Spotting Willie Sherman hurry into the K&B Drug Store at St. Charles and Louisiana Avenue on a rainy Tuesday night, LaStanza pulled his charcoal gray Maserati across Louisiana where he could watch the door and Sherman's pick-up. He checked the Swiss clock in the dash. Eleven thirty.

Three minutes later Sherman jogged out, a six pack under his arm. He climbed into his pickup and drove off up Louisiana. LaStanza figured he'd probably lose the pick-up in the heavy traffic and was surprised to find himself accessing the Pontchartrain Expressway at Claiborne and heading up to I-10.

He followed the pick-up into Metairie where Sherman exited at Causeway Boulevard and went straight up to the bridge. He noticed two new bumper stickers on the back of the pick-up. One was a standard NRA sticker, the other, also an NRA sticker, featured a quote, "You can have my gun when you pry it from my cold dead fingers."

LaStanza smiled. He was just the man to do it.

Switching lanes between cars, Sherman was in a big hurry. LaStanza laid back and followed him across the Causeway Bridge, across the black stormy waters of Lake Pontchartrain to the north shore.

No problem keeping up on a twenty-four mile bridge

in the rain, even in traffic. When Sherman cranked it up to eighty, LaStanza just waited for them to get pulled over. But in the rain, he guessed the Causeway cops had better things to do. Wherever Sherman was heading, he was in a big fuckin' hurry.

LaStanza was certain Sherman hadn't spotted him as they exited the bridge and headed up LA 21 through Waldheim and Bush and Sun to LA 16. Just beyond Sun, the rain increased.

He's probably going home, LaStanza figured as they passed Ruby's Fresh Goods. But Sherman didn't turn down LA 437 to Yellow Tavern Road. He continued on 16 for another mile before finally slowing to take a left down a blacktop road.

LaStanza waited until the tail lights disappeared to the left before following. Not fifty yards down the road the blacktop gave way to mud. The pine forest closed in and the road snaked into a sharp left, then a sharp right, then another sharp left. LaStanza slowed the Maserati but hit a slick spot and held on as the car slid to the left into a ditch.

Coming to a rest up against the door, LaStanza put the car in "park" and looked at a large pine tree not a foot from the driver's side window. He unfastened the seat belt and took in a deep breath.

"I don't fuckin' believe this!"

He hated doing stupid things. He hated proving he was a dumb Guinea. He hated that more than anything.

You dumb Wop. What are you gonna do you? Wait out the rain?

He looked at the clock again. It was pushing one a.m. and he was sitting in a goddam ditch, his right tires up in the air, somewhere in Washington fuckin' Parish. LaStanza closed his eyes and wished he had just gone to bed after he dropped Jodie off.

A long evening following a known sex offender around had made him restless. He'd talked Jodie into using his car, because the fucker had a Corvette. They never lost him. Fat lot of good it did. After dropping Jodie off, he had to pass Norwood's. But Sherman wasn't there. So LaStanza tooled around the neighborhood and found the redneck and look at him now, sitting in a goddam ditch, rain slamming against the windows like it was time for Noah to break out another damn Ark.

LaStanza killed the engine and turned off the lights, folded his arms and waited. Maybe Sherman would come back by and get a good laugh. Sooner or later, he told himself, the rain would stop or someone would spot him, sooner or later.

Fuck! He remembered how Lizette wanted to get him a car phone and what did he say? "Car phone? What the hell to I need a car phone for?" After all, he had his little fuckin' police radio. Fat lot of good that did when he was almost in fuckin' Mississippi, the nearest repeater link-up over a hundred miles away.

LaStanza closed his eyes and made himself as comfortable as possible. He reclined the seat back and folded his arms and tried to calm down. He listened to the rain, to the torrential downpour, to the waves that rolled over the car, to the wind ripping through the tall pines.

Fuck me!

When he woke, the rain had stopped. It was so dark and so quiet, he had to feel around to realize where he was. Turning on the headlights, he leaned forward and looked up at the tall trees. He couldn't see the sky. The clock read 3:10 a.m.

He turned off the lights and climbed out the passenger side, his feet sinking up to their ankles in mud. When he tried to walk, his feet came out of his penny loafers. He was about to reach down for them when a pair of headlights made the turn in the road behind the Maserati and stopped.

He could see by their height it was a pick-up, a light color, either white or yellow. He was about to wave when he felt something along his spine and along the nape of his neck. He felt a pricking, an innate feeling, something he was sure Sicilians had felt for centuries. It wasn't fear, but it was close. It was an early warning system, a little voice that whispered, "Watch out."

LaStanza slowly edged back to the front of the Maserati. Pressing his hip against the right headlight, he reached around and pulled his service revolver from the holster on his right hip.

He caught a movement along the driver's side of the truck. It was the door opening. He saw the same movement on the other side and thought he saw something move into the woods.

The outline of a man appeared next to the left quarter panel of the truck. LaStanza heard a twig break off to his left in the woods. He backed around to the front of the Maserati.

"What's 'sa matter, Dago? You stuck or somethin'?" It was the man next to the truck. LaStanza's pale eyes picked up a movement in the trees across the road. He moved to the left headlight.

"Let me tell you what you're up against, Italian boy." The man pronounced it Eye-talian. "You got two boys in the woods on your left and two in the woods to your right. They sneaked up on you while you was sleepin'."

LaStanza took a step to his right and pressed his back up against the big pine next to the car. He felt his heart racing now and blinked sweat away from his eyes. He worked at calming himself, at hitting that plane, that leveling out when he could ice down his veins and let his mind run things, like a leopard.

"You're in over your head, boy." The man stepped away from the truck and moved toward LaStanza. The headlights of the pickup bathed him in yellow light. He was tall and wide and carried a pump shotgun, resting the stock on his hip as he moved forward. He wore a dark ski-mask.

Where's your fuckin' hood?

"What's 'sa matter? Cat got your tongue?"

A leopard is silent. LaStanza raised his .357 magnum,

squeezing the rubber grip that was tacky from his sweaty hands.

"Shoot him," someone shouted from the woods across the road.

"No," the man in the road said, "I wanna see him beg."

Fat chance.

"Get down on your knees, boy. You're about to die."

Fuck you!

The man stopped about twenty yards beyond the Maserati, resting the shotgun in his folded arms. He laughed. A man laughed in the woods across the road. Another voice laughed behind LaStanza and he remembered and old saying about the Klan. They were a rough bunch, but only rough when they were a bunch.

"Know something?" the man in the road said.

LaStanza felt sweat rolling down his temples, yet his breathing had leveled out. He'd hit that plane. He was all senses now, listening to the woods behind him, watching for any movement across the road and watching the big man in the road at the same time.

"You know what?" the man said. "You're about to be one of them 'disappeared' people."

He moved the shotgun up to his shoulder.

For an instant LaStanza saw Lizette's face.

So this is how it ends, on a muddy road with sweat in my eyes and she's on the other side of the world.

A gendarme would go to her hotel to tell her. Mason would drag his feet up the steps to knock on his parents door to tell his mother that her last son was gone.

For an instant LaStanza saw his brother's face smiling at him.

No! He blinked it away and fixed the sights of his magnum square on the chest of the big man and cocked the hammer. It sounded loud.

He could feel the man's eyes staring at him as he squeezed the trigger slowly, raising the iridescent red sights to the man's head. His hand wavered and he locked his right elbow, his left hand steadying his grip and reminded himself he'd never missed before. At that range, he'd take one fuck with him.

"You know," the big man said.

LaStanza let out his breath and breathed in again.

"If you wasn't a goddam cop you'd be dead."

"Shoot him," the voice across the road said.

"No," the big man argued. "You know the routine. Anyway, goddam New Orleans cops kill cop killers. Even white ones."

"Fuck!"

The big man was already backing toward the truck.

"You're pressing your luck, Dago. You came a cunt hair away from dying, you dumb fucker."

So did you.

Pressed back against the tree, LaStanza looked over the slanted roof of his Maserati as the big man climbed into the front cab of the truck, watched a man cross the road from the right and jump into the rear bed of the cab and another climb into the passenger side. The headlights backed away and disappeared around the curve in the road.

LaStanza waited. He wasn't about to move. Obviously with the tree at his rear and the Maserati in front of him, he didn't provide the easiest target. So he waited and watched the road and watched the woods.

He was thinking that maybe he should get the hell out when he saw headlights on the road again, coming around the curve. *What if they changed their minds?*

He didn't need to be stupid—again.

The headlights approached directly for the Maserati, passing where the truck had stopped and finally stopped just beyond the car. LaStanza sank down as the headlights bathed the Maserati.

He heard the door open and a voice said, "Hey? Anybody there?"

Crouched, LaStanza moved around the front of the Maserati and peeked around the right headlight and saw that it was a wrecker. The driver was out now and walking around the front of the wrecker, his hands in his back pockets.

"Freeze!" LaStanza said, rising and training the still cocked magnum at the man.

His hands went straight up.

"Police," LaStanza said. "Don't fuckin' move."

"I ain't moving!"

LaStanza looked around again, at the woods and the road.

"What are you doing here?" he said.

"I got a call. A sports car in the ditch. I got a wrecker here."

LaStanza listened to the woods for several seconds.

"Who called you?"

"It was on my answering machine. It just said a sports car was stuck in the ditch on Burlwood Road."

He sounded young.

"Step up to the car and put your hands on the trunk."

The boy assumed the search position. He'd been handled before or watched enough TV to know. He had red hair and stood about LaStanza's height, only lighter, wearing a plaid shirt and jeans.

LaStanza touched the muzzle of magnum against the base of the man's skull and searched him. Pulling out his ID folder, LaStanza flashed it in front of the boy's face and said, "Let me see some ID."

His name was Charlie Tatum and he was nineteen, from Sheridan, Louisiana. LaStanza gave him back his driver's license and slipped the magnum back into the holster.

"Sorry about the gun," he said.

"Man, I almost peed on myself," the boy said, a relieved chuckle in his voice.

LaStanza pulled out two fifties and passed them to the boy.

"It only costs fifty," Charlie said.

"Keep it."

It took Charlie ten minutes to get the Maserati out and

that was because he made sure not to mess it up.

LaStanza apologized again about the gun.

"No problem officer."

"You got a girl?"

"Yeah?" Charlie shrugged.

LaStanza handed him another fifty. "Take her out on me," he said.

"Thanks." Charlie bounced on his feet and started back to his wrecker. LaStanza watched the Maserati slip out of the ditch.

LaStanza raised his right foot, rolled up his pants leg and pulled his sock off before climbing into the wrecker. He left both socks in the mud of a road called Burlwood, in the backwoods of a country-ass parish named for the first president of the United States.

"Where's Sheridan?" he asked Charlie as they drove along dark LA 60 all the way to Bogalusa.

"It's between Bogalusa and Franklinton. Blink and you'll miss it."

Charlie checked out the Maserati at his Mobil station in Bogalusa, and hosed it down with a power hose as LaStanza downed a cold Pepsi.

Beneath the darkest sky he ever remembered, LaStanza took LA 21 back down to Sun and Bush and Waldheim and left the north shore behind.

"You all right?" Jodie asked as LaStanza settled into the passenger seat the following afternoon.

"Didn't get much sleep."

"Nice suit," she said, backing the LTD on Garfield to Calhoun.

She was being cute again. They'd worn the same color again. He hated that. For some strange reason, she liked it. In her navy blue skirt-suit and white blouse, her weapon on her hip, she smiled smugly at him as she executed a three-point turn at the corner and took Garfield over to Henry Clay and up to St. Charles.

LaStanza wore the navy blue suit Lizette had given him

for his birthday, his magnum on his hip. He loosened his gray and silver tie and said, "I love Task Force work."

Just as they approached State Street, a beep tone came over the radio, followed by the emotionless voice of a radio operator, "Signal 42 in progress 1637 State Street."

Jodie hit the brakes and swung the LTD hard to the left, through the no-left turn sign, across the neutral ground and punched it up State Street. They were the first unit to arrive, squealing up in front of a stone two-story mansion on the downtown side of the oak lined street.

LaStanza jumped out before Jodie put the car in park. Magnum in hand, he crossed the wide yard and took the dozen brick steps in three strides up to the wooden front gallery. He heard Jodie behind him telling headquarters they were 10-97. The wooden door was open. He saw a hallway with a coat rack to the right.

Pausing at the doorway, LaStanza listened as he waited for his partner. He heard nothing inside. Jodie pressed herself against the other side of the doorway, her radio in her left hand, her semi-automatic in her right. LaStanza nodded and went in low, crossing over to the coat rack. Jodie followed in high and moved to the other side of the hall.

LaStanza raised his left hand, palm out to Jodie because he heard something. He strained to listen and heard it again. Faint, it sounded like someone crying. LaStanza stood and moved down the hall, his magnum raised and pointing up, Jodie right behind.

Peeking through an open doorway at the end of the hall on the left, he spotted a blonde-headed woman sitting in the center of a study, a telephone next to her, a stocking dangling from her neck. He took a quick look around the room, then back at the woman as he stepped aside and let Jodie take the lead.

The woman's face was in her hands as she sat cross legged. She wore a gray sweat suit. As Jodie took another step into the carpeted room, the woman looked up with teary eyes and let out a long sigh. There was a deep red mark around her neck.

"Police," Jodie said. "Is he still here?"

LaStanza stepped back into the hallway.

The woman shook her head no, pulled the stocking down and dropped it, and put her face back in her hands.

"When did he leave?" Jodie asked, going down on her haunches.

The woman shook her head.

"Which way did he go?"

The woman continued to shake her head.

"What did he look like?"

The woman stopped shaking her head, pulled her hands off her face and stared Jodie in the eyes and said, in a scratchy voice, "I know his name."

"You know him?" Jodie said.

"No. He left his wallet. It's on the mantle." She pointed across the room and said, "It fell out of his pants."

LaStanza stepped back in and moved over to the fireplace mantle and looked down at a man's wallet that lay open. A driver's license had been pulled out and lay next to the wallet. He looked down into a full round face of a clean shaven white man with puffy eyes and a receding hairline. His name was Frank K. Hughes, 5'11" tall, 200 pounds, with brown hair and eyes. He lived at 826 Calhoun Street.

"Jesus!" LaStanza turned to tell Jodie the son-of-a-bitch was his neighbor; but Jodie was sitting now, next to the victim, her head bent forward. The women talked in muffled tones.

A loud commotion in the hall turned LaStanza's gaze to the door as Frank Savage rushed in with two patrolmen.

Savage's hair was wet on a dry evening, he wore the same black tie and pants that looked as if he'd been sleeping in them. The patrolmen stopped in the doorway.

Savage walked over to LaStanza who told him it was Pantyhose all right, pointing to the stocking on the rug next to the women. Then he pointed at the mantle and said, "Look at this."

Savage leaned over the wallet and blinked.

"He dropped his wallet," LaStanza said.

Savage's mouth fell open, his brows furrowed as he leaned even closer. He looked at LaStanza, batted his wide eyes, then looked at the driver's license again. His shoulders sank, his chest caved in. He reached over and grabbed LaStanza's shoulder and said, in a gravely whisper, "Son-of-a-bitch. Son-of-a-bitch. Son-of-a-bitch!"

Savage pulled his LFR from his rear pocket and signaled LaStanza to follow him back into the hall. He stormed out, brushing the patrolmen aside. He continued down the hall, calling to Gately, who didn't answer quickly enough for Savage.

"10-19 right away," Savage snapped. Telling Gately to get over there—now.

Turning back to LaStanza, Savage stood up on his toes and said, "I don't fuckin' believe this! Do you know where there's a phone?" Savage looked into a room off to their left.

"Probably wherever the kitchen is," LaStanza said.

"Yeah," Savage brushed past him, back up the hall into the rear of the house. LaStanza found him punching numbers on a wall phone in a kitchen painted bright yellow and brown.

"Yeah," Savage said into the receiver, "it's Savage. I want you to get that fuck from the D.A.'s office, what's her name? Yeah. That's her. Get her on the phone and ask her what the fuck happened to Frank Hughes? Yeah, Hughes. Ask her why the fuck he's not in jail. That's right. He ain't. And call me on the radio." Savage hung up and took a second to catch his breath.

Gately stepped into the kitchen behind LaStanza, who decided to get out of the way. It didn't take a rocket scientist to figure out what was going on, but he didn't want to miss the show.

He almost missed Savage's opening volley because

Gately's outfit *matched* the kitchen colors. The portly dick wore a brown coat with a canary yellow shirt and a brown and yellow striped tie as wide as a hog's ass. To top it off, not that it needed topping, Gately wore green and yellow plaid pants. LaStanza reached into his coat pocket and pulled out his gangster glasses to cut the glare.

"I thought Frank Hughes was in jail!" Savage said, as if Gately had let the man out personally.

"He is."

"No he's not." Savage waved his hands in a wide circle. "He's the fuckin' Pantyhose Rapist!"

Gately rocked back on his heels and looked at LaStanza, who tapped down his gangster glasses and gleeked him.

"Ba...but," Gately mumbled.

"Exactly!" Savage noticed LaStanza's glasses and lost his train of thought momentarily before turning back to Gately. "I put in a call to the fuckin' D.A.'s office to find out how the fuck a man sentenced to *two* thirty year terms for aggravated rape is out after two months."

Gately looked at LaStanza, who couldn't help saying, "Good behavior?"

"Yeah!" Savage said, nodding to LaStanza as if there was some secret meaning to LaStanza's tired joke.

Savage started listing things on his fingers, as he leaned into Gately. "You take this crime scene."

Gately nodded.

"You," Savage pointed to LaStanza, "take your partner and canvass the neighborhood."

Davenport and Wilson stepped into the kitchen as LaStanza said, "Uh, lieutenant. You might wanna let my partner stay with the victim for a while."

"Yeah, good idea." Savage tapped his index finger gently on LaStanza's chest and turned to Davenport and Wilson. "Y'all canvass the fuck out of this neighborhood. Gately, go show them the license."

"What license?" Gately had backpedaled all the way to the door.

"Never mind," Savage said. "I'll show them."

LaStanza followed so he could see their faces. Each looked as if they'd been slapped as they recognized the face on the driver's license. Easing around them, he pulled off his glasses and went and touched Jodie's shoulder. She reached up and touched his hand momentarily, whispered something in the victim's left ear and then looked up.

"I'm going over to Calhoun," he said. "You stay with her, Okay?"

Jodie nodded but said, "Calhoun?"

"That's where Angie Rinaldi's killer lives."

Jodie was holding the victim's left hand. LaStanza turned to leave he heard the victim say, "You're going to catch him?"

LaStanza turned and backpedaled. Putting the gangster glasses back on he said, "I'm gonna shoot him."

"Good."

He hurried into the hallway and ran straight into the coat rack, jamming the hell out of his left shoulder.

Goddam glasses! He couldn't see a damn thing in the dark hallway. *How the hell do they wear these things in barrooms?* He pulled off the gangster glasses.

Rubbing his shoulder, LaStanza climbed into the LTD and drove directly to the 800 block of Calhoun Street, just off Magazine Street. The Hughes house was a narrow shotgun single nestled behind a narrow front yard. The telephone pole in front had a caution sign affixed to it. The yellow sign had a black cat on it with "Cat-Xing" stenciled on it.

Cute.

LaStanza parked the LTD beneath a weeping willow across the street and waited. He rolled down the windows of the LTD to let the evening breeze, such at it was, to filter through the car.

Fifteen minutes later the cicadas started up and continued rising and falling in long echoes down the narrow street. The traffic on Magazine continued to increase while the traffic on Calhoun remained sporadic. LaStanza paid close attention to every car that passed. He jotted down the license plate of every car with a man in it.

A half hour after arriving, headquarters put out an all points bulletin for Frank K. Hughes for aggravated rape. Along with his description, they added a description of the two vehicles registered in his name: a 1979 red Toyota two-door and a 1980 white Honda two-door.

No blue car. He could have painted the Honda. Or whoever Maria Garcia and Jimmy Dore saw on Arts Street just wasn't the killer. So much for pulling over people in sky blue cars.

An hour later Frank Savage called on the radio and asked what was happening.

"There's a woman and a child in the house, but no man. The Toyota is parked in front."

"I'll be there in a minute," Savage said. Exactly fifty-seven seconds later, he pulled his LTD up behind LaStanza and walked over and climbed into the front passenger seat.

He'd lost his tie and there was a black stain across Savage's chest. After a long look at the house, he said, "Fel Jones is bringing the papers."

"Four sets?"

"Fuckin' A."

Which meant Fel had an arrest warrant for the wonderful Mr. Hughes, as well as a search warrant for the house and for each car registered to the wonderful Mr. Hughes.

LaStanza noticed that Savage gripped the dash so hard, his fingers dug into the plastic dash of the police package LTD.

"So tell me about Hughes," he said.

Savage's jaw tightened and he spoke through gritted teeth.

"According to the fuckin' DA's office, the fuckin' judge gave him ninety days to settle his affairs before starting his two *consecutive* thirty year sentences for aggravated rape."

"Jesus Fuckin' Christ. What judge?"

"Feldbruck. The dickless one, himself."

Who else? What other judge except his honorable F. P. Feldbruck would give a convicted serial rapist street time before going to jail? For years LaStanza tried to learn what the fuck the "F. P." stood for. Most cops were certain it stood for "Fuck the Police."

Feldbruck was the judge who made the sheriff's office stop bringing prisoners into court in handcuffs, who led the fight for prisoner's rights as to over-crowding in Parish Prison. No, jail shouldn't be uncomfortable. Feldbruck was best known as the greatest practitioner of quickie bonds, decreeing from his bench, as if he was the fuckin' burning bush, that a prisoner must be processed and out of Central Lockup within two hours, even if the police officer was not finished his or her report.

Hell, no way a prisoner could be rolled out that fast, even on a slow night. It took that long for the strobe lights on the sheriff's office mug cameras to recharge, much less fingerprinting and delousing. It took time.

Feldbruck brought in several jailers who weren't fast enough into his court to publicly scold, but ran up into a brick wall when the criminal sheriff refused to answer his majesty's order, refusing to allow any more of his personnel to be ordered into court, refused to go himself, and told the judge, on TV, to get lost. Feldbruck tried issuing instanzas and bench warrants, but couldn't get anyone to serve them. Bailiffs worked for the criminal sheriff.

Feldbruck turned to the police but ran into another stone wall. The Assistant Chief of Operations ordered that all of Feldbruck's warrants and instanzas be brought to him so he could personally throw them into the fuckin' garbage can.

Feldbruck actually tried the state police. He couldn't get them to even come to his courtroom. Hell, most troopers had no idea where it was, nor did they want any part of Feldbruck's circle jerk.

Now this.

For years LaStanza had dreamed of ways to nail Feldbruck. Sometimes, when riding the midnight shift during a rare calm night in the Sixth District, he and Stan would concoct maniacal plans on how to fuck over Feldbruck. Stan knew where the judge lived and wanted to firebomb the old fuck's house, but Feldbruck had kids.

Stan actually paid a whore once to set up the old asshole, but the judge wouldn't bite. "You can't use a pussy to ambush a man without a dick," Stan concluded.

Sitting beneath the willow, waiting for Fel to arrive, with Frank Savage squeezing the vinyl off the dashboard, LaStanza smiled to himself as he thought of a way to nail Feldbruck. Once and for fuckin' all.

Palmetto Street

Pulling into the parking lot of Panguin Financial Services, along the decrepit section of Earhart Boulevard, not far from the Calliope Housing Project, LaStanza stopped the LTD behind a row of cars parked against the blond brick office building. The cars were all the same, all full sized Buicks, all sky blue.

"Fuck," Jodie said.

"Exactly."

LaStanza parked the LTD in a slot marked "visitor" and climbed out, leaving his navy blue coat and LFR behind. Stretching, he squinted up at the morning sun and yawned. He took a second to readjust his gray and silver tie.

"Let me," Jodie said, moving around the LTD. She straightened the knot and then flicked a fingernail across his chin. "You need a shave, boy."

He was too tired to smile. He followed his partner in through the glass front door of the office building and up to the receptionist's desk. He spotted the phone message pad immediately, easing around his partner as she dug her credentials out of her purse and showed them to an horse-faced receptionist.

"Police," Jodie said. "We'd like to speak to whomever is in charge."

The receptionist smiled and said, "That'll be Mr. Panguin." She picked up a phone and punched out a number and covered the mouthpiece with her left hand and said, "Mr. Panguin. The police are here. This is Trilby up front. The new girl. They want to see you." Trilby nodded and said, "Yes, sir," and hung up.

"Mr. Panguin will be up in a minute." She looked LaStanza up and down and added, "Would you like some coffee?"

Jodie, who looked as fresh as always, said, "Do you take most of the messages here?" She tapped her fingernails on the phone message pad.

"Oh, yes." Trilby smiled nervously. She looked to be in her fifties.

"Is this the only phone message pad?"

"Yes." The nervous smile was replaced by a cautious frown.

The message pad had a spiral side and was the kind that left a carbon copy behind.

A door opened to Jodie's right and a tall man with thick Buddy Holly glasses stepped out and introduced himself as Frederick Panguin. Bald and pushing sixty, the man wore a three-piece dark green suit with a yellow tie. He invited them in.

Jodie nodded to the phone pad and LaStanza sat in the chair in front of Trilby's desk. For the next ten minutes he watched the woman empty her pencil sharpener, adjust the clock on her desk, clean her bifocal glasses with Windex and a Kleenex, adjust the lamp next to the clock, sharpen two pencils, empty her pencil sharpener again and answer two phone calls—one for Mr. Panguin who was in a meeting and one for a Mr. Simmons who was out of the office on calls. She took messages, dutifully noting everything on the phone message pad. She tore out the original messages and slipped them into a spiral ring contraption at the front of her desk.

When Jodie came back out of the same door, LaStanza knew it hadn't gone well. Frowning, she left the door open and stepped up to LaStanza and said, "I'll be back with a warrant." He gave her the car keys and made himself comfortable in the same chair.

Trilby was re-adjusting her lamp again when the front door slammed back open and Jodie stormed back in and handed LaStanza his LFR before storming back out.

LaStanza adjusted the volume and went back to being comfortable.

The phone buzzed on Trilby's desk. She answered it and said, "Yes, sir." Standing, she reached for the phone message pad.

"No," LaStanza said rising quickly. "Don't touch that. It's evidence."

The woman dropped it as if it was on fire and sat back down. When the side door opened again, LaStanza turned and smiled at Frederick Panguin. The man harrumphed, tugged at his vest and tried reaching around LaStanza for the phone message book. LaStanza slapped a cuff on Panguin's extended hand, spun the man around and cuffed both hands behind the man's back. Then he sat the stunned Mr. Panguin in the chair he'd been sitting in and pulled out a Miranda Card from his ID folder.

"Before I ask you any questions, you must understand your rights," LaStanza began. "You have the right to remain silent..."

"You can't do this!" Panguin protested.

"I just did," LaStanza said. "You're under arrest, mister. Capish?"

"Miss Trilby, call Mr. Hanson."

LaStanza turned to Trilby and shook his head no and pointed for her to sit in her chair. She did. He finished reading the Miranda card and then told Trilby that she wasn't to call anyone nor answer the phone.

"Just sit tight," he told her. "You'll be fine."

Standing next to Trilby's desk, LaStanza invited each person who peeked a curious head into the office from the rear offices to come on in. He lined them along the far wall and told them to keep quiet.

"But..." a man in a seersucker suit protested.

"It's a raid," he said.

When he heard a disturbance call at Panguin Financial Services on his LFR, he told headquarters that he was the disturbance and asked them to send a beat unit over to assist in the disturbance.

Two Sixth District Units pulled up outside simultaneously. LaStanza didn't recognize the two patrolmen coming up to the front door, but he sure recognized the tall, blond haired sergeant behind them.

"Hey, hey. Candy-Ass. What it is, boy?" Sergeant Stanley Smith, Stan-the-Man, stood an even six feet. His blond hair was properly moussed so that he looked like a bad Scandinavian hair-product commercial, his uniform shirt properly taken in around the arms to enhance his biceps and triceps.

Looking at the line of people against the wall, Stan said, "What ya' got here? Panty-sniffers? Child Molesters?" Pointing to a man with buck teeth, Stan said, "Wait, it's a Bugs Bunny look-a-like contest, right?"

LaStanza reached over and pulled Stan so hard, the big lug had to catch himself from falling over Trilby's desk. The horse-faced secretary let out a mousy scream.

LaStanza stepped around to the most efficient looking person in the line, a heavy-set woman in a dark business suit and skirt, and said, "Y'all can go back to work now. Just don't go removing files."

The woman blinked at him, but he could see she wasn't afraid, nor even bothered by Stan's shenanigans. She folded her arms as the rest of the group hurried back into the rear office area.

"Where are the personnel files kept?" LaStanza asked the woman with the folded arms.

"Mr. Panguin's office."

LaStanza waved one of the patrolmen over and said, "This officer will go with you. Show him Panguin's office, please."

The woman looked at Panguin, then back to LaStanza, then turned slowly and went into the rear offices with the patrolman.

"Just make sure no one touches the files," LaStanza told the patrolman, "until my partner gets here with the search warrant. Okay?"

The patrolman shrugged as he followed the woman.

When LaStanza turned back around, he found Stan sitting on the receptionist's desk, flexing his muscles for Trilby, who sat in her chair, both hands up to her mouth, her eyes as large as golf balls.

"What's the old asshole doing in cuffs?" Stan asked LaStanza, nodding to Mr. Panguin, who fluffed his cheeks in exasperation.

LaStanza wasn't about to answer. Answering only encouraged Stan.

"He pissed off the police, didn't he?" Stan pointed to Panguin. "You did something to piss off Candy-Ass didn't you?" Shaking his head he winked at LaStanza and said, "He pissed you off. I know. I know you inside and out."

"I..." Panguin stuttered. "I...If you'll take these handcuffs off."

LaStanza put a hand on the old man's shoulder and said, "We can't un-arrest you. Just sit tight."

A wide grin crossed Stan's mouth. He looked at Trilby and said, "Did he bounce on his toes like a bantam rooster? Did he foam at the mouth and put the muscle on the old geezer? Did he pull up your skirt to take a peek?"

Trilby grabbed a scratch pad and put it between her teeth; and LaStanza saw that she was trying to hide the fact that she was laughing.

"Hey Candy-Ass, remember the time we padlocked the Young Men's Social Club and pulled the fuses outta the wall, then started beating on the walls with our nightsticks?"

LaStanza put his hands behind his head, leaned back and closed his eyes. Ignoring Stan rarely worked, but it was better than talking to him.

"Ever been to the Young Men's Social Club?" Stan asked Trilby. "It's on Clio right next to the Melpomene Housing Project. You know the place. It's painted vomit green."

LaStanza peeked. Trilby's eyes were wet. The scratch pad trembled between her teeth now. He was feeling sorry for her. But that's what she got for working in a place that employed a rapist-murderer, especially a place that let the man return to work to make a little extra cash before starting two consecutive thirty year terms, not to mention allowing the man to use a company car for his night prowling.

"Know why we call him Candy-Ass?" Stan had a captive audience with Trilby.

"It's because he ain't."

Fucker's logic was legendary.

"See that little bastard," Stan continued. "He's killed more people than Wyatt Earp." No doubt he'd been talking to Snowood. LaStanza shuddered at the idea.

"Here's my card," Stan said next. He handed a business card to Trilby, then stepped over and dropped one in Panguin's lap, before shoving one under LaStanza's nose.

"I know you ain't sleeping. Look at my new card. Can you dig it?"

LaStanza took the card and read it. In the upper left hand corner was a silver NOPD star-and-crescent badge, in the upper right was a big "6" with blood dripping from it. Across the center of the card was printed: H.A.N.D.A. Along the bottom was Stan's name and the address of the Sixth District Station and phone number. Beneath Stan's name was printed: Playboy Without Portfolio.

"What does H.A.N.D.A. mean?" Trilby asked.

"Have A Nice Day Asshole."

The woman laughed aloud, looked at Panguin and stuffed the scratch pad back into her mouth.

The front door opened and Jodie came back in with Frank Savage who pointed to Stan and the patrolman and said, "Outside."

Stan and Savage never liked one another, ever since Stan fucked Savage's sister then told everyone about it at roll call. It wasn't so much that he screwed her, it was how he told everyone she was a lousy lay, a cold-as-marble fuck. The two leered at one another as Stan walked slowly out.

Jodie checked out Panguin and winked at LaStanza as she moved to the phone message pad and flipped it back until she found the carbon of the message they'd found in Frank Hughes' wallet. It was timed an hour before he attacked the woman on State Street.

Then Jodie led the search of Panguin's office for Hughes' personnel files and whatever logs kept on the company vehicles. LaStanza had his head in a file across the wide office, when Jodie yelled, "Bingo."

On the night Angie Rinaldi was murdered, Hughes checked out a company car and returned it the following morning.

"What about Burgundy Street?" Savage said. They checked the dates together. Another Bingo. Hughes checked out a company car every night the Pantyhose rapist attacked, including Poeyfarre. In fact, he still had a car out, the one he probably used on State Street.

Stan was gone when LaStanza led the way out with Panguin and the files. He passed the old man to one of the patrolmen who'd gathered to see what was going on.

"Can you take him to C.L.U. for me?"

"Why not?"

LaStanza spotted someone beyond the uniformed officers, someone leaning against the side of a brown Toyota.

"Thanks," LaStanza told the patrolman, "We'll be over to book him in a minute." He moved around the police cars to the brown Toyota.

His old high school buddy, George Lynn smiled that familiar, crooked smile and said, "That shit you gave me on Feldbruck checked out. I got independent confirmation. You gonna love tomorrow's paper." *The Times-*

Picayune always needed independent confirmation. Lynn grinned widely and did and little tap dance. "We're really gonna nail that bastard."

"Good."

LaStanza noticed that Lynn had put on even more weight and had lost more hair in the year since he helped with the Batture Murders.

"See this place," LaStanza said, pointing over his shoulder at Panguin's Financial Services. "Get out your note pad. It gets better."

LaStanza followed Jodie through the front door of the Driskeen Psychiatric Institute on Palmetto Street the following evening at six o'clock sharp. Fel and Savage were close behind. But this was Jodie's show. It was her warrant. Gately and Davenport stayed outside with the wrecker driver to search the parking lot for the blue Buick.

The new green glass building, built along a dark stretch of Palmetto near Airline Highway, overlooked the picturesque concrete Palmetto canal that sliced through that part of town like a futuristic eye-sore from an Orwellian nightmare. The canal stank of a mildew and that rich, chlorophyll smell of fungi. It smelled the same inside the Institute.

Wearing a kelly green blouse and black slacks, her weapon on her right hip, her cuffs tucked into her belt at the small of her back, Jodie stepped up to the nurse receptionist and said, "Police. We understand you have a patient here by the name of Frank Hughes."

The nurse was middle aged, black, and stocky. She stuck out a defiant chin and sat down behind a computer console.

"What was that name?"

"Frank K. Hughes."

The nurse typed on a keyboard. Jodie's right leg wiggled nervously. They'd positioned Darlene Wilson and a host of patrolmen around the clinic, in case Hughes tried to rabbit out a window or something.

"His doctor is Dr. Radosti. I'll page him." The nurse reached for the phone.

"What room is Hughes in?" Jodie asked.

"I'll page his doctor."

Fel Jones moved around the large semi-circle desk and pulled the nurse away on her roller desk chair. The phone console clanged to the floor as she spun in a neat circle. Fel looked at the computer screen and said, "Room 1027."

LaStanza waved to the ancient security guard at the front door.

"Where's Room 1027?"

The old man pointed to the right, folded his arms and went back to sleep.

Jodie led the way with LaStanza right behind. They walked quickly, turned into the room and found Frank K. Hughes sipping orange juice and watching cartoons on an overhead TV. He blinked his brown eyes at them and went, "Heh."

Savage and Fel waited by the door. Jodie stepped up with the warrant in her hand and said, "You're under arrest."

LaStanza slapped a handcuff on the burly man's left arm, grabbed Hughes by the hair on the back of his head and pulled him out of the bed, face first to the linoleum floor. Pressing his right knee against the big man's backbone, LaStanza pulled the right hand around and cuffed Hughes in the back. No need to pat him down, his bare ass poked out of the backless hospital gown.

LaStanza smiled at his partner as he rose and said, "Thanks."

Jodie nodded and began reading a Miranda card to Hughes who had tucked his chin down and curled up into a fetal position. Just as she finished, a loud voice rang out behind Savage and Fel as a tall, blond haired doctor elbowed his way in and stopped just inside the doorway.

"What is the meaning of this?"

LaStanza hated it when people said shit like that. He

spotted the doctor's name tag—*A. B. Radosti. M.D.*

"This man's under arrest," Jodie said, brushing her hair out of her eyes. "We also have a search warrant for his medical records. Are you his doctor?"

Radosti pressed the aluminum clipboard he carried to his chest and said, "This man is my *patient.* You have no right to break in here..."

Jodie lunged forward right in the man's face.

"This man is my prisoner!"

Radosti wouldn't retreat an inch. Glaring back he snarled, "This man is under treatment here."

"Not anymore," Jodie said, her right index finger in front of Radosti's nose. "This is a private hospital. He checked himself in. He can check himself out."

Radosti's eyes bulged. He leaned forward and bumped Jodie with his chest. Fel reached for him. Radosti swung the clipboard around and caught Jodie on the nose.

LaStanza saw a streak of blood as his partner fell back, giving him a clear shot at the doctor. He kicked Radosti in the balls and as the man collapsed caught him with a two-fisted roundhouse punch across the left jaw that snapped the good doctor's head back and laid him out cold.

"Home run," Fel said of LaStanza baseball bat swing-punch. He quickly cuffed Radosti behind the back.

Savage helped Jodie to the bed and had her put her head back as LaStanza got a cold face rag from the private bathroom. It took nearly five minutes to stop the bleeding.

"I don't think it's broken," Savage said.

Another doctor, standing out in the hallway, asked if he could help. Indian, the man spoke in a heavy sub-continent accent. Stepping over Radosti and around Hughes, the doctor examined Jodie and asked one of the nurses in the hallway for some gauze and an ice pack.

"It's not broken," Dr. Asoka said. "She'll be fine. I'm not so sure about him."

Hughes lay stiffly now, his legs straight out, his head

curled back, his open mouth dripping saliva on the floor.

"Okay," Savage said as Gately and Davenport and Wilson and several patrolmen appeared in the hall. "Y'all help Kintyre and LaStanza with these prisoners," he told the patrolmen.

"Come on," he told his crew. "We're gonna strip-search this place for his records."

Radosti came to as he was lifted and was taken, shaking his head, out to a patrol car and the waiting camera of the lensman outside with George Lynn. Hughes had to be carried. Fel and LaStanza, assisted by an Irish patrolman named Tooney, dragged the big fuck out to the LTD and tossed him on the back seat.

Jodie kept the face rag against her nose all the way to Central Lock-Up. "Is it red?" she asked when they pulled up in the garage.

"Why don't you just sit here. I'll process him and bring him out. Collect your thoughts for the interview."

Jodie let out a sigh. "Did I get any blood on my blouse?"

"No. Just relax. I'll be right back, Rudolph."

She shot him the bird.

LaStanza pulled off his red and sea-green tie and laid it across his gray suit coat before going around to the rear passenger side door. He was relieved to see Mark Land step out of CLU.

"Give me a hand."

"What's his problem?"

"He's faking."

"Let me," Mark said as he reached a bear claw in and pulled Hughes out in one swipe. Hughes turned his head aside so it wouldn't hit the door jam on the way out.

"See. Faking."

LaStanza and Mark took him into the lock up. Mark did most of the carrying, jamming Hughes against two door frames on the way to the holding cell. LaStanza leaned on a well worn desk and tried his best not to smell the stale cigarette smoke.

Fel Jones came in with a patrolman and Dr. A. B. Radosti. Fel grinned broadly as he announced, "Who wants to fingerprint this fuckin' doctor. He's a psychiatrist." There were six volunteers.

Fel stopped Radosti next to LaStanza and said, "Little guy packs a wallop, don't he?"

Radosti wouldn't look at LaStanza who moved his left hand behind him because it was red and felt on fire from the rabbit punch to Radosti's jaw.

"I want a lawyer," Radosti said as a portly deputy swung him around toward the holding cell, as if they had lawyers around Central Lock-up for the asking.

"Shut the fuck up!"

Two huge black deputies took Hughes out of the holding cell as Radosti was shoved in. They uncuffed Hughes and pulled him to the fingerprint station.

"Say, white boy. We ain't carrying you."

When Hughes sagged and was about to fall, one of the deputies slapped him across the back of the head so hard he stood up straight. The only other trouble they had with Hughes was when they started to take his mug shot.

"He's crying," one of the deputies told LaStanza.

Mark stepped around them and over to Hughes and pressed his nose against Hughes' wet face and spoke in a low, gravely voice. His right paw rose suddenly and grabbed Hughes by the throat and squeezed. Hughes' face turned red, then white, then blue before Mark let go.

"He'll be fine now," Mark said on his way out.

The vulture below the clock leaned to its left again. The clock was crooked too, leaning to its right. It read 10:15 p.m.

LaStanza picked up Spade & Archer and took a sip of the fresh coffee-and-chicory he'd just brewed. He looked at the closed door of the interview room where Jodie had been sequestered alone with the Pantyhose Killer for the last hour. One-on-one. Mano-e-Mano. She'll get him to cop. She'll get him to put himself into the electric chair, just like she did with the Batture Murderer. Give the D.A. a confession and you're home free.

He put the mug down and called the last Pantyhose victim, the woman on State Street. When she answered her phone he identified himself and told her they'd caught Frank K. Hughes. Then he told her the same thing he'd told all the other living victims, as well as the surviving family members of Angie Rinaldi and the Poeyfarre victim—told them they should file suit against Panguin Financial Services and their insurers and how he and Jodie and the rest of the Task Force would voluntarily testify for them.

"Detective LaStanza," the woman said in a low voice.

"Yes."

"Why didn't you shoot him?"

LaStanza rubbed his eyes and said, "Too many witnesses."

Hanging up, he picked up the memo he'd found on his desk when he and Jodie and Mark brought Hughes up from CLU, before Mark had to roll out to help Snowood and Stevens with a misdemeanor murder at another fuckin' barroom. It was from the Chief of Police. He read it again, closed his eyes, and rubbed his temples for a long time.

It was a warning, a reminder from the Chief, in writing, that he was ordered to cease investigating case number H-080791. He was ordered to list the case as unsolved: investigation suspended.

He opened his hands and let his eyes focus on the right palm and then the left, at the small pink splotches there. Sucking in a breath, he remembered the scorched smell of burned flesh, the sting of the gasoline. He'd never forget that smell. He'd never forget the man writhing, his muscles contracting while still alive, his mouth opening and closing as he said something that sounded like, "Kee. Kee."

Who was he? The autopsy report said he had dental

work that was probably military. Was he a Nam vet, like LaStanza? Certainly older, he might have been in Nam during the worst times, Tet, DaNang or maybe even Khe Sahn.

Buried now in Potter's Field, he was a nameless corpse in a nameless grave. Who was he? A loner who died alone. No, he didn't die alone. Someone was there.

In his nearly four years in Homicide, LaStanza had never suspended a case. He'd solved them all. He reached into his top desk drawer and pulled out a vacation form and slipped it into the beat-up Smith-Corona he shared with Snowood.

He turned his left hand over and looked at the red mark along his knuckles where he laced up Radosti. It was puffy and hurt when he touched it, but was worth it.

Fel Jones entered as LaStanza finished and pulled the form out of the typewriter.

"Got a message for ya'," Fel called out as he headed for the coffee pot. "Radosti's gonna sue you."

LaStanza turned and jerked his hand over his crotch in a simulated masturbation move. "He can take a number and stand in line."

They both turned when the squad room slammed open behind them. Frank Savage came in with Gately. "Yo, ho," Savage said as he crossed the room carrying a brown cardboard box. "We have Hughes' records. He checked himself in at noon today, just like his wife said. And we also have Radosti's records."

"Radosti's?" LaStanza said.

"Yeah. He's a doctor and a patient too. He suffers from an overly aggressive personality. He punches out patients and his own doctors regularly. Can't stand authority."

LaStanza leaned back in his worn metal chair and had a good laugh at that. So much for Radosti's lawsuit. "What kind of fuckin' hospital is that?"

"It's a fuckin' asylum!"

Savage and Gately helped themselves to the coffee while LaStanza signed the vacation form, took it to the

Xerox machine to make copies and slipped the original under Mason's door and one into Mark's "In" basket. He put the third into his briefcase, sat back in his chair and kicked his feet up on the desk and let his mind wander back to Pleasant Street.

He daydreamed of leopards, of a svelte cat hunkering down on the low branch of a tree, hidden in the sunlit foliage, its spots blending in with the dapple sunlight, its pale eyes focusing on an unsuspecting gazelle. LaStanza closed his eyes and watched the leopard move in slow motion, crouching and then leaping to drag the gazelle down. The leopard's teeth crushed the gazelle's larynx as it suffocated the animal, then carried it back up the tree, away from the lions and the fuckin' hyenas.

LaStanza floated in a dreamy, quiet state. He felt himself nodding off. He heard Savage and Fel and Gately moving around and talking, but their voices faded until they were gone.

Someone shook his foot and said, "Wake up boy."

LaStanza opened his eyes and saw Mark turn and go into his office.

Groggy, LaStanza tried to pull his feet off the desk, but they were asleep and fell heavily to the floor. Paul Snowood and Steve Stevens stood next to LaStanza's desk, staring at him with blank eyes, eyes that revealed they hadn't a clue—about anything.

LaStanza rubbed his legs and felt needles all the way to his ankles.

Snowood raised the Styrofoam cup in his left hand and spit a glob of brown shit into the cup and said, "I hear you been arresting all kindsa people. Punchin' them too." He wore a dark brown cowboy suit with a dark brown shirt and black rope tie, black Stetson tilted back on his head. Stevens wore a maroon jacket with a pink shirt, a dark red, white and blue tie, and burnt orange pants. LaStanza looked down for the clown shoes, but Stevens had forgotten them.

Still rubbing his legs, he looked up at the clock and

realized he'd slept over an hour.

"Well," Snowood said, "your vacation's over now. No more fuckin' Task Force."

Stevens still had a blank look in his eyes. He nodded, his head bobbing like a blithering idiot, up and down, up and down.

Snowood put his elbow on Steven's shoulder and said, "Can't help but catch 'em when they leave their fuckin' wallet behind, can ya'?"

LaStanza grabbed Spade & Archer and tried standing. His legs wobbled and his feet tingled in sharp pin pricks.

"Thank God criminals are stupid," Snowood said, spitting again into the cup.

LaStanza made it to the coffee pot only to find it empty.

The interview room door opened and Jodie stepped out into the squad room.

"Who wants to take this douche-bag to the john?"

Fel volunteered.

Jodie walked over to LaStanza, rubbing her neck. She winked at him as Mark stepped out of his office with a, "Well?"

"Hammer City," Jodie said. "He copped out. He was crying like a baby." Her nose was still red and there were bags under her eyes. She looked disappointedly at the empty coffee pot and shifted her weight to her right leg and said, "He claimed he killed the two by mistake. He said if they hadn't resisted, like the others, they'd still be alive."

"What a guy," Mark said. "You need any more tapes?"

"No, it's over," she said, reaching for the coffee pot. Mark reached around LaStanza and took it out of her hand and passed it to Stevens.

"Here," their sergeant said, "make yourself useful."

LaStanza passed Stevens the coffee grounds holder.

Mark slammed his hands together and said, "Good work." He put a friendly hand on Jodie's shoulder and said, "I'll write up a daily for Mason."

Savage and Gately and Fel and even Snowood congratulated Jodie before moving off. LaStanza waited until they were alone to ask about her nose.

"It's Okay. How does it look?"

"Like Rudolph."

She poked him in the ribs.

"It's different this time, isn't it?"

Her wide set eyes squinted at him.

"Not like the Batture," he said and a recognition seemed to come to her eyes. When she'd gotten the Batture killer to cop out, she was so high he had to haul her in like a kite.

"You're learning," he said. "To maintain that even strain."

"Hey," Mark called out loudly from his office. "What the fuck is this?"

LaStanza watched his partner as he said, "It's my vacation slip."

"Ninety fuckin' days?"

"I got 'em coming. Talk to Mason."

Jodie's crooked her head to the left. "Vacation?"

LaStanza walked over to his desk and picked up the note from the chief and passed it to his partner. Her face revealed nothing as she read.

In a low voice he said, "You can handle the rest of this."

Nodding without looking up, she said, "I'm on the downhill side."

"And I got a murder to solve."

Looking up, she arched an eyebrow and focused those hazel eyes at his and said, "Not alone, you're not." She shoved the note back at him and pulled her hair back with both hands. "I'm working it with you." She reached over and poked him in the sternum with the knuckles of her right hand.

It hurt.

"Capish?" she said.

"Capish."

"Count me in too," Fel said. He'd come up behind

LaStanza and grinned when LaStanza looked at him. "I want a piece of that Nazi too."

Hughes stood behind Fel. He was cuffed in front now. Hughes looked at LaStanza and smiled and said, "Hi."

LaStanza looked back at the silly fuck and said, "Does your mother know what you do?"

The smile disappeared. Hughes' chin sank. Fel took him back into the interview room. "What?" Fel said loudly as he shoved the big man ahead. "You gonna cry?"

Jodie tapped LaStanza on the shoulder and said, sarcastically, "Does your mother know what you do?"

"I saw it in a James Garner movie."

Prytania Street

A figure slipped away from the Norwood house, through the side gate and ran, hunched over across Harmony Street and up the river side of Prytania. LaStanza leaned out the window of his Maserati and watched the dark clad figure hurry along the wet sidewalk.

Whoever it was had his hands in his pockets and his head down. As he passed beneath a yellow street lamp, LaStanza saw he or she wore a hooded sweatshirt. Not running anymore, the figure walked quickly, not looking around at all.

LaStanza climbed out and tucked his LFR into the rear of his jeans as he moved up the lake side of Prytania and followed the hooded figure across Pleasant and Toledano toward Louisiana. Dodging the standing water on the sidewalk, LaStanza followed silently, his Nike running shoes deadening his footfalls.

The hooded figure approached Louisiana, turned quickly to the left and started running again. When LaStanza made the corner, he was gone. Stopping in front of The Colapissa, LaStanza looked down Louisiana and then across the neutral ground, then turned slowly and looked at the dull brown front door of the pink stucco apartment building.

He walked up to the front door and twisted the knob

and it opened. He looked at his watch. It was 1:10 a.m. He found a large magnolia tree just below The Colapissa on Louisiana and stood beneath it, in the darkness and waited. A drop of rain smacked him on the shoulder of his light-weight black sweatshirt. As the wind picked up, more drops fell on him. They felt good.

The street smell clean after the rain. The quiet was broken only by the occasional car, tires hissing on the wet pavement as they passed behind LaStanza. After a while, he noticed the sounds of the tree, the rubbery dark leaves rubbing together in the breeze, the creaking of the twisted branches.

He couldn't see his watch in the darkness, but had a clear view of the front door of The Colapissa when the hooded figure stepped out and walked away quickly, head down. For a moment LaStanza saw Kaiser Billyday in the doorway, holding the door open momentarily, his basset-hound face gleaming under the bare bulb above the door.

The hooded figure walked slowly back up Prytania, crossing Toledano and Pleasant Street. LaStanza, moving swiftly and as quietly as he could, closed on the figure. Just as the hooded figure started to cross Harmony Street, LaStanza reached out and grabbed its right arm and swung the figure around.

Biff Norwood let out a cat-like cry and tried to pull away. LaStanza squeezed the boy's biceps and held on. The boy's blue eyes looked green under the corner street-light as he stared back at LaStanza with genuine fear. His lower lip quivered. He had trouble catching his breath.

LaStanza let go of the arm. Biff caught himself as he fell back into the street, looked around, and backed slowly across to the black wrought iron fence and the side gate of his parents' house. His head lowered again, Biff went up the side steps and back into the house through the side door.

LaStanza was still standing under the corner street light twenty minutes later when Willie Sherman pulled up in his pickup and parked along the Harmony Street side of the Norwood house. Fitting the pieces into place left LaStanza frozen in place, a chilly spine and the hair standing out on his arms.

Sherman pressed his face against the side window of his pickup and stared out at LaStanza. A large drop of rain hit LaStanza on top of his head, and he looked at Sherman and mouthed, "Fuck you."

LaStanza walked back to his Maserati and drove home. He fired up the Jacuzzi, broke out a bottle of Valpolicella, stripped and climbed into the hot tub with the wine and a glass. He sipped the rich northern Italian wine and let the bubbling water relax his body and let his gray cells work overtime.

Jodie picked LaStanza up at ten Saturday morning. In a dress white shirt and designer jeans, she looked extra nice with her dark red lipstick and her page boy fluffed out.

"Over a week," she said when he climbed into the passenger door of the LTD. She had her wide set cat-eyes narrowed at him. "What happened to Fel and I helping you?"

"I didn't need y'all until now."

She slipped the car into reverse and backed up Garfield to Calhoun.

"Owen and DeLeon told me in court yesterday that you've been on the Norwood house like beans on rice."

She wore different perfume, stronger stuff. He told her it smelled nice.

"It's Parisian," she said. "Lizette sent it. Probably costs a fortune."

LaStanza smiled. His wife had sent him a dozen silk ties and matching socks. 'Zif he would ever wear silk socks. But he wiped the smile away and focused his mind back on the matter at hand.

"I need to talk with Norwood's son," he said as Jodie performed another three-point turn to take Garfield to

Henry Clay up to St. Charles.

"Norwood left town Thursday. His wife just might let us talk to the boy."

"Okay," Jodie said, a puzzled look on her face.

"Yesterday morning around one I caught his son stealing over to The Colapissa to meet Kaiser Billyday." He didn't add that all those long nights sitting and waiting finally paid off. He didn't have to.

Jodie pulled the LTD over and put it in park.

"Wait. Norwood's son and the old arsonist?"

How do they say it in the projects?

"Zactly."

Jodie slipped the car back into gear.

"The kid's terrified of me," he said. "But he just might talk to you, if we can get him to the Bureau." He didn't have to finish it off with how they needed to get the boy away from the security of home.

Nodding as she turned on to St. Charles, Jodie said, "You might want to tell me what I'm supposed to ask the little bastard."

"Turn around," he said. "Let's go to la Madeleine and talk it over some French roast."

"And an almond croissant," she said, making the same illegal left turn at State Street she'd made the evening Frank K. Hughes dropped his wallet.

Two cups of French roast coffee and a hot, sweet croissant later, Jodie parked the LTD directly in front of Norwood's house. LaStanza climbed out, moved between the magnolias next to the street, and led the way through the front gate, across the fine trimmed lawn and up the twenty concrete steps to the wide front gallery. He rang the brass doorbell with the silver crossed-sabers above and below. The faint echo of "Dixie" chimed behind the white wooden door with its two cut glass ovals.

Buffy Norwood peeked out of one of the glass ovals, blinked at LaStanza, and opened the door. Spotting Jodie, she looked her up and down and fixed her eyes on Jodie's badge clipped to the front of her brown belt.

"My-o-my," Buffy said, in her best Sally Field impersonation, "they make partners dress alike now."

Except for the fact that LaStanza's jeans were faded, they were dressed alike, down to the white tennis shoes.

Buffy wore a typical uptown matron's flowing off-white dress, ankle length, with a round neck and no waist. She had her brown hair up in a bun again and wore little make-up, if any.

Turning her gaze to LaStanza, he noticed her eyes looked clear. She put a hand on her hip and said, "Byron's not here."

"I know," LaStanza said, "we'd like to talk to Biff."

Buffy leaned her head forward and said, "What?"

"We'd like to talk to you and Biff. At our office, if it wouldn't be too much trouble."

Buffy raised her right hand. "Wait. You want to talk..." Stopping in midsentence, she gave LaStanza a hard look and rocked back on her heels a second before turning and going back into the house. She left the front door open.

Two minutes later she reappeared, digging in a large baggy purse, Biff standing behind her in a green "Vandeer Academy" tee-shirt and a pair of those baggy white shorts, the ones in which the crotch reached down to the knees. He blinked at Jodie but wouldn't look at LaStanza.

Buffy dug a huge ring of keys out of the purse, pushed Biff out, and reached just inside the doorway to punch the code in the burglar alarm before closing the door and locking the dead bolt.

"Well, lead on," she said, waving to LaStanza.

No one said a word until they pulled into the police garage and Jodie said, "I don't believe we didn't catch a single light."

"You must live right," Buffy said, grabbing her son by the arm to follow Jodie. LaStanza pulled up the rear. Twice Biff peeked back to see if he was still there.

LaStanza pulled two extra chairs into one of the small

interview rooms, laid his tape recorder on the table next to his notes and a Juvenile rights form. He put Biff and Buffy on the other side of the table, while he and Jodie sat with their backs to the door.

"Now," Jodie said as she sat. "We need to get some things clear." She turned on the tape recorder and spoke into it. "This is Detective Jodie Kintyre, New Orleans Police Homicide Division. It is Saturday..." She gave the date and time and listed who was present before she said, "Mrs. Norwood, we cannot speak with your son without your permission. We can only speak with him if you are present, also."

Picking up the rights form, Jodie looked at Biff and repeated the first line of the Miranda warning from memory, "Before we ask you any questions, you must understand your rights. You have the right to remain silent."

"Excuse me," Buffy interrupted. "Is my son under arrest?"

"No. But he is a suspect in a crime."

"What crime?"

LaStanza said, "Murder."

The boy's eyes watered and he looked at his mother.

"May I speak alone with my son?"

"Sure." Jodie noted the time on the tape and flipped off the recorder and went out with LaStanza, closing the door behind them. The squad room was empty on a Saturday, just as LaStanza wanted.

"How about a Coke?" Jodie said. He dug out two dollars and said, "Get four."

Before Jodie came back from downstairs, Buffy came out of the room and said, "Biff's ready to answer your questions."

"We'll be right in."

Jodie began again, turning the tape recorder back on, going over the Miranda warning, having Biff and Buffy put their initials next to each sentence before they signed the bottom of the waiver form.

Background questions were always first, easing Biff

into answering. LaStanza watched the boy and thought how this had better work. No way they'd get another shot at the boy, not once Byron Norwood returned home.

LaStanza popped open his Coke, which caused everyone else to do the same. Biff spilled a little on his tee-shirt when he took a swallow, and wiped his shirt with his hand.

It didn't take Jodie long to catch the boy in a lie.

"Do you know a man named Billy Day or Kaiser Billyday?"

"No."

"He lives in The Colapissa at the corner of Prytania and Louisiana Avenue." Jodie described the man.

"No," Biff said. The boy looked down when he lied, his hands pressed tightly around the Coke can, and he trembled.

"Did you talk to anyone at The Colapissa last Friday morning, around one in the morning?"

"No."

"Didn't Detective LaStanza stop you outside your house that morning?"

Biff looked at his mother and the tears came.

Buffy wrapped her arms around her son's head and said, "Oh, my God. It's Okay, son. It's Okay." Her eyes met LaStanza's and he could see anger there, but the anger wasn't directed at him.

"Biff," Jodie said gently when the boy stopped crying, "Didn't Detective LaStanza stop you outside your house yesterday morning?"

Biff buried his face in his mother's shoulder and nodded.

"You're gonna have to say, 'yes' or 'no'."

Buffy pulled her son's face away and looked at him and told him to tell the truth. "The truth can't hurt you."

He said, "Yes."

"What were you doing out in the middle of the night?" Buffy said.

"I went to see those men."

Buffy looked at LaStanza with bewilderment.

"Which men?" Jodie asked.

Biff described Kaiser Billyday and a man who had to be Reverend Dothan and a man matching the description of Sam Elliot, retired NOPD. LaStanza felt his neck getting red.

Biff eased away from his mother and took another nervous sip of Coke. Looking down at his hands, Biff said, "They won't give it back to me."

"Give what?" Jodie asked.

A tear fell on the boy's hands. He sucked in a breath of air and said, "My Daddy's gun."

"What gun?" Buffy said.

Looking up at his mother, he said, "Daddy's flare gun. I took it from the boat."

Buffy reached over and grabbed her sons hands with both of hers and said, "I want you to tell me all of it." She looked pale and suddenly old.

"When did you first meet these men?" Jodie asked.

A knock at the door brought LaStanza to his feet. He opened it and Mason shrugged at him and motioned for him to come out. In a tee-shirt and jeans, Mason hadn't shaved.

He walked all the way to LaStanza's desk before he turned and said, "You have Byron Norwood's son in there?"

"Mrs. Norwood too."

Mason nodded and rubbed his chin.

"The Chief knows. He called me. He expects me to do something about it."

"Well," LaStanza said, "he's copping out right now."

"To Pleasant Street?"

"He just told us he stole his Daddy's flare gun and remember the arsonist, Kaiser Billyday? Well, he gave it to Billyday. That's the murder weapon."

Mason nodded and said, "I'll keep 'em off your ass."

"Good."

Before LaStanza reached the door, Mason added, "I don't know how long."

LaStanza nodded and went back in.

"...heard them talking about the niggers and the bums in the neighborhood," Biff said. "They said they were gonna torch a couple niggers." Biff stopped and took in a deep breath.

"This was at the barbershop next to the video store on Magazine?" Jodie asked.

"Yes, ma'am. They sit out front on chairs. I heard them. It was like a joke. Everybody laughed. They called them porch monkeys and jigaboos, just like we do. Then I told them who I was."

Buffy let out a squeaky noise. Biff stopped at looked up at her and she waved him on. Looking back down, Biff said softly, "I told them who my Daddy was."

"And then what happened," Jodie said.

"They talked to me. They told me how much they liked my Daddy and how good he is at what he does and how important my Daddy is. They said he was going to save us all from bad things." Biff opened his hands and closed them as he talked.

"They said it was an honor that we live in the neighborhood, how important Prytania Street is and how the niggers had to be kept off of our street." Biff's chin sank to his chest and he said, "They talked about the burning cross and how it symbolized Jesus and how we had to do something about the niggers. So I did something."

Jodie's voice was smooth and sympathetic. "What did you do?"

"I got the gun." Biff opened and closed his hands. "They said they needed something to catch the gasoline on fire. They said they could pour gasoline on a bum, but a match wouldn't light it. They said they needed something like a flare gun. So I got it for them."

"When did you get it?" Jodie brushed her hair back and looked at the tape.

Biff shrugged. "I went with my Daddy to the boat at the lake and I took the gun. I gave it to Mister Billy."

"What did Mister Billy say?"

"He said thanks and he was gonna use it, 'Sure 'nuff,' he said. Then he told me about it the next day after they killed that guy. But he wouldn't give me the gun back. He said they were gonna do more. But I want the gun back because it's my Daddy's gun. But they won't give it back."

Jodie looked at the tape again as she asked, "What did they tell you about the man who was burned?"

"They said he was always sleeping on our front porches. They said he tried to run away. But they got him."

"How did you feel when you heard about the man dying?"

Biff shrugged.

"Did you feel bad?"

Biff shrugged again and said in a low voice, "I just want to get my Daddy's gun back."

Buffy rested her head against the rear wall, her eyes closed.

"Have you told anyone about this? Any of the men who work for your father? Your father?"

Buffy's eyes snapped open as her son said no, he hadn't told anyone.

"What do you think your father's going to do when he finds out?"

Biff sucked in a breath and said, "He's gonna be mad. I shouldn't have stolen his gun."

Buffy stared at LaStanza as Jodie asked, "Do you think he's going to be mad about the man getting killed with his gun?"

Biff shrugged his looked down at the table again.

"Because it was a black man?" Jodie said.

Biff shrugged.

"What if it was a white man?"

Biff looked at his mother and said, "I didn't do anything." He started crying again and sank his face against his mother's shoulder. Buffy raised her left hand and pet him gently along the back of the neck.

Another knock at the door propelled LaStanza out of his chair. Mason pulled him away from the door and said,

"Norwood's lawyers are coming. I'll stall as long as I can."

"He copped. We won't need much longer."

LaStanza stepped over to his desk and pulled out a juvenile arrest report. Biff was crying louder now and Buffy was teared up when he stepped back in. He sat next to Jodie and filled out the arrest report. Jodie leaned over and pointed to the charge and he wrote in: RS. 14:30.1 Second Degree Murder. Jodie nodded approval.

When Biff stopped crying, LaStanza said, "Mrs. Norwood. Biff. I want you to look at this." He passed them the arrest form. "We're going to have to arrest you son."

The color left the boy's face. Buffy gasped.

"But...wait a minute..." Buffy stuttered. "Can't we talk about some kind of immunity. He'll testify against those men. I promise..."

LaStanza made sure his face showed no emotion as he said in an even voice. "The district attorney makes deals. We don't. We have to arrest him. He had knowledge before and after the murder. Ma'am, he supplied the murder weapon. He has to be arrested."

"Then call the D.A." Buffy pulled her son to her breast. "He's a child!" The tears came back.

LaStanza leaned back in his chair and waited. He wanted to tell her that the D.A. would definitely cut a deal. That's what lawyer's did. But without the leverage of an arrest hanging over Biff's head, what was the incentive for the boy to testify? But he said no more. He just waited as both cried.

Buffy babbled about the tragedy, about how the boy had been tricked, how the boy had been misled, how he was only fourteen.

Another knock at the door brought LaStanza to his feet again. He tapped Jodie on the shoulder and pointed to the tape recorder and drew a finger across his throat before going out.

This time two men stood behind Mason. One was tall and geeky, one short and hairy with a handle-bar moustache. Both wore pin-striped blue suits and striped ties.

LaStanza closed the door as Mason read the business cards he held in his hands. "This is Mister Leroy Hall and Mister Donald Haley."

"I'm Haley," the hairy one said, stepping forward, extending a hand for LaStanza to shake.

LaStanza shook the hand but hated it. He hated shaking lawyer's hands.

"We're attorneys representing Byron, Buffy, and Biff Norwood. We'd like to see our clients. Now."

LaStanza nodded slowly, turned and opened the door. Stepping in, he scooped up the tape recorder and the arrest form. Jodie followed him out as Hall and Haley squeezed in.

When Haley closed the door, Jodie let out a long, "Whew."

"Thanks, partner," LaStanza said.

"Anytime."

Jodie rolled her neck around to work the kinks out, and then smiled at Mason who smiled back and said, "Two confessions in a week. Not bad."

"My partner and I solve them so easily," Jodie quipped, snapping her fingers.

"Easy?" LaStanza said. "Yeah. right!"

He only got burned to hell, put in enough hours to solve a dozen murders, helped with the Pantyhose debacle, besides almost getting murdered on the fuckin' northshore, which none of them knew about. Easy? The only thing easy in Homicide was when a body turns out to be a natural death and there's *still* paperwork.

After a while the crying and loud voices subsided in the interview room. LaStanza just came back up with Cokes for Jodie and Mason when Haley and Hall stepped out and called Mason over.

"It's his case," Mason said, waving LaStanza over.

Haley tried smiling first. Then he said, "What are you charging the boy with?"

"RS 14:30.1. Second Degree Murder."

"But he's already given you everything he knows. He's a *witness*!" Haley looked at Mason. "He's cooperating!"

Looking back at LaStanza, he shouted, "Don't you have any compassion?"

"Counselor. We're taking him to Juvenile Detention Center in five minutes." Stepping forward, LaStanza added, "And don't yell at me again."

Haley smiled one of those superior, I-know-what-your-doing-but-you're-still-wrong smiles, shook his head, and went back into the interview room.

Five minutes later, LaStanza opened the door and told Buffy, "Mrs. Norwood, you and your son's attorneys can come along. I'm sure they can arrange to have Biff released into your custody pretty quickly."

Buffy wouldn't look at him.

He turned to Biff and said, "You need to come with us now."

Haley stepped in front of LaStanza and said, "No handcuffs. No press release with his name. No leaks to the paper. No..."

"Counselor," Mason said from over LaStanza's shoulder, "can you come out here?"

LaStanza let Haley pass, reached over and grabbed Biff's arm gently and said, "Come on."

Biff looked at his mother and slowly came along. Buffy followed, with Hall. LaStanza let go of Biff's arm and pointed to Jodie who led the way through the squad room.

"One minute," Haley called out behind them.

LaStanza told Biff to continue.

"I said wait!" Haley yelled.

LaStanza asked Jodie to wait by the elevator for him. He went back to where Mason and Haley stood, walked up to Haley and said, "I told you not to yell at me you fuckin' asshole."

"You can't talk to me like that."

LaStanza took a step forward and pulled the oldest police trick he knew. He stepped on Haley's instep, which caused the attorney to push him, which caused LaStanza to raise his right fist and throw a right cross at Haley's face, which he stopped inches from the backpedaling attorney.

LaStanza looked at Mason and rolled his eyes as Haley fell flat on his ass.

LaStanza raised a finger and crooked his head and said, in a voice one would use on a child, "Don't yell at me."

"You're crazy," Haley said, getting up and dusting off his ass. "Both of you."

"Fuckin A," LaStanza agreed. "And we have guns."

Leopard Street

"So how was your date with Kelly?" LaStanza said as he pulled the LTD in front of The Colapissa later that afternoon.

"What?" Jodie said, pulling her weapon from the holster on her hip.

LaStanza smiled and said, "Just asking."

He climbed out quickly and waved to Mason and Fel, who'd just pulled up and parked behind their LTD. Behind Mason, a Sixth District unit pulled up with two rookies.

LaStanza led the way to the front door, his magnum in his right hand at his side, the search warrant and arrest warrants tucked into the rear pocket of his jeans. It was unlocked. He left one of the rookies at the door and went directly to Billyday's room. The door was locked. LaStanza went to Mrs. Wagner's room and rousted the landlady for the key.

"We have a search warrant," he told the flustered old woman. "We don't want to break down the door."

Mrs. Wagner hurried down the hall with the master key, her slippers flapping, her robe trailing behind her like a sail. LaStanza followed. Whatever she had on beneath the robe, LaStanza didn't want to see.

Jodie took the key out of the landlady's hand when she

arrived and waited for LaStanza to get into position, his magnum raised and ready. Jodie slipped the key into the lock, unlocked the door and shoved it open as LaStanza went in first.

The room smelled like cooked cabbage and sweat. Every piece of furniture was draped with dirty clothes, even the portable TV next to the unmade bed. The bathroom smelled like a Bourbon Street urinal. The small kitchen was littered with Chinese take-out cartons and empty beer cans. Billyday wasn't home, but the flare gun was.

Jodie found it two minutes later in a shoe box under the bed. There were two cartridges in the box and one spent casing.

LaStanza grabbed Fel's radio and called the crime lab immediately for pictures and fingerprints. He tapped his partner on the shoulder and said. "You're on a roll, padna."

Standing up, Jodie stretched, curling her back, which drew Fel's attention immediately as her chest rose. LaStanza looked at her chest and said, "So, how was your date with Kelly?"

"Fine," she said, casually straightening out. "Didn't you find all the blond pubic hair next to your Jacuzzi?"

Fel rocked back as if she'd slapped him, his dark brown eyes wide as silver dollars. He threw his head back and howled like a goddam wolf.

Mason leaned into the room and said, "What is it?"

LaStanza pointed to the shoe box. "Jodie found it."

Mason pointed to Fel who was still howling. "What's his problem?"

"Jodie stretched and Fel got a good look at her boobs."

Jodie poked LaStanza in the sternum. It hurt. She turned to Mason and said, "Men!"

"Don't look at me," LaStanza said, "I just asked how your date was." He didn't want to state the obvious. There was a sexual tension between Jodie and Fel so thick you could cut it with a fuckin' butter knife. He figured Mason had seen it too, when Jodie and Fel looked at each other.

Mason squinted at LaStanza and said, "Why don't we round up the rest of your killing gang?"

They left Fel in charge of the search and went and rounded up Sam Grover and Sam Elliot, before moving over to The Elton to snatch up Sam Perkins and the bewildered Reverend Opp C. Dothan.

Separating the four conspirators in four interview rooms, Jodie took Sam Grover and Sam Perkins, while LaStanza interviewed Dothan, leaving Sam Elliot for last.

Dothan was the easiest to break. Quick to pin it all on Billyday, he sat across from LaStanza and repeated Biff's story nearly verbatim, from meeting the boy outside their barbershop to getting the flare gun. Running his twig-like fingers through his spidery gray hair, Dothan claimed Sam Elliot threw the gasoline on the "future dead man" and Billyday "lit the wick" with the flare gun. He called it a Very Pistol. No doubt Opp C. Dothan had mucho maritime experience.

Meeting Jodie after taping Dothan's confession, LaStanza learned that Sam Grover was playing hardball. He knew nothing of the murder and denied lying to LaStanza. Sam Perkins, however, copped out, also pinning it all on Sam Elliot and Billyday.

Walking together into the last interview room, LaStanza put a fresh cup of coffee in front of Sam Elliot as Jodie sat next to her partner with her own mug. She's picked up a new mug, a *Far Side* mug with two bulls sitting in a living room, one blowing up a blow-up cow. The second bull was saying something about how good she was looking as the cow inflated.

Elliot's green eyes were red. His drinker's nose was still purple, his wrinkled face still dry as a chamois. Picking up the coffee, he said, "Thanks," and took a sip. He left his hands wrapped around the Styrofoam cup.

LaStanza stared through the man's eyes all the way to the back of his skull. Elliot blinked twice, looked at Jodie, then back to LaStanza and shook his head slowly.

"You know I can't cop out on myself," he said. "You know the routine."

LaStanza just stared.

"You do what you gotta do and I'll just get a lawyer." Elliot pointed to the waiver of rights form in Jodie's hand and said, "I'm not waiving my rights. I can't talk to you guys."

"I have a message for you," LaStanza said as he rose. "From my old man."

Elliot closed his eyes.

"He said, 'Fuck you'."

The chamois face recoiled an inch as if an invisible hand had slapped it.

Outside the interview room, Jodie said, "He told Sam Perkins that they were in trouble because you were on the case."

Dothan had told LaStanza the same thing.

"He said you wouldn't give up. Ever. He called you a hard headed Wop."

LaStanza didn't have to say he was right.

Mason was in LaStanza's chair, feet up on the desk, a lit cigarette dangling from his open mouth as he snored. LaStanza pointed to him and said, "I learned how to be a hardhead from our fearless leader over there."

"You mom says you've always been hardheaded."

"When did you talk to her?"

"I talk to her all the time."

Son-of-a-bitch!

"Detective LaStanza?"

"Yeah."

"This is headquarters. Operator Seventy-six. I have an urgent message for you from a Mrs. Wagner on Colapissa Street."

"Yeah?" LaStanza sat up in bed and flipped on the lamp.

"Mrs. Wagner said to tell you, 'Billyday's back'. Does that make sense to you?"

"Yeah. Anything else?"

"No."

"Thanks."

He looked at Lizette's white porcelain clock on her night stand. It was three a.m. He called Jodie and then Fel and then jumped into the clothes he'd laid out before going to bed. Black jeans, black Reebok running shoes, and a gray turtle-neck pullover, his .357 Smith and Wesson in a Velcro-snap canvass black holster on his hip next to two speed loaders, gold badge clipped to the front of his belt over his left pants pocket, LaStanza picked up his LFR on the way out, tucking his cuffs into his belt at the small of his back.

On his way to Louisiana Avenue, he called headquarters and requested a Six District unit meet him at Louisiana and Prytania. Headquarters advised none was available.

Unit 210 volunteered and was waiting for LaStanza in front of The Colapissa. As LaStanza climbed out of his Maserati, Fel pulled up behind him in his dark blue Intelligence Division Chevy.

The uniform climbed out of the Second District unit and LaStanza recognized the thick moustache and balding head of Sergeant Daniel Dravot. He waved at LaStanza and said, "What you got here?"

"Murder warrant," LaStanza said, leading Dravot and Fel up to the front door. He told Dravot about Kaiser Billyday as he opened the front door of The Colapissa. "You can't miss him. He's fifty-five, bald and fat, with a basset-hound face."

"Real looker, huh?"

Mrs. Wagner was waiting in the foyer. Wearing the same robe, she handed LaStanza the key to Billyday's room and said, "He's up there." She put her hands over her mouth and slunked into a dark corner of the foyer.

LaStanza took the stairs two at a time. He caught his breath as he slipped the key into Billyday's lock and thought how he needed to get back to running—soon.

Rushing into the dark room, his magnum in hand, LaStanza moved quickly through the main room and into the kitchen. When he stepped back into the main room, Fel came out of Billyday's bathroom and shrugged. They each took a closet and looked under the bed.

A commotion in the hall caused LaStanza to turn as Jodie rushed in with Patrolman David Carnehan right behind her. She was in all black, which made her blonde hair stand out even more than usual.

"He has to be close," LaStanza told her.

"Yeah," Dravot said from the doorway. "The door's still warm."

LaStanza shook his head and said, "I'll set up a perimeter outside with Fel, can you go room to room with them?" He nodded to Dravot and Carnehan.

"Sure."

"I'll send the landlady up," LaStanza said as he and Fel rushed back down the stairs. He pulled Mrs. Wagner out of the corner and sent her up to Jodie. As the old woman started up the stairs, she called down to LaStanza, "Oh, I forgot to tell you. He has a gun."

"Gun?"

"Yes. He showed it to me. It's big and square and silver."

"He talked to you?"

"He said he was sorry and was gonna pack up and leave."

LaStanza waited at the bottom of the stairs until Mrs. Wagner was with Jodie, then went out the front door with Fel.

He hadn't noticed how damp the air was. A slight breeze rustled the trees along the avenue as he and Fel walked out to the sidewalk and then up to the corner.

Fel turned up his LFR and passed it to LaStanza and said, "Mason's calling you."

LaStanza clicked the transmit button on the side of the radio and said, "Go ahead, 3120."

"You need a hand over there?"

He looked at Fel and shrugged.

"10-4," he said reluctantly. He felt Billyday was still close, but the bastard could be half way to Mississippi by now.

"3122 to 3124, I'm enroute."

"10-4," LaStanza answered Mark Land, who was also coming.

Handing the radio back to Fel, LaStanza remembered something Sam Elliot said about moving back and forth between The Colapissa and The Elton through the back-yards. He motioned Fel to come along and walked back down Louisiana to the side of The Colapissa.

A dimly lit alley ran down the river side of the apartment building, separated from the next building by an unpainted seven foot wooden fence. With his magnum still in hand, LaStanza led Fel down the alley.

The radio made him jump when Snowood's Country-Ass voice called out, "3123 to 3124. I'm enroute with 3129."

LaStanza nodded for Fel to answer and thought that was all he needed, S & S.

He picked his way over the broken cement walkway as the fence separated from the walk into a narrow side yard. He felt Fel right behind him as he moved to the corner of the building.

Peeking around the edge, he saw the backyard was completely dark. He pulled back and closed his eyes to let them adjust to darkness. He felt his pulse in his ears as his breathing eased. After a minute, he turned to step into the backyard and felt the leopard again, prowling inside.

He hesitated and a golden flash of fire came from his left and the loud report of a large caliber weapon slammed him back into Fel. Screaming, someone rushed out of the back yard as LaStanza bent his knees and raised his weapon. A running figure bolted around the corner, hugging the fence and firing point-blank at them.

LaStanza felt a burning on his right side as he leveled his aim and squeezed off three quick rounds at the figure. He saw his rounds strike the man as Kaiser Billyday fell against the fence. Fel was firing too. Billyday looked right at LaStanza and tried raising his weapon. LaStanza squeezed off three more rounds, watched them rise up Billyday's chest to his face, watched the man's head snap back; and Billyday fell straight down, his .45 automatic tumbling forward to the edge of the cement walkway.

LaStanza heard the hammer of Fel's revolver still clicking as the hammer fell on spent casings. The air was charged with the sharp smell of cordite and burned powder. LaStanza's ears echoed as he recovered, opened his cylinder and ejected the six casings and quickly reloaded with one of the speed loaders. Snapping the cylinder shut, he went down on his haunches and peeked around the edge of the building at the back yard and looked around. Nothing.

He heard footsteps running behind him and turned in time to see Dravot and Jodie stopping next to Fel. Dravot stepped over to the body and looked down at it. Jodie's eyes met LaStanza's as he rose and reached down to his right side.

It burned something fierce. He stepped away from the building and turned his side to the faint yellow light of the alley. He found a hole in his shirt, a bullet hole and pulled the shirt out of his pants and saw a red mark, a burn mark on his side.

"You hit?" Jodie pushed past Fel.

He looked up at her and said, "Bullet burned me."

"You sure?" Jodie pushed his hands out of the way.

"It didn't go in," he said. Looking around Jodie, he called out to Fel. "Hey, you hit?"

Fel shook his head no and LaStanza saw that he was pale. He also saw Carnehan arriving, his flashlight dancing around like a seal beam in the air still smoky with gunpowder.

Pulling Jodie away from his side, LaStanza asked Carnehan for his flashlight and found where the shot that grazed him and imbedded itself in the wall of The Colapissa.

Looking back at the body, he saw Dravot leaning over it, his hand on the man's throat. "I count seven, no eight wounds," Dravot said, backing away. "He's 10-7."

LaStanza heard more footstep rushing for them down the alley. He put a hand on Fel's shoulder and said, "Carnehan. You better check the other side of that fence. Fel might have killed somebody over there."

"Say what?" Fel pushed the hand off his shoulder.

"You missed him," LaStanza said. "See the holes in the fence. Those are your shots."

"What?!" Fel took two steps back.

LaStanza looked him in the eye and said, "You missed him."

The color was back in Fel's face as he furrowed his brows. "I didn't miss, you dumb fuckin' Wop. You missed. I saw my shots hit him."

LaStanza turned to Jodie and said, "How much you wanna bet he missed?"

LaStanza felt a strong hand on his shoulder and turned to face Mark Land's astonished face. "Don't tell me."

"Yeah. I got another one."

Mark closed his eyes momentarily and said, "Tell me fast."

LaStanza told him it was him and Fel, actually.

"All right," Mark bellowed. "Dravot, can you stay here?"

Dravot gave him an Okay sign. "Wouldn't miss it for the world."

"You." Mark pointed to Carnehan. "Go up and secure the front of this alley. Mark turned and grabbed Steve Stevens by the shoulder as he arrived. "You secure that backyard. And don't step on any casings."

LaStanza stepped over to the body and looked at Billyday's white face pointing up at the dark sky. His eyes were half-open, and a stream of blood had rolled out of his mouth, along the side of his cheek. A round entry wound stood out neatly between his upper lip and nose. More wounds dotted his chest and belly.

"All right," Mark said, "y'all know the routine. No talking. Don't touch your weapons until the crime lab gets here."

"I'm here," a voice called out up the alley as Sturtz arrived with his camera case.

"LaStanza," Mark said, "you're first."

Mark reached over and took the revolver out of LaStanza's holster.

He looked at his sergeant and realized he didn't remember putting his gun back in his holster. Mark opened the cylinder and showed it to Sturtz who took a picture.

"You reloaded?"

"Yeah," LaStanza said, pointing off to his left. "Over there. And I used magnum loads."

"Jesus!"

Sturtz reminded LaStanza, "Don't wash your hands until I can swab them."

LaStanza felt someone grab his arm. He turned as Jodie pulled him away, back up the alley, past an open-mouthed Snowood who said, "I don't fuckin' believe it. You're closin' in on Wild Bill Hickock's record."

LaStanza spotted Mason at the entrance of the alley.

"Watch out for a poker hand with aces and eights," Snowood called out behind him.

Jodie waved Mason forward and said, "He needs to go to the hospital."

"He's hit?" The cigarette fell from Mason's mouth.

LaStanza pulled his arm away from his partner and walked past Mason out to the curb where the Catahoula hound sat panting and looking at him.

He heard Jodie tell Mason he'd been grazed.

LaStanza went down on his haunches in front of the Catahoula. The dog backed away and growled. Its eyes were sky blue, its spots black and three shades of brown. The dog spread its front paws and put its head down, growling louder now. LaStanza leaned back away from the Catahoula and noticed webbing between the toes of the Louisiana swamp dog.

He heard someone move up behind him. The dog turned quickly, its large ears flapping against its face as it raced off up to the corner and then down Prytania.

"Come on," Jodie said, "I'm taking you to Charity."

LaStanza stood up and looked back at the entrance of the alley, at Mason's back and the others collected there, including several civilians now. He had that leopard feeling again, as if he was looking at a pride of lions collecting around his most recent kill, stealing the kill from him.

"Come on," Jodie said again.

He looked at her and saw she was shook. Her cat eyes were all owly.

"When my victim died," he said, "he said something that sounded like 'Kee. Kee'."

"I know."

"I wonder what the fuck he was trying to tell me?"

A van pulled up next to them, a WWL TV van.

LaStanza went back to the alley and grabbed Mason's elbow.

"I thought you were gone," Mason said.

"Somebody's got to over to North Bernadotte to tell my mother before she hears something on the news."

Mason looked over his shoulder and saw the TV van and said, "I'll send someone."

LaStanza turned to leave, stopped and turned back and said, "Don't send Snowood."

"Obviously."

LaStanza looked at his partner, dug his car keys out of his front pocket and said, "You driving or what?"

Seated on the same emergency room table at Charity he'd sat with burned hands—when was that—a little over a month ago, a long month, LaStanza watched the same nurse work on his new burn wound.

Freckle-faced Andrea, still with the big smile, cleaned the wound and dressed it. Looking up at him she said, "You must lead a charmed life, mister. Didn't even break the skin. What's your secret?"

"Sex."

Andrea laughed softly.

Jodie, standing behind her with arms folded, didn't think it was funny at all. She stared at the wound, chewing her lower lip. When she looked up at him she said, "You exhaust me."

He thought that was funny and laughed.

A small smile crept across Jodie's face. "Well," she said, exhaling loudly, "at least it's all over now."

"If you don't count the Superintendent's Hearing and the goddam Grand Jury."

As if on cue, Sturtz came in with a small black case and said, "I got a message for you from Mason. You're not going to the Superintendent's Hearing. Fel's going. Wounded men don't have to." Sturtz sat the case on the end of the bed and waited.

As soon as Andrea finished, Sturtz swabbed LaStanza's hand for a neutron activation test to determine if he had, in fact, fired a handgun.

"Who's taking my statement?" LaStanza asked.

"Mana–a," Sturtz said. "Mason said he'd call you."

Before leaving, Andrea came in with a tube of Silvadene and instructions on how to clean and dress the burn. LaStanza was a little surprised when Jodie snapped at him after Andrea finished.

"Were you listening?"

"I've done it before."

"I didn't know you were an expert." Jodie was really aggravated.

"Well, now you know."

Andrea knew when to beat feet and did.

LaStanza told Jodie he'd take her back to her car.

"What, you're gonna drive home?"

"Yeah."

"No, you're not mister. I'm taking you home."

"Not until the doctor says so," Andrea said from beyond the curtain.

So LaStanza kicked his feet up on the table, made himself comfortable and closed his eyes and tried to drive off the smell of cordite from his nostrils.

Audubon Park was foggy with early morning dew as a gray dawn crept in from the west. Jodie pulled the Maserati into the garage. She hadn't spoken since snapping at him.

"Why don't you just take the car home?" he said.

She lifted her radio to her mouth and called Mason and said he could send that unit now to pick her up.

"Your partner Okay?" Mason asked.

"10-4."

"Tell him I just left his mother's. Everything' fine there."

Entering the kitchen, LaStanza looked up at the clock on the wall and saw it was after six now. It was one p.m. in Paris. He sat on a stool and looked back at his partner who stared out the French doors at the wet deck and dewy back yard. Her arms folded, her right foot tapping, she stood there tensed in anger.

He knew it was something he'd said or done, but he was tired now and wasn't thinking straight. He needed coffee. He climbed off the stool and pulled a fresh pound of CDM coffee from the pantry to brew up a strong pot of coffee-and-chicory.

The smell filled the kitchen and even turned Jodie's head half-way around. As soon as it was brewed, he pulled the carafe away and poured two cups. He opened a can of pet milk and poured some in his cup, along with two sugars. He left the mixings out for her and said, "It's ready."

She walked over without looking at him and poured in some cream and one sugar.

The coffee revived him immediately.

She wouldn't look at him as she sipped hers, until they heard a horn outside. She went to a side window and waved out the window. Looking at him for the first time, she let out a tired sigh and said, "You know you came a couple millimeters away from dying tonight."

He knew that.

She put a fist on her hip and said, "The Chief's been

waiting for this, you know."

He wanted to say something smart, but couldn't think of anything, so he just nodded.

"You'll probably be transferred by Monday."

She wouldn't look at him as she left. He moved to the window and watched her climb into a marked unit, which turned around at the dead end of Garfield and drove away.

He went upstairs and called Lizette and smiled when she answered after the first ring.

"Hey, Babe," she said, "I was just thinking about you."

"You ready for some company?"

"Really?" her voice rose excitedly.

"It's all over."

"Great!"

"I can come next Saturday, after the Grand Jury." Grand Juries were always called on Friday.

"Oh, Darlin'. That's great. I'll call my travel agent and..." she stopped suddenly and said, "What Grand Jury?"

"We shot the killer. Fel and me." He let it sink in a moment before adding, "At least he thinks he shot him. I think he missed."

"Oh, Dino." He figured she had her head in her hand. "Are you all right?"

"Of course." He'd tell her about the graze on his side when he saw her, just like he planned to tell her about the pink marks on his hands.

"He didn't leave us much option. He shot first."

He couldn't help remember how Lizette's father tried to talk her out of marrying him, calling him a violent man, a dangerous man.

"Oh, Babe," she said in a distant, sad voice. "Are you sure you're all right?"

"I'll show you in a week.

Paris

At three o'clock p.m., Friday, the Orleans Parish Grand Jury returned two no-true bills in the homicide of Billy Day, alias Kaiser Billyday, exonerating Detective Dino LaStanza and Intelligence Officer Felicity Jones in the killing. Officially the case was listed as justifiable homicide.

"Fuckin' A," Snowood said, raising his Styrofoam cup full of brown shit as Mason announced it to the squad.

Stevens, standing next to LaStanza's desk, looked around as if in a fog. No clown shoes today, he wore all brown, including a polyester brown tie specked with dots of red and green and yellow. Facing LaStanza, he raised his coffee cup and said, "I have no idea what the fuck's going on around here most of the time."

LaStanza had to laugh.

"Don't worry. Your partner never knows."

Jodie, in a pale yellow suit-skirt outfit, sat quietly at her desk. Fel Jones leaned against her desk in a new shark-skin gray suit, smiling as if he had something to smile about. LaStanza wore a charcoal gray suit and a red tie.

"Mark's got some information for y'all," Mason said, pointing to the big sergeant who stepped out of his office with several papers in his hands. His hair messed as usual, his tie undone and his shirt and pants looking like an unmade bed, Mark cleared his throat and said, "First, the F.B.I. lab has positively matched Frank K. Hughes' DNA with DNA collected from the Gentilly and Poeyfarre victims, and the live victims too."

"Fuckin A'," Snowood boomed, raising his cup again.

LaStanza watched Jodie for a reaction—she didn't react.

"Calm down," Mark said as he pulled another piece of paper forward. "I have some information on Kaiser Billyday, a clarification of the autopsy results and firearms examination results." Mark waved toward LaStanza and added, "The Grand Jury already heard this."

Fel's head snapped around and he glared at LaStanza who just shrugged.

"I'll just read it, even if some of it's repetitious. Let me see. Here. 'Deceased suffered eight entry wounds. One in the right shoulder. One in the left shoulder. One in the left thigh. Two in the chest cavity. Two in the abdomen. One in the face. The left shoulder wound was perforated. All other were penetrating wounds. Seven projectiles were recovered from the body. One abdominal wound struck the stomach. One struck the lower intestine. The thigh wound shattered the femur. Three were fatal wounds—one heart wound, one pulmonary artery wound, one pellet penetrated the face and lacerated the brain.'."

Mark shuffled the papers. "This is from firearms examiners. 'Six of the projectiles recovered from the victim were fired by Detective LaStanza's weapon. One was from Officer Jones' weapon'."

Fel's eyebrows rose in anticipation as he said, "Go on."

Mark glowered and continued reading, "Um, 'LaStanza's bullets struck the heart, the brain, the stomach, the intestine, the thigh, and the right shoulder."

Fel's mouth fell open.

" 'Jones' bullet struck the pulmonary artery'."

"All right!" Fel jumped up and pointed to LaStanza. "I told you I hit him in the chest. It's a tie! He said *three* fatal wounds. We both killed him. *It's a tie!*"

Fel tried to moonwalk and bumped his ass against Jodie desk.

You'd think the silly fuck won a lottery.

He hadn't seen Fel so happy before. He felt good for him actually. Fel had taken a beating when they learned all six of LaStanza's shots hit Billyday and only two of Jones'—one through the shoulder and one listed as a "torso shot" on the preliminary report. It was especially hard on Fel after the crime lab recovered four projectiles on the other side of the fence, all his.

He'd killed the fence while LaStanza killed the killer.

Jodie got up and took her cup to the coffee pot while Fel danced and Snowood waved his cup around and Stevens looked lost and Mark went back into his office. She moved slowly and purposefully, never looking at LaStanza.

Mason stepped up behind LaStanza, tapped him on the shoulder and said, "No word from the Chief, yet. He might be waiting until you get back from vacation."

"Well," LaStanza said, rising and closing his briefcase. "I'll catch y'all later. I'm off."

"Have fun," Fel said.

"Slip Liz a boner for me," Snowood said.

"Where 'ya going?" Stevens asked. He had no fuckin' idea.

"Paris. My man. City of Light."

And LaStanza left, glancing back at his partner who wouldn't look back.

"Wait," Snowood yelled. "Nobody move. We ain't found out whose been stealing LaStanza's fuckin' memos!"

The phone rang as LaStanza the copy of *A Moveable Feast* into his suitcase. It was Jodie.

"Quick, turn on Channel 4. Norwood's on. Quick. I'll call you after."

He grabbed the remote control and flipped on the

portable Sony in their bedroom bookcase. Byron Norwood's face filled the screen. He was making a speech.

"...and we hope this tragedy will bring us closer together," Norwood said as the camera pulled back to show Buffy Norwood at his right, and attorneys Haley and Hall on the other side of a mournful Norwood, who continued, "I wish to announce that my lovely wife and I, as well as my son, have been born again."

Interrupted by applause, and shouts of "Praise the Lord," Norwood raised his hand and said, "My son, the true victim in this horrible incident, is undergoing the very best in professional counseling. We hope this error in judgment by...a child...will not destroy such a young life. We hope and pray to the Lord for strength. And we are so very grateful for all the sympathy and support we've received from our friends throughout Louisiana."

"Mr. Norwood, will this affect your candidacy for governor?" a newsman asked.

"I don't know," Norwood said as sincerely as he could. He looked straight into the camera with those big blue eyes, blinked back a tear, and said, "We'll let the Lord and the good people of Louisiana decide that."

Smiling shyly, Norwood took his wife's hand and waved to an hysterical crowd who began to chant, "Nor—wood! Nor—wood! Nor—wood!"

Fucker knows how to land on his feet.

Norwood's image was replaced by a solemn anchor who told the viewing public how Norwood's juvenile son had been charged, along with several men, in the apparent murder of a "street person" about a month ago.

When Jodie called, LaStanza answered with, "There was nothing 'apparent' about it. It was fuckin' murder."

"Right," she agreed.

"Coulda guessed he'd use this to his advantage."

"What a slime ball," Jodie said, then asked if she could come over for a minute.

"Sure."

He had a bottle of Valpolicella open and breathing, two glasses on the kitchen counter next to the stuffed artichoke Brulee had left for him, when Jodie knocked on his kitchen door. She still had on the same yellow outfit. LaStanza had pulled on a tee-shirt and jogging shorts and was barefoot.

She put her purse on the counter and grabbed a glass for him to fill. She took a sip as he poured his own glass. She held her glass up for a toast. They tapped glasses as she said, "To Paris."

"To Paris."

He reached for an artichoke leaf, pulled it away and said, "Ever hear of *folie a deux*?"

She shook her head no.

"It's French. It mean the folly of two. I looked it up in one of Lizette's books." He bit the artichoke leaf, scraping the garlic and bread crumb stuffing into his mouth before dropping the leaf back on the plate.

"It's an old legal term used when two people subscribe to the same extremist view, usually political. A husband convinces his wife, or a father convinces a son, that witches are evil and the wife or son goes out and burns some women—it's a shared crime. The perpetrator was driven to it."

He took a sip of wine.

"It was used as a defense mostly, to show how vulnerable perpetrators were coerced into committing crimes."

Jodie's left eye was narrowed.

"Like Biff," she said.

He nodded and reached for another leaf of artichoke.

"That boy received subliminal messages all his life that blacks are evil," she said.

"Subliminal hell. Overt."

Jodie agreed and reached for a leaf herself.

LaStanza thought of the writhing body again and the smell of burned flesh. He took another hit of wine.

"Oh," Jodie said as if she'd just thought of something. "The Stupid Lupert Case is over."

"What?"

"He copped out to Second Degree yesterday."

"Why?"

"Couldn't get any psychiatrist to declare him insane. At least that's what that ADA Daka told me."

"Good, even if Lupert's stone fuckin' nuts." LaStanza said. "Fuck the insanity plea."

Jodie was quiet for a while. He watched her play with her artichoke leaf, then trace her finger over to her wine glass to tap her fingernails against its base.

When she looked up, her eyes were filled with emotion.

"I'm gonna miss you," she said in a voice forced into firmness, faintly adding the word, "partner."

"I'll be back."

"Will you?"

Lizette stood along the left side of the concourse, just beyond the security gate, her face beaming. In blue jeans and a white dress shirt tied at her waist, her hair down over her shoulders, she looked *beautiful.*

LaStanza squeezed past a priest and a French sailor through the gate, dropped his carry-on and snatched her in his arms and kissed her. He kissed her for a long, long time, pressing his mouth against hers, feeling her tongue work back against his, feeling the length of her body against him. Catching his breath, he kissed her lips softly again and again, looking into her gold-brown eyes, feeling her breasts against his chest now and her right leg working against his crotch. He reached down and grabbed her ass with both hands and pulled her closer as his tongue worked against hers again.

"Oh, Babe," she gasped when they finally came up for air. Her eyes were wet. "I'll never leave you again. Not for a minute. Ever."

"It's a deal."

Draping his carry-on over his left shoulder, he held her close as they walked down to baggage claim. Stumbling several times, because he couldn't stop looking at her face, they moved slowly, stopping now and again to kiss. Before turning the corner from the concourse, he pressed her up against a wall and kissed her until they were both light headed.

"Come on," she said. "Let's go the hotel."

Nuzzling her head in the crook of his neck, she poked a finger into his side as they walked again. He flinched and she pulled away.

"What is it?"

"Nothing. I'll tell you about it later."

"You're hurt."

"I'm Okay. Really."

She took his face in her hands and kissed his lips ever so softly and said, "I want you to tell me everything."

Walking arm in arm, he thought back to that unseasonably cool night when he turned the wrong way down a one-way street named Pleasant, about the burned man lying curlcd up likc a burncd inscct, about Angic Rinaldi's tiny dead hand, about the dead feet of the Poeyfarre victim, and the way the woman on State Street looked at him when he promised to shoot Frank K. Hughes, about knocking Dr. Radosti out with one punch, about Billyday's basset face beaming out of the front door of The Colapissa, about his weapon recoiling as he gunned the down the fucker, about how it wasn't enough. How it was never enough.

His wife pressed against him as they waited for his luggage. His heart raced in the anticipation of getting to that hotel, but he couldn't stop his mind from drifting again—back across the long miles to the dark streets of New Orleans, to his town, to a town of unending murders and long nights spent hunting those who hunt humans.

The End